The Tomorrows After You

A Small Town Suspense Romance

Annie Ritter

CONTENTS

To my cat, Dallas, who insists on sitting directly on my laptop keyboard.
So, if you find any errors?
Blame Dallas.

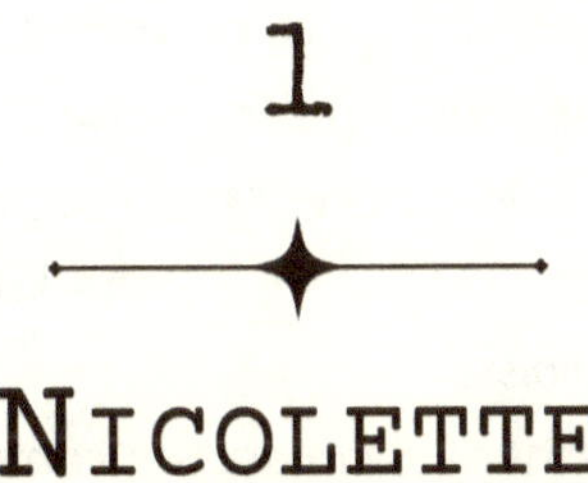

1

NICOLETTE

My car engine sputtered to silence; a mechanical representation of the death my career currently faced. The rusty road sign towered above me, offering little consolation.

Welcome to Godot, WV
We're what you've been waiting for!

A deranged Big Boy cartoon with a miner's helmet gave an exaggerated wink and thumbs up with a pickaxe over his shoulder on one side. I cringed at the other side featuring a female cartoon resembling a gratuitously endowed Olive Oyl holding out a pie with a salacious grin.

If my journalism career wasn't dangling by a frayed thread, jeopardizing my life's work, I wouldn't be caught dead back in this town. A town that clearly hadn't changed a bit in the dozen years since I'd left at seventeen. I had been so anxious to leave my backwoods hometown that I left the summer before my senior year, jetting off to New York to enroll in an early degree program so I could start an internship at the Independent American News Network upon graduation.

The vibration of my phone cut through the oppressive mediocrity of the landscape in front of me.

"Hey, Mel," I answered. "Please tell me you're calling to let me know you found me *any* other assignment?"

She chuckled into the phone. "Sorry, hon. I'm calling to make sure that old Caddy didn't crap out on you halfway through Pennsylvania."

With a sigh, I narrowed my eyes at the patriarchal cartoons, their antiquated eyes mocking me from the billboard. "Yeah... I'm here."

"I'm going to level with you. When I dropped your name to the producers, they were hesitant. Your body of work is strong, there's no doubt. But they're wary after the most recent... *noise*."

"No, I understand," I said quickly. "And I appreciate you going to bat for me." I punctuated my response, so she knew I didn't need to be reminded of my recent *noise.*

Melody worked for Athena Studios, the company behind the hit docuseries *Beyond Bizarre: Real Weird Real Stories*. When she gave me the assignment that would send me back to Godot, the only thing that poked through the impending sense of dread was the shred of hope I could resurrect my recently marred career. From a journalistic integrity standpoint, the docuseries was drivel. But it was popular drivel. And the same producers had hands in some legitimate documentary studios.

"You built a strong following in Easton," she said. "It's a big city and you covered some real topics in your podcast. The studio was impressed with the content... But they don't exactly hire off YouTube followers. You need a home run here, kiddo."

My cheeks burned at the reductive summary of how I'd spent the last seven years. I opened my mouth to argue, but snapped it shut. Melody was sticking her neck out for me. I knew *she* took me seriously. It was her bosses I had to convince.

"This could open a lot of doors, Nicolette. No one has gotten through to Riot Asher in over ten years."

"And you think I can?" I asked.

"If anyone can, it's you. Put on that high school sweetheart smile and get him to open up. The guy must have a side to this story."

She made it sound so easy.

Nausea crept up my throat. I'd heard about Grace Asher's murder. I already moved to New York, but it had made national news because of how goddamn bizarre it really was.

When Riot Asher confessed to killing his mother, it stunned everyone. A murder hadn't occurred in Godot in decades.

He was only a year older than me in school, but I don't think I'd spoken five words to Riot Asher during the eight years I spent in this town.

Despite living in Godot since nine years old, I never felt a part of the community. My affinity for asking questions was frowned upon. I'd kept to myself and never looked back once my bags were packed.

I was an outsider now. And Godot didn't like outsiders.

"What if I can't get him to talk?" I asked.

"You? The Bloodhound of New England? Can't get someone to talk?" I almost smiled at the old nickname.

"Okay, what if he talks and his story is the same as his statement? He's never strayed from it."

"We don't need him to change the story. We need a psychological portrait. Was he *really* a golden boy who snapped under the immense pressure of collegiate expectations? Or was he a silent predator all along?" She paused. "Or was Mama Asher a bible-thumping bigot who beat her sons into loving the Lord until finally the youngest snapped?" I heard a sharp intake of breath. "Oh, I like that angle. Go for that one."

I frowned. "You know that's not how it works. You collect the facts. Gather the empirical data. Then piece together motives and a narrative."

Melody chuckled before clucking her tongue. "Your news world might've operated that way. But this is the entertainment business. We need streams." I blew out a humiliating breath. "Plus, everyone loves a good redemption story. Look. I'll mail you the treatment for the episode once it's finished. We've got three storyline options for how to end it. We need you to paint us a picture of why he did it. And Nicolette?" She paused and I let the silence swell. "You get him to go on the record? I can't *tell* you what doors that could open."

I let the reality of that swirl around me.

"Okay... But really, Mel. Shoot me straight. If I can't get a story out of him, what happens then?"

She hesitated and I could practically hear her chewing on her lip.

"Then you'll need to come back with a bigger story to tell."

White clapboard siding covered Jacob Maxwell's quintessential southern farmhouse, which featured a sprawling wrap-around porch. The massive landscape beyond was immaculately manicured.

My eyes fell to a piece of lawn art peeking out of a bush next to the porch stairs. It looked like a bird made from recycled metal and it spun in the wind, making its limbs come alive. A faint chime emanated from inside it. A twinge of familiarity reminded me of similar pieces popping up all over the northeast coast.

Jacob came sweeping down the porch to greet me.

"Oh, Nicolette, how *wonderful* it is to see you! Look at you." He appraised me for longer than necessary. "You've turned into quite the woman, haven't you?"

"Good to see you, Jacob," I muttered, pretending to root around for my bags.

"Oh, come now. You can still call me *Uncle Jacob!*"

I grimaced. I had never called him "uncle". Even when he had married my Aunt Shirley shortly after her lung cancer diagnosis took a turn for the worst. It was same summer I got my driver's license so I didn't spend a ton of time getting to know him. My mother never cared for her brother-in-law. She called him an opportunist.

Still, he was the only quasi-family I had left in Godot since my parents retired and now spent their days traversing the country in a rehabbed camper van.

"That's all you've got?" he asked when I hoisted a backpack over my shoulder.

"I'm not staying long..." I drifted off.

Shit. In my reluctance to come back, I never came up with a cover story for why I was here. I couldn't very well waltz into town and allow Riot Asher to shut me out before I got close enough. I wondered if I'd recognize him. His dark hair had framed a soft baby face that featured brilliant blue eyes. He was a looker.

But he'd also been in prison for ten years. Who knew what that did to a person.

My laptop bag slid off my shoulder and hit the ground with a clunk.

"Oh, let me." Jacob bent down to pick it up. He eyed the laptop. "I guess I should have warned you. I don't get wireless internet out here." He cocked his head and shrugged.

"You don't have internet." I wanted to cry on the inside. How was I supposed to get any research done?

"I have one of those desktops in the office upstairs. You're welcome to use that!"

I blew a breath out. This was going to be a long couple weeks.

I tossed my backpack on the bed, scattering novelty throw pillows like dust bunnies before wandering into the computer room next door.

Once the dinosaur tech booted up, I opened a browser and shot off an email to Melody, giving her Jacob's address to mail me the episode treatment.

I opened up the email I sent to myself containing all the news links I had found in my brief research on Riot Asher. Most of the articles were from ten or eleven years ago and the distant memory of the story came flooding back to me.

Golden boy and star quarterback, Riot Asher was ready to put Godot on the map when he won himself a full scholarship to play football at West Virginia State College. As a starting freshman, he led the team to an undefeated season. The night before the final homecoming game, he left campus, drove three hours back to Godot and stabbed his mother three times before burning her body.

To be fair, he lit the whole house on fire. Her body just happened to be in it.

That same iconic photo that had made front-page news in almost all major publications was still the first image to populate.

Riot knelt on his front lawn with his hands behind his head, his childhood home burning to the ground behind him. I don't know who was smart enough to snap a photo of that, but by the next morning, that image was *everywhere*.

Outside that, I found nothing new published about Riot Asher in the last ten years and there were certainly no current photos. Plenty of follow-up articles with other townsfolk, but every single article ended the same way. *Riot Asher did not respond to our requests for an interview.*

It *had* been an open-and-shut case. He confessed. Didn't even get a lawyer until the court assigned him one to cut the plea deal.

The story went that his brother, Brennan, called upset because he and their mother had an argument.

Riot had been going to college for only a few months and getting Brennan's call put him at the end of his rope. He drove home to confront them both. His mother was defensive and angry, and Riot *snapped*. It didn't make total sense, but for over ten years he swore by every single detail of those events.

I considered my angles for approaching the assignment. I had never shied away from addressing my subjects head-on. *Impulsive* is what they had called me initially, but when that impulsiveness ended in truths no one had ever uncovered, my critics were quiet.

But Riot Asher was going to be different. The rumor mill was that he shut down every media outlet that tried to approach him. *20/20. Dateline.* Even ESPN had made him offers for an exclusive special. But Riot Asher never let anyone get past the "Hi, my name is..."

No, as anti-media as Riot Asher was, I would have to work this differently.

"Hey!" Jacob's voice jolted me out of my vortex. I jerked to face the door and accidentally closed out the entire browser.

"Shit," I muttered to myself. It was going to take another twenty minutes for all those tabs to reload.

"Didn't mean to startle you, but dinner will be ready in five minutes!"

I groaned at the blank screen. Wanting to protest, but not wanting to be rude, I pushed away from the desk and joined Jacob for dinner.

"So, Nicolette, what made you decide to leave Easton?" Jacob slurped pasta into his mouth, and I cringed at the little tendrils of spaghetti that slithered between his leathery lips.

"Oh, you know, just time for a change of scenery," I said.

He paused, regarding my expression for a beat. "Not getting into any more trouble, are you?" His features darkened.

Fuck, had *he* heard about my latest *noise*?

My expression remained impassive. Jacob might have caught wind of it. The World Wide Web *was* a big place, but the fine people of Godot still believed the internet was for pedophiles and democrats.

"Oh, you know me." I gave a phony laugh. "If trouble were a compass, I'd be the navigator."

He cackled out loud as if it was the funniest thing he'd ever heard.

"Any boyfriends to speak of?"

I would have laughed if my love life hadn't been so pathetic.

"No, I haven't exactly prioritized personal relationships," I said, noting the bitter undertone in my own voice.

"Well, now that's no way to find a husband."

This time I did laugh. Because I knew he wasn't kidding.

"I have a few more aspirations in life than becoming a wife," I said, trying not to sound too bitter.

"Gosh, Nicolette, you were the youngest evening news anchor to ever make it on national television. How many more aspirations can you have?" Jacob laughed and shoved another forkful of pasta in his mouth.

A nostalgic yearning gurgled in my stomach at the memory of my early IANN success. The entire world had been at my disposal. I had travelled the globe. I'd presented breaking international stories and drawn TV ratings an independent news network could only dream of. I was the Bloodhound of New England.

And then I lost it.

All because it was the one time in my entire life I *had* prioritized a personal relationship. I jeopardized everything back then because I listened to my naïve heart instead of my head.

I never made that mistake ever again.

I didn't dignify his question with an answer. Instead, I shoveled down three more bites of pasta before standing up.

"I'm going to get some work done then go to bed early. I appreciate you letting me stay." I offered a polite smile.

"Please, Nicolette." His smile held a weird expression. "The pleasure is all mine."

I brushed my teeth and got ready for bed, eager to wash the day of travel off me. I could hear Jacob downstairs, blaring some war movie. He'd offered to watch something else if I wanted to join him but I declined.

Sitting down at the antique computer, I moved the mouse to wake it up. I opened the browser and went to History, hoping I could relaunch all the tabs I had had open.

My stomach lurched when I spotted it. My recent *noise.* Clear as day, scattered across Uncle-fucking-Jacob's search history. Not just once. Not twice. But at least seven different searches and visits over the last two weeks.

Noise. I scoffed. What a great euphemism for an illegally taken sex tape of me that had been unapologetically released.

Shame. Embarrassment. Disgust. All of it rolled off me in waves. He'd been looking at it. Watching it. For weeks.

Jacob's cackle from downstairs made me jump and I felt like I might throw up. My heart hammered in my throat.

Fuck this. Fuck him. And fuck this house.

2

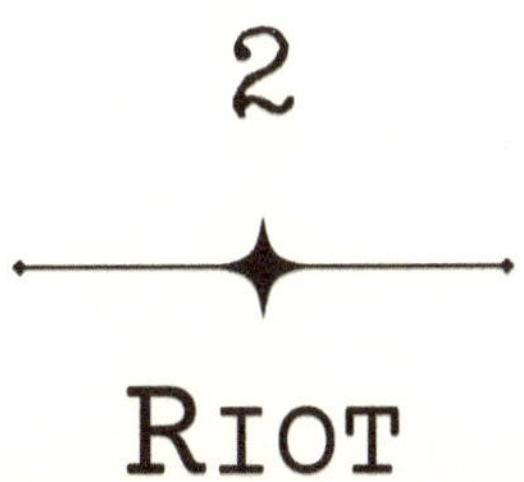

RIOT

My five a.m. alarm felt like a cruel joke. I silenced it, wondering when had been the last time I'd slept in?

Probably before the weight of my life's greatest mistake weighed me down every night.

I cursed the little prick of a police deputy, Jeremy Blackwell, for giving me the earliest community service assignments.

Thankfully, I didn't mind today's work. I liked groundskeeping. It offered immediate gratification, and I found the rhythm of mowing, edging, and trimming soothing. I'd picked up a few side jobs for a local landscaping business earlier this spring to make some extra money. That is, until one of the customers found out *I* was the one pruning their roses and had me fired. *Fucking Cherry Mitchell.*

I pulled on my work clothes and emerged from my bedroom like a baby bird hatching into the world.

Only I was hatching into my large, luxurious double-wide park model.

As I brushed my teeth, I was once again confused by the stranger staring back at me in the mirror. My beard grew unrecognizably long. It was scraggly and unkempt, and made me appear crazier than everyone thought I was. But Katie told me not to shave, so I suppose I kept it overgrown as some show of disobedience.

Katie, my great redeemer.

I sighed, splashing water on my face. A few years back, I found myself on the wrong end of an inmate fight and I cracked my chin open. Medical wasn't top of the line and the stitches had been a pretty gnarly chop job. I shaved when I got home, happy to have a real razor and shave gel for the first time in a decade. But Katie told me I needed to keep a beard to cover the scar.

"It would be one thing if it were somewhere you could cover up, but Ry, if you don't hide it, the evidence of your past is literally all over your face. Anytime someone looks at you, they'll see the scar and think 'prison'."

Katie made me her pet project since the day I got home, showing up on my doorstep with a basket of muffins. I appreciated it, even though it gave me a false sense of how the town would receive me. She secured me a job at her dad's auto body shop that paid well, and the guys didn't treat me like a convict, so I'd been grateful.

Part of me suspected it might be her way of living out some buried high school fantasy. She'd had a crush on me but, at the risk of sounding like an asshole, a lot of girls had. I only had one love back then, and that was football.

But now I had nothing and although I found her overbearing, I'm ashamed to admit I was happy for the attention. Katie was kind and pretty, but even after everything she'd done for me, she didn't stir anything emotional or otherwise inside me except gratitude.

And that was saying something, considering I hadn't been with a woman in almost twelve years now.

I considered throwing a pot of coffee on, but decided against it, grabbing a bottle of Gatorade instead. Downing the sugary drink, I gazed across the sprawling landscape of my backyard. It had been in my father's family for generations.

And then I fucked it all up.

The church offered to buy it and lease it back to us so it wouldn't go to the land bank. I still held hope of buying it back, but, quite literally, only *God* knew how much they'd ask for.

The land extended beyond eyesight. My double-wide was supposed to have been temporary. My brother Brennan laid out plans for a nice sprawling farmhouse, but the money ran out before he finished the drawings.

I loved my brother, but I couldn't live with him and his quirks. So, I made him a deal… if he laid out the plans for a small one-bedroom, I'd build it. It would be the same cost as another manufactured home, and I knew he'd like it better if it were up to his very high standards of specifications.

And God bless him, did he lay out those plans. It stood like an adult treehouse and pride bloomed within me. I had no experience as a carpenter, but I spent the last ten years working with my hands and all kinds of tools, so it wasn't hard to pick up. Especially with the building plans Brennan drew.

I mean, down to the exact directions.

Ensure the circular saw is connected to power.

He priced out lumber, plumbing, electric, all of it. Down to the goddamn *shelf* that the materials were found on.

Home Depot Store 4802- Aisle 27 Bay 005.

Yes, he was *fucking* brilliant, but he was also trying.

Still, it was nice to work with my big brother on something *tangible* that served as evidence we'd built something together.

I gazed at my watch. 5:23 a.m. *Shit.*

I hopped in my truck and pulled into the back of the library right as the clock struck 5:30.

"Asher," Mr. Meaney regarded me.

"Mr. Meaney," I said.

His eyes were flat. "You can call me Kevin, now, Riot. I'm not your wood shop teacher anymore."

I nodded. He led me to the enclosed trailer. Riding lawn mower, edger, pruning shears. The job was straightforward. Upkeep the grounds around the library. *Serve the community.*

"Not just the bushes you have to prune." Mr. Meaney gave me a knowing nod before swiveling his eyes to the entrance of the library where I spotted movement.

He walked over, tilting his head for me to follow him.

"Up and at 'em! Look alive!" He barked and started clapping. I peered around him to see a young man, maybe a few years younger than me, strung out in the overhang of the library entrance.

The boy opened his bleary eyes as if he didn't know where he was. I was once again struck by how rampant the drug problem had become during my time away.

"Sorry, son." Mr. Meaney helped him to his feet, grabbing him around the upper part of his arm, which was littered with track marks. "Library is closed and there's no loitering. The Center is open 24/7. You know that."

A pang of pity cut through me, watching him stumble away.

Mr. Meaney gave me a quick rundown before leaving, and I went to work.

After finishing in the back, I was drenched with sweat. I wiped my face with the bottom of my grass-stained shirt, hauling all the materials to the front.

Shit. I pulled up short, spotting a parked car. Shielding my eyes from the sun, I noticed someone passed out in the driver's seat. *Double shit.*

As I got closer, I cleared my throat and dragged the edger against the pavement, hoping the driver would wake up and take off before I had to play *bouncer* at the local library. But no such luck. A head of long blonde hair pressed against the window.

A woman. *Great.*

I could get along with the men in town. Their disposition remained impassive, disinterested. They left me alone for the most part and weren't afraid to pass me in the grocery store. If engagement was unavoidable, they'd ask me about football scores and I'd ask how they thought the Steelers were primed for the upcoming season, cautiously steering the conversation into comfortable small talk.

Women, by contrast (save Katie), regarded me as if I were wearing a necklace made of puppy skulls and children's teeth. They crossed the street when they noticed me coming. They avoided the grocery aisle I stood in, and they *certainly* never engaged in small talk.

For the most part, at least. A handful of busybodies would ask about the weather or my brother so they could report back at teatime that they were brave enough to converse with Riot Asher, Mother Slayer.

I took a breath, irritated I had to interrupt my work to shoo away another addict, before rapping three times on the window.

The woman lurched forward and snapped her head, scowling as if *I* were the one inconveniencing *her*. When our eyes met, a twinge of familiarity struck me.

"Jesus Christ, you scared the shit out of me!" she scoffed, rolling down her window halfway. I hid my surprise at her aggressive response and regarded her with skepticism.

She didn't look like a crackhead. Her teeth and skin were impeccable despite dark circles under her eyes. Maybe she was a dealer.

She blinked rapidly, as if she could clear me out of her eye line.

"Well?" she snapped. "Can I help you?"

Okay, she wasn't a drug dealer. A bit of an asshole, maybe.

With narrowed eyes, I tilted my head to a sign on the front of the building indicating the hours.

"Library's closed," I muttered.

A pit in my stomach formed, waiting for her to recognize me. For the inevitable wide-eyed, fear-stricken silence. But I only received an impatient, irritated huff.

"Okay. Then, what are *you* doing here?" She smirked like she'd caught me. She had stones. Spoiled little *princess* stones, but stones, nonetheless.

I waited for a beat. Then blinked and held up the edger in my hands.

"Work."

A faint rouge colored her high cheekbones before the indignation returned to her expression.

"Oh," she said, pushing her chin into the air. "Well, me too." She gestured toward a laptop that sat askew on her lap. It left red indentations on her toned thighs, and I couldn't help but notice she was wearing pajamas. *Tiny pajamas*. Something stirred in my gut but I shoved it down. "Turns out, no one's heard of wireless internet here except for the library. I was working and must have fallen asleep."

I raised my eyebrows and blinked once. Twice.

"Okay, I'm leaving. Jeez, you'd think the library would be *thankful* that someone *actually* finds their resources *useful*," she said.

Without another word, she gassed up the engine. It turned over hard. She cast one glance behind her and sped in reverse. I took a step back to avoid getting my toes run over. Her long blonde hair caught the wind as she took off.

Brat.

3

NICOLETTE

What a dick that John Lennon-wannabe was with his scraggly facial hair and dirty grass clippings stuck in his beard.

I was tired. And dirty. And did I mention tired?

I slid, unceremoniously, into the bathroom of the Piggly Wiggly. The minty toothpaste refreshed my attitude, albeit slightly. I applied a little makeup to cover the dark circles under my eyes, still reeling and bitter from the night before.

I was about to storm down the stairs and mother-fuck my pervert uncle up and down the Big Coal River, but I stopped myself. I was pissed, sure. But what was I supposed to do? Watching an adult video on the internet wasn't illegal. We weren't related, not really, and I was twenty-five in the recording. Confronting him would only bring more *noise* I couldn't afford to make.

Watching his quasi-niece's sex tape didn't make him a predator. Just a real fucking creep and I wasn't going to let him occupy any more of my time than he already had. So instead of facing my slimy demons, I twisted my ankle in the jump from the upstairs window before driving away from them.

A disgusted shiver went down my back. I growled to myself in the mirror before brushing my teeth again.

I emerged into the store, tossing some items into a basket before heading to the checkout. The cashier's eyes followed me, doing that obnoxious thing where she tried to figure out who I was by staring *harder*. I pulled my sunglasses down and smiled at her.

"Find everything okay, dear?" Her chubby cheeks were red, her eyes bloodshot. Her hair was thinning and teased in an attempt to appear thicker.

I felt as haggard as she looked.

"A phone charger?" I held my phone up, showing her the port. I left mine plugged in at *Uncle* Jacob's house, and I was certainly not going back for it.

The cashier turned around and spent an inordinate amount of time rifling through the little hanging boxes.

"I think it's that one," I piped in, pointing to the one she'd touched three times already.

"Oh, yes. Thank you, dear. My eyes aren't what they used to be." She gave me a sheepish grin, ringing me up before I threw my credit card on the counter.

"Nicolette Parker... is that you?" a voice shrieked behind me. I cringed and turned, but blew out a relieved breath.

Chelsea Rhodes had been my best friend in high school and the only person I missed when I left town. Guilt scratched at me for how we'd lost touch over the years. I watched her life progress over social media. She'd invited me to her bridal shower, her wedding, her baby shower, but I'd opted to send expensive gifts instead.

And now here she stood in front of me with a baby on her hip and a toddler in her shopping cart. She looked the same, only older, a bit paler, and very tired.

"Chelsea, you have no idea how glad I am to see you!" I hugged her like a lifeline. The smell of her shampoo brought me back to all the nights we snuck out of our houses and met up to smoke cigarettes and drink cheap beer in the shed of the water tower. "Oh my, is this Amelia?" I put a hand on the toddler's shoulder. "She's so big!"

Chelsea laughed nervously. "Um, this is Olivia. Amelia is seven now. She's in ballet class. And this is Erin." She rubbed her nose against the baby in her arms. "We're doing a little girl's shopping until Amelia gets done."

A pang of guilt struck me. She had a *seven*-year-old? How was that possible?

"Wow..." I exasperated. "That's so—"

"Sorry, honey, this declined."

I spun around where the red-cheeked woman held out my credit card. I frowned at her. "Can you try it again?"

"I tried it twice already. It says to call the bank." She offered a timid glance.

I dug through my purse for my debit card and slid it over to her before returning my gaze to Chelsea.

"I'm so glad you're the first person I ran into. This whole trip has been one headache after another."

Chelsea pouted at me. "What brings you—"

"Excuse me, sorry, this one declined too."

I turned around to face her. What was going on?

"That's... impossible." I pulled out my phone and swiped to find my banking app.

"Here you go, Edna." Chelsea handed a fifty-dollar bill to the woman, and I smiled with gratitude.

"I'm sorry, my bank must have frozen the cards. I'll pay you back, I've got cash in the car—"

She waved at me dismissively. "Please, you supplied *all* the booze and nicotine in my teenage years. Bill's working the night shift tonight; you should come over after dinner to catch up."

My spirits lifted a beat. "I'd love to. Where are you living?" I asked.

"Oh, same place." I raised my eyebrows. "Mom and Dad retired to Savannah and sold us the house for a dollar."

"Oh," I said, offering a supportive nod. "That's cool." She still lived in her two-bedroom childhood home? With three little girls?

She pressed her lips together in a thin smile. "I better get these girls in the car before meltdown o'clock."

I wasn't sure what that was but I gave her a hug and thanked her again for picking up my tab.

As I got back in my car, I scrolled through my email and, sure enough, my accounts were frozen for fraud suspicion. The irony of American National Bank not recognizing *Godot, West Virginia.*

I had a handful of hundred-dollar bills stashed in my glove compartment. That would have to last until I got a hold of a human being. My fingers perched over the 1-800 number but froze when two voices chattering on the park bench arose a few feet away from me. I leaned toward the open passenger window.

"Is it true the Asher boy is dating Katie Plainbottom? I heard she's over at his house every night."

"No, no. She told me in church that she's trying to help him get back on his feet. She even got her dad to hire him at his auto shop. That girl's always taking on too much. I don't know *how* she can stand to spend so much time with that man. I told her to be careful." Disdain radiated off the woman who shook her head, out of the corner of my eye.

"I never thought I'd see the day that Riot Asher showed his face back here." I pulled out my small notebook, scribbling notes down.

Katie Plainbottom.

Her name sounded familiar, and I was fairly certain she was in my grade, but if she was who I thought she was, we never crossed paths.

There had been nothing remarkable about her. She wasn't one of the smart girls. She didn't play sports. No musical talent. But she was involved in the church and Junior League and Daughters of the American Revolution and every other community activity. She wore fake pearls and long skirts and pastel-colored *headbands.*

So, Little Miss Perfect Katie Plainbottom is shacking up with a convicted killer.

The idea almost impressed me.

I started to search for *Plainbottom Auto Shop Godot* when my phone went black. Groaning a sigh of frustration, I plugged the new charger into the cigarette lighter.

I spotted a liquor store across the street. I grabbed some cash from my glove compartment, letting my phone charge while I picked up wine for the night.

The sun was already warm and a thin layer of sweat started to humidify my back as I jogged across the street. I pulled the door handle but fell backward.

Of course, it wasn't open yet. I rested my hands on my hips and cursed at the sky before re-crossing the street to my car.

I grabbed the driver's side door handle and once again fell backward.

No, no...

"Ughh!" The frustration broke from my chest. My keys were in the ignition, powering the car that powered my phone. And I was locked out.

Fighting the overwhelming sense of defeat, I sank to my heels, pulling my hands through my hair so I didn't punch something.

"Are you alright, sweetheart?" I peered up at an elderly woman who gazed at me with such concern I felt self-conscious.

"I locked my keys in my car," I said, deadpan.

"There's a garage one block down. I'm sure one of those handsome young boys can help you. They're so good. They helped me reprogram my radio last week." She smiled as if it were the greatest kindness in the world.

I stood up. "That's not the garage that Mr. Plainbottom runs, is it?"

"Well, I don't think he does much work himself anymore, what with the cancer and all, but yes that's his."

The auto shop was just as the old woman described, a garage with *lots* of handsome young men. I pulled my hair into a loose braid that hung over my shoulder and I shifted my boobs in my bra, so my cleavage popped. I smacked my lips with the cheap tube of lipstick I bought at the Piggly Wiggly.

I strutted into the garage and walked up to the front desk. The back of a desk chair faced me, and a low voice grumbled into the phone cord. I looked around and smiled at a few of the gazes through the glass window that peered into the work bays.

I waited for the person to get off the phone.

And waited.

The phone clicked back on the cradle. I turned my smile up a watt.

But I still waited. Whoever was on the phone hadn't turned around.

Maybe they hadn't heard me walk in. I shuffled my feet and coughed, calling attention to myself. But they still didn't turn. My impatient shoe tapped the cement floor. The chair turned a few degrees but then turned back.

My patience snapped.

"Excuse me, can you tell me where I can find Riot Asher?" I said in my sweetest, damsel-in-distress voice.

The chair spun around. My smile fell to a scowl. The same moss-faced man from this morning stared at me, his expression bored. His fingers were peaked with his elbows on the side of the chair.

"Not here," he said, impassively.

Rude.

"Well, can you tell me when he'll be in?" I smiled, reaching a hand up to stroke my braided hair.

The man-beast followed the motion for only a second before scowling at me.

"I locked my keys in my car," I waved like *what a silly wench I am*, "and I heard he's practically a magician with a Slim Jim."

The Chewbacca narrowed his eyes at me and blinked, considering. He stood with a grunt and brushed past me. I couldn't help but catch the smell of motor oil, grass clippings, and something else familiar I couldn't put my finger on.

He disappeared into a small room, and I opened my mouth to yell "excuse me" when he returned with the flat tool in his hand. He paused at the front door.

"Where?"

God, did this walking carpet only speak in one and two-word sentences?

"Outside the Piggly Wiggly."

Without looking at me or saying another word, he stalked in that direction.

"If it's an inconvenience, I can wait for Riot to get here," I said, skipping to keep up with his long, brisk gait. I hissed when my ankle reminded me that it was still sore from my midnight second-floor escape.

Captain Whiskers twisted his head slightly at my sound but kept moving forward. I almost demanded he stop and answer me about Riot, but I reminded myself I was here on a delicate mission. I had to remain professional and not show my hand. I didn't have the luxury of alienating anyone. Even though this guy had certainly not extended *me* the same courtesy.

He stopped in front of my car.

"Got ID?" he asked.

"Are you fucking kidding me?"

His eyebrows twitched with surprise.

"How do I know it belongs to you?" he asked.

"So, he *does* speak in actual sentences!" I put my hand to my chest, feigning shock.

He glared in response, but I caught his eyes move briefly to where my hand was pressed below my throat. Professionalism be damned. I wasn't going to get any kind of story with *Fuzzy Wuzzy* standing in my way.

"You woke me from a dead sleep by pounding on this window a few hours ago." I smacked my hand against the driver's side.

One side of his lips twitched. But he didn't flinch, only crossed his grizzly arms over his muscled chest and stood his ground.

Heat crept up my neck. Did he have that many muscles earlier this morning?

Stomping my foot, I winced again; how had Grizzly Adams managed to turn me, Nicolette Parker, the Bloodhound of New England, into a petulant child?

"My ID is in the car." I made overt gestures with my hands and enunciated my words. "If you open it — then I can show it to you."

He narrowed his eyes again, and I reminded myself that I still needed him to open my car.

Just like I needed Chelsea to pay for my groceries.

Just like I had needed Jacob's house to stay at.

My throat tightened. I was suddenly tired and sad and angry with the foreign feeling of being so goddamn dependent on *everyone else* all of a sudden.

"Look, I've had a really bad night and morning. Please, can you just *help me?*"

At that, Hairy Houdini pressed his lips together reluctantly, or I think he did, it was hard to tell through all that *fur.*

He took one stride and towered over me, his defined chest inches from my face. His arm brushed mine, and we both looked down as if the connection had created something tangible to examine. I took in another deep breath of his musk before stepping aside where he went to work on opening the car door.

When it popped open moments later, I let out a giant breath I hadn't realized I'd been holding.

"God, thank you..." I whispered. I ducked in to grab my wallet to show him my ID but when I turned around, he was already walking back toward the garage.

"Hey, what do I owe you?" I called, holding up a few bills.

He stopped walking and turned his head to the side, so I only caught his profile. He paused a long beat, ignoring my question.

"Riot's out of town all week. You should move on."

I scowled at his back, stalking away. *Yeah, no shit, Fuzzy Wuzzy.*

If only it were that easy.

4

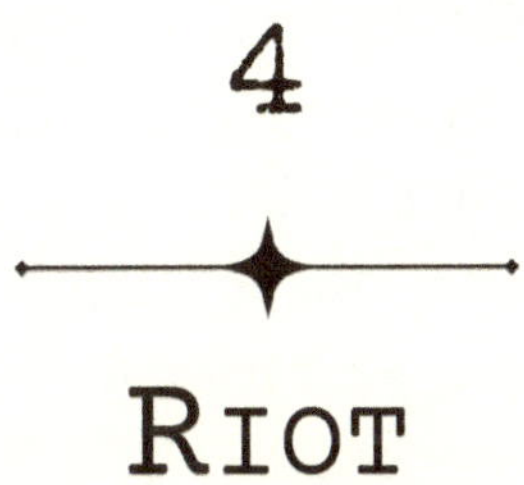

RIOT

Katie sat on the edge of the front desk when I reentered the auto shop, her suspicious eyes fixed on something beyond me.

"Oh, my gosh! Was that *Nicolette Parker?*" she said with interested eyes.

"Who?" I asked, trying to sound uninterested.

"You remember Nicolette Parker. She was in my grade." Katie pressed her face to the glass door, craning her neck to try to catch another glimpse of the bratty little witch. "She was always camped out in the broadcast journalism studio. She left right before senior year for some big fancy internship at a TV station in New York." Katie rolled her eyes, feigning like she was unimpressed.

"I remember her getting busted for smoking weed at the water tower with Chelsea," said Amber, our accountant, sauntering into the shop.

Katie turned her attention. Good, I was glad she had a partner for the gossip. I knew what it was like to be the subject of small-town chatter and didn't care to partake.

Part of me had been itching to know who the blonde was since I caught her sleeping in her car this morning. But now that I had confirmation she was, in fact, a reporter, like I had guessed when she walked in here asking for Riot Asher, I wanted even less to do with her.

"I heard she was fired from the TV station for sleeping with her boss," Amber hissed. "It was a whole big affair, like, ten years ago. The guy was *married*. Had two little girls at the time." She turned her nose up.

"How do you know?" Katie prattled on.

"Ladies," I regarded them. "As much as I would love to hear all about Where Are They Now, I do have some quotes to write up." I nodded to the desk Katie was sitting on. She gave me a flat expression and hopped off, following Amber into her back office.

"She's been hosting some video podcasts in Easton. Like, how *embarrassing!* You used to be on TV." Amber's voice drifted off and Katie clucked her tongue.

I flipped on the radio to drown out their scandalmongering before scribbling on the quote sheets.

I don't know why Nicolette Parker was back in Godot. But after the barrage of media my brother and I had faced over the past twelve years, I was too cynical to believe it had nothing to do with me. A knot formed in my stomach, picturing the stubborn way she stomped her foot and the bratty toss of her silky blonde hair.

The two exchanges with Nicolette had been brief, but they left an impression on me. The only vague memory I have of her from high school is when she interviewed me after a handful of big wins for the morning announcements. I was pretty cut off from the outside world after I went to prison, so I knew nothing of her career after high school.

My curiosity got the better of me and I pulled out my phone and searched for her name.

The first few articles and videos were all old stories from ten or eleven years ago. Most had been written by her for the former media conglomerate, The Independent American.

Sex Trafficking Suburban Nightmare Exposed

Guess Where the Charitable Donations Really Went

Hedge Fund Manager Dethroned for Embezzlement

Fuck, these were serious exposés. The knot in my stomach grew tighter.

A series of videos with a younger version of her behind a news desk were followed by more recent videos with lower production quality of Nicolette up close. She had hundreds of thousands of YouTube subscribers, but nothing had been posted in the last few months.

I kept scrolling until I spotted an old article that was from some women's magazine.

IANN Investigative Journalist Wrongfully Terminated for Misconduct, Predatory Producers Strike Again

I scanned the article. Nicolette had barely turned eighteen when she met Bentley Upton, the VP of the floundering network. He was more than twice her age and the article credited her with the resurgence of ratings the network experienced after giving her feature opportunities.

"I was weak and fell victim to the young woman's advances," Upton was quoted admitting. The article tore him apart for the sexist douche he sounded like. My gut wrenched at the last line.

Nicolette Parker was not at fault but paid the price with her career and future.

I groaned internally and the girls' chattering suddenly took on a different meaning.

Don't put your guard down now, I reminded myself.

Pulling a hand over my face, I returned to the second page of the search results.

Nicolette Parker Nude Photos Leaked!!

My tempted finger hovered over the link.

"Whatcha doing?" Katie's voice snapped me out of my vortex. I swiped the browser away.

I leaned back in my chair and tossed my phone down on the desk, raking my hands through my hair. "Finishing up the quotes." I shook my head and stifled a yawn, noticing her inquisitive expression. "It was an early morning. They have me on groundskeeping at the library for community service."

Katie put a hand on my shoulder.

"Ry, that's great." I winced at the nickname that I'd never cared for. She frowned. "Although I wish it was something a little more public. It'd be good to have people see you out volunteering."

Volunteering. She had an amazing way of spinning things to make it sound like I wasn't a convict.

"Maybe I can talk to Jeremy and see if you can switch to helping the church with the annual Field Days coming up—"

"No!" I said, a little too harsh. Guilt struck me for the startled look on her face. "No," I said, softer. "I like the groundskeeping. I can do a good job with it."

The idea of being paraded around like some zoo animal on display was bad enough. The thought of it being in front of my mother's parish was mortifying.

Katie's gaze was laced with sympathy I found too condescending to appreciate. She ran a hand over my cheek. The physical contact was comforting but my mind flashed to that brief brush of Nicolette's elbow. The jolt of electricity it sent through my body.

"Riot, you're going to have to face the church sooner or later. I mean, you see these people every day." She gestured out the window where the town was bustling. "What's the difference if you see them all at once under the roof of Redeemer's?"

I gave her a dark look. "You know it's not the same."

She pressed her lips together. "I know it feels that way now. But we'll give it more time. They need to see you as one of *them*. And you'll never be one of them again if you keep avoiding the church."

Shame and something like irritation ripped through me. I hated this conversation, and it was happening more frequently.

She spun the chair to face me head-on, putting her hands on either side of my face. I closed my eyes at the tender warmth even if it didn't feel genuine.

"The town needs to stop seeing you for what you did and start seeing the person you could be." She took her hands back and turned her head. "I know you think your presence at the church feels… *wrong*. But eventually, it's going to be noticed. People want to believe in you, Riot. I'm doing everything I can, but you'll need to meet me halfway."

My knotted stomach turned to stone. None of that sat well with me but as I looked up into her wide, well-meaning eyes, I reminded myself she was trying to help.

I nodded, which seemed to satisfy her.

"We'll get there, together. I promise." She patted my hand and kissed me cordially on the cheek before walking out the front door.

Each minute dragged on for hours the rest of the afternoon. I put a hand over my abs where the knot was growing. I picked my phone up to check the time, and it opened the search results page I had been on.

Nicolette Parker Nude Photos Leaked!!

I'd be lying if I said I wasn't curious, recalling that light sheen of sweat on her neck that had made her skin glisten. But for some reason, particularly after Katie's conversation, it seemed perverse to open Nicolette up to that kind of scrutiny, even if it was just in my head. I closed out the browser.

Besides, the URL was skinflix.me. It would probably give my phone a virus.

When I got home that evening it wasn't quite six but I was ready to call it a night. I was looking forward to taking a shower, cracking a beer, and going to sleep.

My luck continued to dwindle when a bunch of crashing noises emanated from the storage pod that sat a few yards off our houses. What didn't get ruined in the fire was ruined *putting out* the fire and the rest we kept in a storage pod.

"Brennan?" I called out a few feet away, so he'd know I was coming.

He had rifled through almost every box and was sitting on the ground with books and notebooks all around him.

"Wrong," he muttered, ripping a page out of a Bible in his lap.

"What are you doing?" I asked.

"It's all wrong," he repeated scribbling something out. He picked his head up and cackled his signature robotic laugh. "Ha! Ha! Ha! Look at this, Riot. Mom circled this passage."

He held the book up without looking at me. It was a passage from Genesis. A little heart was scribbled in the corner with my dad's name, *Scotty*, inside. My heart twisted at the familiar handwriting.

"Did she really believe she was made from Dad's *rib?*" He shook his head in disbelief and took the book back from me.

"What are you doing in here, Brennan?" I asked gently.

"Did you know that there was a rare and powerful microchip built into the Snapmaster 700?"

I furrowed my brow. "The digital camera?"

Brennan had gotten one for his birthday when we were kids. I remember because he was so excited he wouldn't open any more presents. I had asked my mom to get him Rock 'Em Sock 'Em Robots so we could play later. But he'd spent the rest of the weekend locked in his room, taking photos of his model action figures and posting them to online chat rooms.

He looked up, unblinking. "I was fourteen. It was a Thursday evening, and I had filled the entire memory card with the most wonderful images 1.4 megapixels could take," he said wistfully.

"Did you find it?"

"No." He snapped back to his hunched position. "No. I did not. No, I did not. Not. Not!" He threw the Bible on the ground.

"Okay, okay," I said gently. "How about I make us some dinner and then I'll help you look tomorrow after work?"

He gazed up at me with those open, blue eyes like I was offering him a kidney.

"Yes. Please."

I offered a hand to help him up, but he somehow rose to his feet from a cross-legged position without so much as a twist. I used to tease him and tell him that he was an alien. Or a pod person.

Of course, he would then proceed to spend half an hour telling me all the reasons why extraterrestrials wouldn't be able to survive in our atmosphere. But if they could, the pod person theory would be the most likely. However, if the aliens were discerning then *I* would be the one more likely to be body-snatched due to my fuller physical stature and more symmetrical facial features.

I think he was trying to say I was good-looking. But it had been hard to understand at the time.

"What do you want for dinner?" I asked him, sliding the storage pod door closed with a grating sound.

Brennan halted his mechanical walk and turned to appraise me. He stared at me for a long time, expressionless, blinking in front of the setting sun.

"SpaghettiOs. Over the fire pit," he replied before taking calculated steps toward his bunkhouse.

I smiled. SpaghettiOs started on a camping trip when we were kids. That camping trip was one of the few real memories I had of our dad, the firefighting hero.

He had taken us camping at Alum Creek State Park. We all slept in one tent and had the time of our very young lives. We hiked along a creek that led to some cave-like overhangs. It was like we'd stepped into a different universe. Each turn, a discovery. Brennan was overjoyed looking at the rocks, naming each layer of rock and sediment.

We planned to catch fish for dinner, but it had not been a successful session, hence the SpaghettiOs. We had been hiking and fishing all day and we were starving. I remember those cans of pasta and sauce with sliced hot dogs tasted like the best thing I'd ever eaten. I was happy. I was five.

Brennan got frustrated with the fishing. He had done all kinds of calculations with how far to cast the line, how deep to rig the sinker, but nothing was biting. My dad laughed, creating a distinct crinkle at the corners of his eyes when he smiled, calf-deep in the water.

"Sorry, kiddo, not a lot of logic and planning when it comes to fishing. You have to be patient and *feel* the fish. *Will* them to come to you," he had said. Brennan appeared confused, which was surprising because my big brother always had *all* the answers.

"That doesn't make any sense, Dad."

Dad smiled again, casting a line far into the center of the creek.

"Sometimes things don't always make sense, Brennan. There are some things we can't put to logic. But they work out anyway. Or they don't." He tilted his head back and forth. "But usually, they do. If you believe they will. That's the magic of it. You never know. You can chase after something your entire life and never catch it. But the moment you stop chasing and start picturing what it'll look like when it's yours, well, you might discover that it'll end up finding you."

A few minutes later, a tug on Brennan's line made his eyes go wide.

"Dad!" he shout-whispered, afraid to scare the fish. "What do I do?"

"Be smooth, don't tug. Lean back and then reel in the slack, nice and slow."

It had only been a tiny smallmouth bass, but I'd never seen Brennan so excited. At the time, I was grumpy that my brother had all Dad's attention. I had a small children's pole, and it wasn't catching *any* kind of bass.

I remember being surprised when our dad made him throw it back.

"That's just a little guy, not even enough meat on him for little Riot here. Would be a waste and it's a shame to waste a living thing." Brennan pouted. "How about this? We come back same time next year and that little sucker will be so big and fat that when you catch him again, you'll be able to feed all three of us."

Brennan's eyes lit up at that.

Unfortunately, we never made that trip back to Alum Creek State Park. A few months after that camping trip there was a huge fire in the valley. It was the poor section and all the houses still had old knob and tube wiring. Nearly the entire block burned down, and it took my dad with it.

Brennan had begged my mom to take us back to the campground, but after the funeral, she had become a recluse, despondent. She was never the same after losing him. None of us were. Brennan didn't know how to process his feelings. He never cried. He just looked surprised. Surprised that he was suffering something he didn't understand. Still, he begged Mom to bring us back to Alum Creek. Time and again, she said no. It wasn't something she was comfortable doing.

When I was old enough to understand what that trip had really meant to him, I promised, no matter what, we would go back once football ended my freshman year of college.

And like so many years earlier, Brennan was once again let down by his family. I was already in jail by then, awaiting sentencing that would take another several months to be made.

It wasn't Alum Creek State Park, but that night as my brother and I cooked SpaghettiOs over the open fire pit, halfway between my house and his, I knew we both felt closer to Dad.

5

NICOLETTE

I rolled up to Chelsea's house at eight-thirty, astonished by how familiar everything still was. Aside from the plethora of children's toys scattered around the yard like landmines, it was exactly as I remembered, down to the rockers that we had spent hours on, giggling about the way cute boys did or didn't give us attention.

My heart pulled at how much of her life I had missed.

I knocked on the door and the running water cut off before Chelsea pulled the door open a moment later.

As we methodically went through almost two bottles of wine, I relaxed at the ease with which we fell back into conversation. As if it were the summer after junior year. We were busy waxing nostalgic when a wave of sadness came over me. I reached across the table and took her hand.

"Chels, I'm so sorry I haven't been back to visit you and the girls. And I'm sorry I wasn't at the wedding. Or the baby shower."

She laughed into her wine glass. "Honey, do you know who was at my wedding?" My blank stare told her I didn't. "Because I don't. I remember moments but I couldn't tell you who was at the wedding or the showers." She waved dismissively, shrugging. "You're here now and I'm glad to see you're doing so well." She patted my hand.

"Where's Bill?" My eyes scanned the tiny, cluttered house. Who knew kids needed so much... *stuff?* "I was hoping to see him."

"He works as the night maintenance guy at the Center."

I frowned. "I thought he was a shift leader for the coal mine?"

Chelsea shook her head. "They laid everyone off almost ten years ago. Pastor Blackwell got some reports that Godot had the highest rate of lung cancer in almost the entire country, so he outsourced the whole operation to some management company. I guess they only hire within their union so no one in Godot actually works in the Godot Valley Coal Mine anymore." She offered a flat look.

"Pastor Blackwell? Good to know Jeremy's dad is still large and in charge." My stomach turned sour at the thought of my old high school prom date. "How on earth did he manage to convince the coal mine to outsource?"

"Well, because he owns it. The church owns the land the mine is in."

Had I known that? I knew it owned a large amount of the land in Godot, but it seemed bizarre for a church to manage something like a coal mine. "Really?" I said.

"Yeah, the whole mine acreage right up to the airfield, the *entire* valley, and half the town center. The only part they don't own is all the big farmhouses on the east side."

I nodded. It seemed weird for a *church* to own so much property, but it was run by a nonprofit with a board of directors and everything, so I guess it was perfectly legal. I turned to her. "What's the Center?"

She assessed me like I was crazy before her expression softened. "Oh, right, I guess it opened right after you left. It's a soup kitchen, a homeless shelter, and a drug rehab resource all in one. Oh, the drug problem? Got so bad in the last fifteen years that the Center began handing out free, clean needles just so that Godot wouldn't become ground zero for the next AIDS epidemic. You wouldn't believe how many people that we graduated with are cracked out in the Godont Valley."

I chuckled. "The what?"

"The Go-Don't Valley. That's what we call it now. Because we Don't Go to the Valley. They're all those pre-manufactured homes that went up after that big fire ripped apart half the Valley."

"Yeah, I remember hearing about that. People were moving into them when my parents moved here." I pictured the interconnected buildings that stood almost like barracks from the outside.

"They're all dumps. Remember we went to that rager at one of them the summer before you left?" I remembered, but barely. It had been a wild night. I had tried ecstasy for the first time, so my memories of that party consisted of blinding strobe lights, dance music, and trashed furniture that sat on top of sticky floors. "Yeah, that's how they all look now. The entire neighborhood is a smack den. Honestly, I think that the Center is the only thing keeping any of those people alive." She shook her head and *tsked*.

"Jeez," I blew out a breath. "I heard Godot had gone downhill, but that's kind of insane. Is it just meth?"

She shook her head and frowned like she didn't know. "I thought so, but Bill said some new drug spread like wildfire over the last ten years or so. He sees ODs at the Center all the time. It's a mix of stuff, I guess."

Something inside me ticked. That strange instinctual feeling I get when the coincidences begin to outweigh the facts. It's almost like seeing a bunch of random stray puzzle pieces but then a few start to match and you realize a whole game was coming together.

I had to check out this Center tomorrow.

Chelsea offered me the couch for the night but literally as she did, the baby started crying, which woke up the toddler and I was an asshole for not remembering their names.

"You've got your hands full," I said. "We'll catch up again soon."

As I got in my car with nowhere to go, a feeling of disquiet settled over me. I had been so used to being the fearless one, the one in charge, the one other people found formidable. And here I was, holed up in my fifteen-year-old car in a town where it was nearly eleven p.m. on a Friday and everyone was already nestled in their beds, snuggled down with their families.

I thought maybe driving past my old house would make me feel better. It would give me proof that I had a home once. A life here. People who loved me.

It was a five-minute drive from Chelsea's, and I still had it memorized. I slowed my car, rolling the window down and gazed out to see it had changed quite a bit. It had been re-sided to a different color. The lights in the kitchen were on and I could see that too had been remodeled. I idled for a minute until a small motion caught my eye.

In the corner still hung my favorite part of the house; the two-person porch swing. I could make out the silhouettes of a couple cuddled on the seat; the woman's legs pulled beneath her, resting her head on a man's shoulder, his arm wrapped around her body.

I drove circles around the town, feeling ruthlessly alone before finding myself back at the town's water tower. It had been Chelsea and my go-to spot for sneaking around with boys. It had a breathtaking view of the valley and mountains beyond and the clearest view of the night sky.

The ladder rungs on the water tower were rickety as I climbed to the top.

Back in my investigative days there had always been a moment — right at the cusp of blowing a story wide open. A moment when I got to sit in front of the *bad guy* and ask him the question I already had the answer to and watch his or her face pale while their brain raced for an adequate lie. They had been lying for so long that on a rare occasion, there was a flash of relief. The lies were over. They'd been caught. They could rest now in the deterioration of their "after" life. I called it the Gotchya Moment, and I used to live for it.

Watching the soft lights of the town below me continue to flicker out, I sat on the water tower, looking down at all the lives that had moved on without me. The weight of the loneliness felt like it might crush me.

"Gotchya," I whispered ruefully to myself.

The deep tug of displacement was like an anchor around my foot, dragging me into the pool of water I huddled next to.

The rumbling sound of a car engine stirred me from my pity party.

"Shit, seriously?" I groaned.

Below me, a commercial truck pulled up to the base of the tower. Two men hopped out. One went around back and started to unravel a hose. The other climbed on top of the truck, hooking up the other end. One started shouting as the other turned on the hose, spewing some kind of colorless liquid all over the ground.

They were treating the water at this hour? I waited until they were preoccupied with hooking up the hose to climb down the ladder.

I was about to sneak back through the strip of woods where I'd parked when I got a closer look at the truck. An unfamiliar symbol that didn't belong to the Spokane County Water Authority decorated the sides.

Echo Chemicals

That internal tick went off again, and I snapped a quick photo on my phone and scooped up a few wet leaves with a tissue I had in my pocket before scurrying off back to my car.

6

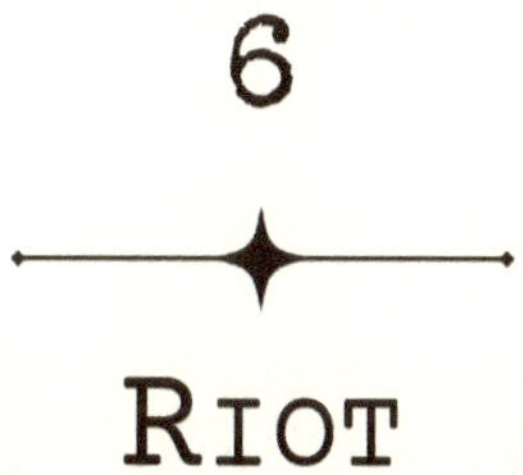

RIOT

It wasn't my morning to mow at the library but I had left a bizarre spot in the front bushes yesterday. I hedged them best I could but there was an awkward empty space where the branches grew in the wrong direction, leaving a little alcove that begged to be filled.

I woke up early, grabbed the materials I needed, and headed there.

The spring sunrise was beautiful that morning and I stood up straight, pushing my shoulders down to let my face warm against the rays. I took a step back to appraise the small contraption I'd arranged. I fiddled with the bolts before feeling accomplished enough to put my tools back in my truck.

As I pulled the tailgate down, I spotted her. Her car at least. I was too far away to see inside but when I squinted in her direction, the engine started up. It turned over so rough I was surprised to see that dinosaur of a car peel out so fast.

Weird. Yesterday morning she said she was working on her computer and fell asleep. It was possible. But two nights in a row? I began to wonder if she had somewhere to stay. I remembered the look in her eye the day before when she had dropped that armor of a façade for a split second and genuinely asked for help.

That moment had stirred something in me. I *wanted* to help her. And that made me nervous. This girl could be here for ulterior reasons, and I didn't need more occasions to engage with her. Still, she didn't seem to know who I was, so as long as that held, I was safe.

She peeled out, slowing down when she passed the entrance where I had been working. Had she seen me? My nerves ticked up a notch.

After chugging the remaining hot Gatorade in my car, I gave my face a quick slap. I had to keep my guard up; she was still *media,* after all.

Six hours dragged by at the auto shop before my shift manager told me I could go home a little early if I had gotten all the necessary quotes out, which I had. Four hours ago.

I was about to pack up when the office line rang. It was the regional AAA affiliate. There was a disabled vehicle right on the outskirts of Godot and it was *just* too far for them to cover.

"Riot, can you check it out? Last job of the day then you're good to take off," my manager, Rodger, said.

I scanned the wall of keys to the tow trucks and service vehicles.

"We got a tow here?"

"Nah, Evan had to take it out about an hour ago. It probably just needs a jump. Grab some cables and try to get it back here and we'll take a better look."

I sighed. My truck bed was still full of all the materials I'd used that morning but if it was an easy jump, it would be quick.

Or so I thought.

As I turned the corner, I spotted the car on the side of the road and recognized it immediately. I groaned and cursed under my breath.

I rolled to a stop, parking in front of Nicolette Parker who leaned one hip against her relic of a Cadillac and shielded her eyes.

"I don't know what happened, it just cut to a stop, it's never done—" She launched into her story but stopped short when my feet hit the pavement. She dropped her arms and tilted her head toward the sky. "You gotta be kidding me. Of all the garages in this entire county, they send *you*?"

My feet cut to a stop and I bristled at the sneer on her face. I turned to get back in the truck. *Fuck it,* she didn't want my help, she could call one of her many resources.

"Wait! Fine, I'm sorry." She threw up her hands. "Can you get it going?"

I bore my eyes into the whiny little witch. Her fingers ran through her blonde hair, glinting off the sun. A light gleam of sweat glistened across her chest—

I pulled my attention back to her car, walking over and popping the hood up. *God, how old was this thing?*

"Jesus..." I said under my breath. She took a step toward me, and I caught the brief scent of lilacs. "When was the last time you drove this thing?"

"Easton's a big city. I didn't need it much, and it got me from there to here, didn't it?"

I hung my head between my shoulders and growled to myself to take deep breaths. If I could deal with convicts in prison and the judgmental people back in Godot, I could deal with a petulant city girl.

I checked the batteries and the fluids but to be honest, I wasn't good with Caddies, especially ones this old.

"Gonna have to get a tow back," I said.

"Isn't that what you're here for?" she asked, her tone laced with attitude.

I turned and caught her peering into my truck bed. She dropped the tarp she had been poking around.

Nosy, little asshole.

I glared at her. Her arms crossed under her chest, which pushed a bit of cleavage over the top of her neckline. Her skin was flawless. A little paler than the rest of us but smooth and perfect, nonetheless. She probably had a nightmare of a skincare routine. A girl that beautiful had to be high-fuckin'-maintenance.

"Do you see a tow cable?" I chided, pointing to where she'd been snooping.

I shook my head in disbelief and turned back to the engine in front of me, poking around another minute before pulling out my phone.

"Evan," I barked. "Need a tow on 79 North before the town border."

He grumbled something while I stole another glance at Nicolette who was now shamelessly rifling through the parts in my truck bed.

"Hey!" I shouted at her, but she wasn't startled in the slightest. She turned her face to me, looking bored, before rolling her eyes and leaning against my truck. She bent one of her long legs and rested it on the tire behind her. I turned my attention back to the phone where Evan muttered something about forty minutes.

Slipping my phone back into my pocket, I jerked my head to tell her to get into the truck.

"Wait, we're leaving my car here?"

"Evan has the last tow truck and he'll be here in about forty minutes. You can either *ride* back with me, wait for him in your hot car, or you can walk six miles back to town." I gave her a pointed glare before she ran both hands through her hair, bunching it in her fists. I saw her eyes flit to her ankle, which she gave a quick rotate before moving back toward her car.

For a second, I thought she was going to wait inside it for the tow truck and I don't know why I was let down by that. Instead, she ducked inside, grabbed a stuffed backpack, and slung it over her shoulder before shooting me a glare and moving toward the passenger side of my truck.

I caught her stealing another glance in the truck bed before she got in. An anxious tick moved through me.

Had she figured out who I was since our last encounter? If she had, what was she looking for? Did she think I carried dead bodies around in my truck?

When I got in the car, the walls of the truck cab seemed to close in. I was painfully aware of the warm body next to me, despite how *cold* and prickly she was.

I was content to drive in silence but a minute after we got moving, she spoke up.

"What is all that stuff, anyway?"

Something inside me ached to tell her the truth. The way she spoke to me. The attitude. All of it was so refreshing compared to the blatant avoidance I was used to. She was so "un-Godot", I found myself pulled to her in an inexplicable way. But I had to remember who she was.

A reporter. The media. The enemy.

She was not the person to find a kindred spirit in.

"What stuff?"

She scoffed. "All those half-built pieces in the bed of your truck?"

My heart skipped a beat, but I remained neutral. "They're spare auto parts. I work for a garage, remember?" It came out more sarcastic than I meant it, but I was hoping if I gave her enough attitude, she'd drop it.

"Do you often fashion auto parts into lawn spinners and wind chimes?"

My head snapped to her. I couldn't help it. How had she seen those shambled, half-built whirligigs and deduced they were wind spinners? I had to give her credit, she was brighter than I thought. *You need to be more careful, Riot.*

She looked at me with a smug half-smile on her face. My eyes darted to her lips and the small, arrogant dimple on her cheek. I didn't know if I wanted to push her out of the car or kiss her and my stomach tightened.

I opened my mouth to reply with something snarky but, thankfully, my phone rang. I recognized it as the garage and hit the answer button. It connected to my Bluetooth automatically.

Before I could answer, Rodger started talking. "Hey, Cherry Mitchell has a dead battery at the elementary ballpark, can you swing by on your way back to the shop?"

I hissed a curse under my breath. First Nicolette Parker, now Cherry Mitchell. Could this day go any better? I tensed at the anticipation of the look on Cherry's face.

"Cherry doesn't particularly care for me, Rodger," I warned.

"Sorry, you're the only one out in the field and if you're driving back on 79, you should drive right past the ball field."

I closed my eyes. It was only a jump. It'd be easy. It'd be quick. I quirked an eyebrow in Nicolette's direction, asking if she minded.

She rolled those obnoxious gray eyes and shrugged her shoulders before fixing her annoyed gaze out the window. *Little pain in the ass.*

"Alright, be there in five."

"Great, thanks, Riot." He clicked off.

I froze. I held my breath. Nicolette took a sharp breath in. I stared out the front windshield like my life depended on it.

"You..." her voice dripped with venom, "are Riot Asher?"

I didn't turn my head, but I could tell she gaped at me, glaring daggers at the side of my head. I stayed silent.

"Why did you tell me Riot was away for the week?" she asked but the tone of her voice told me she already knew the answer.

I stayed silent. She scoffed again and threw herself back into her seat, small waves of that blonde hair dancing across her bare shoulders as she shook her head.

"Wow, you are a real piece of work..." she muttered. The anger bubbled up my throat, tightening my grip on the steering wheel.

"Can you blame me?" I asked. "You're a reporter, no?"

I whipped my head in her direction, and she narrowed her eyes, hesitating as if trying to figure out how to answer that.

Let the lies begin.

She opened her little pink, heart-shaped lips but snapped them shut. She looked nervous. Caught. I clucked my tongue and shook my head, surprised by my disappointment.

"Right." I moved my focus back to the road. "Just like all the others..." I muttered.

"You don't even know me—"

"And I don't care to!" I interrupted whatever she was going to follow up with. The quick, wounded look on her face sent a pang of shame through my chest.

She's a reporter, don't get soft now.

Her expression fell to something resolute, and our eyes met, tangling for a minute like two tigers circling, each waiting for the other to attack. She nodded once and frowned, accepting the fact that I didn't want to know her.

I expected her to push. To defend herself. To try to get a rise out of me so I'd say something newsworthy. That's what all the others did when the soft approach hadn't worked.

But not Nicolette.

She sat back in her seat and turned her whole body away from me, looking out the window, not saying a word for the rest of the ride. Guilt snaked up my throat. I found my hand drifting halfway across the cab, eager to apologize for the shitty words my mouth had spoken. But before I reached the warm heat of her skin, I pulled my hand back.

When I pulled into the ball field, I spotted Cherry's bright red hair next to her Chevy Tahoe.

I hopped down from my truck, ignoring Cherry's abhorred gaze but it was impossible to ignore her reaction. Her audible gasp wasn't subtle. She turned away, pulling her phone out, angrily tapping the screen with those venomous fake nails.

My eyes wandered to the passenger mirror to see if Nicolette was watching Cherry's reaction. Not only was she watching, but she had rolled the window down to better examine the exchange. My chest tightened when I met her eyes, squinted in my direction, and my face burned.

Great, the *one* woman in the entire town who, not only *hadn't* been afraid of me but hadn't been afraid to *piss me off*, would now start ostracizing me like the convict I was too.

"Why... *him*... here... Rodger," I caught only a few angry words Cherry Mitchell was hissing into the phone. ".... *kids* here." I rolled my eyes. It's not like I'd killed a child... A shiver went down my back, remembering the look in my first cellmate's eyes. He *had* murdered a child. And there I was, sharing a room with him, no better or worse.

Equals.

Suddenly being outside in the open air made me feel incredibly vulnerable.

Cherry hung up and stalked toward me. "That's fine, please stop. My husband is on his way," she said, almost like a warning. "I don't need y—"

"Oh, my God, Cherry Mitchell!" Nicolette's voice sounded different. It was so high, almost patronizing. Leaping down from the passenger side, her long legs hit the pavement and *fuck, she looked good jumping down from my truck.* My dick twitched, and I cursed it under my breath.

Nicolette intercepted Cherry Mitchell's charge toward me and gave her a big hug. Cherry looked confused. "Nicolette Parker." She touched a hand to her chest to remind Cherry who she was. "I went to school with your daughter, Lanie? Wasn't she the captain of the cheer squad? Oh, my goodness, you look so *good!* Is one of these handsome boys yours? Oh, you have to show me!"

Something foreign bloomed in my chest at Nicolette's save. I made quick work out of jumping the massive Tahoe, but I couldn't help myself from stealing glances at Nicolette. She nodded like a looney bird and the dumb toothy smile fixed on her face was so phony I stifled a chuckle.

I coughed to signal Nicolette I was done. She wrapped her arms around Cherry. When she moved to walk away, Cherry pulled her back in, whispering in her ear while giving me a death stare, undoubtedly warning her about me. Nicolette's mouth dropped open, and her eyes went wide.

Fuck, what did she say to her? A thin hand went to cover her mouth, her horrified eyes going wide in my direction.

I couldn't watch this. Leaping back into my truck, I gassed up the engine. Cherry still had Nicolette in her vice grip with a serious face. A disparaging groan rumbled in my gut. We were back in town. Nicolette could walk to wherever she was staying. The image of her peeling out of the library came back to me.

Where *was* she staying?

Nicolette waved backward to Cherry and turned to follow me. Her phony expression dropped like a boat anchor. She stuck her tongue out like she had eaten something rotten. I suppressed a chuckle at the 180.

I watched her climbed into my truck. Because I couldn't help myself. And why did that turn me on so much?

When I hesitated after she settled in, she looked over at me with a wry expression.

"Old friend of yours?" I asked dryly, my eyebrows tinged with mild amusement. She rolled her eyes. I put the truck in drive but hesitated another second. "Thanks," I muttered quietly, not looking directly at her.

"Just drive," she said, casually ignoring me.

But I didn't fail to catch a suppressed smile on her lips as I drove us back to the garage.

As we made our way down Main Street, I spied her scrolling her phone, narrowing her eyes. Was she looking up the things Cherry told her? I could only imagine what she had said about me.

"I knew it!" she exclaimed, and my face felt colder, devoid of color.

She spun toward me and shoved her phone in my face. I winced in anticipation of my mug shot or maybe that awful picture they'd taken of me, my house burning in the background.

But I was taken aback when I realized that it was a picture of an art gallery. I squinted, unable to focus on the photo while keeping my eyes on the road. She zoomed in and shoved it closer. My heart stopped.

"You're the goddamn mysterious Motion Mechanic. I *knew* I recognized those wind chimes!"

She held up a photo from an art show I had been featured at on Hanniqua Island. Right after I'd been released, I was allowed to bring several of the whirligigs I had left from prison to sell at an art show. My lawyer argued that I had a right to make a living, and the art show was crucial for my ability to make said living.

I hadn't used my real name. I didn't need people searching for my work only to find that goddamn photo of me on my knees in front of the fire, hands already above my head. I went by The Motion Mechanic. I insisted on no photography and most of the upper crust from Hanniqua Island had thought it was some mysterious, quirky, artist thing. But someone had caught a candid of me from the side, my chin scar laid plain for all to see.

"I don't know what you're talking about. That's not me," I tried lying. She gave me a sarcastic, knowing smile.

"I've seen them around town, and I saw you install one at the library this morning," she snipped.

"Where you were sleeping in your car again?" I bit back, trying to throw her off but her smile just became more satisfied. "That was just some leftover piece the landscape company had. It's cheap shit from China."

"Nope. No cheap shit from China is that well-balanced."

How did she know that's how I tell the difference between real parts and fake "art" parts?

I gave her a discerning once over. Her satisfied expression made my stomach tighten. Not only was she *brighter* than I thought. But she was far more curious than I gave her credit for. I had assumed she was a washed-up influencer trying to relive her former glory days as a news anchor.

No, she thoroughly enjoyed putting these two pieces together, and, goddamn, had she done it fast. Nervous energy coursed through me.

"You can't tell anyone," I said.

"Oh. My. God. It *is* you!" Her eyes went wide, and I cursed myself again when I realized I had confirmed her suspicions. "Why are you doing oil changes and jumping washed-up soccer moms' overly jacked-up SUVs?" I suppressed a chortle. "Your work is *huge* in the northeast. Why aren't you selling it here?"

I gave her a flat look. "Godot isn't exactly the mecca for modern art appreciation."

"So, what? You just sneak around, sticking them in random places like some dirty, artistic Santa Claus?"

The chuckle caught in my throat. When I worked for the landscaping company, we integrated them into our quotes. The library was a leftover wind spinner that had been shaped like an owl and I found it fitting.

"Seriously, why aren't you selling this stuff?"

Heat crept up my neck. There were lots of reasons I wasn't using it as active income, although the demand was there. After the art exhibit on Hanniqua Island, my email inbox was flooded with custom requests. I entertained the big ones but didn't have the means and time to get back to them all.

Then there were my parole restrictions. I couldn't leave the goddamn county without a request and signed *permission slip* from Jeremy Blackwell, and I didn't very well fancy writing down "arts and crafts" as my reason for wanting to leave.

"Not really any of *your* business, is it?" I bit off with a knowing glare. She narrowed her eyes at me before sitting back with a *harumph*.

We pulled into the parking lot of the auto shop. When I killed the engine, I heard her mutter, "I saw the eagle in Jacob's yard. It looked nice."

Was that her attempt at complimenting me? She unbuckled her seat belt and hopped down.

"Not an eagle," I muttered before she slammed the door.

"What?" Our eyes tangled. This time, like two tigers working together to take down prey.

"It wasn't an eagle," I said. She looked at me curiously. "It was a vulture."

Inside the shop, Rodger wrote up Nicolette's ticket as I gathered my stuff to head home.

"Do you have a card you want to put on file when we get the diagnosis?" he asked, not looking up.

I looked at her in the reflection of the window when she hesitated.

"My cards are frozen at the moment," she said, pushing her chin in the air.

Rodger lifted his head, giving her a flat look before letting his eyes roam over her chest and hips, which turned a sour taste in my mouth.

She threw her hands up and her voice rose. "I'm sorry, but apparently not even a *national* bank thinks Godot, West Virginia is a real place!" she said.

Rodger leaned back, putting his palms up. "It's alright, just asking..." Another slow gaze landed on her rib cage. "You're staying with that uncle of yours, right, sweetheart?"

She narrowed her eyes. "How did you know that?"

"Aw, come on, you're all Jake's been talking about since he knew you were coming back."

Nicolette shuddered.

What was that *about?*

"Alright..." Rodger stood up. "Well, sweetheart, it looks like you're going to need a ride home then."

"I'll take her," I said, immediate regret slapping me in the face.

Fuck, why had I offered that? I needed to limit my time with her. Rodger looked at me like I had taken the last slice of cake.

That's why I offered that. Sit down, old man, something carnal in me growled.

"Jake's place is on my way," I shrugged, trying to make it seem like that's all it was. She did me a favor by distracting Cherry Mitchell. Offering her a ride home was simply returning the favor. That was all.

"It's fine," Nicolette cut the tension that thickened between me and Rodger. "I have a few places to stop. I can walk. Thank you, gentlemen. Call me when the car is ready!" She flew out the door before either of us could protest, which I found bizarre.

If she was trying to get some kind of quote from me or dig around my past at all, she would've jumped at the chance to accept my ride. But there she went, running out of the garage like she couldn't get away fast enough. Maybe I'd misunderstood her. The knot in my stomach loosened, and I started to feel guilty for the way I'd spoken to her.

The image of that quick flash of hurt that had crossed her face ate at me. As I left the town center, I took the road that would lead me home. Lost in thought, I almost missed the small blonde head bobbing down one of the side roads that led toward the valley. She hitched her backpack up and cracked her neck. One of her long, slender arms swiped across her forehead.

Something squeezed my heart, watching Nicolette walk alone down the valley road. I warned myself that this could all be a ploy to earn my trust. But as I tried to convince myself that she and her kind were still the devil, I had to resist every urge in my body that called me to go pick her up.

She waltzed into your place of work yesterday specifically asking for you, I reminded myself.

Raking a hand over my face, I kept driving straight.

Despite my best efforts, later that night, Nicolette plagued my thoughts and dreams like a melodic jingle that got stuck in my head. I replayed each of our interactions, trying to piece together why she was back. Why she seemed to cross my path so often. I tried convincing myself she was a threat but the memory of faint lilacs wafting off her skin and hair pushed my thoughts into a very different direction.

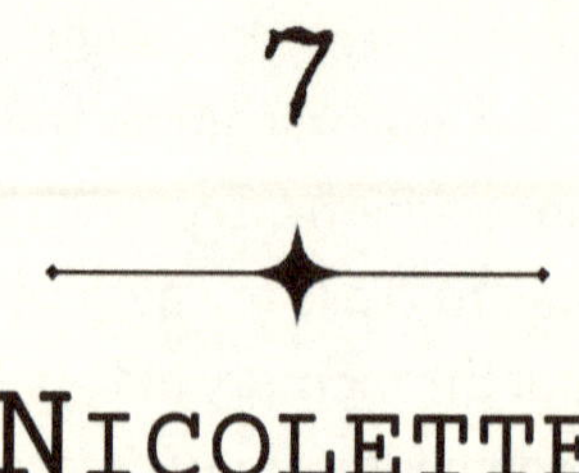

7

NICOLETTE

I must have read and re-read the welcome sign for the Center for Support and Recovery at least a dozen times.

Come to me, all who are weary and burdened and I will grant you rest.

Matthew 11:28

I had never studied the Bible. My parents initially sent me to Sunday school to try to make some friends when we first moved here, but after I'd been kicked out for dancing on the altar, my parents enrolled me in sports instead.

Still, that reassuring passage from Matthew wrapped itself around my chest and made my heart long for... *something. God, I wanted to rest.*

And now without my car, I had nowhere to go. I couldn't let Riot or that fat manager drive me back to Jacob's house.

I still had a job to do and finding out that gigantic furry man-beast was the guy I was supposed to be profiling made me realize how close I'd come to botching this entire assignment before it even began. I had to make a contingency plan in case I've blown my chances with Riot altogether.

Then you'll need to come back with a bigger story to tell.

I didn't know if the highest rates of drug use or lung cancer in a mining town in West Virginia counted as a *bigger story.* But I needed a cover story and my instincts *had* told me to keep digging. Which is what brought me to the Center.

As I entered, I was still distracted by the fact that Riot Asher, convicted mother killer, was also the biggest up-and-coming kinetic artist in the northeast. It would be an interesting angle to take for the documentary for sure. But I pushed the thought away to appraise the task at hand.

Green cots littered the open space like it was a FEMA shelter. Strung out residents of all ages scattered across the cots. I scanned the giant corkboard hanging on the wall next to the entrance. It was covered in flyers for recovery programs and meeting schedules. I moved down the row to a large section advertising compensated donations.

We Buy Blood - Blood Bank of Virginia

Get Paid for Extra Plasma - Plasmatose

Get Compensated for Participation in our Cancer Study - Echidna Pharmaceuticals

Drug Trial Seeking New Volunteers - Compensation Available - Echidna Pharmaceuticals

The little tags were nearly gone from the drug trials.

"Hello, miss, can I help you?" An elderly woman with soft, weary, eyes greeted me.

"Do a lot of people qualify for these things?" I pointed toward the flyers.

She tilted her head back and forth. "The blood and plasma shops don't get much out of us, unfortunately. The drug trials are quite popular. We have a shuttle that takes people to the teaching hospital twice a week, if you're interested?"

I smiled and shook my head. "No, I was here wondering if I could speak with someone regarding the increased drug problem?"

The woman cocked her head at me, suspiciously.

"I'm writing an article, trying to draw attention to the opioid crisis and the different measures communities have taken to help improve the problem. Who would I need to speak with?" I cringed internally. It sounded rehearsed but it was the best I could conjure up.

"Well, I guess that would be me. I'm Miriam, I'm the executive director. I—" But she stopped short, excusing herself to jog over to an older man who began to unbuckle his belt, about to piss right in the middle of the room. Miriam put a hand on his back and gestured to the restrooms.

Tiredly, she made her way back to me.

"Somehow, I have a feeling 'executive director' doesn't exactly cover it." I gave her a warm smile, and her hesitancy melted away.

Miriam had been working at the Center since it opened over ten years ago.

The building had been an old elementary school that sat empty for several years after it had been used for temporary housing following the Valley fires.

"They decimated the Valley. Wiped out an entire block of houses. Dozens of families lost their homes."

"That's right. Everyone got brand new houses?"

"Yes and no. The church commissioned the Valley Housing Project. They hired some up-and-coming building company that was supposed to revolutionize affordable housing. The deal was that they could live rent-free if they paid the county and state taxes and took a job in the coal mines."

I furrowed my brow. "The church paid for the entire Valley to be rebuilt? And then forced people to take jobs at the mine?"

Miriam shook her head. "I know how it sounds, but it was quite the opposite. Many of the folks who lost their homes needed work anyway. Pastor Blackwell piloted an apprenticeship program and before you knew it, people had a home *and* a job. It was one of the best times to live in Godot." She looked wistful.

"But didn't Pastor Blackwell shut down the mine years later?"

"Oh, he had to. Half the valley was developing some form of lung cancer, asthma, or some other health problems. He offered those who were still willing to work a job through the church but by that time, most of the valley had already fallen sick. Then, of course, came the Chimera." She shook her head with a rueful expression.

"Chimera?" I asked, but she seemed lost in thought.

"Hm? Oh, yes, the Chimera. It's the street name for a hybrid drug that popped up several years back. Horribly addictive. Some kind of cross between methamphetamine and heroin." She looked around, and I followed her gaze.

As I surveyed the Center, the weary bodies passed out on the cots, I realized they didn't look like the meth addicts that I stumbled across on the streets of Easton. They were more haunted, gaunt, lifeless.

That instinctual tick landed in my gut like a rock.

"Any idea where it came from?"

She frowned at me. "No, but these things tend to spiral like this. A few health problems in the more underprivileged communities lead to a rise in opioid use and when the money runs out, they switch to cheaper alternatives or whatever they can get." She swirled her finger in circles. "Eventually they have kids that are already predisposed to addiction and before you know it, an entire community is pitched into a hole too deep to dig out of."

I nodded.

"Do you guys have Wi-Fi?" I was already itching to do some research on this drug.

Miriam almost laughed. "Sorry, sweetheart. We operate on razor-thin budgets here. I'm the only paid employee we have outside the maintenance crew."

"You run on volunteers?" I asked.

"Oh, yes. We need all the volunteers we can get. Breakfast is always a struggle. It's one of our busiest meals and it's hard to get volunteers up that early."

There was my opening. "Do you need an extra hand tomorrow?"

Miriam smiled with appreciation. "Always, my dear."

I shrugged. "I don't have a lot of culinary experience, but I know how to wash dishes... I was going to find a hotel tonight," I lied, "but I'd be happy to stay here if you've got an extra bed so that I can help out in the morning."

Miriam gave me a tight-lipped smile and I could tell she saw right through me. My face burned and I looked away, acting casual.

She patted my hand. "Of course, dear. Come, I'll show you where you can put your things down."

The next morning, I whimpered to myself before I even opened my eyes. I had tossed and turned all night. I sat up, eyes still closed, twisting the soreness out of my neck.

When I opened my eyes, the Center was bustling already. I looked at my watch. Not even six a.m. I groaned again, digging my phone out, hoping I had an email from my bank. I don't know if I could do another night of this.

I tapped my phone, but it remained black. I tapped again as if pressing the screen harder would make a difference. I dug through my bag before remembering I left my charger in my car, which was still at the auto shop. A whiny sob escaped my lips. Pressing my palms into my eyes, I hung my head.

God, this was a mistake. A huge fucking mistake. Maybe I can call Melody and beg for a different assignment. I can cut my teeth on something else to earn back a shred of dignity because this shit wasn't doing anything *for my dignity.*

But I knew that was a nonstarter. I had exhausted all my connections and favors before Melody reached out to me with the docuseries opportunity. If I couldn't come to the table with something, I'd have to resign my life and career to something *ordinary.* And that was out of the question. I didn't work my ass off my entire life, sacrificing any semblance of a social or romantic life so that I could work a floundering news desk at some call-letter affiliate in podunk market ninety-four.

"What are *you* doing here?" the low tenor of a male voice asked. I felt it in my core. Muddy boots stood in front of me before I looked up, already wincing as the last of my dignity disintegrated. I lifted my head to see Riot, arms crossed over his defined chest, scowling in that signature way.

I leaped to my feet.

"What are *you* doing here?" I shot back.

"Community service," he replied without hesitation. A crinkled hair net dangled from one of his fists.

I rolled my shoulders back. *Of course.* "Oh, well. Me too." I stuck my chin higher in the air praying my mascara from last night wasn't running down my face. "I mean, not mandated or anything."

Riot's eyes darted to the green cot I had slept on, my belongings strewn about, making it obvious I wasn't here to volunteer. When his glare floated back to my face, I could feel my cheeks burning red. I averted my gaze, looking around as if trying to decide where I should help.

"Good thing then," he said, bringing my attention back to him. "One of the volunteers called in sick this morning." He took a step forward and pushed the hair net into my chest. Our fingers tangled momentarily when I took the hair net. "Wash up. Meet me in the kitchen."

"Wash. Cut. Tray." He pointed to the fruit on my left, the giant cutting board in front of me then to the large metal serving tray to my right. Riot picked up a butcher knife, and I grimaced sarcastically, leaning away. He frowned at my reaction but there was a twinge of surprised amusement. He spun the knife, handing it to me handle-first.

"Yes, Riot," I said, taking the knife. His eyes fluttered to me at the sound of his name. "I may be from the big city, but I know how to cut *fruit.*"

He shot me a look of doubt. "Once the tray is full, bring it out. Rush starts around seven-thirty."

And he wasn't kidding. The doors had been open since five a.m. but around seven twenty-five, people began to stream in by the dozens. Once I was done cutting the fruit, I graduated to the serving line.

My stomach grumbled. I had snuck a few pieces of cantaloupe while I was dicing it up, but my pride was too afraid of the judgment I'd get if Riot caught me taking advantage of the charity I, myself, was doling out. I don't know why it bothered me so much that he thought I was a resident here.

But wasn't I?

I looked around at the harrowed faces of our guests. As I took them all in, one by one, I started to pay attention to the families. Had I gone to school with kids like these? I couldn't remember it being this bad twelve years ago. There were poor kids and rich kids, sure, but these parents' faces had the poverty-stricken years painted all over them.

If less than thirty years ago, the impoverished population was refreshed with new homes and new jobs, how had things ended up this badly?

When the rush began to slow down, Riot's warm body sidled up beside me and started to wipe down the counters, sliding scraps of food into the garbage bin he held in his left hand. His forearms flexed and I watched his shoulder muscles ripple as he reached under the sanitary partition.

"Miss, may I have another scoop of eggs? They were simply delicious today!" a woman interrupted my ogling. She was probably in her mid-fifties but didn't look a day younger than sixty-five.

My stomach growled, the eggs *had* looked good. I reached for a scoop just as Riot slid his hands under my elbow, reaching for a sausage stuck between the warming tray and rider. His forearms brushed my elbow, and my body hummed, leaving a trail of heat where our skin touched. His eyes flicked up to me but I ignored him, unwilling to let him see the reaction he'd caused.

But I couldn't ignore his scent. It was this strange mix of masculine sweat, leather, motor oil, and clean citrus. I found myself taking a deep inhale. Realizing his eyes were still on me, I jerked away, knocking the eggs off the spoon, and sending them rolling down his shirt.

"Sorry," I said under my breath before piling the last spoonful of eggs on the woman's plate. I stole a glance at Riot who was still looking at me with narrowed eyes. I wondered if he thought I was afraid of him. Was that better than thinking I found his scent invigorating?

I felt a greasy piece of sausage hit my arm.

"Sorry," Riot said, mimicking my tone, one corner of his lips tipped up. I picked the sausage off and flung it back at his chest. It bounced off his hard stomach and into the garbage bin in his hand.

What a fucking child.

I glared at him, but he met my unwavering gaze. His eyebrows separated, amused. Was this Riot Asher's attempt at flirting? And why did his attention feel so *good*?

The two-dimensional human in me knew I should be wary of him. He admitted to killing a woman. Not just a woman. His mother. I should be afraid. But the distant, unfamiliar look in his eyes didn't strike me as guilt. It doesn't mean he didn't do it. Nor does it mean that he wasn't capable of it. Still, something inside me couldn't help but find him intriguing. Compelling.

I hated the way Cherry looked at him. The way she spoke to him. Like his mere existence offended her. Like he was a danger. Perhaps Riot Asher had me fooled. Maybe he *was* dangerous. But as he stood next to me, fighting a grin when I wiped away the grease mark the sausage had left, I felt more kindred toward him than I had with anyone else in a long time.

"Nicolette Parker, as I live and breathe!" A male voice bounded up to me from behind. I spun around and my stomach dropped.

Jeremy Blackwell.

Where Riot had been the All-American football hero, Jeremy, a year older than me, had been the class do-gooder; student body president for two years running, organizing recycling drives and the like.

He had a crush on me on and off throughout high school. I frequently interviewed him for his various community efforts for my broadcast journalism classes. He was cute and nice, but I found him incredibly dull. If I was being honest, I found all the volunteer stuff a little phony. It was almost too much, but he *was* Pastor Blackwell's son. I guess the Good Boy thing was in his blood.

After a barrage of asking, I let him take me to his senior prom. Later that night, the entire group spent the night at his parent's camp on the other side of the lake. I hadn't wanted to sleep with him that night. Or any night, really. But I had gotten drunk and when he virtually confessed his undying love for me, it had struck a chord. Either way, it was easier to go along with it than to say no and have it be awkward the rest of the night. When he went to college, I hadn't even said goodbye to him.

And now here he was, like a ghost of my past, clad in shiny new sneakers, sucking on an iced coffee that had way too much cream in it. He lifted his sunglasses to his head, stopping about six inches too close to me. I took a step back, brushing against Riot's arm. He didn't waver and I was surprised to acknowledge that his presence provided something akin to comfort.

"Jeremy. Been a long time..." I pressed my lips together with a thin smile. Riot's eyes moved between us.

"Yeah, no kidding." He smiled and dragged his eyes over me, sucking up the last bits of the iced coffee. The way it slurped up the straw made me cringe. "What are you doing here?"

I took a breath and shrugged. "Oh, just... volunteering. What about you? What brings you to the Center?" I stole a glance at Riot, worried he might blow my cover, but he only stood taller, his eyes boring holes into Jeremy's head.

Jeremy's eyes danced between the two of us. "Dad asked me to drop off a check. Monthly donation of some sorts." He gestured to an envelope in his hand before taking another step closer to me. I leaned backward, his coffee breath assaulting my face. "You know, I asked you to volunteer with me *hundreds* of times in high school and you never *once* joined me." He flashed a million-dollar smile, his white teeth perfect and straight. He was like a fish out of water in this room filled with people the town had chosen to forget.

"Yeah," I forced a laugh. "I wasn't much for volunteerism, was I?"

He tilted his head and gave me a smug grin. He reached out and put a hand on my elbow. "Most ambitious people aren't." He gave me a wink and I could almost hear Riot snort under his breath. Jeremy looked up as if just noticing him standing there. "Oh, hey, man..." he said, as if talking to a child.

"Jeremy." Riot nodded his head.

"Good to see you, Riot. Looks like you're doing well here. Katie mentioned the yard work wasn't your speed," he crooned. Riot didn't reply or look up. Jeremy widened his eyes at me as if saying, *What's his problem?* "Anyway... what are you doing back here? I never thought I'd see the day that the New York-famous Nicolette Parker would return to our little hamlet."

Ugh, I wanted to hit him. I hadn't lived in New York for almost a decade now.

"I'm just here for a few weeks." I tried to turn and help Riot with the cleaning, but it was already clear.

"Well, I'd love to catch up. What do you say I take you out to breakfast?" My stomach growled again, and I thought about the diner and a giant pile of steaming hot frittata. I clutched my gut to mask the empty mumbling. "Looks like things are winding down here. I'm sure Riot wouldn't mind if I stole you away a little early. Right, Riot?"

At the same time Jeremy said his name, he tossed the empty iced coffee cup into the garbage bin Riot was still holding. It landed on the bottom with a noisy *plunk,* sending flecks of watery ice droplets up his forearm.

Riot froze. His knuckles whitened with the grip on the garbage can. I held my breath, expecting a hideous reaction from the burly man. But, to my surprise, he blinked and stood taller, not meeting my gaze. He started to walk back into the kitchen.

"I don't care what you do with her," he tossed over his shoulder. My throat burned with the sting of his words.

What an asshole. I glared after him before returning my attention to Jeremy's hopeful expression.

"Sorry, Jeremy, but I had a big breakfast before I got here this morning." His shoulders slumped and out of the corner of my eye, I could see Riot's head turn toward us. My face burned with the indignity of him knowing I was lying about such a basic necessity as breakfast.

"Another time then." It should have been a question, but it wasn't, almost like my interest should be inherent. I didn't have the energy to fight him.

I nodded once. "Sure, I have to start washing dishes. Good to see you."

As I picked up the empty egg tray, I brushed past him and got a whiff of his cologne. *God, he even smelled the same.* I had a flash of his young, teenage face on top of me and I let a disgusted shiver roil my empty stomach.

He would hold me to the breakfast. Why had I said "sure"? I didn't want to spend time with him. My heart fell, realizing I had said "sure" for the same reason I had slept with him twelve years ago. It was easier to agree so that he'd go away.

Visceral disappointment made my arms feel thick. I had only been back in Godot a few days and already the weight of my hometown's expectations was eroding the self-confident shield I'd worked so hard to construct, reverting me to the girl who would do anything to just get out as quickly and peacefully as possible.

Riot was washing dishes when I approached. I scraped the last bits of eggs into the garbage with a little too much aggression. His head tilted in my direction.

"I can take care of this if you want to go to breakfast with him." His voice was unnaturally even. He didn't look me in the eye as he reached over and took the tray from my hands. I once again caught a whiff of his skin. He moved back to washing dishes, the steam rising to create a shiny layer of dampness over his ropy forearms.

I don't care what you do with her. Why had that stung so much?

I stayed silent, unwilling to dignify his response. The image of Jeremy, slurping up the iced coffee, was fresh in my mind. That awful grating noise coming from his lips, sucking on that plastic straw. I remembered how vehemently he had pushed those lips against me, mistaking his eagerness for passion.

I almost wretched, muttering under my breath, "Words cannot describe how much I don't want to go to breakfast with *him*."

If Riot had heard me, he didn't respond. We went back to work, shoulder to shoulder, him washing dishes, me drying them and putting them away in the industrial kitchen. The measured rhythm had a calming effect. The reassuring scent and presence of the warm body next to me combined with the calculated cadence of our movements had me surprisingly relaxed for the first time in several days. We matched each other's movements. It was like, without words, our bodies knew how to work together.

A sinister thought drifted past my mind. If our bodies worked this well together doing dishes, what else could they be capable of?

By the end of the cleanup, I had almost forgotten about Jeremy altogether.

When I dried the last pan, Riot stood at the sink, angled toward me, deliberating something. I stole a glance and found some internal conflict mapped all over his features.

He looked down at me, his brows knitted in a firm gaze.

"What're you doing here?" he asked.

"I told you," I said, trying to mask my irritation. "My cards are frozen—"

"No." Riot's jaw ticked, and I felt myself swallow, watching the flex. "Why are you back in Godot?"

My heart fluttered.

"Chimera," I blurted out, trying to keep the red from rising to my cheeks. "A colleague of mine said there's a hybrid drug raging through West Virginia." I looked off to the side and ran a hand through my hair. "When they heard I was from here, they asked me to look into it."

It sounded plausible. Realistic even.

"Why did you come into the shop asking for me?"

My lips rolled together. "I locked my keys in my car. Some old woman told me you helped reprogram her radio and said I should ask for you." I held my breath before daring to steal a glance at him. The conflict on Riot's face seemed to resolve. His head bobbed slowly.

"You shouldn't be staying here," he said with resolution.

I almost laughed, picturing the kids' faces that had come in with their parents. "Nobody should have to stay here."

Riot gazed above my head, his focus unfixed on anything in particular.

"But *you*... shouldn't be here." He dragged out the word *you* like it was clear I didn't belong here.

My insides burned like they had yesterday when he had told me he wasn't interested in getting to know me because I was a reporter. It had made me feel like the lowest, dirtiest piece of shit on the planet. Now

I wasn't even good enough to stay at the town *homeless shelter?* Anger gripped my throat, and I parted my lips to unleash my fury when he continued.

"This place does a lot of good." He paused. "But it has a way of enabling people. Keeping struggling people all in one room together…" His head shook ever so slightly before casting it downward. "If you tread water long enough in the same pond, eventually you all sink to the bottom."

His icy blue eyes met mine and there was an empathetic sadness in them.

Was he *concerned* for me?

His pity made me want to cry. I pushed a greasy strand of hair out of my face. What I would do for a hot shower and a fucking meal right now…

"Yeah, well… My options are running a bit low these days," I snarked.

Something crossed his features. I turned the last pan over in my hands even though there wasn't so much as a drop of water left on it.

Riot let out a long exasperated sigh, turning his eyes to the ceiling as if he already regretted what he was about to say. "Alright, I have a proposition for you."

My eyes snapped to him. I turned my nose up, and he rolled his eyes.

"Not *that* kind of proposition, Jesus. You're not even my type."

For the second time that morning, my pride was stung by Riot Asher. The guy had been in prison for ten years. Was I that undesirable not even a freshly released convict was tempted? I averted my gaze, biting back something equally hurtful.

"It's a business proposition," he said. My gaze rose, but I didn't meet his eyes, unable to stand one more look of pity from the man. Instead, my eyes stared straight ahead where his tanned neck met his muscled shoulders. "Look, I don't know about you but I'm starving. I'm going to grab a bite at the diner across the street. If you come with me, I'll tell you the terms and you can decide for yourself."

My stomach growled right before it did a little flip.

"Okay. Business discussion it is," I said, squaring my shoulders to him. A twitch of amusement crossed Riot's face. As we turned to leave, I was viscerally aware of the gentle hand that brushed my upper back, guiding me out of the kitchen.

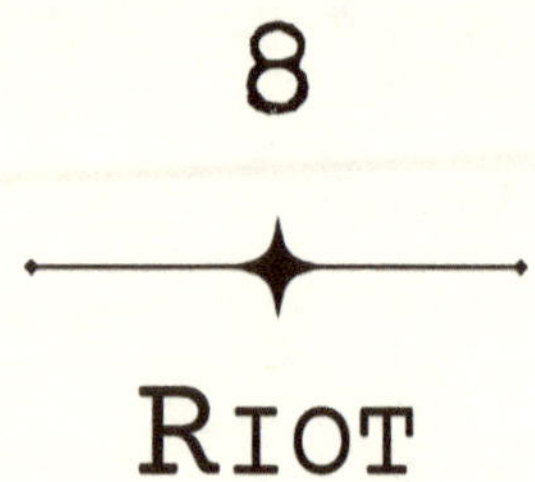

8

RIOT

My chest thrummed with regret before I even thought it through.

Nicolette made me uneasy. Beyond being a bratty city girl, she was a *reporter*. A crop of people whom I'd spent years fighting off. I thought a decade in prison would have made me "old news" but still at least a dozen showed up, unannounced at all hours, wanting to "tell my side of the story". It set Brennan off into a tailspin each time. I'd been more aggressive toward them than necessary, but I needed it clear around the media circuit that Riot Asher was not someone willing to speak.

I bought Nicolette's story the first time about working late at the library and falling asleep in her car. I didn't buy it quite so quickly the second time. I found it bizarre when I spotted her walking in the direction of the valley instead of her uncle's, but I told myself she was busy making those "stops" she had referenced.

Nothing surprised me more than finding her sleeping on a cot at the Center. Surprise was quickly replaced by remorse, watching her wake up and sink her head into her hands, her straight blonde hair disheveled and wrapped around her face like it was the only shield she had left.

She didn't belong there. It was bizarre to see her against the backdrop of all the addicts, homeless, and downtrodden, and for whatever reason, I didn't like the way it sat with me.

"I was thinking about what you said," I said through bites of breakfast burrito, still accustomed to having to wolf down food.

Nicolette was being polite, trying to restrain herself from scarfing down the frittata she'd ordered. I could tell she was hungry and the fact that she'd turned the offer down from Jeremy fucking Blackwell while her stomach audibly growled gave me this weird mix of satisfaction and sadness. She ordered a half portion of the diner's frittata. When she slipped into the bathroom, I asked the waitress to make it a full order, feigning surprise when the massive plate was put in front of her.

"Hm?" She raised her eyebrows at me, her wide gray eyes now filled with notably more life. Color had returned to her high cheekbones and a slight flush rose up her neck and down toward the top of her shirt, which was just low cut enough to reveal the rounded tops of her—

I brought my eyes back up to her face, clearing my throat.

"About selling my work." I steered myself back on track. "I can't do it myself." I wiped my mouth and squared my gaze. "There's a farmer's market on the edge of town every Saturday during the summer. It's big but everyone still knows everyone. If *I* set up at the farmer's market, no one will buy anything. They won't even approach the booth. If anyone knows this work is mine, it'll never see the light of day."

Clasping my hands together, I closed my mouth and stared at her, daring her to make a snide comment, or worse, try to deny that it was true.

She put her fork down, took a long sip of coffee, and met my gaze. There was a softness in her eyes that made my heart do a quick skip. It wasn't pity like half of the town or terror like the other half. No, it was something more empathetic, like understanding.

"You want to hire me to man your booth and sell your artwork?" She nodded, considering, and I watched her silky neck swallow a small bite of her breakfast. "What's the wage?"

"Nothing," I clipped. She rose higher in the booth, about to raise her voice before I put a hand up. "And in exchange, you can rent out my lanai. It's not much, but it's got its own entrance and a full bathroom with hot, running water inside the sliding glass door."

At my words, her eyes widened a little and my chest constricted. When was the last time she'd gotten to take a shower? The image of her in the shower flashed in my mind. What shade of blonde would her hair take on when she was wet? Blinking away the disgraceful thoughts, I shifted in the vinyl booth, hoping my body wouldn't betray me.

"You want me to live with you and work for you... But you don't *care to know me*," she said flatly.

"I'm offering you room and board in exchange for half a day's work on Saturdays. I'd say that's pretty fair." I raised an eyebrow, ignoring the last part of her sentence. I could tell in her face she knew it was more than fair.

God, I hope I don't regret this.

"What if nothing sells?" She stirred her ice water with the plastic straw. "Then you don't make any money and I wouldn't be holding up my end of the bargain."

I almost laughed but let out a humorous grunt instead. "It'll sell."

She narrowed her eyes. "You seem pretty co—" She paused, reevaluating her word choice. "You seem *confident*." I smirked at her, knowing my arrogance would get a rise out of her and bring back that red flush to her smooth collarbone.

Nope, nope, nope. Don't go there.

"The art will sell." I took a long sip of coffee. "If it doesn't, it's just a matter of finding the kind that does and letting word spread. It's lawn art, after all. It advertises itself." I flashed her a phony grin, and she startled at the expression.

I braced myself for indignation, expecting her to accuse me of making her a charity case.

Instead, for the second time today, she surprised me by extending her hand across the table.

"You've got yourself a deal, Riot Asher."

My lower abdomen tightened at the sound of my name on her lips. Her fingers were long and slender, and her skin was soft, my hand wrapping around hers with a firm pump. She looked at me without a fleck of fear in her eyes.

Fuck, I hope I don't regret this.

"And the terms of the deal *are* the terms," she said with finality, going back to her plate. "I'm your tenant. Don't get any ideas that I owe you anything *more.*"

Anger bubbled inside me, offended by her insinuation. *The nerve… This girl assumes because she's beautiful and city-sophisticated that everyone is trying to fuck her.*

Heat crept up my neck at the memory of the way both Rodger and Jeremy dragged their beady little eyes over her. I bit my tongue, realizing it was very well possible that had been her experience back in Godot.

"I told you before," I dismissed. "You're not my type." A flash of hurt pinched her eyes. I almost backtracked but she sat up straighter and tossed her hair arrogantly over her shoulder.

"Good. You're not mine either." Even though there was a tinge of doubt in her voice, my chest deflated a bit. I guess it always hurt a little when someone told you they weren't attracted to you.

Even if you had no interest in them, anyway.

We ate in silence for a few more minutes. I tried running through my mental inventory of the pieces I could have ready to sell in a few weeks but every few minutes, my eye wandered to the reflective window where I studied her profile, the elegant shape of her neck.

"What happened to your uncle's place anyhow?" I asked, clearing my throat, desperate for a distraction.

Don't ever think I owe you anything more.

I was insulted, sure, but something in her voice made it seem at some point in her life, someone *had* made her feel like she owed *more.* Plus, it *had* been burning me up all day to know why she wasn't staying in Jacob's sprawling, five-bedroom farmhouse.

She slowed her chewing but didn't look me in the eye. Her face paled.

Nicolette shrugged. After wiping her lips with a napkin, she relaxed a bit. "I was hoping he'd be visiting his cousin in San Diego for the summer, but I was wrong."

"You two don't get along?"

I was prying but if this woman was going to live in my house, I should find out why her last residence didn't work out. She was quiet for a long time, and I resigned myself to being left in the dark. I wasn't going to pry into her life and make her think I wanted her to open up.

This was a business trade, nothing more.

"It's not that," she said, sitting up and pushing her plate away. Nicolette's gaze drifted out the window and I was once again struck with how soft her neck looked. I pictured running the pad of my thumb over her collarbone.

"Sometimes it seems like he wants to get along *too* well." Her voice was barely above a whisper. She moved the coffee mug in front of her face, hiding her emotions behind the ceramic.

My chest constricted and the blood in my veins turned prickly with a foreign feeling of defensiveness.

This girl, despite her bratty tendencies, had left the home of the only family she had remaining in her hometown, had been sleeping in her car and then in a homeless shelter all because her fucking uncle couldn't keep his eyes or hands to himself.

It pissed me off more than I expected it to.

My anger must have been written all over my face. "It's not like he *touched* me," she followed up. Shrugging it off like it wasn't a big deal, which only stoked my anger. "Just... I don't know. I found some unsavory internet search history." She shook her head, sending blonde waves over her delicate shoulders. A shiver pulsed through her body as if she'd landed on a specific memory. "It's not a big deal or anything, I just didn't feel like sticking around. That's all." There was an edge of defensiveness in her voice.

I held up my palms. "You don't need to convince me. Wanted to make sure you didn't get kicked out for leaving the stove on or anything."

The smile I tried to plaster on my face fell flat. My teeth gritted and some innate protectiveness gripped my chest.

Let that go. You are her landlord now, nothing more.

She smirked sarcastically. "I've got a lot to do. You probably won't even see me much. And besides. It should only be for a couple of weeks tops. I'm not trying to spend any more time in Godot than I have to."

And despite my better judgment, there was something that *really* bummed me out about that thought.

Something caught her attention out the window and dread washed over her expression. She leaned her elbows on the table, rubbing her eyes with her palms. I followed her line of sight to see Jeremy rolling past the diner in his cruiser.

"Of course, he's a goddamn cop," she groaned.

Distinct satisfaction flooded my soul when the police cruiser rolled by. His head was turned toward us but he had his sunglasses on so I couldn't tell if he spotted us through the glare of the window. If he did, he didn't show any signs of recognition.

Regardless, I gave a subtle wink.

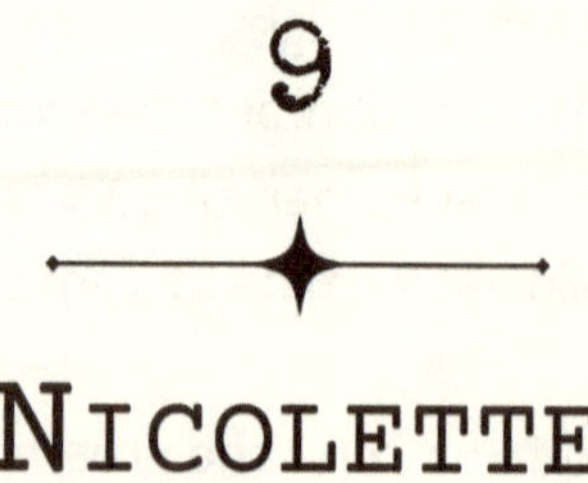

9

NICOLETTE

After swinging by the auto garage to grab the rest of my things from my car, we drove the short distance to Riot's home, which was located on a sprawling landscape down a dirt road.

The inner, ambitious conniving bitch in me was floating with glee. I had somehow weaseled my way into staying at the house of the subject I was supposed to reel in.

This job should be a walk in the park now.

So why did the thought of my original assignment fill me with dread?

And why did my lie about why I had returned sit like a rock in my gut?

Because he'd been kind to me. Because he was offering me help in a way that didn't make me feel pathetic. For no other reason than he'd been the one to notice what a tight spot I found myself in and I'd been the one to put together the art he made in his spare time.

My bank sent me an e-mail that my accounts should be unfrozen by tomorrow. But I'd keep that part to myself for now.

Riot's lanai was small but cozy. It was a simple screened-in porch off the side of his double-wide park model. After he gave me the very short tour and house rules ("Keep the kitchen clean. Don't ever go into my bedroom."), I excused myself to take a shower.

An audible sigh escaped my chest when I turned the hot water on. I must have stood under the cleansing water for at least half an hour.

When I emerged, feeling remarkably more human, Riot was sitting at the breakfast bar at the kitchen island.

"You know '*endless* hot water heater' is just an expression, right?" he grumbled, scowling. The apology froze on my lips when I detected a playful lilt in his voice, so I shook out my wet hair and smirked at him instead. His eyes followed the motion of my hair like it was a hypnotist's watch.

"Who are you?" I turned toward the voice that emerged from the front door. A taller, skinnier, goofier version of Riot stood ramrod straight in the threshold to the kitchen. Riot sucked in a breath and bristled, trying to block my view.

I always knew Riot's brother was *different*. About four years older than me, I remembered catching rare glimpses of him around town. My conscience ached for the guy. He possessed no social skills whatsoever, and I sometimes wondered if he was an outcast because he was different or if he was different because people treated him that way.

"Brennan, this is Nicolette Parker. She's renting out the lanai for a little while." He swiveled his attention from me to his older brother. "Under no circumstances are you to speak to her. Ever." He shot me a warning look, all levity from his expression vanished.

Shame burned my cheeks and I fought to bite my tongue. He had already made me feel like dirt. Telling me I wasn't allowed to so much as speak to the only other person living on the property felt like a new low.

I stalked over to him, jutting my chin out and thrusting my shoulders back. My nose was mere inches away from his puffed-up chest.

"If you think so little of me, why did you invite me here? There has to be someone else on the planet who can sell your artwork." The ensuing silence grew thick between us. I found myself preoccupied with the muscle that twitched in his jaw, defined even under all that beard. I was idly aware of Brennan standing a few feet away, head spinning between us like an owl.

Riot's jaw worked up and down. His breathing picked up and his eyes darted over my face, but he remained silent.

"He finds you attractive," Brennan stated, leaning toward me. I stammered, caught off guard with his honesty.

Riot blanched. "Brennan!" he growled. "That's not true, why would you say that?"

"Because you're grinding your teeth, which isn't altogether an indication of attraction but coupled with your increased respiratory rate and your notably dilated pupils, particularly when your focus falls to her—"

"Alright! Brennan, that's enough!" Riot cleared his throat looking wholly uncomfortable. A childish snicker erupted from my chest. I took a step back, assessing the brothers.

"I like him," I snorted, grinning victoriously, pointing to Brennan before spinning around, swaying my hips, and strutting back to the lanai.

I spent the next hour organizing my little space. When I cracked the sliding door, Riot and Brennan were still in the kitchen, looking through some papers.

"Katie's bringing over dinner tonight, after service, so don't go eating an entire bag of chips," Riot warned Brennan.

"There's a service tonight?" I asked, interrupting them. "Isn't church usually in the morning?"

"Both," Brennan said mono-toned. "Did you know that there are enough people in Godot to warrant two live church services each day? And that Sunday yields the highest data usage from Godot residential properties because the services are also streamed? Makes you wonder if we can't fit a couple hundred people into a four thousand square foot building, how could they fit two animals of every species on that boat?"

He looked at me like he expected an answer before breaking out in what I could only guess was supposed to be an amused smile. But he looked crazier than kidding. He bared his teeth in a grin, but it made him look maniacal. I stifled a laugh, realizing it was his attempt at a joke.

I examined him. His demeanor, his stance, his speech. I didn't know enough about autism to draw a conclusion but if he wasn't on the spectrum, he was certainly parallel to it.

"You know, I hadn't drawn that conclusion, Brennan," I smiled. He beamed with my acknowledgment at his joke.

Riot stepped in between us, pushing that firm, muscled chest in my line of sight. "Did you need something?" He glared at me, clearly agitated and overcompensating for Brennan's earlier remarks.

"What time are those services, and can I borrow your truck? I'd like to attend to see what the buzz is all about."

He smirked. "Sorry, I've got errands to run tonight." He started to walk away before adding, "There's a bicycle in the shed. Maybe you can dust that off."

His snicker made me growl, and I resisted the urge to kick him in the head.

My dad had taught me to ride a bike when I was young, but it had been *years* since I'd ridden one. Riot had peeled out minutes earlier, still smirking at the idea of me on a bike. I wasn't above riding a bike like he probably thought.

Well, I would show him.

Or maybe I wouldn't.

I pulled the bike out and couldn't get the pedals to turn. I cried out in frustration.

"The chain fell off the drive train."

Brennan's voice startled me, and I dropped the bike, the handlebars landing on my bad foot.

"Shit!" I shouted, hopping on my good foot.

"My apologies, Ms. Parker..."

I rubbed my toe, glowering at him. "Nicolette is fine, thanks, Brennan." He stood a little too close and leaned over me like a giraffe, craning his neck down.

"Yes, Miss Nicolette. Can I assist you?"

"Can you teach me how to fix and ride a bike in the next thirty minutes?"

Brennan's weird, maniacal grin stretched across his pale face.

"Of course I can."

Brennan Asher, in short, was un-fucking-believable. He had handed me the tools and given me very specific instructions on how to realign the chain on the drivetrain and a weird sense of pride lit up in me after I'd gotten the pedals to start turning.

After that, he spent twenty minutes talking about center of gravity, balance, and aerodynamics.

"After you establish a vertical posture, you must maintain static balance with one foot on the pedal and the other on the ground before you can propel the mechanism forward."

He spoke like an astrophysics textbook, yet I still somehow understood what he was saying and was able to apply it to what my body was doing. I made it up and down the road in front of their house a few times before coming back and dismounting.

"It's coming back to me now, thank you, Brennan." I offered him a grateful smile.

"Well, there is a reason for the proverbial saying 'it's like riding a bike'. Your muscle memory should retain the information at least until you are too old to manage your faculties." He looked at my confused expression. "Hah! Hah!" His laugh actually consisted of the two words, *hah, hah.*

Before I took off, I gave him one last regard, "Do you have another bike? Do you want to come with me?"

He frowned at me. "Oh, Miss Nicolette, I can't ride a bike."

With that, he turned around mechanically and shuffled back to his little treehouse in the backyard.

I was half an hour late for the service. I tried sneaking in, but the damn door was heavy and creaked with every motion. I cringed at the sound it made.

The place was *huge*. Bigger than I remember, and I wondered if they had remodeled. The front lobby was larger than three of Riot's double-wides and the actual room where Pastor Blackwell stood at the chancel and delivered his sermon was the size of the entire town square.

Every seat in every pew was taken.

I stared back at the eyes that had swiveled toward me. I smiled and wiggled my fingers in a sheepish wave. A few *tsks* went through the crowd. Pastor Blackwell paused.

"Would someone kindly squeeze in to let our guest join us?" he commanded from the front. Magically, a seat on either side of the aisle opened up.

As he delivered his sermon, I studied Pastor Elias Blackwell. I had met him plenty of times back in school and he seemed like a nice guy. He was always busy and surrounded by people, but he had made a point to come to say hello to me, even though I'd never attended his services. He still knew every single person by name. Knowing how far his influence reached in this town, I reminded myself to keep a discerning eye.

He was handsome, a better-looking version of Jeremy with dark hair that had a smattering of salt and pepper behind his ears. And, boy, was he charming.

Pastor Blackwell moved methodically down the aisle toward me. I scanned the eyes in the room where everyone sat enrapt with his words. Heads bobbed. Guttural noises of agreement popped up. Everyone looked so... content. At peace. The sense of belonging here was palpable, and I envied it.

Eyes turned toward me when Pastor Blackwell finished his sermon and planted one hand on my shoulder with fatherly affection. The congregation's eyes fell on me, and I heard muttering through the room.

"Katie is going to start passing around the collection plate. If you feel called to donate whatever amount you can spare, please do so responsibly. Thank you all for coming, feel free to stay for the potluck downstairs in the function room. I believe Ms. Plainbottom also has a few community announcements if you could give her your attention, please."

The collection plate moved through the congregation. Every single person pulled out money or checks and placed them into the plate. My eyes landed on the man I recognized from the night before who had almost urinated on the Center's floor. He pulled out a few crumpled dollar bills and coins and placed them in the basket.

My eyes turned to the podium where a petite brunette was barking into a microphone, failing to command anyone's attention. As people started chatting and getting up to leave, she grew more flustered.

Katie Plainbottom, the girl that the woman on the bench mentioned in relation to Riot. Were they dating?

I eyed her up and down with suspicion. Riot had said I wasn't his type. Was *she* his type? Still clad in one of those dumb headbands, she hadn't changed much. She was a slight thing with a floral dress buttoned up to her chin. I couldn't picture her with Riot's scruffy, overgrown face. A stab of something I couldn't put my finger on echoed in my gut.

As people shuffled out, I stood to face Pastor Blackwell. He shook hands with congregation members but moved toward me, his arms outstretched.

"Nicolette Parker!" He beamed at me, and I embraced his hug with a quick pat. "I was so thrilled to hear you were back in town. More so to see you join us today."

I smiled. "It's good to be back. I saw that Jeremy works for the police department now."

"Deputy Chief." He beamed. *Wow.* This family *really* had a grip on this town. "Are you staying for the potluck?"

"Well, I was hoping to schedule a time to sit down with you."

"Of course, anything for Jeremy's *favorite prom date*." He winked at me and my stomach turned.

Elias Blackwell's office was surprisingly drab. I had expected ornate, granite furniture with walls lined with bookshelves and religious relics. But it was a small room with fluorescent lighting and a chipped oak desk.

I sat across from him.

"What brings you to town, Miss Parker?"

"Chimera," I said. I waited but Pastor Blackwell just blinked. "It sounds like a pretty vicious drug."

His head bobbed. "It is. I lead a support group at least once a week but I'm afraid nearly the entire Valley has been consumed by it." I studied his face. Sincerity was etched all over his downcast expression.

"You lead support groups at the Center?"

"Mm," he nodded.

"You also fund it, don't you?"

"Oh, *I* don't," he corrected. "The church does. I am but its humble servant." He smiled, and it looked genuine, but I noted it could very well be his way of alleviating responsibility. "Yes, it's just one of the great works the church does."

I nodded. "Yeah, it's quite the operation," I scrunched my face. "That has to be quite the heavy financial commitment." I finished my sentence and sat in silence waiting for him to fill it.

His smile faltered briefly. He blinked at me. "We do what we can." He pulled my move and sat in silence with a thin-lipped smile. I had under-estimated him. He wasn't fooled by my playing dumb. He knew I was after information, and he was going to make me work for it. Time to try something new.

I dropped my façade and sat straighter in my chair putting my elbows on his desk. "Where does all that money come from, Pastor Blackwell?" I tilted my head.

He examined me and I studied his face.

Watching Pastor Blackwell maintain his thin-lipped smile, the Gotchya Moment was subtle, but it was there. I tried to suppress a smile. He broke our stare down and leaned back in his chair.

"Did you know I'm not originally from Godot?" he asked.

"I did not."

He nodded. "I was born in DC. My parents were military, and we moved around a lot before landing in Baltimore." He paused, studying me. "I've seen a lot of this world, Nicolette. Some might say more than I cared to." A genuine sadness passed over his eyes. "What I hope you'll understand is that when I moved here from Baltimore thirty years ago, I had a much more worldly view than... most. And I knew the town was going to need more support."

I'm not the dumb, Bible-thumping redneck you think I am, girl.

"So, you're funding all these projects out of your own pocket?"

He smiled and shook his head. "No, not exactly. In the beginning, yes, but then the need grew too great, and I knew it wouldn't be long before the resources demanded more than I could give. We needed a steadier source of income."

I nodded. "The mine." He hummed in assent. "So why outsource it?"

"The mine was profitable in the early years. But its profitability waned when the health problems arose. I can't say which came first but by then I couldn't very well ask these people to keep going into those mines day in and day out. The money was irrelevant; it was producing itself by then anyhow." His eyes darted around the room before landing on me.

"Producing itself?" My head tilted and Pastor Blackwell studied me before blowing out a sigh.

"The day I was elected Board President and senior clergyman over twenty-five years ago, I knew this town needed more than it could feasibly support on its own. I took a careful look at the finances. I brought in some chosen experts, and we began... investing. Everything we could spare. Into properties and businesses. Eventually low-risk hedge funds. *Housing and healthcare. The only two consistencies people will always need.*" His tone mimicked whomever had first spoon-fed him that phrase.

I pictured the man from the Center handing over crumpled dollar bills.

"That's what you're doing with their donations," I said out loud, more to myself. Elias shifted in his seat. "So, all the money that funds the Center... all the money you spent rebuilding the Valley... It's *their* money."

"It's legally the church's money," he corrected. "They give to the church because the church gives back to them. But make no mistake, they don't have enough money to make the kind of difference that's needed here." He waved his arms as if describing the town.

"So, you invest it into hedge funds. And that's enough to pay for the entire Center *and* the entire Valley being rebuilt?"

"Some years the market is kinder to us than others, but gosh darn it, if my advisors weren't right about housing and healthcare." He paused as if considering something. "Well, we were in the lucky few who shifted their investments out of the housing market before it collapsed in 2008." He shrugged.

I sat back. That was the big secret? He invested poor people's money to make more money to pay for the town that was too sick to work and too broke to afford healthcare?

Not much of an exposé there.

"Do they know? Do you tell them where their money goes? How much it yields, where the profits go?"

Blackwell frowned and almost looked ashamed. "Nicolette... I am not blind to the ignorance you think you see here. I know you are a woman of the world and you've seen more of this planet, the good and the ugly than that entire congregation might ever see combined. There is a certain... *skepticism* surrounding things that aren't easily understood. And hedge funds?" He shook his head with a frown. "Aren't easily understood. Heck, *I* don't even totally understand them. But if I told them their money was going to Wall Street, they'd stop giving and then we would no longer be able to help. And within five years this entire town would look like the Valley." He ran a hand over his chin, a forlorn expression decorating his features.

"Don't you think they have a right to know where the money goes?"

He bit the corner of his mouth and looked down before nodding. "Yes, they probably do. I know that. But sometimes, as leaders, we have to make decisions for the better of our community when they can't make those choices themselves."

My head swam. His words made sense; perfect, logical, infuriating sense. But I still sat unsettled. I stood up and thanked him for his time.

"Miss Parker," he said before I exited. "I tell you these things out of respect for you and your time. You are a bright young woman, and you have a choice. Now, I can't, and I won't stop you from making any of this information public. That is a matter you will have to settle for yourself. But I hope you'll consider what the future might look like either way. *Think* about the people who will have to live in it. And if you decide that candor is the more important route..." He looked away and the momentary look of hopelessness on his face stabbed me with hesitation. "Well, I respect your decision."

I held my breath, needing to get fresh air before digesting any of this. I nodded and turned but when I opened the door, I smacked right into Katie Plainbottom.

"Oh, gosh! I'm so sorry!" She scanned me up and down. "Oh, Nicolette, I heard you were back." Her smile was sweet but there was a tightness to it. She breezed past me, not waiting for a reply and she already rubbed me the wrong way. "Pastor Blackwell, I wanted to let you know that we're still down a body on the marketing committee but I'm confident I can fill Mrs. Coleman's place as the chair."

Blackwell sighed. "I appreciate that Katie. I can't tell you how important this year's Field Days are for winning that tourist grant from the state." His eyes darted to me. Katie turned around as if surprised I was still standing there.

"Do you... need some help in marketing?" I asked.

Katie's patronizing smile was like sandpaper against my eyeballs. "Oh, Nicolette, that's okay, we really need someone who we know will be here through the Field Days on Memorial Day Weekend. I'm sure your *busy* schedule wouldn't lend itself to the demands of the job." I opened my mouth to protest, but she went on. "I mean it as a *good* thing, honey. You're just so successful, I mean... You're way too *big* for Godot now." She flitted her eyes over me, and I blanched.

"I don't know," Pastor Blackwell offered. "I think Miss Parker's resumé might lend itself very well to contributing some new ideas." Something in me warmed at his fatherly defense of my honor.

Katie spoke through gritted teeth. "Well, yes, but if you remember, Pastor Blackwell, Nicolette was never much of a joiner—"

"I'll do it," I quipped, jolted with instant regret. I needed more distractions like I needed a hole in the head. But the way she told me what I *was* or *wasn't* irritated the shit out of me.

"Great!" Blackwell clapped and beamed at Katie. "That settles it, you have your full committee! If you'll excuse me, I'm starved. I think I'll see what's left at the potluck."

He breezed out, and I gave Katie a quick, overzealous smile. She shoved a piece of paper in my hands with the committee details.

It was a pink paper with strict agenda items and too many smiley faces.

Ugh, what had I gotten myself into?

10

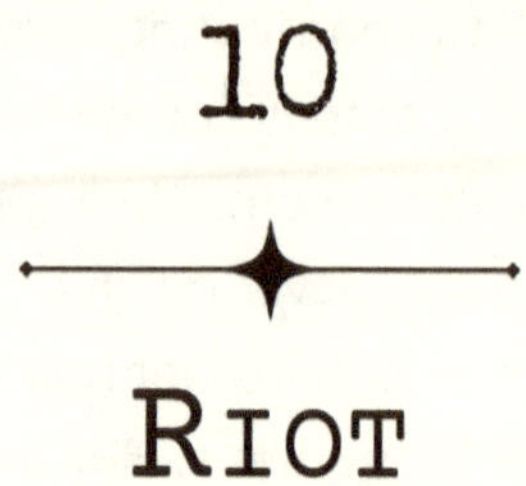

RIOT

I had been half teasing when I told Nicolette she should ride a bike to church but lo-and-behold she continued to surprise me when she pulled into the driveway at eight p.m. on Brennan's old bike. I gritted my teeth. Had he helped her with it?

The idea of the two of them spending time together unsettled me. Brennan was immune to female charm, so it's not like she could flirt information out of him. But, still, there were other reasons I wasn't quite ready to admit to myself why I didn't want them getting too close.

I was in a good mood when I got home from the scrap yard. And my mood was tickled more when Nicolette's blonde little ponytail stumbled, getting off the bicycle. I went to greet her at the door, a bottle of water in hand.

"You must be thirsty," I mused, extending the water bottle.

She growled but snatched it from me and took a long swig. I drank in the gleam of sweat that coated her neck. I could practically taste her salty skin from where I stood.

"Dick," she enunciated. I withheld my chuckle. It wasn't until she moved deeper into the kitchen that I caught an imbalance in her gait.

"Are you limping?" I swirled to face her. She glanced down at her ankle, rotating it.

"I'm fine." But the wince on her face said otherwise. I pulled out the two chairs at the kitchen island.

"You're not. Sit down. Let me look."

"You a doctor now, Riot?" she asked with an edge to her voice before sitting down in the chair across from me, toeing off her sneakers.

"No, but I've seen enough injuries on the football field to know that healthy ankles don't make people limp." I absently pulled her foot into my lap and gingerly removed the black ankle sock. One hand gripped her heel, and I heard her suck in a breath when my other hand moved to hold her calf in place.

"Sorry, does it hurt there?"

"No," she said, too quickly. "I mean, I didn't... I just wasn't ready for—" My eyes caught her lips, stammering to complete the sentence. "Your hands are cold, that's all."

My hands weren't cold. But it was a cute attempt to cover up the little gasp she made. "Sorry," I muttered, appraising her ankle more carefully. I was suddenly aware of how much of her skin was touching mine.

"There's no bruising... So, it's probably not sprained." She had delicate feet. Bony, yet elegant. "Do a quick rotate?" She swirled her pointed toes, gently brushing against the crotch of my shorts. I felt my cock jump instantly. I picked her foot up, praying she didn't notice. "You should have told me you couldn't ride a bike. I didn't mean for you to get injured."

She snorted. I tilted my head to look at her. "I know how to ride a bike just fine, thank you. This is from jumping out *Uncle Jake's* second-story window in the middle of the night." She said his name like it tasted bad.

Nicolette huffed humorlessly and took another long swig from the water bottle.

But I was frozen still, some emotion I couldn't describe racing through me. I felt my scowl grow darker, my eyes burning into her. She came to stillness when she spotted my expression.

For a long moment, our eyes tangled. The air grew heavy with all the things she wasn't saying. My hands tightened around her foot, gripping it possessively. Her lips parted gently and her eyes widened. I was keenly aware of my breath and hers, blinking only when I realized I was gripping her foot tight enough to feel its pulse.

I shook my head to get rid of the image of her scrambling out of a second-floor window.

"Sorry," I muttered again.

I loosened my grip, trying to push down the rage that image stirred up. Why did I have the overwhelming urge to be there to catch her?

"It's okay. I'm fine," she repeated. "I was stuck in Saudi Arabia with a broken toe riding around on a camel for half the summer once." Her eyes dart to where I'm still holding her foot. "This is nothing." Her words are bathed in reassurance like she's trying to calm the caveman that reared its head inside me.

I rested her foot on my chair before moving toward the freezer and pulling out an ice pack. I wrapped it in a dish towel and made my way back to my seat. Carefully, I wrapped the ice pack around her, muttering, "Probably just a soft tissue strain."

There was a bottle of ibuprofen in the junk drawer within my reach. I shook out two pills. She held her palm up, and I covered it with mine. Once again, my attention was snagged on those haunted gray eyes. A discernible energy passed between our fingers so quickly, I might have imagined it. She snatched her hand back, as if burned, and looked at the table.

"I met your girlfriend," she said abruptly, pushing a pink piece of paper across the kitchen island. I recognized Katie's Field Days committee meeting agenda.

"She's not my girlfriend," I grumbled. Nicolette took her foot back. "She roped you into the Field Days, huh?"

Nicolette scoffed, finishing the water and throwing back the pills.

"Quite the contrary," she said but didn't elaborate. "What's the big deal with these Field Days?" She pulled a yogurt out of her bag and started scooping a small spoonful into her mouth. I tried not to stare at her tongue, darting out, licking the spoon.

"They started a couple years ago. It began as a little family fun competition. Tug of war, relay races…. It got bigger the next year, and they started adding more to it, shopping vendors, an artist village, local bands and musicians. Then last year Katie had the idea of adding a carnival to the Saturday after the family games and it was pretty huge. They were up for a tourism grant that the state gives out but lost it to the Lowville County Talent Showcase. They said if we proved that we could draw a crowd from people *outside* West Virginia then we'd have a better chance of winning." I shrugged.

"We're thirty minutes from the border so that shouldn't be too difficult."

I shrugged again. "We don't exactly have a lot of influence with neighboring cities."

She was quiet for a long minute before a mischievous smile crossed her lips and I hated the way it reflected right off me, tugging at my own mouth. I cleared my throat, running a hand over my beard to straighten out my expression.

"This town is *so* lucky I decided to stay for a while... I gotta get to work."

"So... you're staying for a bit then?" I tried, poorly, to mask the interest in my voice.

She spun around and looked at me with wide eyes. "Oh, um, yeah if that's okay... I mean I know we didn't put a timeframe on this." She studied me. "I can check into a B and B—"

"No," I said. "I mean... no," I repeated softer and shrugged, hoping I looked cooler than I felt. "The farmer's market opens in a week or two." Her eyes danced in the dimly lit double-wide. "I'm really interested—" I cleared my throat. "I'm eager to see how that goes." Her eyes glittered brighter with something unspoken. "Stay for however long you need to."

Nicolette masked a smile. "Won't be forever. Definitely until the Field Days." Her eyes darted around. "But Godot isn't my home anymore. I'm just here to get the information I came for..." I couldn't place the expression on her face. "And then I need to be getting back to..." She drifted off and part of me was dying to know how that sentence ended.

Where was she going back to? What did her life look like there? Was someone back there waiting for her?

She rushed into the screen room, leaving the door ajar, but not before shooting me an appreciative smile that hit me square in the chest.

Fuck.

I hung my head in my hands. She was staying for a while. But then she was leaving.

And I don't know which idea I disliked more.

Half an hour later I had taken a cold shower and was toweling off when a soft knock landed on the door. *Shit.*

That was Katie, right on time, as always. I hadn't told her about Nicolette moving in yet. It only happened this morning. Also, I was an adult, who was semi-free to make *most* of my own choices. Still, some part of me felt indebted to her and, in a way, I was. My brother and Aunt Jen were the only people who greeted me when I was released. I had tried applying for jobs, but no one would look me in the eye. At least until Katie heard I needed work. She was the reason I had official employment and her company was comforting, albeit a little overbearing.

I pulled the door open, rubbing my head on a towel, and greeted her.

"Hey!" She grinned ear-to-ear, standing on the top step, her arms overflowing with Tupperware. "How was your week—"

"Riot, can you write down your address? I need to mail out—" Nicolette emerged from the lanai just as I pulled my shirt on. Katie's eyes went wide at Nicolette, who had changed into small sleep shorts and a tank top. I could make out the outline of her pert little nipples in the tank top and the image went right to my groin.

Katie's mouth dropped to the floor, her eyes darting between the two of us. "Um," she cleared her throat. "Can I please have a word with you, Riot?" Her glare yanked me outside and I had a distinct memory of being dragged to the principal's office. She put the Tupperware on the steps and fixed her hands on her narrow hips.

"What is *she* doing here?" Katie hissed.

I ran a hand through my hair and hung my palm off the back of my neck. I shrugged.

"She had nowhere to go. So, I'm letting her rent out the lanai." I tried to make my voice sound confident, like an adult, like a man who knew what he was doing. Like a man in control of his own life.

"What were you thinking?" she asked, sounding distinctly like my high school football coach after we'd all been busted at a field party. "We're working toward something here, Riot. Nicolette left Godot and never looked back. She's not one of us and I'm not sure being associated with her is the right move for your *image*." Her eyes bore into me and her pout tugged at my conscience. My palms rested reassuringly on her shoulders.

"She's just staying until she gets her finances together, then I'm sure she'll want to move on somewhere else."

It was a lie. All of it. And I couldn't help but wish that her bank never unfroze her card if it meant she'd walk around in that tiny little pajama set every night.

Katie softened at my reassurance. "I wish you'd told me. Have you heard about the things she's done? She's a man-eater, Riot. A home-wrecker and a snake." Anger and irritation bubbled in my chest when I recalled the gossipy way Katie and Amber had twittered about her. "You need to be careful what you say to her—"

"Katie, it's temporary!" I cut her off. "And while I appreciate your concern, I would think that *you* of all people might be a little more willing to give someone with a *reputation* a chance." I fixed her with a hard stare, and she frowned.

"I'm just trying to protect you," she said and the softness in her words cut through me.

"I understand that, but I also need to be able to make my own decisions, okay?"

"It's just that… I know what the people in this town are like, okay? I've watched them all grow up. I know how their minds work."

"I grew up here too, Katie," I said with a tone.

She huffed a laugh. "Yeah, and you grew up being celebrated on the shoulders of everyone in town. You were a leader, people looked up to you. You can't see who people truly are when you're at the front of the pack." Her eyes started to glisten. "Not me, okay? I was fixed firmly in the background no matter how hard I tried. I had a much different view of Godot. It's incredible what you can learn when people forget you're there."

A loaded silence passed between us.

"You're right," I said with defeat, though I wasn't sure she was right at all. "Can we just have a nice Sunday dinner? Please? I haven't eaten all day." I flashed an elusive smile hoping to put the issue to bed.

She suppressed her smile and nodded. "Fine."

I spun around and pulled the door open for her. She glowered but acquiesced.

When we went back inside, I found Brennan and Nicolette on the floor, on their stomachs with their heads together and giggling like teenage girls.

"What's going on in here?" I asked.

Brennan turned around and I couldn't remember the last time I'd seen him look so elated.

"I found it! I found the camera and would you believe there are still pictures on here!" He leaped up and I tried to avert my eyes from Nicolette's neckline as she bent over, rising to her feet.

Brennan bounced over and shoved the digital camera in my face.

"Hey, remember what we said about space, Brennan?" His eyes turned down, and he took a calculated step back. He lifted the camera a normal distance from my face, and I recognized the party we'd thrown after high school graduation at the lake a few miles away. A smile crept across my face at our young, dumb expressions.

I almost didn't recognize myself. I was nearly thirteen years younger, sure, but there was a levity to my smile, a youthful glow that I hadn't felt since that night. I scrolled through the photos, landing on the one Brennan had been in.

His arm was around me and he had that mechanical grin on his face but he looked *happy.* I looked happy. I wondered if we'd ever get back there.

Katie's hand landed on my shoulder. She reached for the camera.

"Dinner's getting cold, guys. Why don't we sit down while the ziti is still warm." She shot Nicolette a look. "Sorry, I guess I only packed enough for three." But she didn't sound sorry.

This was not going to be an easy few weeks. I shot Katie a glare but if she noticed, she paid no attention, busying herself setting three place settings at the dining table.

Nicolette stood in front of the fridge, lingering in Katie's way, taking her time pouring milk into her cereal. I rolled my eyes. *Women...*

"Ready when you boys are!" she called out in a sing-song voice. She was playing it up. She'd never once invited Brennan to eat with us for Sunday dinner. I tried to get them to interact more. If she was going to be part of my life, I needed her to at least be comfortable at my house. But Brennan steered clear of her, once telling me she looked at him like a quadratic equation with two unknowns. Whatever that meant.

He awkwardly shuffled to the table and sat down, his back ramrod straight with his palms resting on his thighs. He reached for his fork, but Katie rested a hand on his arm.

"We say grace, first, Brennan." His eyes went wide, and his face paled. A slight shiver went down my back, but Nicolette broke our attention with a quick snort before exiting the room. I breathed a sigh of relief, hoping she'd stay in her room until Katie left. "Do either of you want to say grace?" She looked between the two of us but my eyes were locked on Brennan's quickly paling expression. "Okay, I'll do it. Bless us, oh, Lord, for these Thy gifts, which we are about to receive, from the bounty of Christ, our Lord, Amen."

I peeked up from my bowed head at Brennan, who had lost more color and began to twitch. His eyes were big and unfixed on seeing something that wasn't there above my head. I tried to catch his attention while Katie raised her head and did the cross over her body, but he didn't look at me.

Katie started up small talk about the church services that day, taking up most of the space in the dining room.

"How did it go at the Center this morning? I'm so glad they could reassign you so quickly to finish up those community hours."

"You didn't have to do that, Katie. I was fine doing grounds mainte-nance."

"Oh, it wasn't a problem." She waved but didn't understand my tone. "Plus, the Center is so much more *visible*." She placed her hand on my arm and patted it with a sheepish grin.

I waited to feel the same electricity that I had when Nicolette's hand brushed mine. I tried to manufacture it in my head, picture what it would be like. But it was hard to suppress the irritation I still harbored for having her meddle with my community service in the first place.

"Brennan, aren't you hungry?" She enunciated each word, and her voice turned an octave higher like it always did when she spoke to him.

His eyes swiveled to her. "Not hungry. I'm not hungry. Not hungry!" I held my breath and tried to give him a reassuring look, but he pushed the plate of food away.

She frowned and examined him like her sensibilities had been offended by his outburst.

At the same moment, Nicolette walked back into the kitchen, and I wanted to yell. She took her time rinsing the bowl. Katie glared daggers into her head and suddenly my lonely double-wide felt very small.

"Grace! Not hungry, Grace!" My heart clenched at the sound of our mother's name. He pushed the food further away. A meatball fell off the side, and I raked my hands down my face. Katie moved to clean it up. I put a hand on her arm and shook my head. It wasn't going to help.

"Hey, Brennan, weren't you gonna show me those pictures from *your* graduation party?" Nicolette called from the kitchen. She was leaning over, cleavage spilling from her shirt as she bit into a Twizzler. The thickening tension in my neck prevented me from checking her out. I didn't want Katie to see Brennan's forthcoming freak out.

But to my surprise, it didn't come. At Nicolette's words, Brennan stood up, took his plate, and brought it to the trash, dumping the entire dinner, plate included, into the garbage. The ceramic shattered and Katie startled, a hand fluttering to his chest.

Brennan disappeared with Nicolette around the corner and the desk drawers began to shuffle. Katie looked at me like I owed her an explanation. I shoved another spoonful of ziti into my mouth to prevent from having to answer.

"Is he always like that?" she whispered. I shrugged, eager for this night to be over.

After a few more minutes of eating in silence, we cleaned up the table. I walked into the kitchen to find Nicolette spread out on the couch, her ankles crossed on Brennan's lap. She cackled at the photos she shuffled in her hands. She looked relaxed and, more importantly, *he* looked relaxed, and I tried to suppress the bubbling jealousy at how her smile touched her eyes when she was around him.

Katie cleared her throat, entering the living room with a tray of cookies.

"Are you feeling better, Brennan?" she said again with her voice in that singsong tone.

Nicolette's eyes narrowed, and she scowled at Katie. "Why are you talking like that?" I sucked in a breath, stifling a laugh while trying to stifle my nervous energy. The tension rose with the pressure.

Katie looked at her, taken back. "Excuse me? Like what?"

"Your voice." Nicolette snorted, pushing Brennan's shoulder with her bare foot. "He's socially awkward, Katie. He's not a slow adult hard of hearing."

Katie gasped, a tiny hand flew to her mouth. She glared at me with accusation before dropping the plate of cookies on the table, grabbing her bag, and storming out the door. Nicolette had an amused look on her face, and I wanted to smack it off her.

I followed Katie, the screen door almost hitting me in the face.

"Katie, wait!"

She spun around, biting back tears.

"All I do is try to help, Riot! That's all I want to do for you! And you invite this woman to live with you and it ruins everything!" She threw her hands up. "And what is wrong with your brother, where did he learn those table manners?" I opened my mouth to defend him, but it wasn't the time. She didn't understand, and she wasn't going to.

"I'm... sorry," I exasperated, throwing my hands up.

She took a step toward me. "Get your priorities straight, Riot." Her voice was softer but still stern. With one last withering look, she got in her car and sped off.

A better man would have gone after her. A better man would have respected her input after all she'd done for me. But I wasn't a better man. I was a tired man. And I was pissed.

I stormed back into the house where my brother and Nicolette were still giggling on the couch.

"Really?" I demanded, boring holes into Nicolette's head. She narrowed her eyes at me. "I knew I was going to regret this and thank you very much for wreaking havoc on night *one!*"

I roared and her momentary look of hurt made my chest ache. But she leaped to her feet and stalked toward me, her indignant expression spurring me on.

"You couldn't have just been *nice,* could you?" I could feel my blood pressure rising and the vein in my neck throbbing, but Nicolette didn't seem bothered by it, crossing her arms under her chest, which only pissed me off more. "From now on, I would appreciate it if you stayed clear of the house when she comes over."

She was inches from my face, and I could feel her hot breath on my skin. Her chest heaved with anger and her milky neck was flushed with red blotches. After a beat, she took a step back, wounded and resigned.

"Right," she nodded, and I thought I detected a crack in her voice. "There's no place for a man-eating snake like *me* in the house."

She threw me a final accusatory look. My chest sank, realizing she had overheard my conversation earlier that night. She slammed the sliding door shut. My resigned head fell back.

My focus drifted to Brennan who sat on the couch, watching everything unfold. A moment later he stood up and approached me. "I feel as though I need to tell you..." He leaned in and whispered, "that part was a bit mean."

He, too, found his exit. And I was left alone to absorb the overwhelming silence of my double-wide.

The following morning, I awoke to the sound of angry clattering and objects banging from the screen room. What was going on now?

Wiping the pathetic grogginess from my eyes I pulled on sweatpants and stepped outside my dark hole of a bedroom. I caught flashes of Nicolette moving around the room and I leaned into her doorway. Brennan's old mini fridge sat in the corner. Above it was a busted-up microwave from the storage pod. The side door swung open, and Nicolette stormed in, toting a rusty coffee maker, and placing it on top of the microwave.

"What are you doing?" I asked, masking my dread.

She whipped around, startled, and froze when she spotted me, taking in my groggy appearance, before narrowing her eyes and going back to adjusting the small appliances.

"I am outfitting this screen room with my own kitchen, so I don't continue my reign of home-wrecking terror. Can't wreck a home you don't step a foot in, can you?" Her words were laced with hurt and my chest tightened.

Everything inside me wanted to stop her, wrap my arms around her shoulders, say I was sorry. Breathe in the lilac smell of her hair.

"Nicolette..." I began, but the words didn't come.

How should I know what to say? People avoided me. No one spoke to me. I haven't had to be conscious of someone else's feelings in a long time. I certainly wasn't used to explaining myself or apologizing and why had I invited this chaos into my life?

"Can you please stop?" I pleaded. But she was like the Tasmanian devil, swirling around the room.

I walked in and put my hands on her shoulders. "Stop, please?" *God, her skin was smooth.* Her eyes were tired and hurt and my stomach clenched knowing I had made them that way. My thumbs ached to draw circles on her upper arms, so I dropped my hands to my side.

"Why? I was always just *temporary*, right? That's what you said."

I sighed and sat down at the small round card table in the corner of the lanai and put my head in my hands.

"I'm sorry," I said, still gripping my face. When I looked up at her, she had stilled and watched me cautiously. "Look... Katie? For whatever reason, has been trying to help me... *reintegrate* into the community. When I got back, no one would look at me, let alone speak to me. I... I owe her." I half expected Nicolette to say something snarky, but she was quiet. She sat down on the bed and crossed her arms, listening to me. "She convinced people to see past my conviction and got me a job at the garage. She was the only person that would even *talk* to me or look me in the eye like a real person."

"That's because these people suck." I blinked away the chortle that threatened to bubble up my throat at her bluntness. "You know that, right? She's not special, everyone else just sucks that bad."

The chortle escaped. Her body relaxed, and she pulled those toned legs up, tucking them underneath her.

"Yeah," I nodded. "They pretty much suck." She was quiet for a long minute, avoiding my gaze. The angry tension settled into a softer kind of tension. "You know this room isn't wired to handle that kind of electric, right?" I nodded toward her stack of appliances.

She snorted, defeated, and shook her head. "Brennan wasn't even sure if they work," she muttered at the ceiling, and I bit back my smile. "I need a ride to the hospital."

I looked up at her, raising my eyebrows.

"That's where I was going the other day when my car broke down." She fiddled with her small toe. "I have to talk to someone there about Chimera and the lung study they did."

I had the whole day off but the idea of spending it in such close proximity to her made me nervous. And excited.

"I would ride the bike but it's pretty far—"

Still, my head nodded. "I can take you. I've got a quick errand to run but... I'll go with you."

11

NICOLETTE

My insides were still reeling from Katie's little Sunday dinner visit. I couldn't explain it but as she moved around that kitchen like she owned it after spewing such nasty things about me, I grew increasingly infuriated. Especially after Riot's only response was to remind her I was *temporary*.

Which meant *she* was permanent.

That hurt more than I was willing to admit. I had spent all night stewing on how angry I was and the more I thought about it, the more incensed I became. I even started typing a biting little profile on how Riot wasn't some golden boy, he was just a heartless jock. I had no intention of showing it to anyone, it was more of a diary entry, I guess. I didn't know how to get back at him, so it felt good to let my anger flow through my fingertips even if I was the only one who ever read it.

Still, Melody's assignment niggled at me. Nothing I had seen from Riot Asher so far would lend itself to a profile on why he killed his mother. Confusion swirled inside me. I never let a subject get to me like this. I always remained indifferent. Unaffected. When did I become invested?

Riot appearing in my doorway, shirtless, in dark gray sweatpants had melted my resolve. I felt my face flush at that moment, standing there, drinking him in. I knew he had muscles. That was obvious. But there was something intimate about seeing him this way in the morning, groggy and half-naked, and I had the resounding urge to run my fingers over every inch of his abdomen.

It's just temporary.

I shouldn't spend the whole day in the car with him. He was off limits now.

Not that he was ever "on" limits but after last night, it was clear that Katie's claws were in him. Deep. My face puckered at the thought of him being her little resurrection project. There was so much more to him.

Those piercing blue eyes were dark and haunted and although his face was mostly covered in hair, I could tell he had a firm jaw. That permanent scowl that was his standard expression was harsh, but I had seen some levity in those eyes. His eyebrows relaxed when he flipped through those photos on Brennan's old digital camera.

Until Katie pulled it away.

I pushed her petite frame and mousy little nose out of my mind, promising myself I would focus on the job at hand.

"What's at this hospital that's so important?" Riot broke the silence that had filled the truck cab for the last twenty minutes on the way to the teaching hospital. His shoulders relaxed and his eyebrows fell further apart when we left the town border, and my heart filled with tenderness that I tried to tamp down.

"A doctor I used to work with at IANN. He was our resident MD any time we needed a 'professional opinion'. Because, you know, people need to know you have a doctorate to believe you when you tell them to wear sunscreen."

I caught the edge of Riot's lips twitch.

"Why do you keep your beard that long?" I asked before thinking better of it. His cheeks reddened. "I just mean, facial hair is in, sure, but if you're trying to *reintegrate* into society, a seven-millimeter trimmer might do you well."

I could tell from the crinkle of his eyes he wasn't offended. But I could also tell from his posture he didn't want to talk about it.

"I'll take that under advisement," he said.

"It covers your smile, that's all," I said quietly. His eyes met mine and for a split second, the world around us seemed to pause. The air in the truck thickened with a warmth that hadn't been there a few days ago. A car horn jolted us back to reality.

When we pulled up to the hospital, Riot didn't get out. "I'm going to run some errands in town. How long do you need?"

"An hour?" He nodded and started to roll up his window. "Hey," I called. He paused and leaned over the seat to look at me. "You're totally going dump scavenging, aren't you?"

He didn't answer but I swear I got an honest-to-God smile out of Riot Asher. Our eyes met, tangling for a few seconds and at that moment, I wished more than anything I could see more of that smile.

Dr. Leland Moore had been a friend of my father's in med school so when I had told my dad I was interviewing him he had been overjoyed. The rapport we'd generated on camera was genuine. He reminded me a lot of my dad; good-looking, charming, and smart as hell.

He gave me a warm hug when I spotted him. He still smelled like Old Spice and coffee, his silver scruff scratching at my chin.

"How are your folks? Where are they this week?" We sat down at a table in the cafeteria.

"Mom sent me a video last night. I think they're in Bozeman at the moment. Making their way down to my dad's brother in Yellowstone."

"Still living out of that camper van?" He raised his gray eyebrows, still flecked with the original black hair he used to have.

I nodded, smiling at the fond memory of my parents' excited grins after buying that camper van. They spent an entire summer gutting it and building their dream home on wheels.

"Yes, they are. Retirement is treating them well."

"That's great to hear, what brings you back to Godot?"

I opened my mouth to give him one of the excuses I'd concocted but his fatherly interest melted my exterior. I blew a breath out.

"Honestly, I don't know. I started with an assignment. A big one. With big opportunities."

I pictured myself packing my bags and moving to the documentary studio in California, big sunglasses on my face, strolling the red carpet into the screening of the Riot Asher Story.

"But... now? There's something about it that feels... misguided." I shook my head, realizing how confused and cryptic I probably sounded. "But after coming back and seeing how half the town deteriorated... I don't know, it just gave me that old feeling of something being off."

"And what can *I* help you with?"

I bared my teeth and dug through my bag, pulling out the plastic baggie of leaves I had collected from the water tower.

"For one, I was wondering if you could have these tested?"

He raised his dubious eyebrows. "For what exactly?"

I pressed my lips together. It was important not to lead him in any specific direction, but I had to give him something.

"Any kind of chemical that might not organically belong in the woods of West Virginia?" My hopeful voice went up.

Dr. Moore laughed. "There's that old Nicolette Parker evasive line of questioning. You know being purposefully vague in hopes I'll reveal something doesn't work on an old man like me?" He leaned in and winked.

"It could be nothing, and I could be barking up the wrong tree. Literally. But it's a hunch."

"Well, if I've learned anything in my lifetime, it's floss twice a day and never ignore a Nicolette Parker hunch." His smile touched his wrinkled eyes, his tan skin was weighed down with more gravity than the last time I'd seen him. "Do you think this has something to do with the health reports?"

I remained quiet for a moment, hoping he'd go on, but he didn't. "Which ones were those?"

"Godot hasn't exactly had the best luck when it comes to keeping its people healthy. The cancer rates are astronomical and climbing. The reports come out every couple of years."

I nodded, measuredly. "Godot's lung disease and cancer rates have been higher than any other county in the country. It got so bad, they shut the mine down because of it."

Dr. Moore gave a short chortle. "Really?"

"Yeah, the church owned the land, so they outsourced it to another company to manage. It displaced a lot of people's jobs, I guess."

He regarded me intently. "Seems unnecessary, but I can see how the church wouldn't want to be liable."

"You don't think the coal mine has any relation to the increased cancer rates?"

He gazed up into the fluorescent lights of the hospital cafeteria and tilted his head back and forth.

"Extended active coal mine exposure presents an increased risk of lung disease, there's no doubt. But unless we took a hard look at the makeup of that specific coal mine to see if there were any extenuating factors... I wouldn't draw a direct correlation to it, no."

I frowned. If there was no direct link between the cancer rates, why would the church outsource it?

"Think about it..." he went on. "Your aunt passed away from lung cancer, right? Non-smoker if I remember correctly?" I nodded. "Did she ever work in the mine?"

I chewed on my lip. She had been a librarian.

"She used to take kids on a field trip once a year but otherwise, no."

He tilted his head in my direction. "There are a *lot* of active coal mines in this country. Outside the expected hazards of the job, no other area suffers with the rates Godot does."

I sat with that for a moment, trying not to feel dejected. All I had were a bunch of unlinked circumstances that made no sense.

"Have you ever heard of Chimera?" I asked.

He squinted one eye, searching his memory. "The Greek fire-breathing monster?"

"No, it's some new drug that's completely overtaken the Valley in Godot, some hybrid between meth and heroin."

Dr. Moore grimaced and shook his head. "Eesh, I haven't heard of it but it's not surprising. That could certainly be a contributing factor to the aggressive progression of the adenocarcinoma cases."

"How's that?"

"Early detection and screening are crucial to cancer treatment. Most people in areas like Godot don't really have preventive health coverage. They don't go see a doctor until something's wrong. And if this Chimera is a blend, the heroin could suppress any discomfort and the methamphetamine would provide energy, I suppose. They might feel leveled out. Until they weren't, of course, and by then the carcinoma has probably spread to other organs."

"You really haven't heard of Chimera or anything that sounds like a new hybrid drug out there?"

His eyes studied the table as if it held answers and shook his head.

"Not personally, but I've been off the floor for a while. Teaching caters better to my aging limbs now." He smiled. "I've got a colleague that consults for the DEA. I can put you in touch if you'd like?"

"I'd appreciate that, thank you."

I found it strange that a new, deadly drug was rampant in Godot, and it wasn't even on the radar of the teaching hospital not an hour away. My thoughts drifted to the harrowed faces at the Center.

"I've seen a few flyers around town, recruiting volunteers for some new cancer drug trials. Are any of those looking encouraging?"

Dr. Moore tilted his head back and forth. "There is one study from Echidna Pharmaceuticals that's looking very promising. It's been years in the making and is finally getting presented to the FDA this summer. It was hard to find volunteers who meet the criteria, though, and with the addiction problem as big as the cancer problem, I wouldn't imagine the folks from Godot were viable candidates."

I narrowed my eyes. "The Center said they send a shuttle van full of people here twice a week for the trials."

His expression fell to concern. He paused and considered that.

"Odd..." He shook it off and sat straighter. "Well, perhaps there are more clean lung cancer patients than we think?"

"So, in addition to being positive for lung cancer, one of the requirements to volunteer for the trial is that you have to be clean?"

He nodded. "Yes, the presence of substances like meth or heroin could skew the results." Dr. Moore's heartfelt look was laced with sadness. "If this drug gets passed, you can rest assured that it'll help a lot of people. I'm not well-versed in it but it's caused quite a buzz in the pharmaceutical world." At that moment his beeper buzzed.

I thanked him profusely before promising to give my dad his regards.

"What kind of unexpected factors?" I asked before he started walking away. He looked at me with a question in his eyes. "You mentioned we'd have to test the mine to determine if there were some unexpected factors. What might some of those be?"

He turned his lips down in thought. "Oh, just the normal things they would have had to test for when they opened the mine. Certain carcinogens, asbestos, radon..."

When Riot pulled up to the hospital parking lot a few minutes later I felt a pull at the edges of my lips. Something foreign and wholly unfamiliar tugged at the corners of my mouth and my heart fluttered when his truck rolled to a stop. My ego still ached from the way he'd yelled at me the night before, but I could understand the stress of the new situation we found ourselves in.

I was the new factor here. *I* was the one who was interrupting Riot's regularly scheduled routine. He had thrown me a lifeline, and I was all but tying us up in it. He deserved better from me.

That realization sat like a block of ice in my gut, freezing me from the inside.

I busied myself with my phone. I had a message from Chelsea with a photo of Jacob next to his truck, getting towed away.

> Your uncle's truck totally just blew the bed. Brand new engine — shot!

Something familiar tugged at my memory.

"Wow," I said out loud, baiting Riot.

Respectfully quiet at first, he finally asked, "Everything okay?"

"Yeah, it's my Uncle Jacob…" I waited for a reaction that didn't come. "Apparently his engine blew up."

"Hm, really." Riot muttered but I couldn't help noticing the small twitch in his lips.

"Yeah, which is weird because he was bragging about how it was brand new, and he'd just had it tuned up." I pictured the metal tray under the carport I'd spotted before we left. The one filled with thick, dirty liquid.

"Hm, yeah?"

"Yeah, you're a mechanic. What would make an engine die like that?"

Riot raised his eyebrows and shrugged. "Plenty of things, I guess." He kept his eyes fixed on the road ahead and I kept mine fixed on him. He was good at giving nothing away.

"I mean, it's almost like someone drained the oil out of his car."

His eyebrows went up, seemingly impressed. But then his right shoulder shrugged.

"You wouldn't know anything about that, would you?" I was goading him, but I couldn't help it. His profile was steady, unwavering while the highway passed us.

His exaggerated frown directly contradicted his amused eyes. His head drifted from side to side. "Nope."

The little pop his lips made on the end of the word *nope* warmed my insides and I felt that block of ice begin to thaw.

12

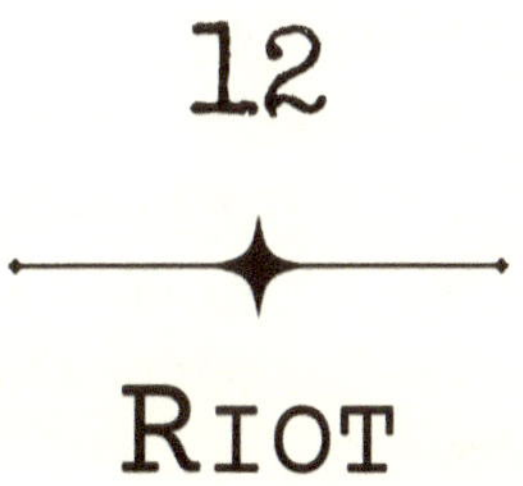

RIOT

The ride home was quiet after she'd asked me about her uncle's car. I wasn't a good actor, which was why I was glad my beard covered up my shit-eating grin.

I ran a hand over my face. I should shave it. I never gave much thought to it before. Katie told me to keep my scar covered, so I did, never offering myself a second thought as to how *I* felt about it.

It covers your smile, that's all.

Those words hit me like a truck because I couldn't even remember the last time I smiled. And now I felt I was working overtime to keep a straight face around Nicolette. She made me want to smile more, and that made me want to shave this beard straight off, reveal my whole, full face to her and everyone else, and let their judgment fall where it might.

A thin tendril of dread wove itself around my brain. Nicolette made me want to uncover myself like no one ever had and that realization terrified me as much as it gripped my heart in sadness. I'd never be able to uncover myself. Not wholly. Not completely. Not to her. Not to anyone.

I flicked the radio on to drown out my quickly spiraling thoughts. I flipped through the channels, glancing in her direction to see if anything sparked interest. When I landed on a station, the slow drums of The Wallflowers' "One Headlight" pumped through the speakers, and I smiled. My dad loved this song. I was young but I remember him playing the air drums every time it came on the radio.

A smile crossed Nicolette's lips too, so I let the song play. The music grew when I clicked the volume up a notch. Nicolette's eyes fell to the dashboard and her head began to bob. She reached a tentative hand to the volume, turning it up one more notch when the guitar came in. I tried to suppress the smile on my lips, but I couldn't help it. Her silent challenge had me all but forgetting about the self-pity that consumed me moments before.

When the vocals began, I hit the volume up again from the controls on my steering wheel. Her fingers started to drum on her thighs and the sleepy, wry grin on her lips warmed me from the inside out.

When the first chorus came in, her delicate hand cranked the volume up to the point I needed to roll down our windows. The smile that stretched across her face was giddy and unbound.

We let the music and air assault us and I couldn't remember the last time I'd felt this unbridled. I stole a glance over and reveled in the way she let her arm hang out the window, her palm catching the wind. I imagined what it would have been like to hang out with her in high school, young and unburdened by the darkness the world would throw at her.

My heart thudded when she peered up at me through a thin curtain of blonde hair that had fallen in front of her eyes, wisps of untamed hair whipping around that ponytail she always wore. I let my mind wander to what her hair would feel like all around my face and chest. How easily my fingers could slide through it.

Her lips moved with the lyrics, and I found myself humming. Her gaze caught on the words I was mouthing but hadn't given voice to. She leaned over and nudged me with an elbow to loosen up.

Even though she screamed the chorus, her voice was almost inaudible over the music, but it made me want to join in. So, I did. Throwing all reservations out the open truck window, not caring how off-tune or ridiculous I looked.

We shouted the familiar chorus in unison. Her laugh was infectious, the music blaring.

As she sang, she tapped my beat up truck's dashboard, and I gave her a sarcastic frown, which only lit her smile up further and my heart beat like it might jump out of my chest. As the song went on, my guard began to drop. The way her head nodded, how her foot tapped, unforced. When our eyes met on the last lyrics, it was as if the black cloud of the last ten years was dissolved by that one headlight.

I'd be lying if I said that car ride home hadn't changed something between us. I wasn't delusional enough to think she was interested in me but she had warmed to me in the days that followed. It was strange how one little moment, one song, one lyric, one simple shared experience could shift the tenor of the connection between two people.

We'd developed a light contentious battle of wits, each of us trying to one-up the other any time we interacted, which wasn't altogether that much. I had to work a good amount after one of the guys called in sick all week.

It took some getting used to, having another person share my space. I reminded myself that I had lived in a six-by-eight cell with another person for ten years. Sharing a kitchen shouldn't be that difficult. But she tested my patience. The morning after the hospital, I'd gotten up early to make a pot of coffee.

"Dear God, you call this coffee?" Her face twisted with disapproval.

"What's wrong with it?" I took a sip to make sure it brewed correctly. "Tastes fine to me."

Her eyes rolled dramatically. "This is *so* Godot. Just accepting shitty standards because they're present."

She still drank the coffee every morning, she just made sure to groan audibly enough so that I knew she wasn't happy about it.

As the days went on, the more opposite I realized we were.

I used one dish. She used all the dishes.

It took me two hours to do laundry.

It took her two days.

I wondered how on Earth she had gotten anything done before. And what her old apartment must have looked like.

"I had a laundry service," she'd said after I asked her how green her clothes got when they sat in the washer at her apartment in Easton.

I scowled at her, throwing a ball of wet clothes her way when I told her that *I* wasn't her laundry service.

She'd stuck her tongue out at me and I'd wanted to bite it off.

For all the grief I gave her, I found myself looking forward to getting out of bed in the morning. To coming home at night. Her presence filled my little double-wide with things I didn't know it was missing. Air. Life. Color. Laughter. *Heart.*

Platonic, temporary heart. But heart nonetheless.

Brennan came around more often too. I was still wary of their friendship but I missed my brother. He'd spent so much time holed up in his little adult treehouse that it was refreshing to have him stop over each afternoon while Nicolette barked answers at *Jeopardy!*

It became a nightly routine, and it was just another item on my new list of things I looked forward to. The three of us made a drinking game out of it. The first person to answer correctly chose someone to drink. I was far out of my league with those two and went through a lot of beer.

Nicolette insisted her ankle was fine and was still bicycling all over Godot. She hadn't complained once until this afternoon when a knock landed on my bedroom door.

Fresh out of the shower, I was clad in a towel, pulling my bedroom door open. She stood in front of me, soaking wet from head to foot, her golden hair plastered to her face. I tried to keep my eyes on her face but the way her nipples beaded under the thin material made my groin ache and what I wouldn't do to drag my tongue across—

"Can I *please* borrow your truck? I tried riding to my Field Days committee meeting and there's a goddamn monsoon happening outside." She pouted, holding her clasped hands in front of her.

"Nope," I smirked, enjoying the way the fury crept up her neck.

She stomped her foot in that bratty little way she had the first day I'd met her.

"Fine, but if I get the flu I am going to sneeze all over every piece of food in that fridge!" She took a step closer to me, pushing my bare chest with her index finger. I grabbed her finger and glared into her heated eyes.

Her face was so close to mine that I could smell the rain on her skin. The deep gold of her wet hair left droplets running down her chest, disappearing into the crevice between the swell of her breasts. I let go and backed up a pace, aware I was in only a towel and it was about to get tented if I didn't step away.

The bratty attitude had all but ebbed away and was replaced by a slow smirk that crept across her face. As if reading my mind, she took a step back, raking her eyes down my body.

"Careful, Riot." Her tongue darted out, pulling her bottom lip into her mouth, trying to mask the satisfied smile on her face. "Your pupils are dilating."

My face grew hot. She swaggered away like she had that first day and I was acutely aware my cock had thickened against the rough towel. "I'll be waiting in your truck," she tossed over her shoulder.

I opened my towel and gazed down at myself.

"Traitor," I muttered.

After I dropped Nicolette off at the church for the committee meeting, I sped away quickly. I hoped working together on the Field Days would quell the tension that seemed to simmer between her and Katie.

Back at home, I decided to work on a few pieces for the opening weekend of the Farmer's Market. I had acted confident, but the truth was I had no idea if any of it would sell.

My work had been a hit among the socialites and New Englanders who had two homes to furnish but Godot was a crap shoot. I was hopeful the seasonal tourists from Lycon, the resort town on the other side of the lake, would find their way over. The Farmer's Market was on the outskirts of Spokane County, which meant I *could* go but I would be too anxious and I wanted to let Nicolette know I trusted her with this.

My thoughts surprised me. Did I trust her? The woman had an innate need to ask questions, I had figured that much out. So, what would happen if push came to shove, and she started asking questions about me? About that night?

I pushed the idea from my head and focused on my work. I had about a dozen wind chimes that I put the finishing touches on and about ten medium-sized wind statues that were ready for display. They were woodland-creature-themed and I was pleased with the way they turned out. I turned on the industrial fan to see how they all looked when they moved together and I had to say, it excited me.

I went inside to wash up when my phone vibrated.

Katie

> The Field Days committee is walking over to get a drink at Benny's after the meeting, would you like to join?

The text surprised me. Katie didn't invite me places, not public anyway. She'd said I should make *calculated* public appearances, and that didn't often include social gatherings. The excuse was already at my fingertips. But something about the idea of going to a bar with a group of people seemed so *normal* that I found myself putting a little extra effort into my appearance.

I hated the way I looked with my beard this long. The scar hadn't bothered me, I didn't even notice it anymore. But to Katie, and the rest of the town, it was a blatant reminder of my past.

It covers your smile, that's all.

It was the second time that week I let Nicolette's words come back to me and a sudden feeling of decisiveness washed over me. I was tired of hiding. I pulled out my trimmers and made quick work of cleaning myself up, bringing my beard down. It was still full, but at least it looked kempt. I didn't know if Nicolette would be there but she was on that committee now and butterflies hummed in my stomach.

When I pulled into the parking lot of Benny's Bar, I ignored the whispers and looks I got. It had been a long time since I'd been out socially and there was a levity in my chest I couldn't quite explain.

I wasn't sure why I questioned whether Nicolette would be out tonight. Benny's Bar was not Katie's scene and when I walked in, I could tell Nicolette had been the ringleader in setting it up.

Her tall blonde ponytail was the first thing my eyes landed on. People surrounded Nicolette. Her voice was full of laughter, speaking animatedly with her hands. She was like the bright flame they were all attracted to, her barstool fixed in the center while committee members circled her, enrapt with her story and charm.

The local dive bar was dark, but still, our eyes met and I swore something brightened in her. A slow smile crept across her face as I nervously ran a hand down my chin, shuffling my feet in place. She slid off the barstool, raking her eyes over my face as she began to move toward me like I was *her* flame.

Our eye line was severed when Katie ran up and threw her arms around my neck.

"Riot! I'm so glad you came!" I could smell a slight tinge of beer on her breath and I'd never known her to drink anything stronger than coffee, but here she was.

My eyes flashed back to Nicolette, who had sat back down and was returning to her conversation. Purposefully ignoring me. She tucked away a playful smirk and my chest tightened.

"Yeah, thanks for the invite." I pulled Katie's arms down and gave her a friendly nod. "How'd the meeting go?" I asked, casually walking toward the group of people surrounding Nicolette. Katie followed close on my heels, explaining how well everything was coming along and that despite her initial skepticism, she was impressed with how much Nicolette could add to the group.

I stopped in front of Nicolette. It had only been a few hours since I left her, but against the backdrop of the bar, something seemed different. It seemed *right.* Familiar. Not in the sense she reminded me of the past. But familiar like she felt like *now.* A promise of safety.

"Hi," I said, shoving my hands in my pockets.

"Hey," she said, too casually, taking a sip of a beer, masking a wry grin. I know she was trying, but *fuck*, she looked cool. I don't know why it made me want to smile. "This looks better." She twirled her finger, motioning to my face, still unwilling to make eye contact.

"What's that?" I played dumb. It was childish, but I was eager to hear the words my ego so desperately craved. I caught a brief eye roll before she tilted her head to meet my gaze. The air vibrated between us. Her eyes looked just a hint droopier. From the beer or otherwise, it made my groin tighten.

"This." Her eyes dipped to my mouth. "I like what you did with it." I expect her to go back to her conversation but her eyes stay pinned on my lips. Or beard. Probably beard. It makes me smile nonetheless.

I leaned toward her like she was gravity. "Careful, Nicolette." My words come out more gravelly than playful. "Your pupils are dilating." Her breath got caught on a muffled giggle and we were close enough that I could lean in so easily to press my mouth to her—

"Okay, so Nicolette, you'll finish the press release and I will scrub the distribution list," an older woman interjected, pulling us out of our little bubble.

"Think we'll get some coverage this year? Since we were runner-up for the grant last year?" asked another older gentleman.

"I wouldn't count on it. I've submitted and called every year but no one ever answers me," Katie whined. Nicolette's eyes narrowed in her direction before she pulled her phone out and started tapping. "I think we're better off concentrating our efforts on flyers and getting them posted on community boards in the neighboring towns. I can take—"

"Donnie?" Nicolette's powerful voice cut Katie off. She rose from the barstool and stood up, her phone pressed to her ear. "Hey, it's Nicolette Parker, how *are* you?" She paused, and I cringed at how high-pitched her voice sounded. "It's been forever, yes I was in Easton for a while. Well, hey the reason for my call..." The sound of her voice drifted out of the bar.

"Can you believe her?" Katie scowled at one of the women to her right. "I get it, you worked in media, whatever." She rolled her eyes dramatically.

"I mean, it's kind of nice to have the additional help..." a younger woman offered.

"Are you taking her side?" Katie accused.

"Aren't we all working on the same side?" the gentleman asked.

As Katie began to protest, Nicolette swept back in. "You are *such* a doll, thank you. I will send you the pitch story by tomorrow morning at the latest!"

Everyone's eyes were fixed on her and it was hard for me to hide my smile when she sat down, ignoring everyone's stares. She took a long sip of beer, letting it land back on the bar.

"We'll be in the Sunday edition of the Huntington Herald. I need some high-quality photos from last year, please."

One of the guys high-fived her. "How the heck did you get that done so fast?"

Nicolette shrugged. "One of my old co-workers from my internship is the associate news director for AB Media, which owns all the newspapers in the tri-state area."

The pleased smiles were hard to ignore and even though I had no right to be, I'd be lying if I said I wasn't proud of her.

As the evening wore on, a strange sense of home settled in. I never had the chance to feel like an adult, to drink, legally, with friends, and feel somewhat of a grown-up. I'd spent my twenty-first birthday in prison. And by now, all my high school and college buddies had moved on. Married. Kids. Something I was unlikely to ever have. A pang resonated in my gut when I thought of all the life I'd missed out on.

I had never welcomed boring conversation more than when Nicolette and I played a little game of tag with our eyes, stealing glances at one another but unwilling to get caught staring.

There was an unease to the comfort I was settling into and I wondered how much of that was *me* getting back to my life and how much of it was Nicolette, making me *want* to get back to my life.

As I watched her, casually listening to her committee members, I studied the way the dips and curves of her neck arched when she threw her head back. Golden strands of hair danced over her shoulders and the urge to pull out that ponytail and weave my fingers through it gripped me.

Shut that down. You're her landlord and she's leaving.

It felt wholly unfair. I spent ten years sitting still while life went on without me. The idea of watching Nicolette walk away from Godot, probably forever, felt like I was getting cheated. I wanted to be near her and it felt refreshing to admit that to myself.

Her back leaned against the bar when I sidled up next to her. Her elbows rested on the oak surface behind her. Leaning over the bar, I let my shoulder brush against her arm. Small goosebumps appeared on her forearm.

"Seems like you found a nice little niche here." I nodded to the rest of the committee members.

Nicolette gave me a sarcastic glare. "It's amazing what people don't know they don't know."

"Still," I gazed up at her through a few strands of hair that fell in front of my face. "It's generous you're doing it. I can't imagine you're getting much out of the Field Days committee for your big drug story." She stiffened slightly, gazing down into her near-empty beer bottle.

Unspoken words hung on her lips like icicles. Her jaw moved up and down. Her lower lip was still damp from her last sip and I resisted the urge to swipe it with my thumb. She rotated toward me and her eyes lifted to mine.

"You're going to have to pick up a copy of the Huntington Herald at the grocery store, though," I said, trying to ease the simmering tension that had thickened. She quirked an eyebrow up. "They had some of the worst, most aggressive reporters." I shook my head at the memory of the gossip columnists camped on my lawn. "I forbid the mailman from leaving any of their rags in our mailbox." I offered a chuckle but Nicolette's face paled slightly before twisting her lips into a forced grin.

I chastised myself, hoping I hadn't offended her. "I didn't mean—"

"Hey, did you eat?" she interrupted me.

I shook my head. "Grab a pizza on the way home?"

She smiled, the tension from moments ago melted off entirely. "If we hustle, we can catch the repeat of *Jeopardy!* and see how aggravated Brennan gets when he can't answer the pop culture references."

I couldn't help but warm with the familiarity in her voice. As I made a quick round of goodbyes, I could tell Katie wanted to talk more. But I didn't give her the opportunity.

The hushed whispers and wide eyes that followed Nicolette and I leaving together didn't go unnoticed. It would cause the rumor mill to start swirling. We spilled out into the cool, late spring nighttime. I pulled the passenger door open before she climbed into the seat.

What would people say? What would they think?

As she pulled the seatbelt across her body, almost in slow motion, no part of me could muster the concern to care.

13

NICOLETTE

For such a small town, the Godot Farmer's Market was huge. Three rows of long, repurposed barns housed booths from several surrounding towns. By seven a.m. the line to get in was wrapped around the entire barn and the parking lot was at capacity.

I don't know why I was nervous to sell Riot's artwork. He had been pretty liberal with his instructions.

"Take the prices as a recommendation." He'd shrugged, tying on little tags to each of the pieces. "Feel free to go low, buy one, get one, throw in a wind chime, whatever you need to get them in people's hands. Just make sure to note which ones people are drawn to first."

Our relationship was changing. Our interactions felt weighted. It was a strange feeling, being so conscious of someone else's thoughts and feelings. Not just considerate. But eager. I *wanted* to do well today. I *wanted* to impress him. Something inside me craved his approval and the irony of needing validation from someone I was supposed to be studying was not lost on me.

When he'd walked into the bar with his beard cut tighter, it was as if he was offering me something. Opening himself up. Peeling back his layers. I wanted more of him and not out of journalistic interest.

The war inside me raged on. He was offering me his trust and there was something in that vulnerability that made me want to protect him, so I told myself I would follow the Chimera clues. But I knew there was a small piece of me still profiling Riot in the back of my mind.

"Wow, honey, look at this one!" a woman crooned in a thick southern dialect, dragging her husband over to my table. "These are gorgeous, did you make all these, sweetheart?"

I almost laughed. "No, but a friend of mine did, he's all the rage on the upper East Coast right now." I turned on my reporter voice, trying my best to command authority when I had nothing to back up my statements.

"These are just wonderful. Harry, listen, this one has a wind chime *inside* of it, how clever! Honey, go pull the truck around."

After several minutes of hemming and hawing, she selected three large whirligigs and a wind chime. She'd drawn some attention and before I realized it, it wasn't even ten o'clock and my table was cleared out.

This weird sense of pride lit up inside me and I was excited to get home. *How* I was going to get home was another story. Riot had dropped me off and wasn't planning to come back until noon when the market ended.

I was about to text him to come get me early when I bumped into Jeremy Blackwell.

I cursed under my breath, stooping down to pick up my clutch with over a thousand dollars in cash.

"Hey, you." Jeremy leaned in for a big hug. "What are you doing here?"

I swallowed. Riot didn't want anyone to know about his work. "Just browsing the local talent, you know us girls, never stop shopping!" I said.

He gave me a wink and leaned in. "Don't I know it. Hey, don't you still owe me a breakfast date?"

I opened my mouth to protest but realized it might be my best shot for a ride *and* some Chimera intel.

"Yeah, why don't we get that over with?" I said.

"What's that?" He leaned in.

"I said, yeah why don't we head over to the diner in town?" I forced a smile and he looped his elbow with mine, escorting me to his cruiser. I shot Riot a text and let him know I'd gotten a ride home.

"When did you decide to be a cop?" I asked with my mouth half full of toast.

"I studied criminal justice in college and, I don't know, it just sort of felt right. Protect and serve, you know?"

I didn't. I was distracted by my fork, remembering the way Riot had drummed the same fork against his fingers at our first breakfast. He had tapped it against the plate, his glass, a coffee mug. I had thought it was a nervous tick at the time but now I understood he was testing it out for a piece. I absent-mindedly pocketed the spare fork next to me.

"Didn't want to follow in your dad's footsteps?" I asked. He ran a hand through his perfectly coiffed dark-blonde hair and shook his head.

"No, no, the pastor's life wasn't for me."

"Who's on deck to take his place?"

Jeremy shrugged. "Who knows? I know Katie Plainbottom was going to seminary school but put it on hold to take care of Riot when he got home. Aside from her..."

"Wait, Katie dropped out of school because Riot got out of prison?"

Jeremy shrugged. "She's already got a paralegal degree. Seminary school was to ensure she could take over when my dad retires."

My face twisted. "She's got a paralegal degree?" I was getting sidetracked but suddenly Katie felt more formidable.

Jeremy snorted. "When she took over... um, *Grace's role*, she said the church was paying way too much in legal fees to alter the non-profit's bylaws. Said it'd be cheaper if she just got the paralegal degree so that she could prepare all the paperwork herself." A reverent smile touched Jeremy's lips. He gazed down into his mug, lost in thought. "It was pretty impressive, actually." His face twisted as if he was just realizing it. "Riot's lucky to have her. Hope he knows it."

My insides burned. I wasn't accustomed to feeling insecure and I sure as hell had never experienced jealousy over a man. At least not in the last ten years. The image of them sitting down at the dinner table together tightened the knot in my stomach. It reminded me how *temporary* I was.

You're not here for Riot to like *you, anyway.* I was here for a story. I gazed down and realized I was twisting the fork in my hands, rubbing my skin raw.

"So, if Katie's a dropout then who's going to be in charge?" I asked, compartmentalizing Katie for another day.

He shook his head helplessly. "A lot of people love the church, but there's not a lot of leadership left in Godot." He frowned.

"Yeah, what do you think happened? I mean, thirty years ago, the church built those brand new houses in the Valley, and people were offered jobs. It seems like Godot should have flourished. But that's not how it went." I tilted my head, the familiar investigative inflection resounding in my throat, settling back into exactly where I was comfortable.

"Unfortunately, there was a big strain of bad luck. The illness rate skyrocketed after they all went to work in the mines. Once the illnesses hit, then came the drugs, and it was a vortex from there."

"You know, a doctor friend of mine said that it's probably unlikely the coal mine has something to do with the high lung cancer rates."

Jeremy looked up at me, a doubtful expression crossed his face. I let my face soften, tilting my head and pushing my shoulders back. His eyes darted below my chin, and he loosened up.

"Well, that's just one guy's opinion."

I frowned as if having the thought for the first time. "Right, but I mean, he's still a doctor."

Jeremy shrugged, and I was irritated with his lack of response, so I kicked it up a notch. "I mean, it just seems a little preemptive to *fire* everyone and *outsource* their jobs without some kind of medical study. There were probably a lot of people that were put out."

Jeremy regarded me for a moment, something twitched in his jaw. He looked around and that little jolt of energy coursed through me. I'd hit something.

"Look, this is all off-the-record okay?"

I nodded with wide eyes. *Of course, it was.*

"I'm not sure of the specifics but the mine had been getting less profitable every year. Back then, as Dad tells it, the mine was the town's largest employer and biggest economic resource. The taxes from the mines literally paved the roads here back then. If people knew that the biggest source of income was starting to dry up, they would have freaked. So... maybe Dad exaggerated the health reasons a bit so that people wouldn't lose confidence in Godot."

"It's empty then? There's no company managing it?"

"Oh, there is." He shook more hot sauce on his eggs. "They move in for six months outta the year and they keep largely to themselves. They give us a percentage of the profits, but they handle all the operations."

I chewed on the end of the plastic straw. I remember Brennan babbling about a drone he'd used to find metal scraps for Riot once. Maybe he could let me borrow it to do a quick survey of the mine area.

"What company is it?" I asked.

"Hm... Something Industries? Titan? Triton, maybe? I dunno, I honestly try to stay out of it. My concern is cleaning up the streets so pretty things like you feel comfortable walking home at night without getting assaulted by meth heads." He grinned at me, and I forced a smile.

"I heard that it isn't just meth," I said. His fork froze mid-air. I examined him with a critical stare, and something passed across his face.

"We try not to publicize that." His words were low and held a hint of warning to them. I arched an eyebrow. "Look, the town already has enough bad press with the illness rate. The last thing Godot needs is to get pegged as the town crazy enough to splice meth with morphine, okay?"

"So, you've heard of Chimera?"

"Of course, Nicolette, I'm the Deputy Chief of Police. And *being* the deputy chief, it's my job to try to keep the peace. There are a lot of good people here. The last thing we need is mass hysteria to spread about some drug that will probably be old news soon."

"Is the DEA aware of it?"

He shrugged. "They came around asking about it a few years back when it first showed up, but no one was able to pinpoint a pattern. Last I heard the feds dropped it."

His radio buzzed. I waved to our waitress for the bill.

"Looks like I gotta pay a visit to the Valley for a domestic." He rolled his eyes before looking at me. "Can I give you a ride home?"

"Oh, that's okay, I can walk." Jeremy didn't know I was staying with Riot and I didn't feel like explaining myself to him.

"Nonsense, I insist. Your uncle's estate isn't that much out of the way."

"I'm not staying with *Jacob*," I grumbled.

Jeremy furrowed his brow. "Okay, so where can I take you? Do you need a place to stay? Because my house could use the touch of a woman." He grinned his million-dollar grin.

"I'm settled in." I took a long sip of ice water. "I'm renting out the screen room on the Asher property."

Jeremy froze.

"No way." He shook his head like he had a say in the matter. "No way you're staying with Riot Asher, Nicolette. I won't allow it."

It was my turn to freeze. I sat up straighter and gave him a scathing pointed look. *Excuse me?*

He softened. "I mean that it's not safe. *He* is not safe. His looney tunes *brother* is not safe."

"But it's safe enough for Katie Plainbottom? I can handle myself." Irritation crawled down my spine like a spider and I threw down two twenty-dollar bills, eager to get out of the diner. "But I appreciate your concern," I said despite my tone making it clear I didn't. I stood up, and he grabbed my hand.

"I'm sorry, okay? I forgot you hate the whole white knight thing. I just don't think it's a good idea for you to stay there. He *murdered* his own mother, who was nothing but a saint. I hate to think of you in that kind of danger."

My shoulders made an exaggerated shrug. "It's not your choice. And it was voluntary manslaughter."

"What?" he asked.

"He didn't get convicted of murder. The official sentence was voluntary manslaughter."

Jeremy gave me a flat look before his eyes lit up. "You're doing a story on him…" He gave me a wicked grin, and I felt my heart rate surge.

"No. No, I'm not," I stammered quickly, forcing a chuckle. "I have no interest in *voluntary manslaughter* cases. Especially ones that were nearly twelve years ago."

Jeremy squinted a doubtful eye. "Sure." He put his hands up but didn't look convinced. "But I'm still going to give you a ride there."

14

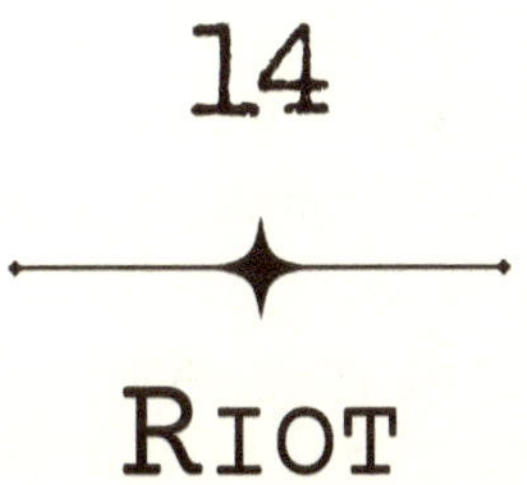

RIOT

Childlike eagerness pulsed through me, anticipating Nicolette's return from the Farmer's Market so I could hear how everything sold. Getting all those pieces loaded up and out of the backyard provided me with a sense of cleansing. The extra space gave me a small surge of inspiration. I was working on a new line of birds when a vehicle rumbled to a stop in the driveway.

When Nicolette said she'd gotten a ride home, I had been curious who she'd run into but I assumed it was Chelsea or one of the committee members. When I peeked around the corner, a shot of fear ripped through me, spotting Blackwell's police cruiser parked in my driveway.

Did he know I had left the county to take Nicolette to the hospital? It was a stupid chance to take but it was right on the border, and she needed the ride. Did someone tell him I'd had a beer at Benny's? There were no policies against it but I knew it was frowned upon. *Fuck,* Nicolette made me forget myself. Made me forget what I was supposed to be working toward.

As Nicolette hopped out of the passenger side, a small wave of relief eased my tension but quickly simmered into something darker. An unfamiliar feeling withered around the knot in my gut. She gave him a friendly wave, bouncing toward the house. He grinned back at her, lowering his sunglasses.

He wasn't here for me. That meant he was here for her. Was she interested in him? That would be bad news. Only because that meant Jeremy would be around more often, of course.

A few minutes later, the smack of her screen door jolted me, and I tried to shake the dark cloud that matched the size of the dust cloud that Jeremy's cruiser made, gunning down my road.

What was wrong with me? A minute ago, I was chomping at the bit to see how the Farmer's Market went, now I couldn't look her in the eye.

"I have to give it to you, Asher. I thought you were one cocky son-of-a-bitch, but you sold out within two hours!" Nicolette came bounding up to me, a wad of cash in her hands. "I didn't move on a single price." Pride radiated from her and my chest tightened.

I nodded and muttered "thanks," burying my attention into the piece on my bench. She stood, shifting her weight back and forth, waiting for more from me but I kept working.

"Who peed in your cornflakes?" she asked, frowning.

I sat up and let my eyes rake over her. Her hair was pulled up into a messy knot and she had rust stains on her shirt along with grease marks. But her smile was loaded, almost like she was trying to rein it in. She tapped a fork I recognized from the diner in one hand. *So, they'd gone to breakfast.*

"I brought you this," she said, notably less enthused after taking in my brooding scowl.

"Thanks?" I offered.

I was playing it down like I didn't understand but I was once again floored at how observant she was. When we went to the diner that morning after the Center, I noticed how well-balanced the forks were. They would make great strikers, but it had been my first meal out in public, and stealing from a restaurant wasn't the first thing I wanted to do.

But here she was handing me one. She really noticed me toying with it? A small shred of guilt planted itself in my ribs at how I'd greeted her.

She ignored my sour attitude. "Hey, is Brennan home? I have a favor to ask."

"No," I clipped, going back to work on the hubcap that was in front of me.

She shifted her weight to one leg, crossing her arms.

"No, he's not here?" She drew her words out, irritated.

"No, you can't ask him for a favor." I stopped and looked up, ignoring the momentary look of surprise on her face. "I told you when you moved in. You and Brennan aren't friends. You're not going to be buddies. And he's certainly not going to do any favors for whatever you and Jeremy Blackwell are up to."

I punctuated my last words, standing up and moving around to the other side of the workbench. She narrowed her eyes at me but I averted my gaze, catching the light scent of lilac and metal on her. *God, she smelled good.*

She shifted her weight to the other leg and I could feel her eyes boring into me. The air in the tent felt warm and it emanated from her like a brewing hurricane.

"Well," she clipped, turning to leave. "*Someone* needs to be his friend because the only other house guest he gets to interact with is your little girlfriend and *she* treats him like he's mentally challenged and you, of all people, should have corrected her."

I opened my mouth to argue, but she held a hand up, silencing me. "And don't piss on my leg and tell me it's raining. *She's not my girlfriend.*" Her voice mimicked mine, and I felt my breath quicken with my angry heartbeat. I threw daggers at her with my eyes. "I heard her talking at the bar before you got there. Your little redemption project? Ends with you proposing. So, congrats. Sorry if I spoiled the ending for you. But I hope you live happily ever after."

My skin grew hot. There had been a time in my life when marriage and a family were *all* I ever wanted. I should be happy. Grateful, even, to hear that someone like Katie could see a life with me. But all Nicolette's words did was turn the ugly shade of dread into more anger.

Nicolette spun around and shoved the curtain back, disappearing around it. I had more questions about what she heard Katie say but now was not the time and, truth be told, Nicolette wasn't the source I should be hearing it from. It was a conversation I needed to have with Katie but Nicolette tossed it out there so callously, it made my frustration boil over.

"Hey!" I stalked after her, catching up just as she reached for the screen door. "I don't need you spreading fake rumors, okay? I don't know what you *think* you heard, but it's none of your business."

She met me toe-to-toe and I could feel her hot breath on my neck. My stomach clenched again. From rage, of course.

"I'll tell you what I heard." She took a step toward me, pointer finger outstretched. "I heard *all* about her plan to make you the ultimate redemption story of Godot. You'll spend a few more months doing community service until she's ready to start dating you publicly and then by next Christmas, you're going to propose in the town center. Then you'll build a large house and you'll move in together and pump out at least four children." Her mockery rang louder with each word and she was hard to hear over the rushing blood in my ears. "But you'll have to get to work on *that*," she gave a lascivious wink, "as soon as you're engaged because time's a tickin'." She scoffed. "God, it was pathetic and basic and just so... *predictable.* No surprises, no nothing. Who, in their right mind, *wants* that life all laid out for them?" Her disgusted expression evaporated what was left of my restraint.

"Me! Okay? *I* wanted that, Nicolette," I said her name derisively, and the skin on her neck started to flush. "I wanted *all* of it. All I wanted was to play football in college, maybe warm a bench in the NFL for a few years until I saved enough money to buy a massive piece of land for my *sweet, homemaker wife* and our *basic, predictably* beautiful *litter* of children."

I was using all the words I knew would piss her off, and I took a step closer to her with every breath. The fury in her eyes blended into something sadder. I continued spewing all the things I had kept bottled up over the last few years.

"I wanted that life, Nicolette! I couldn't *wait* to live out my days, fat, happy, and *predictable*. I wanted lots of babies and I wanted to coach Little League and host garden parties, okay? *I* wanted it. And if that makes me *pathetic* then so be it!"

I had to turn around and clench my teeth to keep from screaming. It wasn't fair. I was being unkind and it shouldn't have been directed at Nicolette. These were all things I had kept gurgling inside of me and I wasn't sure why I was hurling it all at the one person who didn't tap dance around me. The one person who treated me like an equal.

I raked my hands through my hair and my stomach did furious flips. I took a breath and stalked inside, half expecting the little pain in the ass to follow me so she could get the last word.

But she didn't.

And that was almost worse.

The next morning, I got in my truck and drove around, trying to clear my head. I had tossed and turned the rest of the night, replaying my outburst over and over like a skipping record and I still didn't know what to say when I saw Nicolette. I knew I owed her an apology, but she had been so judgmental, turning her nose up at the idea that someone would want to settle down here and raise a family.

My anger was misplaced. Katie never came out and said it, but somewhere I knew she expected the two of us to end up in a relationship. So I was mad at her for helping me and then holding it over me. For trying to mold me into some little Play-Doh Ken doll, despite the fact that her dream for me had been my own once upon a time.

I was mad at my mother for being the reason I couldn't have all those things I had wanted. And I was also a little mad at Nicolette, for showing me a hint of a world beyond, dangling new possibilities in front of me that I'd never considered, never knew I could have.

Pushing my conflicting thoughts to the side, I took my time at the scrap yard and then took a long way home, still feeling anxious about how I should apologize to Nicolette. *If* I should apologize to her.

When I got home, I didn't find her in the house or her screen room. Her room was empty and her laptop was still open on the breakfast bar, a half-drunk cup of coffee sitting next to it. Brennan's digital camera sat in a few disassembled pieces on the other side of the breakfast bar and nervous concern washed over me.

Faint shouts cut through the backyard. I didn't see anyone and my stomach dropped realizing the yelling must be coming from Brennan's place.

I threw open the screen door and sprinted across the lawn, my heart hammering in my chest. The only sound piercing through Brennan's carnal roars was the high-pitched sound of Nicolette screaming.

15

NICOLETTE

"Die! Die! Die!" Brennan shouted, slamming the buttons on his blue alien robot.

"No!" I was so close to winning our best four-out-of-seven. Adrenaline raced through me as I hammered my thumbs so hard against the levers I thought they were going to fall off. I gave up and started slapping them with my palms.

The head of my red robot popped up and I let out a painful wail. Brennan cackled that robotic laugh.

"Okay, best five out of nine!" I whined.

"Nope!" Brennan yowled. "Pay up!"

I tried scowling at him but his ridiculous grin was infectious. I threw a handful of Twizzlers in his face.

We both flinched when the door crashed open.

Riot flew in with wild eyes, his firm chest heaving big gulps of air. The horror on his face weakened as he took in our scene. His eyes narrowed at me.

I laughed. "Riot... you're going to have to teach your brother to be a gracious winner if—" But I didn't get the rest of my sentence out.

Without warning, Riot wrapped a thick hand around my arm, tearing me off the floor, and pulled me outside into the bright sunshine.

"Riot, what the fuck?" But he didn't respond, just continued pulling me toward the main house. "Hey! Slow down!"

I tore my arm from his grip and stopped in my tracks. He spun around, rage and something else indecipherable in his eyes.

"What is your problem?" I asked.

"I told you to stay away from my brother!" he roared. "His place is off limits. Are you deaf or just dumb?"

The sting of his words immobilized me but I recovered, feeling the rage pounding in my ears. His hurtful words from the day before came hurling back to me and my expression darkened.

All the things he'd said to Katie about me being temporary. Her hard words of accusation. All the things he said he wanted that I'd never be able to give him. It all flooded back to me at once.

I shoved passed him and stalked toward the house. He followed me close behind with heavy, angry steps. I slammed the screen door in his face. My heart thrummed in my chest and my throat tightened. He was never going to see me as someone he could trust. I was always going to be some snake in the grass, lying in wait to strike.

Well, fuck that.

I started to shove clothes into my backpack.

"What are you doing?" he demanded.

"I'm leaving, Riot. What does it look like?" I hated how shaky my voice sounded but I couldn't help my body from trembling. "I've been kidding myself. You made it clear I wasn't welcome here the very first night and like an *idiot,* I didn't listen." I spun to face him and found his nose inches away from my face. "I guess I'm deaf *and* dumb!" I spat, going back to burying my stuff with chaotic, angry, fistfuls, hoping the motions would also bury the hurt burrowing into my chest.

He grabbed my arm, gentle but firm, and spun me to face him. "Why didn't you just listen to me?" His warm breath blew over my face. We were so close and my chest heaved from the emotional turmoil.

"Why didn't you just trust me?" I asked.

Because you don't deserve his trust.

And somewhere a part of me knew that was true. I had lied to him about why I came back. I've stretched truths plenty in my career but none of them felt as rotten as this one had. Tears sprung to my eyes. *No, oh, no.* Besides my father, I had never let a man see me cry, and I wasn't about to let Riot Asher be the first one.

Mixed emotions crossed Riot's face. He was breathing hard but fire still spilled from his eyes. I couldn't help myself from dropping my gaze to his mouth. I didn't deserve his trust, which meant I didn't deserve him. And the fact that I *wanted* that meant I was never going to be neutral when it came to him.

The Riot Asher Story was dead for me now, which meant I had no reason to stay. The lump in my throat grew, and I tore myself away from him.

Blinking away the sting in my eyes, I stormed into the kitchen and yanked my laptop cord from the outlet.

"Will you just stop for a minute?" His voice was calmer, but I needed to get out of this house, away from his unbearably intoxicating presence. I whirled around and found my nose an inch from his heaving chest. He still smelled like leather and citrus and sunshine and it took everything in me to hold my breath.

"And why should I? You don't want me here, Riot and I'm not—"

But my words were cut off by the firm press of his lips against mine. Everything inside me came alive. The words we had exchanged dissipated and I couldn't remember what we'd been talking about.

The world disappeared. All the anger. The disappointment. The guilt.

All of it evaporated because his presence consumed me.

Before my body had a chance to respond he pulled back slightly and the sense of loss overwhelmed me. His chest pressed against mine more firmly with each heavy inhale. His eyes were full of fire, darting over my face. Searching? A glint of longing and concern flashed in them when I realized he was asking permission for more.

I responded without another moment of hesitation and wrapped my hands around his shoulders, pulling him so close I thought he might disappear into my body. The thought sent shivers down my back. The growing need to touch him consumed me. I felt his hand slip into my hair, fisting it gently before pulling me closer like I might slip through his fingers.

His lips were wild and untrained against mine and my brain went blank, letting my body mold itself to him. My lips parted in response and his other hand wrapped around the back of my head, pulling my face harder against him with vicious need. My fingers felt their way up his midsection and a small moan escaped my lips. I fisted his shirt in my hands, desperate to bring his body closer to mine.

Every layer of my skin was brimming, all my senses heightened from the fight just moments ago. Our bodies moved like an animal of its own accord, crashing into the wall behind me.

His warm tongue slipped between my lips and I tilted my head to the side, trying to consume him entirely. A growl vibrated his chest. I moved my hand up to his neck and the blood coursing through his veins surged with desire. His mouth felt so *right* against mine.

Stealing a glance, I pined at the sight of his face, so close. I was astounded at how much I had underestimated my attraction toward him. Hot blood ran through my limbs, surging toward the center of my body. My hips pressed tight against him, desperate to alleviate the pressure I didn't know had been building for the last several weeks. I felt his erection pierce through his jeans as his hips met mine with the same force.

His hands explored my body, running down my rib cage, leaving shadows of fire on my skin. My back arched, willing him to explore further. His hands trailed down the edge of my hip.

I raked my hands through his hair and his chest exhaled a long breath accompanied by a small moan of relief. His brow stitched together. He yearned to be touched. Anywhere. Everywhere. It crushed me to think of the last time he'd been kissed by a woman. The image of Katie passed through my mind and I wanted to touch him, anywhere, everywhere, hungrily claiming his lips for myself. He tasted like salty sunshine and I was drunk on desire.

Our reckless bodies ping-ponged off furniture carelessly until we made it to the dining room. We crashed into the wall that separated the dining from the kitchen. My back hit it with a thud and something crashed to the floor.

Our faces separated an inch. I felt his smile against my lips and I let the warm breath of his laugh tangle with my own. His swollen lips called to me and I wanted him on top of me more than anything in the world. His droopy eyes still burned into me but I had never seen Riot look so carefree. So unburdened and I wanted to give him more of it.

I studied his mouth, committing every dip and curve to memory, running my fingers over his lips.

"I wish I could see more of that smile." The feathery truth escaped my lips before I realized I'd spoken.

Riot's grin widened, his eyes meeting mine before faltering. He blinked and his expression shifted to sadness. To confliction. My body was still alight with the desire he inspired. But I could feel my heart ache for the inevitable words perched on his lips when he pulled away from me.

He squeezed his eyes shut and shook his head, remorse contorting his features.

"I'm sorry," he said.

I held my breath. I didn't want him to be sorry. I didn't want him to stop. He took a step back and grimaced at me with sleepy eyes. I could see the self-resentment shoot through him like the head of my defeated red robot.

Frozen to the floor, catching my breath, all I could do was watch him spiral away from me. It stole the breath right from my lungs.

"I don't know what came over me." He shook his head, stammering. I narrowed my eyes at him. "I think... I think it's just been a really long time."

The little air left in my lungs exhaled with a huff like a gut punch. That was it? The best fucking kiss of my life and all it meant to him was ten years of pent-up blue balls?

The bridge of my nose stung and hot tears pricked my eyes again. I couldn't let him see how much he'd affected me. I pushed off the wall, angrily brushing past him. I stormed back to my room.

"Don't leave!" he called, pleadingly.

Riot didn't follow me. I could tell he was still glued to the position I'd left him. My feet stopped despite my pride screaming for them to keep storming away. "Please. Stay." His voice was gentler, imploring and I winced. "Please don't leave."

I took deep breaths trying to *will* my throat to open so I could say something, anything. But I had no words because I had no thoughts. My body was humming with desire and disappointment and I didn't trust myself to speak. Dragging my fingers over the laptop I'd left on the counter, I grasped it with a shaky hand, pulled it into my chest, and glided into my room where I stayed for the rest of the day and into the night.

16

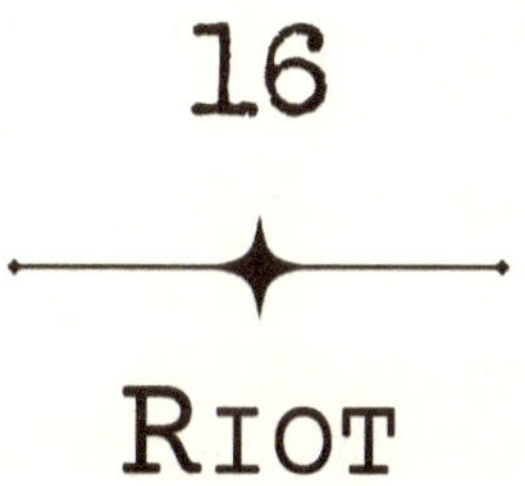

RIOT

I got into my handful of scuffles in prison. They were unavoidable. The wound that left the scar on my chin had been a doozy. But it didn't come close to the searing pain in my chest when I saw the look on Nicolette's face after I'd halted our kiss and said, like an idiot, I didn't know what came over me.

I had tried telling myself that I wasn't attracted to her. That it had just been twelve miserable years since I'd been with a woman and even a bratty city girl like Nicolette was starting to be desirable. But it was a lie.

Because *of course,* I knew what came over me. *She* came over me. And I wanted her to come over me again. Under me. On top of me. I wanted her. I wanted every inch of her. I wanted her all over me and I wanted to keep her forever.

That kiss. *God, that kiss.* The discomfort in my jeans was outstanding but, goddamn, if that wasn't the best kiss I'd ever had. I felt like a pathetic nobody, begging her to stay. I wasn't sure why I'd done it. It would be easier to go back to my regularly scheduled, Katie-programmed life if Nicolette wasn't sleeping thirty feet from my bed every night.

All I knew was that if she left, I would have to come back to this empty house, void of the hope and life that she had brought with her. I would go back to living in slow motion. In black and white. It would happen eventually. A woman like Nicolette Parker was destined for bigger things than Godot. Bigger things than me.

I wrapped my arms around my uneasy stomach, dropping onto my bed. I closed my eyes and relived every moment of the past half an hour. Hearing her screaming terrified me to my bones but then the relief that flooded my body when I saw they were just playing Rock 'Em Sock 'Em fucking Robots was too overwhelming to process and I snapped, dragging her out like the petulant brat she used to be to me.

And then she started packing and every cell in my body needed her to stay put. To turn around. To not be upset.

Why was I always upsetting her?

So I kissed her. I had to. I think I would have dissolved into a heaping pile of flesh and bones if I hadn't kissed her in that moment. I had wanted to apologize. And now I had made things worse. I prayed she would stay. Not because I needed her at the Farmer's Market, but because I needed her to *want* to stay. I needed her light. I needed the chaotic colors of her personality to paint the empty walls of my heart.

I think it's just been a really long time.

God, I was such a fucking idiot.

The days that ensued were moving in reverse. Whether it was on purpose or by happenstance, I hardly saw Nicolette once. I would be up and out early before she woke up, and she'd be gone every night when I got home. She used her outside entrance to come home, which hurt my soul because she had always used the front door before. I would hear rustling now and then and I would make believe she was making noise to tell me she was here and got home safe for the night. We were like ships passing in the night and I couldn't help but feel like she was avoiding me. Not that I blamed her. Kissing her had been foolish but telling her the kiss was a result of being a celibate jailbird for ten years was downright asinine.

She had to know that wasn't the truth, right?

After the kiss, uneasiness crept through me the first time Katie came over. I told myself I had nothing to feel guilty for. Katie made it clear we were not romantically involved (yet). But still, I had that guilty, jittery energy when she brought dinner over.

I hadn't addressed the little tidbit of information Nicolette told me about Katie's plans. I knew I needed to but my entire soul was consumed at the moment and the idea of another heavy conversation almost broke me.

As Katie laughed obnoxiously loud, staking her claim in the kitchen, I didn't hear a peep from the lanai. Not even a floorboard creaked, and I wondered if Nicolette was home. She usually was at this hour and I couldn't help but run through the possibilities of where she might have gone. The uneasiness spilled over into anxiety. I had to talk to her.

"What's going on with you?" Katie asked as I walked her to her car later that night.

"Hm?" I wasn't good at playing dumb but I didn't care. I was already concocting an excuse to knock on Nicolette's door. But I froze when I saw a black Infiniti SUV idling on the street outside the house, Nicolette stood outside the car and leaned in the open driver's side window, blocking the view of the driver.

"You've been distracted. All week. What's up?" she asked, but I wasn't paying attention. Had the car dropped Nicolette off? And who the heck was driving?

"Nothing..." I muttered, trying to see, but the windows had an irritatingly dark tint. "Just haven't been sleeping great."

"Okay, well I was thinking, maybe, if you didn't have plans already..." A jolt went through me when Nicolette spun around smiling, looking happy, more than happy. "... go to the carnival together?" She turned back to the driver and tilted her head, giving whoever it was a big smile. She started toward the house with an envelope in her hands when she spotted me and froze. She was several hundred feet away.

But I could have felt her eyes on me from across an ocean.

I saw her focus dart from Katie to me. She pushed her hair behind her ear and cast her eyes down. My heart clenched and the veins in my arms grew prickly. "... wouldn't be a date or anything..." I was half-aware of Katie speaking but I was too focused on the brief profile of a man in sunglasses, rolling up the driver's side window. "But maybe a trial run?

See what kind of reactions we might get and work from there…" The car pulled away.

"Riot?" Katie grabbed my chin and forced my attention on her.

"Sorry, yes that sounds good," I said, trying my hardest to bring my attention back to the small woman speaking to me.

"I'll be at the church and I need to get there a little early, so pick me up around ten?"

"Sure." I shook my head as Nicolette disappeared behind the house. "Sorry, when?"

"Saturday — for the carnival?" She started tapping her foot impatiently.

"Right," I nodded, giving her my full attention. "Yes, I can do that."

When her car door slammed, I booked it inside.

Nicolette's sliding door was closed, but the curtain was open. I listened, but it was quiet. I took a breath before knocking on the door. She appeared a moment later and pulled the sliding door open a few inches.

Her high cheekbones were sun-kissed but her eyes were tired and I hated that she might have lost sleep over what transpired between us. She peered up at me with raised eyebrows but her lips remained pressed in a thin line. I tried not to look at those lips, tried not to remember what they tasted like.

"Hey, I was going to order a pizza. Are you hungry? Did you eat?" I asked. She suppressed an amused smile at my nervous shifting.

"Um, thanks but I'm all set." She blinked at me a few times. Does that mean she had eaten with whoever was in that car? *God,* I was spinning out. I had no claim to this woman but here I was, analyzing every man she shared a meal with.

Because I want them all to be with me.

I nodded, shuffling my feet, trying to come up with a reason, *any* reason, to keep her talking to me.

"Oh, okay," I started to turn away. "Hey, did the last of the woodland creature pieces sell this morning? I was thinking of rounding out the bird line for the Field Days — maybe a couple more of the Northern Cardinals?"

"They did. And that sounds like a great idea, Riot." She nodded and there was a finality to her voice. I offered a weak smile and turned to go. "Chelsea said she'd help out with the booth on Saturday. I have a few committee member duties — so she's going to tap in."

I clutched her gaze with my eyes and wanted to hold on forever. After the shitty way I'd treated her, she had still thought of ways to help me.

"Thank you, Nicolette. Really." I hoped she recognized the sincerity in my voice.

"Of course. I have to..." She pointed her thumb over her shoulder.

"Right, good night."

She offered a weak smile and slid the door shut, taking all the beautiful colors of her personality with her.

17

NICOLETTE

I sank back down into my bed, clutching my wounded heart. After the gut-wrenching rejection I had suffered last week from Riot, I was too embarrassed to show my face around him.

I think it's just been a really long time...

Every time I let my head wander, every time I'd let my heart hope that kiss had meant something more to him — I replayed that sound bite on repeat, drilling it into my soul night after night, reminding myself what I really meant to him.

I didn't cry over boys. Ever. I remember Chelsea sobbing into me when her boyfriend dumped her right before our junior year. I had criticized her and told her to be stronger than that. He wasn't worth the tears. She looked up at me through bloodshot eyes and said, "The ones who move you are always worth the tears."

Was that what Riot had done? Had he moved me? I don't know about moving me but, he had reached a part of me that no one else ever had. A part I didn't know existed.

After the affair with my producer left my life, heart, and career in shambles, I promised myself I would never let a man affect me like that again. When I entered into a relationship with the guy who filmed me, it was purely sexual. I thought that might empower me somehow but lo and behold that rebound came back to smack me right in the face. *I know how to pick 'em.*

I gave myself one day. Twenty-four hours was all I took to sulk over my wounded pride that was Riot Asher. He couldn't have any more than twenty-four hours. At least that's what I told myself. I was burying myself in work, going down every rabbit hole to find out how all the problems in the Valley could be interconnected.

Today, I was hoping I struck pay-dirt. Dr. Moore had called back with some information. He was leaving town for a few days but wanted to drop off the results in person since my request had been "off the record".

Riot must have been curious about the car I'd gotten out of and I could have cleared it up right away but hadn't I earned a little retribution? I'd be lying if I said I didn't get a little satisfaction out of watching him squirm.

Pushing his shy smile and deep blue eyes to the back of my mind, I tore open the envelope Dr. Moore had given me. The first piece of paper I pulled out was the results of the leaf samples I had given him. It looked like gibberish to me but he had circled the bottom where the paper indicated the sample tested positive for a high concentration of...

"Fluoride?"

I sat back. That wasn't much of a scandal. Not that I was *trying* to conjure one up but healthy teeth didn't exactly link back to lung cancer or drug addiction. So why was Echo Chemicals treating the water with fluoride in the dead of night instead of the county water authority during normal hours?

I did a quick search for the Spokane County Water Authority and brought up their website, scrolling down to find the names of the executive team.

Geoffrey Brown, Executive Director

Arthur Plainbottom, Director of Operations

I clicked on Arthur's name and was given a headshot and a brief bio. It was Katie's father, and I was struck by how... *severe* he looked. Powerful but with a violent undertone. Then I remembered back to what that elderly woman had mentioned. He had some kind of cancer and didn't work anymore.

I searched Geoffrey Brown's name, but the results were thin. I found him on Facebook. He didn't have much posted, just a bunch of outlandish posts that were probably meant to be searches. I clicked on his friends list but it was private.

I took a long sip of red wine, clicking on his photos. I scrolled through them until a familiar face halted me. It was an old photo that had been scanned in.

Geoffrey was standing at the front of Redeemer's Church, holding a small baby in a white gown. He embraced another man his age; Elias Blackwell.

Geoffrey Brown, executive director of the water authority, had been Elias Blackwell's best friend and was Jeremy Blackwell's godfather. A smile crept across my face.

The next morning, I dismounted my bike in front of the county office building.

I walked into the office building like I had a purpose so no one would stop me. It was a dusty old building that looked like it hadn't been updated since the eighties.

"Hi, I have a nine a.m. meeting with Geoffrey." I offered the receptionist my sweetest smile. She frowned, looking at her computer. I didn't have a meeting, but you'd be surprised with how many people you can get through to if you acted like you knew what you were doing.

She pushed a few buttons and lifted the receiver. "Your nine a.m. is here." She paused, eyeing me up and down. "No, I'm not sure. I don't see anything." She listened again before putting the receiver down. "You can go right in."

Geoffrey was plenty older than his headshot. He was a round man with a thick neck and a red nose. He opened his eyes, surprised to see me sweep into the room and sit right down in the chair in front of his desk. He had stood to greet me but sat down, amused at my forwardness.

"Good morning, I'm sorry I don't seem to have you on my calendar, Miss..."

"Nicolette Parker, nice to meet you, Geoffrey." I sat back and clasped my hands over my stomach, gazing around at the updated office furniture that didn't match the old building.

"Well, what can I do for you, Miss Parker?"

I took a breath, chewing on my tongue as if I wasn't sure where to start.

"My parents moved us here when I was nine, but you know, before that I went to this real hippie-dippy elementary school with a girl who had the *worst* allergies, ever. I mean you name it, she sneezed at it." I observed his amused expression while he listened, confused. "But there was one particular allergy they couldn't figure out. Every night, she'd get these mouth sores and hives all over her face and they could not, for the life of them, figure out what was causing it." I stared at him, waiting for anything to register. "Turns out, she was allergic to her toothpaste. In particular the *fluoride* in her toothpaste. But did you know that less than one percent of the population has a fluoride allergy? That's what makes it so popular and commonplace for adding to a municipality's water supply."

I paused and cocked my head, watching for his reaction. He sat still. He wasn't clueless, I'd seen his eyes widen when I said the word *fluoride*. He shifted in his seat.

He smiled and held his hands out. "Like you said, it's quite a common practice."

"Except, the town voted down the proposition that would have added fluoride to the water eight years ago." His jaw clenched.

"Well, then they must have bundled the prop with another vote in the last few years because I have a signed work order from the mayor himself."

I felt myself start. I had looked up every bill and every item that had been put to vote over the last eight years and nothing approved the motion. I took a deep breath, ready to call his bluff.

"That's great, could I see a copy of that work order?"

All amusement fell from his eyes but he kept his mouth in a toothy grin. "Of course," he said through gritted teeth.

I followed him down the stairwell into the basement, lined with rows and rows of file cabinets. It was dark, only a few free-hanging light bulbs lit the hallway. Geoffrey led me down to the far end. I watched him unlock a small wire door that held a bunch of cabinets labeled *County Records*. He grinned, opening the door for me.

"Ladies first."

I narrowed my eyes, a prickly suspicion putting me on edge. This was Godot, I reminded myself. Not the Middle East.

I took a cautious step inside. My stomach sank at the sound of the door swinging shut behind me. I spun around just in time to see him jamming the key back in the door.

"Hey!" I shouted, but he was already taking off back down the hallway.

"We'll see what the boss wants to do with you," he threw over his shoulder, menacingly, before disappearing up the stairs.

18

NICOLETTE

G etting locked in a strange basement should have made me nervous, but I'd been held at gunpoint during my month in Saudi Arabia after a misunderstanding about a few choice words I'd had for one of the leaders.

Okay, I'd called him a misogynistic, slave-trading pig and his security guard detained me for six hours.

I pulled out my phone. One bar of service blinked on and off as I moved about the small space. A wave of sadness and insecurity crashed over me, realizing I had no one to call. Chelsea had three girls and I couldn't ask her to bring them into this. Whatever *this* was.

My thoughts went to Riot. I could call him. I *should* call him. He would be here in an instant, I know, and I tried not to let what that meant distract me from my task at hand.

I think it's just been a really long time...

My finger hovered over his name on my phone when my eyes caught one of the file cabinets labeled *Land Permits & Geological Surveys*. I recalled what Dr. Moore had mentioned about needing to do more extensive research on the mine to determine whether there were other carcinogens.

I scoured the files for anything that referenced the coal mine but there wasn't much. It was private property after all. There were surveys for the land around the mine but nothing for the mine itself.

The coal mine was suspicious, but it wasn't the common denominator. Too many people who never stepped foot in that coal mine had gotten sick for that to be the root cause.

Leafing through the folders and drawers, I landed on the year of the fires. I wasn't sure what I was looking for so I pulled my phone out and snapped pictures of every page I could find that had information about the fires and the homes that were built as a result.

As I shuffled the pages, I paused to listen but there was silence. My heart started to pick up. I looked at my watch. Half an hour had gone by. I glanced down at my phone. One little bar remained for the moment and I wished Brennan had his driver's license.

He had been helpful when I'd asked him for help the other day before his rude brother found us and freaked the fuck out.

I had been hoping he could fly his personal little drone over the coal mine land to check out what kind of activity was happening there.

"I can do better than that." He swirled in his desk chair and started tapping into his computer. "The coal mine ends on the edge of the town. Right over the town border begins the UAS test field."

"The what?"

"Unmanned Aerial Systems, better known as drones," he summed up somewhat pedantically. "There is a brand new Airborne GPR that can give us a thermal image of not only what's happening on the coal mine but inside of it."

"Really?" I asked, bending over to see better at his computer but the code was all gibberish to me.

"Yes, I'll need to hack into their intranet to navigate the launch systems but I can run a scan protocol that should break in by tomorrow." He spun back around and grinned at me. "Do you want to play a game while we wait?"

So we had pulled out Rock 'Em Sock 'Em Robots and started betting Twizzlers when Riot flew in like a madman. And then that kiss.

I think it's just been a really long time...

Regardless of what had transpired between us, I needed to get out of here. Who knew what Geoffrey Brown, or whoever the boss was, what their intentions were. I steeled myself before hitting Riot's number. It rang once and as soon as he picked up, the line went dead. *Call Failed,* my phone mocked me.

I tried one more time and again it rang but this time Riot picked up halfway through the first ring.

"Nic?"

"Riot, I need your help. I'm stuck in the basement of the county office building," I rushed out.

Silence.

Call Failed. I knocked a couple of folders to the ground in frustration. I groaned with irritation, moving to type out a text message.

> Locked in basement of county office building.

I hit send and waited to see if it would go through. The little service line disappeared. I hung my head and flopped down on the ground, cluttered with papers.

Hitting my head against the file cabinet wall, I cursed Melody for ever sending me here. But then my heart clenched at the prospect of never getting to know Riot and that idea produced an unexpected wave of melancholy.

I was about to try my phone again when I spotted a paper on the ground. I picked it up and examined it. Sifting through a few more pages of the report, I took a careful photo of each one, my adrenaline starting to pick up.

The far door creaked open, followed by the pattering of what sounded like a couple of pairs of feet coming down the hallway. I folded up a few of the papers and shoved them in my back pocket. I held my breath as the footsteps came closer.

I spun around, preparing myself for anything when around the corner came Geoffrey and Pastor Blackwell. I narrowed my eyes at him; I knew he'd be at the center of this.

Elias stopped in front of the closed door with a surprised look on his face. He regarded me before spinning to Geoffrey and holding his hands out.

"Really, Geoff? You locked her in the records room? Give me that." He snatched the keys out of Geoffrey's hand and turned to unlock the door. "Sorry about this, Miss Parker." He shook his head in disbelief. "Geoff fancies himself a bit of a prankster." He shot a scornful look at Geoff who smirked at me with two *guffaws*. A silent rage coursed through me. If I hadn't just hit pay-dirt I would have lit him up but Geoffrey Brown had just locked the wrong girl in a room with information she shouldn't have.

Pastor Blackwell led me upstairs into an empty office. "Can I get you anything? Coffee? Water?"

"No thanks, I've had my daily dosage of fluoride, thank you." I was baiting him, but I saw no reason to play games.

Pastor Blackwell stilled, but he just gave me a flat look before holding his hands up like I was a cop. "You got me, Nicolette. I asked some friends at the water authority to put fluoride in the water. I am guilty of caring too much about this town's enamel."

He sat down across from me. He was shaking his head as if I were his teenage kid who had just been busted for shoplifting.

"So why was Echo Chemicals dumping it in the dead of night?"

Pastor Blackwell sighed deeply. "There's no official work order, so the county can't touch it. Geoff asked some connections there to help us out." I kept my lips pressed tightly together. He looked tired. "Honestly, Miss Parker, you are trying to make me out to be a bad guy... I'm sorry, but there's no story here."

"You don't think people have a right to know what's in their water supply?"

"It's a perfectly safe additive."

"So why not tell them?"

Pastor Blackwell looked off, appearing defeated. He took a long pause and a brief expression of regret passed over his face.

"I was disappointed when the bill was voted down some years ago. I've always done everything I can to try to bring select progression to Godot. But I'm often met with resistance. People don't like change." His eyes drifted off as if lost in thought. His mind seemed to land on a sad memory. "The fluoride in the water is harmless. It's administered by a reputable company and is perfectly safe." He looked at me like the matter was closed so I reached back and pulled the papers from my back pocket.

"Were the massive amounts of radon in the Valley perfectly safe when you built a whole community on top of it?"

I tossed the paper down that contained the land surveys of the valley right before the houses were built. He looked down at them and then back at me, remaining expressionless.

"I'm sorry you had to find that." My heart thrummed in my chest.

My phone buzzed in my pocket, a barrage of messages coming through now that service returned.

"I assume since you're such a *worldly* man that you know radon is the second leading cause of lung cancer?"

He pressed his lips into a thin line. "The company we contracted with to build the homes *overlooked* the mitigation systems."

"They *overlooked* one of the most standard practices in home building?" I asked, the doubt clear in my tone.

He sighed before a thick swallow rolled down his throat. "They were a young, up-and-coming real estate company that sought to revolutionize pre-made manufactured housing. But startups often cut corners and radon hadn't been much of an issue in Northern California where they originated." A tick of familiarity tugged at me and I let my brain rewind, taking advantage of the silence. "There is already a massive class action lawsuit pending in hopes to make it right for those that got sick."

Finally, I tilted my head. "This real estate company wouldn't happen to have been a company you had investments with, would it?"

Pastor Blackwell remained stoic and blinked at me. Once. Twice. "Housing and healthcare. That's what you said, right?" I reminded him.

"It's not a crime to either hire or invest with companies that you believe in."

His words from our first meeting came swirling back to me and I thought about the influx of cash it must have taken to pay off the financing for a project the size of rebuilding the Valley. A devious warmth spread through me and I tried to conceal my nervous excitement.

"But it *is* a crime to short a stock when you have inside information. Let's say that information is about a massive impending class action lawsuit for failing to install radon mitigation systems."

Pastor Blackwell blinked with a blank expression. The pregnant pause was nine months large, and I drank in the Gotchya Moment.

His face reddened. "Nicolette, I am the pastor of a church in rural West Virginia." He shook his head at me. "I leave the investments up to my consultants."

"You weren't *lucky* to pull out of real estate before the housing collapse. You just knew one of your funds was about to face a massive lawsuit. You shorted the stock then pulled out of real estate entirely to make it look like an overall strategic move." I nodded, piecing it all together, clucking my tongue like I was impressed. "Very well done," I regarded him.

"Nicolette, if you are going to make these kinds of accusations, I'm afraid I'm going to have to excuse myself from these conversations. I was trying to entertain you as the bright, intelligent young woman you are but your ideas are becoming... *outlandish*." He stood up and gestured toward the door. "If you have any more questions, there is a hotline dedicated to the class action. I'm sure their lawyers will be *happy* to get you a statement. Our community members who were affected by the radon are already on the list of potential recipients."

I opened my mouth to reply but a distant shout halted me. My head swiveled toward the door. It almost sounded like Riot.

"Nic!" It was definitely Riot.

Moving toward the door, I peeked my head out to see Riot standing at the front desk, the receptionist on her feet, scowling at him. His head snapped in my direction and his expression registered immediate relief. He sprinted toward me.

"Excuse me, sir, you can't go down there without an appointment."

"It's fine, Susie." Pastor Blackwell stepped into the hall and raised his hand toward the woman who frowned and sat back down.

"Are you okay?" His words rushed out while he crushed my body against his chest. My breath hitched from fierce tenderness of the gesture. He finally pulled back but kept a hand on my elbow, anxiously scanning me. It reminded me of the wild way he dragged me out of Brennan's house.

I don't know what came over me. I think it's just been a really long time...

"Yes, I'm fine." I pulled my elbow out of his grasp and he deflated. "What are you doing here?"

"I got your message about being locked in the basement," he said, darting his suspicious eyes between me and Pastor Blackwell. The concern in his voice tore open that wound I spent all week stitching up.

"A misunderstanding." Elias Blackwell put himself between us. "Now, I think it's time for you two to let everyone go back to their regular business." The tone of his voice was tight. And Riot put a protective hand around my shoulders to lead me out.

"Oh, Mr. Asher?" We turned around and Pastor Blackwell gave Riot a heartfelt smile.

"I would love to see you back in my congregation one of these days."

19

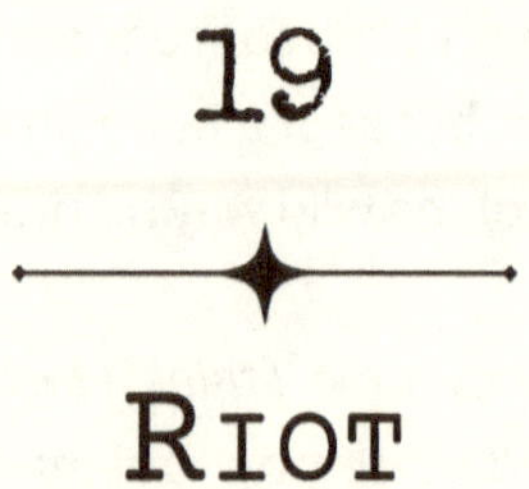

RIOT

Teeming with anger, I pushed the county building doors open. The sick little smile on Elias Blackwell's face when he invited me to my mother's church almost made me snap. But I remembered the last time I let my emotions go and how much I'd hurt Nicolette, so I inhaled my fury and stalked to the truck, listening for her steps behind me.

I could feel her hesitation as she approached the truck, but I'd already stashed her bike into the bed of my pickup.

Reluctance emanated from her, but so did that wonderful lilac when she spun her head to put her seat belt on, her blonde hair twirling around her like a curtain.

"What happened in there?" It came out more demanding than I intended but, truth be told, I had been worked up and on edge since her first attempted phone call. I spent the last half hour having Brennan hack into her mobile carrier to remotely turn on her location sharing but it was taking too long.

When I'd gotten a text message that she was locked in the basement of the county office building, I sped to the office, blind with adrenaline. I tried convincing myself that this wasn't my problem, but the only thing that echoed throughout my brain was her asking for my help before the phone cut out.

"It was nothing. Like Pastor Blackwell said, it was a misunderstanding." But she didn't meet my eyes, keeping her body closed off to me and facing the passenger window.

"Elias is a liar and I don't trust a word he says."

Her head snapped to meet my gaze, but she didn't speak. Her slate gray eyes were big and filled with things I wish she'd say out loud.

"Nic, I'm sorry..." I said, utilizing the chance to look her in the eye. Her chest hitched a bit, and I reddened, realizing I had used the nickname out loud.

"I'm fine, Riot. Really, it's fine. Can we just go home now?" she said, devoid of emotion.

I didn't know what else to say. If she didn't want to talk about the kiss, I wasn't going to force it.

She   probably hadn't even thought about   it. She'd probably kissed several guys and never gave a second thought to plenty of them. My fingers tightened on the steering wheel at the image. We drove the rest of the way in silence.

Nicolette retreated to her room when we got back, the clacking of her keyboard and the faint sound of her voice created a rhythmic din. It sounded like she was leaving a message for her parents.

My anxiety had grown tighter and tighter with each passing second on the ride home.

I pictured the wounded look on her face when I told her I didn't know what came over me and an overwhelming urge to hear the sound of her laugh punched me in the chest. I approached her door, the curtain pulled back an inch.

I shouldn't interrupt.

If she had wanted to talk to me, she would have. I retreated to my bedroom. She didn't want to hear my excuses and, really, what had changed? She was still only here for a few weeks and my life was already mapped out for me and it included marrying the pastor's right-hand woman.

Although, the more I thought about Katie, the more irritated I grew. I should confront her about her plans for me but I didn't want to open that conversation yet. If what Nicolette had told me was wrong, I would look like an asshole for assuming Katie wanted to be with me. If Nicolette had been telling the truth, then I would have to have the awkward conversation of trying to let her down gently. If I was being honest, I was a little nervous about the possible repercussions.

After a month or two of her showing up with dinner at least twice a week, I realized she wasn't going away. And I had been okay with it back then. But despite my best effort, I struggled to feel anything deeper for her. She was attractive and kind and, for whatever reason, she wanted to spend time with me.

So, I told myself to give it time. Maybe it was just *me.* Maybe my time incarcerated deadened me inside. But after the kiss with Nicolette it became painfully obvious, I was *anything* but dead inside. I didn't know what Katie's hair smelled like. Was she odorless or had I just never noticed?

Then I remembered the way Nicolette had smelled like lilacs and when she was close to me, I could detect some kind of sweet berry at the base of her neck. Her lips had tasted like salt and Twizzlers and I remembered the way she'd smiled against my mouth. I had opened my eyes to look at her in that moment and been awestruck by how beautiful she was and how *blissful* she appeared. Her face typically carried the weight of concern but she was relaxed, carefree.

I recalled the way she pressed against me after feeling how hard I was, which was impossible to hide. I hadn't *wanted* to hide it. I wanted her to know how badly I wanted her. I wanted her to see what she did to me, how my body came alive in her presence.

Before I knew what was happening, my hand had slipped underneath the waistband of my boxers. I stroked myself to the memory of her mouth and the possibilities of where that kiss could have gone. After I came to the fantasy of her beneath me, a deep melancholy settled through me, realizing I might never feel this for anyone else, no matter how long I was given to try.

The following week, the town was in full Field Days mode. Everyone's windows were polished. The signs were cleaned, the streets swept, and the dead light bulbs replaced. I knew because I'd been asked to replace them all.

"You did such a great job with the library landscaping, the town council asked if you could do the town square. You know, the little park with the benches and the bushes?" Mr. Meaney said through the phone. "It's a paid gig, kid, so don't screw it up. They only ask that you wait until after the shops have mostly closed so that the noise doesn't disturb customers."

I almost snorted. Yes, of course, it was the *lawnmower* they were worried about making people nervous. I assured him I'd be there prompt and quick under the cover of night.

"Oh, and bring one of those little metal, spinning statue things. That looked good at the library. Where'd you find that?"

"Just a local artist at the Farmer's Market," I said.

"Well, stock up, the library has gotten a lot of questions about where people could find something similar."

A grumpy feeling bloomed in me, knowing I couldn't tell them it was my work. That my art would suffer because it was aligned with my name. I wanted to create something I could be proud of. I wanted to put something out into the world that would help people see me as more than just a monster, just a killer. I had been working on a grand piece to display at the Field Days Art Showcase and had planned on entering it anonymously.

But lately, I was tired of feeling anonymous.

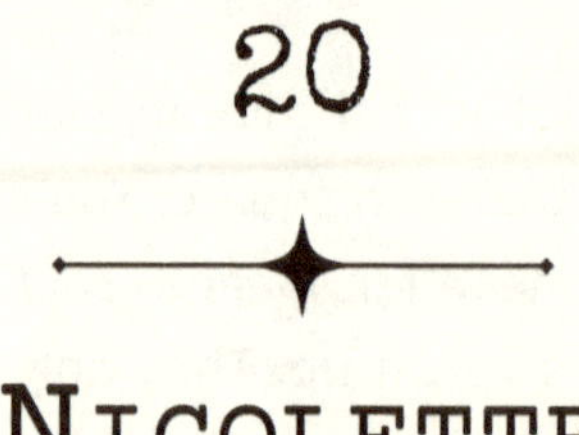

20

NICOLETTE

I had butterflies in my stomach the day before the Godot Family Field Days and I didn't know why. I had only volunteered to piss off Katie and prove I wasn't just some self-centered outsider. But somewhere along the line, doing a good job with this stupid carnival began to mean something to me.

I had done my due diligence on the class action lawsuit. It was still wrapped up in courts and after a quick trip to the Center to talk to Miriam, she confirmed that everyone affected was already aware and they were all on the list of award recipients if the lawsuit ever closed. It would be years, but it would be something.

It wasn't just the radon that did the damage. The building company had cut a lot of corners. The reason they were so profitable in the beginning was because they never paid for supplies . They repurposed old building materials that contained lead paint, asbestos, you name it. The radon just accelerated the problems.

There was still the mystery of Chimera but I hadn't heard back from Dr. Moore's DEA colleague so I was running out of leads.

Beyond that, I had a hard time finding a reason to stay in Godot after these Field Days. For a fleeting moment, I considered Melody's original assignment. I had *some* additional information that *could* yield enough of a personality profile for the Beyond Bizarre episode. But none of it resonated well, and I berated myself for entertaining it.

So, here I was, a bruised heart, a broken ego, and no story to be written.

It was best for me to stop Riot's apology because when Pastor Black-well had mentioned the class action, my story was dead in the water and there was no reason left to stay in this town. I would leave after the Field Days were over. And I didn't need to open my heart up to any more hurt. The auto garage had said my car would be ready by Monday and once that was settled, I would be able to go.

As resolute as I was, each time I reminded myself of that, the hole in my chest got wider.

Before I left for the final walk-through of the Field Days, I stopped at the main house to grab a bottle of water. I spotted a newspaper on the kitchen island. It was a copy of last week's Huntington Herald. It was folded open to the article I'd written. I had forgotten about it after I'd submitted it. There was a sticky note next to my name.

"You should be proud. I know I am."

My heart clenched, and I clutched the paper to my chest.

I think it's just been a really long time...

I reminded myself that I was leaving. But I kept the note as proof that something had been real here.

The final walk-through made sure all the rides, games, A/V, and ven-dors were all set up. I gave an interview to one of the regional TV stations and the buzz around the event was surprising to all of us. The planning and last-minute setup had all gone so smoothly that it was hardly an hour before I returned to Riot's house.

I pulled a fresh shirt on and caught a glimpse of him inside his work tent, with the flaps pulled back, letting air blow through the space. He was holding a drill, sweat dripping from his forehead and a small darker stain trailing down his back. He was reaching up, twisting a bolt into what looked like the blade of a ceiling fan. His biceps flexed under his tan skin and my mouth went dry. It hurt to even look at him.

Making a quick decision, I grabbed two beers out of the fridge and let the screen door to the lanai slam shut to let him know I was coming.

He looked up, that signature scowl on his face, squinting into the sun. When his gaze landed on me, I could have sworn I saw his eyes soften just a bit, but I shook it off, chalking it up to the sudden cloud that drifted in front of the sunlight. I appraised his work.

"This is incredible... what'll it be?" I asked.

He almost cracked a grin and gave one of the fan blades a little spin.

"Not quite done yet." I handed him a beer, and he took it with an appreciative nod, slugging down almost half of it in one gulp. "Everything teed up for the big day?" he asked, wiping his hands on a rag.

I nodded, relieved we were settling into a comfortable, albeit mundane, conversation.

"Surprisingly, yes. I'm a little nervous, waiting for the other shoe to drop or something but, knock on wood, everything is ready to rip. Are you selling this piece?" I noticed his booth was still empty during the walk-through.

"No," he said, turning his gaze on me. "I'm not letting this one go."

His eyes pinned me with a hard stare and I sucked in a quick breath. He didn't elaborate, so I didn't push.

I gave him a tight-lipped smile. It still bugged me that he didn't feel like he could sell his own art. I hadn't thought about what he might do with the Farmer's Market booth when I was gone, and a remorseful sorrow nestled in my gut.

Shading my eyes, I studied the whirling metal. It was a beautiful shell. Compiled of imperfect pieces, arranged to come together for something incredible. But it felt absent of something. Like its heartbeat was missing and just needed one last contribution to make it come alive.

"I'm going to bring the load over shortly," he said. He hesitated, meeting my gaze. "Want to come with me? Direct me to the booth?"

I wanted to say no, but maybe this was the ideal time to talk to him about my moving out.

"Yeah, happy to." I nodded, and I saw one corner of his lips twitch.

The ride over was silent. My hands itched to turn on the radio but I didn't want to risk hearing that stupid "One Headlight" song again. I don't know if my wasted heart could take it. As soon as we parked, I spilled out of the truck, needing space.

As we unloaded his pieces, I was viscerally aware of his body moving around mine like we were dancing. We worked together harmoniously, and I was reminded of the way we worked in tandem, washing dishes at the Center.

At one point I moved right, he moved left, and we did that awkward dodge where we both tried to move in a different direction. I let out a chuckle, coming to stillness in front of him. Without thinking, I put my hands on his hips and spun us 180 degrees.

Something in his eyes jumped when I touched him, and a bolt of electricity shot through my body. Our eyes met and my lips parted, trying to suck in more air, feeling lightheaded. But that only brought back the smell of sweat, musk, and metal filling my lungs.

Shit, he still smells good. Like man and machine and safety and sturdiness. My chest constricted and a warmth spread between my hips. The air began to feel thick.

I was struck with a need to make things better between us. With my departure looming, it was the right thing to do, the least I could offer us both. The idea of leaving without some kind of resolution seemed wrong. All the while, a part of me yearned for the way he'd wove his fingers through my hair during that "mistake" of a kiss.

He broke our gaze as if just realizing something and moved to shut his tailgate. I busied myself with arranging and rearranging the artwork on his table. He needed more display materials. The pieces sat haphazardly on the table and ground. I made a mental note to grab some of the old crates and burlap that I'd come to use for displays at the Farmer's Market.

Maybe I could load them in Riot's truck and we could go to the carnival together. The thought made my heart leap. *Like a date?* No, that would be ridiculous. But still, I did want to grab those crates, and I certainly couldn't carry them on the bike.

My heart thudded in my chest, an adolescent insecurity gripping my throat about asking him for a goddamn ride.

"Would you, maybe, want to head over in the morning? Together? Like, in one car, I mean," I stammered, my face reddening.

Riot turned toward me and I had a hard time looking him in the eye. Why did I feel like a pubescent teenager asking a boy out for the first time? Something I didn't recognize flashed behind Riot's eyes, something soft and amused and happy but then uncomfortable.

"Oh, um... I—" he shifted, and I could tell he was off balance. "I kind of promised Katie I'd give her a ride tomorrow." The words rushed from his lips like a confession.

A stale sensation spread somewhere between my ribs. I should have known. But it still hurt. Probably because I was a grown-ass adult with nothing but a fucking bicycle who was bumming rides off her convict landlord who'd let her stay out of pity.

I waved dismissively. "Oh, of course, no worries." I turned away to move toward the passenger door, eager to get out of his line of sight.

Riot took a step forward. "I'm sorry; she asked a while back. I don't mind dropping you off early. Or I'm sure she wouldn't care if you rode with us."

I pressed my lips together, failing to dodge his words, each one hitting me harder than the last. I suppressed a laugh and offered a tight-lipped smile.

"It's okay, Riot. Really." There was something in his eyes that almost looked like regret or guilt and the injury just kept piling on top of the insult. I gave him my best genuine smile and pulled the car door open.

Silence hung in the truck like stale air. It was a loaded silence, one teeming with quiet humiliation. It shouldn't bother me that Riot was taking Katie to the carnival. I'd heard her little three-year plan. Still, the image of her sitting in the very seat I sat in now churned my stomach and made my throat feel a little hollow. I picked a piece of fabric on the seat.

I could feel Riot's gaze on me. His jaw worked up and down, at a loss for an appropriate topic of conversation. Unwilling to share my disappointment, I kept my gaze out the window. He didn't need to feel guilty. Katie was a nice girl. I was glad that he had her.

Glad. That was it.

When we got back to his place, Riot broke the steely silence at the door. "Hey, thanks for... tagging along," he said with too much phony enthusiasm. "It was a big help. It would have taken me way longer without you... So, thank you," he finished, and his expression faltered.

I suppressed another dismal laugh. *Tagging along.* God, I felt pathetic. I was nothing more than the annoying little sister who tagged along, inserting herself where she wasn't needed or desired.

I wanted to slap myself across the face. *You are Nicolette fucking Parker. You have brought down billion-dollar companies and exposed corrupt government officials and you're feeling sorry for yourself because a hot convict asked your arch-nemesis to dance.* I scoffed at myself. I took a breath, resigned to pushing it far from my mind. I had to focus on my future and that meant coming clean with Melody about my failure to write anything usable.

As I made my way through the main room toward the lanai, Riot didn't close himself in his bedroom and slam the door like usual. Instead, he dropped his keys on the table and made his way to the kitchen, idly leafing through the mail that had been sitting on the counter since I arrived.

I walked through the main room to the sliding door to my lanai.

"Want one?" Riot's voice startled me. He stood with the refrigerator door open, holding a beer with a glint of hope in his eye. "There's a boxing match I might stay up for. If you're interested, I mean." His eyes darted to the living room TV, which had remained notably dark since our evening *Jeopardy!* games came to a halt.

Again, my throat twisted. I wasn't fooling myself; he didn't want to hang out with me. He just felt guilty. Why he felt guilty was beyond me. The man owed me nothing. I looked at the beer in his hand for a beat and then into his eyes.

"No, thank you. I'm going to wrap up some work." I jerked my head in the direction of the lanai and although his expression didn't change, he deflated the tiniest bit.

"Oh, okay," his deep voice sounded softer, and I wanted to press my ear against his chest to hear it resonate. "Good night, Nicolette."

My steps faltered at the sound of my name and it did unwelcome things to my insides.

Be fucking cool, I scolded myself. I turned on my million-watt smile and nodded once. "Good night, Riot."

I didn't work on anything. Instead, I curled up in my bed and let the deep melancholy I'd been keeping at bay wash over me. I pictured Riot getting ready in the morning, brushing his teeth, styling his hair, picking an outfit, and then getting in his truck to go pick up a different girl for their date to the carnival. I pictured him winning her some obnoxious stuffed animal, his arm thrown around her shoulders.

Why was I doing this to myself? I should get up. But just like the night after our first kiss, our first and probably only, I allowed myself to dwell in miserable self-pity for just a bit longer.

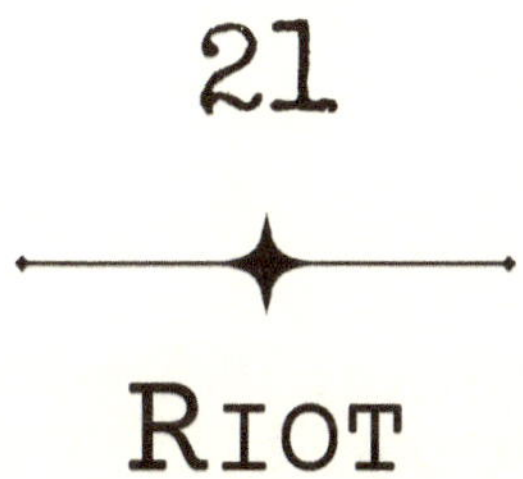

21

RIOT

I hated that look on her face. Why did that look on her face twist me up so much? Katie had asked me to take her to the Field Days carnival when I wasn't paying attention and I kicked myself for ever saying yes. I considered telling Katie I'd meet her there, but it would be a bigger shithead move if she saw me pull up with Nicolette. But, *fuck*, if I didn't hate that look of disappointment I caught in her eyes.

I also hated this TV. I never turned on the living room TV unless it was with Nicolette and Brennan. Now it felt empty, watching it alone. Still, if she changed her mind and came to join me, I wanted to be here.

But Nicolette Parker didn't change her mind. She stayed holed up in that tiny screen room all night. The longer the night wore on, the more jittery I became. I tried drinking a beer. I tried making tea but the hollow way she said "Good night, Riot" echoed in my brain. My legs ached to walk to her room. My hands ached to knock on her door. I wanted to hold her. I wanted to tell her she was the only woman I'd thought about since the day she arrived.

I wanted to pull her outside. I wanted to build a fire and sit next to her, tell her everything I was thinking and not thinking. I wanted to kiss her. Pin her to the ground next to the fire. I wanted to fuck her all night under the stars and fall asleep to the sound of cicadas in the wind. I wanted to wake up with her in my arms, breathing in the soft scent of her hair.

But I wouldn't do any of those things.

Even if I told her how I felt, I had no real way of knowing if she wanted the same things.

Frustrated, I flipped the TV off and retreated to the darkness of my bedroom.

The next morning, I expected to find her awake already, but she still hadn't come out of the lanai. Usually, she was out here by now complaining about my shitty coffee and being a royal pain in my ass at the breakfast bar. Her empty seat cracked my chest open, and I already wanted this day to be over so I might steal another chance to talk to her.

Closing myself in the confines of my bathroom, apprehension ran through me. I splashed water on my face. I glared at the stranger in the mirror and suppressed a disgusted scoff.

I wish I could see more of that smile.

I had trimmed my beard down, but it still didn't feel like enough. I dug through the drawers until I found what I was looking for.

Twenty minutes later, I finished getting ready and was pulled out of my spiraling thoughts by the buzz of my doorbell. I frowned. No one ever stopped by here.

My irritation grew when I saw the police car parked in my driveway like it belonged there.

I pulled the door open for Jeremy Blackwell and crossed my flexed arms in front of me, leaning against the doorframe. If he was intimidated, he sure didn't show it. Jeremy's wide smile mocked me.

"Good morning, Riot. How are you?"

I grumbled at the niceties. "What can I do for you, Jeremy?"

"I'm here to talk to Nicolette. Is she home?" He grinned wider and something in me turned a little cold. Defensive. I puffed up to block the view of his craning neck.

"I haven't seen her up yet so I'm not sure. I can take a message and let her know you stopped by when she wakes up."

"She's awake," Nicolette muttered groggily behind me, taking a sip of coffee. She grimaced with distaste and I wanted to smile. She paused her next sip when her eyes landed on my face. Her hair was tousled in a knot on top of her head and I couldn't help but rake my eyes over her body in those tiny pajamas again. *God, the woman is pure torture.*

Something delicious crossed her face, almost like a smile, more like intrigue. Our eyes tangled and my heart skipped a beat. I ran a hand over the lower half of my bare face, self-conscious of the very short stubble I'd left behind.

Nicolette's head tilted to the side. I wanted her to know I'd done it for her. Because she had said she wanted to see my smile and even though I had obligations with Katie today, I wanted her to know my smile was all hers. It wasn't much, but it was all I had left to offer.

"Oh good!" Jeremy's voice severed the moment. "Hey, sorry to just drop by but I was in the neighborhood and figured it was too nice of a day for a text message." I tried to compute that but just frowned. "I wanted to ask you, Nicolette, if you'd let me give you a ride to the carnival later this morning? I ran into Katie last night and when she said she and Riot were going together, I didn't want you to be left high and dry."

He flashed another smile with a subtle wink at me and I wanted to break all of his beady little white teeth.

I can't explain what infuriated me more; the idea of Jeremy fucking Blackwell taking Nicolette anywhere, or the fact that he made an in-person stop to ask her like he was marking his territory.

My molars ground together, not wanting to turn around to see her expression. I shouldn't care. I couldn't care. But still, I listened for her response, holding my breath.

"Oh, um, you don't *have* to do that, Jeremy. I don't mind walking." The way the pitch in her voice went down when she said *walking* did something funny to my chest.

"Nonsense, you're a co-chair. Besides, I *want* to. I'd be *lucky* to walk in with *Nicolette Parker* on my arm." He flashed another cheesy grin.

The rushing of blood in my ears might have drowned out her answer so I turned around. Her gaze dropped when my eyes landed on her. There was a sadness that wasn't there a moment ago and my fingers hummed to hold her. She felt stuck, but there was also gratitude. She knew his flattery was phony, she was too smart not to. But still, he'd made her feel like a priority and I *fucking* hated everything about this moment.

"Okay, yeah, there are some crates I needed to bring to one of the vendor booths if you don't mind."

My spirits plummeted.

Was that the only reason she'd asked me to take her yesterday? Mixed emotions warred inside me. But the overwhelming one was despair. She was going to be gone soon. And I wanted her here. It didn't matter that she'd be riding in Jeremy's cruiser today. I'd let her ride with Jeremy every day if it meant he was driving her home to me.

"I'll let you two coordinate," I said, stalking away. But I'll be damned if I didn't eavesdrop on the rest of their conversation.

"Great!" Jeremy exclaimed. "What time should I pick you up?"

Nicolette hesitated. *Half past go fuck yourself.*

"Maybe eleven-thirty?"

"Great!" he repeated "It's a date!"

My fists balled up. I could practically hear Nicolette rolling her eyes.

"It's not a date, Jeremy." My mood lifted. That's my girl.

No.

No, not my *girl*, I reminded myself.

"Oh, it's a figure of speech," he laughed dismissively and I was certain he didn't mean it as a figure of speech.

What was I doing? This was pathetic. She was free to do whatever she wanted with whomever she wanted to. Just as I was, I reminded myself. I should be more grateful to Katie; she was a sweet girl, and she was looking forward to this day.

I promised myself to honor that commitment and show her a good time. Let the Nicolette and Jeremy chips fall where they may.

22

NICOLETTE

I didn't want to lead Jeremy on, but I *did* need a ride if I was going to bring the crates to Riot's booth. I still wasn't sure why I was doing it. Someone like *Katie* should be doing this for him and I idly wondered if she even knew about his art.

She's helping me re-acclimate *to the community.*

And that included telling him he had to hide his face from the world because of a measly scar.

Riot had left to pick her up nearly an hour ago and *holy fuck* did he look good. I began to drool when my eyes landed on him. At first, I couldn't help but feel like maybe he'd shaved for me. I had told him a few times I wish I could see his smile more and the way he'd regarded me made my heart stop.

I noticed the little scar on his chin. Was that what he was so worried about people seeing?

"Excited for today?" Jeremy kept looking at me and it was irritating, like he was waiting for some reaction that would never come.

I gave him a tight-lipped smile. "Yep," I replied, gazing out the window. The town was buzzing and there was significantly more traffic through the streets. I couldn't believe after everything, I found pride in seeing this event become successful.

"After the mayor does the welcome, I'll need to go on stage, I was hoping you'd join me." I raised an eyebrow.

"Why would I need to go on stage?"

"I feel like Godot is on the brink of a little renaissance, you know? Good things are happening, like these Family Field Days. And I think you are a big part of it. We need to highlight the bright things happening in Godot. The *successful people* that have come out of here and no one is a better example of that than you. There's too much press about the drug problem and the health issues." He waved his hand dismissively.

"Don't you think those things are worth addressing so that maybe someone can root out the cause to correct the problem?"

Jeremy faltered but recovered. He tipped his head back and forth.

"Of course, but those issues are generational now. We're past the point of being able to eradicate the drug problem."

"Yeah, I heard about the class action from the homes built after the fire." I was baiting him but if he had any new information for me, he didn't give it away.

"Those poor people will be lucky if they're even alive when they finally see that payout. You know how those things go, deny and delay." He waved another hand dismissively. I parted my lips to speak, but he threw the car in park. "We're here!"

Tearing off my seatbelt like I couldn't get away fast enough, I came to stillness when my feet hit the ground.

Riot's gaze met mine across the parking lot. The petite brunette tugged on his hand and *they were holding goddamn hands.* Jealousy gripped me and I'd never felt so unbelievably temporary. I was already looking forward to this day being over so I could go back and pack.

"So, what do you say? Be my Vanna White on stage?" Jeremy came around to my side and held his arms out, expectant.

"Okay, sure." He beamed. "Thanks, Jeremy, and thank you for the ride. I really appreciate it. I have some set up to do. But I'll see you in there?"

His smile faded when I began to unload all the items I brought.

"Do you need a hand?" He moved to help me.

"Oh, I'm alright, I just need to get these set up before the vendor booths open!" I flashed him another smile but the phoniness was apparent, even to me. I saw him frown and scuff his shoe and a pang of guilt struck me before I disappeared to take care of Riot's booth.

An hour later, I'd checked on all our sponsors, gave a few comments to bloggers, and refilled approximately three large tumblers with rum and Diet Coke. The event was running smoother than I could have predicted.

Everything felt like it was wrapping up in Godot and that sense of finality filled me with a surprising amount of sadness. I sucked down whatever was left in my cup and tossed it in the garbage. Maybe it would be better if I just took off tonight. Better to sober up.

I found myself wandering into the artists' showcase. I idled past the children's section and stopped in my tracks when I came to the end.

It was the twinkling sound of metal chimes I heard first.

They filled my ears and brain with the reminiscent sound of adolescent summer. The sound somehow sprinkled its way down my entire body. I felt like I could float away. But I was viscerally grounded by the harmonious carousel of sparkling colors that caught the tent walls. The shimmering display called me forward and the crowd that had gathered around it parted like they'd been commanded to.

My mouth fell open when I reached the front.

The whirligig was made of all kinds of scrap metal and glass shards to form the body of a pickup truck.

Riot's pickup truck.

An empty jug of cheap wine was broken into pieces and added to act as the truck's doors. There were old cigarette ads decoupaged on the metal hood of the truck.

The real punch to my heart, though, was the old Barbie doll in the center of the truck bed. Her long blonde hair pulled up into a high ponytail. Half of her face was marred in black dirt, which only somehow made her more spectacular. She was wearing a dirty blue gown, and she spun, positioned like a ballerina. The back of the truck came alive with pieces of stained glass cascading off the back. Slivers of a mirror behind it made it look like it was burning. One small, round light emanated from the front.

The twinkling that emanated from it was hypnotic. Everything about it was magnetic.

My breath caught in my throat, which was quickly tightening when I let my eyes drift to the card beneath it.

ME & CINDERELLA - *Riot Asher*

He used his real name. My chest burst with pride I hadn't earned and when tears sprung to my eyes, I didn't blink them away. They were evidence. That something, no *someone*, had moved me.

I'm not letting this one go, he had said to me last night, referring to the piece before me. At least that's what I had thought he was referring to. Now it didn't feel like that.

Not even a little.

I sucked in a shaky breath, unable to tear my eyes away.

Even when the familiar scent of leather, clean citrus and a hint of motor oil came wafting from the strong body now standing next to me.

"It's an old, beat-up truck..." I whispered almost inaudibly.

"With one headlight," Riot finished for me.

Heart in my throat, I tore my eyes away from the whirligig and gazed up at him. The carnival fell away, and it was just us. Back in his truck, vying for the volume of the Wallflowers' "One Headlight".

Only we were facing one another now. No pretense. No façade. Only the deep reverence on Riot Asher's expression, his eyes sweeping over my face.

"You used your real name." My voice was tight. I pulled my bottom lip in between my teeth to keep the tears from spilling over. His jaw twitched.

"I wanted everyone to know it's mine." He said the words with such conviction, I lost my breath. Riot's eyes grazed my lips. The air between us crackled with all the things we weren't saying. All the things we'd kept inside. I felt something shift inside me like waking up in a brand new time and place. And there I saw it all over his face. That same feeling of newness breaking through a long, dark and cold night. A night that lasted forever. But here we were. Together, bathing in the sanguine hues of a brand new morning.

I was never temporary for him. Like he was never temporary for me. No matter what happened Riot would be a permanent stamp on my heart.

"Riot..." I rasped. His chest rose, inching closer to me. The weight of everything he'd left unsaid poured from his icy blue gaze.

"There you are!" Jeremy's voice was like a bucket of cold water. "Nicolette, I have to introduce you to the mayor. Let's go!" I felt him grab my hand. He didn't wait for a response before dragging me away. My other hand shot out for Riot, almost instinctively. I clutched a thick bicep, the rigid tension of his body relaxing under my palm. I clung to him for as long as I could before ultimately, my fingers slipped away.

"Godot is on the cusp of becoming an even more incredible town than it once was and will be again." Jeremy sounded like he was running for president.

Everything in my body hummed, and it was almost like I'd been hit by Riot's artful truck. All I wanted to do was go home. See him. Talk to him. I didn't know what I would say. I just needed to be near him. In his orbit.

All I had left to do was join Jeremy on stage to be his little case study and then I would duck out. I'd walk, no, *run* back to Riot's house.

"We're going to continue to bring fresh, new, invigorating ideas on how to bring more visitors and more businesses to the town. We have an unbelievable amount of talent and leadership in Godot and I want to highlight one special leader who not only calls Godot home but has made an incredible impact in the world outside our humble hamlet." Jeremy grinned and motioned for me to join him. "If you didn't catch her on the national evening news, you might have seen her work hosting the Godot High School morning announcements." A chuckle rumbled through the crowd, which by my calculations, consisted of the entire town population. "It's my honor to reintroduce Nicolette Parker!"

I walked across the stage, realizing I didn't know if he expected me to speak. I took slow, regretful steps across the stage, scanning the crowd for Riot. He stood a few rows back, a head taller than everyone around him. He shifted his weight to the other foot as Katie wrapped an arm around his waist.

"I know I, for one, am looking forward to the resources and relationships that people like Nicolette can bring to Godot," Jeremy continued. I smiled half-heartedly out into the crowd. I had come here to blend in, to root out a story and now here I was being paraded in front of the entire town like some sort of beauty queen and it turned my stomach.

"And we have a little surprise for you," Jeremy pulled me into him, giving me a tight side hug and my stomach turned sour. "The Family Field Days committee wanted to put together a little highlight reel, honoring your success. You left before graduation, which is when students usually get the chance to be celebrated. We never got the chance to applaud you in person and it's important you know how proud we are to call you one of ours."

My skin flushed. My eyes glided over to Katie who had a strange look on her face. Riot's jaw was tight, but I never wanted to look away.

The projector screen came alive behind me. My face was huge and *everywhere* as my own voice came out of the speakers. They were all clips of my early newscasts. God, it had been so long since I'd seen these. They elicited a sad wave of nostalgia.

My career at IANN had gone down in such disastrous, embarrassing flames that I had never had any interest in looking back. The work I had done, the stories I had covered, they made a difference. They gave a voice to people who'd been robbed of theirs. Watching the highlight reel, that same wave of pride I'd felt for Riot came back. But this pride — I'd earned.

I *had* worked hard to get where I was that early and I had never been celebrated by anyone. I wanted to turn around. I wanted to share this moment with Riot and see what he thought of my work. But the walk down memory lane had my eyes fixed on the screen.

The video cut from my newscast to an onsite interview I had conducted with the county prosecutor about a sex trafficking ring that had been busted after I followed a few tips on some bizarre solicitation arrests. The reel then cut to a few of my most viewed podcast videos, including the one that had exposed an embezzlement scheme in Easton.

Finally, as the reel wound down, I gazed out at the faces that were all beaming and smiling at the screen. A wave of guilt for all the judgment I'd passed crashed over me. I had assumed they would reject me because I had left. I never considered the thought that they might be proud of my success, hailing from their hometown.

As the background music started again, Jeremy turned back to the microphone.

"One of our hometown heroes, Nicolette Parker!" He started a large round of applause and I finally caved in and found Riot again. He was standing there, hands in his pockets. Katie clapped her hands, still clinging to him. When his eyes met mine, they softened and I caught a small nod. He slowly clapped three times. A smile stretched across his bare face and I'd never been so appreciative of beard clippers.

"Thank you—" Jeremy began again, and I moved to the right to step off stage when an audible gasp spread through the crowd. I scanned the townsfolk. Eyes went wide and parents wrapped their hands around their children's eyes.

It was a sea of incredulous gasps.

"My heavens…"

"Oh my goodness!"

"What is this?"

"What in the Sam Hill?"

I frowned, confused, and I couldn't help but flit my gaze to Riot whose eyes were fixed beyond me. There was confusion in his expression before realization passed over him. His jaw clenched in a hard line and his whole face took on a dark, dangerous visage. Next to him Katie's mouth dropped so far open I thought it might hit the grass.

My heart hammered in my chest when familiar, animalistic noises came from behind me. Every inch of my body went rigid.

Oh, God, no...

The world moved in slow motion. A cool breeze pushed a wisp of hair in front of my face and I blinked. I somehow managed to turn around to see the unforgiving sex tape of me plastered in live action over the giant screen.

My heart stopped and for the first time in my life, I had no words.

23

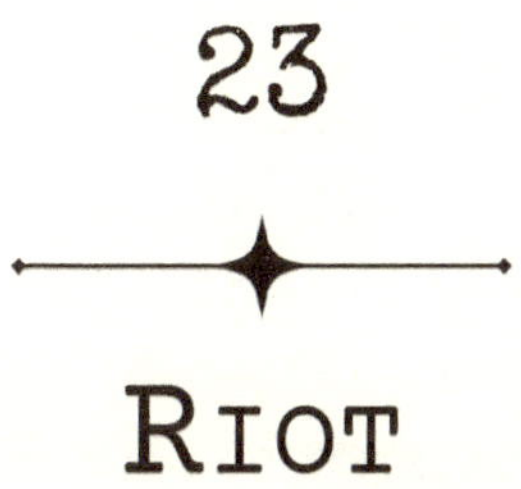

RIOT

I blinked several times to understand what I was watching. It was a black-and-white video with a high vantage point, like from a security camera. And it was porn. Part of me wanted to snort a laugh. Some kid had inserted a skin flick as a joke to light a fire under these uptight ass-hats.

On the screen, a young woman was strapped to a bed while a tall man with dark hair hit her with some kind of instrument. He slapped her hard on the ass and the woman cried out.

All the oxygen left my body at the familiar cry.

No fucking way... The man flipped the woman over and moved aside. It was Nicolette, a bit younger, but it was most certainly her.

My heart stopped. My stomach clenched and hot rage coursed through my veins, lighting up every limb and every space inside my chest.

"Who did this?" Jeremy fucking Blackwell said over the loudspeaker. "I demand to know who put this in there. We do not treat our citizens this way!"

He pulled Nicolette into him, holding her head against his chest and I don't know what made me angrier; the fact that Nicolette was being publicly humiliated, or that Jeremy was acting like a phony goddamn hero. He grasped her face with both palms and whispered something. He stroked her hair and I wanted to pull him off stage so he landed on his ass of a face. He didn't deserve to touch her hair.

"Turn it off! Someone turn it off!" he exclaimed heroically.

A bustle of people fumbled at the A/V booth. Katie put a hand on my chest.

"Ry, you can't let her stay with you anymore. You're so close to earning a respected space back here. You can't be associated in any way with that woman. Look at that!" Katie jerked a hand in the direction of the screen, which was *still fucking running.* "That is despicable, and she's never going to be accepted here. I know you felt bad for her and it was generous to let her stay but she *has to go.* Ry!" Her small hands shook me. "Riot, are you listening to me?"

But I wasn't listening to her. I wasn't listening to the horrified *tsks* in the crowd. And I sure as hell wasn't focusing my attention on the screen.

No, I couldn't tear my eyes away from the hopeless expression frozen on Nicolette's face. The round little *o* that formed on her lips. Her eyes were large, unfocused, pointing to some undetermined spot in the distance.

My chest constricted. Her heart visibly shattered before my eyes and I would rip my own heart out to stop her suffering right now.

My body coiled. Every muscle tightened. An eternity passed before the video cut from the screen and the entire fairgrounds was dead silent.

Nicolette shoved Jeremy away from her. He stumbled back, confused.

"Riot, please tell me you'll make her leave. She can stay anywhere," Katie hissed.

Nicolette's bleary eyes blinked before floating in my direction. Katie grabbed my face and yanked my attention away.

"You can't afford to be associated with her, not anymore. Not after this."

Katie's eyes were fierce. The hair on my arms stood up. Her hands were hot on my cheeks and I still couldn't concentrate on what she was saying. "Riot!" she yelled.

A split second. That was all I gave to consider what she said. What it meant.

Katie represented the only thing I had hoped for over the past dozen years; a pathway back to being the man people revered. The man they loved and *wanted* around. A man people trusted. I considered what it would be like to walk away from that. Choose a different, direction-less path. No promises. No guarantees. The dangers were endless but so were the possibilities.

When I pulled my focus away from Katie, it was just in time to see Nicolette run down the steps and take off behind the stage. When she disappeared from my eyesight, I knew there were never two op-tions.

Not even fucking *close*.

There was only ever one ending for me since the day Nicolette stormed into my life. Regardless of what she chose, I would choose her. If she walked out of my life tomorrow, I'd spend the rest of my days chas-ing the colors she painted my heart. My heart. So wretched and wrecked, I wasn't sure why it still bothered to keep beating. I would chase the color of her beauty. Her danger. I would spend the rest of my life shielding that vibrancy from the deep unkindness that seemed to follow it.

I took a breath and pulled Katie's hands from my face. Her con-fused expression fell.

"Thank you for everything, Katie."

I didn't wait. I didn't look back. Not one more split second before turning to run after Nicolette.

My neck shivered with the fear that maybe I had hesitated too long. I sprinted in the direction she ran but didn't catch any glints of that obnoxiously perfect blonde ponytail. I kept moving through the vendor booths, still empty from gathering at the welcome presentation, until I heard the familiar clanks of metal and chimes.

I paused a few yards short of my vendor booth when I spotted Nico-lette violently trashing the scattered pieces. She swept the table with both arms, knocking everything to the ground, before stomping on the wooden crate that she had brought to help decorate the space. When

I noticed the way she had made the booth come to life with the extra touches, I was floored.

And now everything was in pieces on the ground. I didn't care about the art. It was made of metal, it would be fine. I could rebuild all of them in a day if I wanted. I understood her fury, I just hoped she didn't hurt herself.

I approached her with caution, like a wild animal. Visceral, throaty screams rumbled from her chest, as if caught inside her body, refusing to erupt from her mouth, unwilling to make it real. Once the table was clear and there was nothing left to throw, she came to stillness. Her shoulders rose and fell rapidly with exhausted, breathy pants.

Her eyes fell downward, landing on the *Godot Family Field Days* tank top that all the committee members wore. I stood, stunned, as she yanked the neck of the shirt, splitting it down the middle, tearing it from her body like the Hulk.

She balled it up and shoved the wad of cotton in her mouth and, finally, let out the most desperate, heartbreaking scream I had ever heard from a human.

Nicolette fell to her knees, exhausted. She inhaled a breath and let out another cry, this one laced with fury and grief.

I turned to see a small crowd gathering, peering around the entrance to the vendor row. Jeremy Blackwell scowled at me from the front of the group.

My focus returned to Nicolette. Her screams subsided to shallow wails, still muffled by the shirt she stuffed in her mouth. She was left wearing just a black bra and as the crowd grew, something fiercely protective in me came alive. I unbuttoned my plaid shirt and removed it, leaving only my white t-shirt underneath.

I took careful steps toward her, trying to use my body to block most of the view of her shirtless form. My heart hurt to think she might not want to see me but the need to get her far away from here eclipsed my fear of rejection.

She didn't look up when I draped my shirt around her shoulders. She didn't look up when I put an arm around her and used the other to help her to her feet. And she didn't look up when I guided her in the direction of my truck, away from the onlookers. She pulled the shirt from her mouth and used it to wipe the tears that had started streaming from her red, puffy eyes.

Nicolette's shoulders continued to hitch, remaining curled in on herself. I didn't take my arms away, fearing she'd collapse if I let go. I pulled her tighter to my body and her shoulders relaxed causing something in my heart to bloom. Her careful steps kept time with mine and although I wanted her to look at me, wanted to ask how she was doing, wanted her to know it would be alright, I had to let her be the first one to speak when she was ready.

I pulled the passenger door open, and she didn't hesitate before climbing in, eager to lift her feet from touching the earth that had just viciously torn her heart to shreds. When her sobs subsided, she took a deep breath, leaning back against the seat, devastated and defeated.

Godot had taught me the harsh reality of what it was like to be a pariah in this town. The façade of southern hospitality was laced with judgment and I knew how she was feeling right now, at least partially, because I felt it the day I returned and every day since. It was a horrible sensation to feel unwanted. Especially in a place that was supposed to be your home.

A few minutes after I began driving, she lifted her head, blinking as if she just realized we were moving. She wiped away a tear and turned to me. "Where are we going?" she asked.

"For a little ride." I finally let my focus drift to her and my heart broke all over again at her deep, wounded eyes, swollen and bloodshot, her flawless skin splotchy and red.

I had seen her defeated. I had never seen her wrecked.

"Are you dumping me on the outskirts of town with all the other trash?" She sounded so sad and bitter it made my chest hitch.

"Nope," was all I said. And kept driving.

The lake was serene as dusk settled over it. The water reflected the hot colors of the early sunset and for a moment it looked like one endless sky. I almost smiled, breathing in the air that came off the small lake. Nicolette pushed her door open.

"Hang on." I jogged over to the passenger side and pulled open the glove compartment where I kept a small first aid kit. I pulled it out and gestured for her hands. She looked confused, gazing down at her hands and wrists which were oozing blood from tiny cuts. Her palms extended toward me.

I opened an antibacterial wipe and patted her skin. She sucked in a painful breath, the chemicals stinging the wounds. I lowered my lips to hover over her bare arms and blew cool air on the stinging cuts. Goosebumps ran down her skin. I kept my hands on her forearms, trying to warm her from the outside in.

"I'm sorry about the pieces, Riot," she rasped, her gaze still fixed on the bandages I was applying to the larger lacerations. "I'll pay for them or help fix them or..." she drifted off. When I finished, I held her hands in mine, silently pleading for her attention.

"You needed to hit something. And it was the most familiar something nearby." I dared to lift her chin to look me in the eyes. "Don't worry about the artwork. Not even a little. Those are easy fixes."

I helped her down off the truck and she came to a stop, mesmerized by the sunset too. I halted at the way the golden light reflected off her skin. She pulled the elastic out of her hair, letting it cascade over her shoulders and back. I held my breath, afraid I might give away how unbelievably beautiful I found her at that moment. She wrapped my shirt tighter around her body and my stomach twisted. She looked good in it and I let myself imagine she was pretending it was me.

My phone rang in my back pocket. The last thing I needed was to be distracted by calls right now. I pulled it out and tossed it on the driver's seat at the same time I saw Nicolette throw her lit-up phone through the open passenger window. They both landed on the fabric seats at the same time with a soft thud. She looked up and our eyes caught for a moment of silent understanding.

Wordlessly, I grabbed a backpack out of the back seat and began hiking down an embankment. Nicolette followed close behind.

The path down to the lake was steep. When we reached the bottom, I turned to offer her a hand down the last boulder. She hesitated but took it and her soft hand was so warm in mine it almost made me feel drunk.

As both her feet hit the sandy leaves, I didn't bother letting go of her hand. Warmth spread through me when she didn't pull away.

There was a small row boat upside down on the bank. I flipped it over, landing it in the water and holding it from floating away with my foot. I looked back at her, once again extending a hand to help her in the boat.

This time she stood fixed where she was, continuing to dart her uneasy attention from me to the boat to the water, back to my hand, her eyes wary.

I dropped my hand to my side and softened my gaze.

Come on, Nicolette, trust me. Come with me. Her eyes tangled with mine, fixed in a warring standoff, not with me, but with herself. I raised my hand again, pushing it out, beckoning her closer.

With a tentative step, she reached out, and I wrapped her hand in mine.

24

NICOLETTE

My soul felt like it had been torn from my body. I pictured Katie going pale when the last video ran and I fucking *knew* she had something to do with it. I knew *he* was the one to blame. He'd been the one to record us having sex without my knowledge. But why was it always other women who had to weaponize it?

A hollowness consumed me. Humiliation consumed me. Not from the video. I can wholeheartedly admit I had sex with the guy. I wasn't ashamed of that. I was ashamed that I had, for just a moment, let myself feel the glow of appreciation. I had let my guard down and thought maybe I could find a comfortable existence here.

The video had been leaked months ago. I was foolish to think it hadn't made its way here. His mother had been the one to leak it. She was pissed I had dethroned her son after he'd been voted mayor and her last act of vengeance was to try to discredit me. To paint me as nothing more than a scorned ex-lover.

Well, she was wrong. I was pissed he created video evidence of it, yes, but we were grown-ass adults. Releasing the video had backfired. Easton was a big city in New England. It was progressive, and no one shamed women for enjoying sex.

They did, however, villainize her son even worse. The video was aggressive. He enjoyed inflicting pain, and to top it off, he had recorded it all without my consent. So, all in, Mommy Dearest's attempt to paint me as a promiscuous harlot only made her son look more like the vicious animal he was.

I left Easton because the video had backfired *too well.* I didn't get death threats or harsh messages of criticism. But I did get a lot of calls. From women's groups. From lawyers. From media. They all wanted me to go on record for an exclusive story. They all wanted me to raise my flag of attack and help pioneer the movement for harsher punishments when it came to revenge porn and recording without consent. *Your story could help thousands of women down the road!* they'd said.

I was a feminist, sure. I would always uphold that women should have the same respect as men. But I had no interest in being a martyr for the rest of my life. The idea of being the next poster girl for revenge porn nauseated me.

It was inevitable the leaked sex tape would make its way into *some* of the men's inboxes, but I had thought, or hoped, that it would be too scandalous to share amongst the wholesome townsfolk of Godot. Outside Jacob's frequent internet searches, no one had mentioned anything.

There was plenty of gossip about why I was back, why I was living at Riot's house. Even a little about my defunct television career. I had lulled myself into a false sense of security, thinking I could escape the latest black mark on my record.

But here I was, once again, stripped bare of all my confidence and pride, watching Riot hold a hand out to me like some tiny beacon of light in an unkind darkness. The rowboat he stood in looked a hundred years old. It creaked and appeared as if it would disintegrate when it hit the water.

But looking into his eyes, those blue stoic beams of reassurance, I was reminded that Riot was one of the most steadfast humans I'd ever met. If he was confident in the strength of the wooden boat, I could be too.

So, without another moment's hesitation, I slid my fingers into the palm of his warm, capable hand and stepped into the boat. He pushed us off with brute strength and I couldn't stop my eyes from roaming his upper arms, flexing underneath the flimsy cotton t-shirt that clung to his tanned skin.

A warmth spread through my lower abdomen and how the fuck could I be turned on at a time like this? I didn't have the energy to overthink it or fight it. I was just pleased to feel something other than the gut-wrenching disappointment with this entire day.

Riot dipped one arm into the water and fished around. He pulled up a thick, algae-ridden rope that was tied to a tree trunk on the shore and extended to a strip of land a few hundred feet away. The sunlight glinted off the water that sparkled on his skin. Without a word, he started pulling us across.

"When we were kids, we used to take boats over to this little island to party." His soothing voice cut through the silence of the early evening. "For some reason, we thought because it was only accessible by boat it would be harder to bust up the parties. Back then we didn't know water carries voices like a microphone." He shook his head foolishly. "We used to come over here to drink and there were a few clowns who thought it was funny to throw the oars in the water, stranding us." Riot gazed back at me, rolling his eyes at the memory. "It used to set Brennan off."

"Brennan came to the parties with you?" My voice was weak and my throat dry but I couldn't help my curiosity.

Riot paused, eyeing me over, he nodded. "Yeah, a few times. But he couldn't swim." He was silent for a beat. "Brennan hated the water and I'm pretty sure they hid the oars just to mess with him so we'd all have to swim across." Riot's expression darkened briefly. "So, Brennan and I came down here one morning and bolted this rope into the trees and hid a few blow-up floaties around the island so there was always a safe way to get back home."

Riot's lips pressed into a thin, elusive smile and the warmth it created inside my body caught me off guard.

He was trying to distract me from what happened at the carnival. Normally, I'd hate being tip-toed around, but Riot didn't make it feel that way. He wasn't treating me like I was glass. He caught me staring at his mouth. I dropped my eyes.

"It's kind how you take care of your brother," I said.

His gaze lingered on me. "He's my family. We're all we've got."

We settled back into a comfortable silence, watching the surrounding water, listening to the birds and gentle lapping of the water before the boat hit the other side with a jolt and slid up on land. He led me up a small hill where the land leveled out and the view made my breath come up short.

The far side overlooked the seemingly endless valley where the sun continued to plunge, being pulled down into the deep crevice of the land. The light sank, as if drowning, but continued to cast a warm glow on the never-ending valley. I found it amazing how something as big and powerful as the sun could look so helpless, sinking deeper into the nadir.

Riot stopped walking and slid the backpack off his shoulder. He pulled out a small blanket and let it float to the forest floor before plopping down on top of it.

Without a word, he stuck his hand back into the bag and pulled out a flask. His calloused hands twisted the top off. He took a small pull from it, wincing as he swallowed. His Adam's apple bobbed on his neck and I felt it between my ribs. Maybe it was the view. Or maybe it was just the day I had, but every motion he made was sensual. He held the flask up in offering without looking at me.

I sat down next to him. The blanket was small and our thighs brushed against each other. I brought my knees to my chest, taking a long draw of the liquid. I coughed as the whiskey burned going down. A chuckle escaped Riot's throat. I threw a scowl in his direction and his ensuing laughter was oddly comforting.

A long breath that I'd been holding for weeks escaped my throat. I let my shoulder press against his, handing the flask back. When he didn't move away, my whole body inhaled the small warmth of his upper arm. I flashed back to that one impassioned kiss, and I remembered how quickly I had lost control of my body when it was wrapped around his.

"Got any more stories about this place?" I asked, eager for a distraction from my wandering thoughts.

"Do I..." Riot grinned.

I had tears in my eyes. Happy fucking tears. Tears of laughter and I didn't care my mascara was running, listening to Riot's story about the rope swing that used to dangle between the island and the mainland.

"Brennan's ankle got wrapped in one of the little loops and he was too afraid to jump off." Riot's voice was high and tight, trying to hold his laughter back to get the words out. "But he couldn't hold on any longer so he just dangled there, upside-down, grazing the water, screaming his nuts off." Riot wheezed and wiped away the amused dampness from his eyes.

I sucked air in through my nose to catch my breath, my stomach muscles aching. Maybe it was the bourbon, but I couldn't remember the last time I laughed hard enough it hurt. I pushed the tears out of my eyes as we settled back into silence, the last of the golden light dipping below the horizon. I caught the final glint of warm light as it bounced off Riot's face. He settled back into his signature pensive expression. What was he thinking about?

What do you think *he's thinking about?*

I took one more steadying swig from the flask.

"I didn't know he recorded it." My voice was quiet, but it still cut through the silence of nighttime with sobering truth.

When Riot didn't reply, I stole a glance up. His forehead was tight, his scowl even deeper than usual. The muscle in his jaw flexed. He took the whiskey from me without looking and put it to his lips. I held my breath. Riot put the flask down on the blanket and gazed over at me, his expression remarkably warmer.

"Recorded what?" he asked. I blew a breath out on a smile. Another brimming quiet fell before he looked down at his feet, his voice lower and softer. "Really though... You don't have to explain or justify anything." He hesitated. "But I'll always listen if you want to talk about it."

Always, he'd said. Almost like I wasn't so temporary after all.

He twisted his head to offer me a soft expression.

Did I want to talk about it? Not really. I never felt compelled to justify it and even though the little glow of jealousy I thought I spied in Riot's eyes amused me, I didn't want to bring that ugliness into this space.

I was having too much of a good time with him here, so I stayed quiet. But I offered him an appreciative smile, letting my knees fall toward him gratefully.

"Can I ask one thing?" His voice was low, almost shy.

I nodded, my chest tightening with anticipation. That stern, locked-jaw expression was back. He looked as if he could light a fire with only his eyes.

"What happened to the guy? Did he at least get what he deserved for taping you?" I almost laughed. It was an interesting question to choose.

I tilted my head back and forth. "Yes and no. The investigation is ongoing, but he's in a coma last I heard."

Riot raised his eyebrows, amusement crossed his face. "So... really no point in draining the oil from his car." He squinted one eye at me with a charming smirk. Maybe he really could start a fire with only his eyes because my insides were, sure as hell, melting.

"No, he's very much handcuffed to a hospital bed as a murder investigation swirls around him." I bit my bottom lip, trying to contain the warmth Riot's defensiveness over me inspired.

He barked out a chuckle, shaking his head. "Where the heck did you come from, Nicolette Parker?"

"I live a complicated life," I teased, pressing my shoulder more firmly into his. I inhaled the extra sweetness the whiskey brought to his rustic scent.

His blue eyes pinned me, suddenly a deeper shade of longing. "Yeah..." he whispered. "I'm getting that."

We were impossibly close and his eyes dipped to my mouth. My heart raced. I parted my lips, inviting him to kiss me. I shivered with anticipation. He suddenly blinked and leaned back. My shoulders slumped.

"Are you cold?" His eyes ran down my body, making the shiver worse. Before I had the chance to answer, he leapt to his feet. "Come with me."

He pulled me up. He led me deeper into the woods. The moon was almost full and the stars were bright, guiding us through the darkness. A little house came into view.

"This is a warming hut the snowmobilers use in the winter. It usually stays open…" He drifted off, pulling the door open with a creak. He let out a victorious hiss. He lit two of the gas lanterns in the corner and it was just enough to see the small room.

It was about ten by ten and had one window that overlooked the valley side of the forest. "It's got a solar-powered heater but they disconnect it in the summer." I stood in the middle of the room and wrapped his shirt tighter around my body. He took a step closer and put his hands on my shoulders, rubbing my upper arms. "Sorry, it's still a little cool."

I wasn't cold. The whiskey and desire ran hot throughout my body, but I wasn't going to tell him that. I was thoroughly enjoying the feel of his hands on me.

"We can head back if you want—"

"No," I cut him off. "I don't want to go back yet, Riot."

My voice came out huskier, more pleading, than I expected. I took a step closer to him, letting the tips of my beaded nipples graze his chest. He sucked in a quiet breath and for a moment he was frozen in a look of consideration. His tongue darted out before he pulled his bottom lip in between his teeth.

Before I could blink, his mouth was on me. His lips parted mine, kissing me with uncontrollable force. His fingers slid up my neck before cradling the back of my head, fisting his hand through my hair.

Where our first kiss had been heated, angry, passion-fueled, and hungry, this one, while just as desperate, held a tenderness that the other one hadn't. Before, we had been trying to prove something, trying to take whatever we could get from the other person. Now it was about giving. Surrendering everything.

I pushed my hips into his, fusing our bodies. I felt him harden between us. A low hiss escaped his lips when I pressed more firmly. He walked us backward until my back met the wooden wall of the hut. Every inch of my skin relaxed at the security of being pinned between his body and the wall.

Our kiss deepened when I invited his tongue into my mouth, letting my own sweep his bottom lip. A low groan rattled in his chest and

I separated my feet a little wider, pushing my core into him, desperate for any kind of release in the pressure building between my thighs. He met me with the response I wanted as his hips pressed into me, his erection exactly where I needed it.

I sucked in an audible gasp, my head tipping back. Riot trailed his lips down my chin and my body shuddered when he found a spot on my neck that sent shockwaves through my skin. My hands explored his chest beneath the white cotton. His erection twitched against my core. Every muscle in our bodies strung tight. He trailed his warm mouth across my collarbone, and I reveled in the humid way his breath lingered on my skin.

Every dip and curve of his body was firm and warm and somehow soft under my fingertips. I explored every inch of him, heated with the excitement of touching the body I'd spent so many days admiring.

His lips snaked down the center of my chest and my back arched into him. He sank to his knees in front of me. I ran my hands through his thick, dark hair and a sigh escaped his lips. He paused, leaning his head into my fingers, raking through his scalp. His lips parted, head tilted backward. All at once, I recognized the boy I had gone to high school with, vulnerability painting his perfect features.

I wanted to shield him, protect that vulnerability, and keep it for myself. Reclaiming his mouth, I ignored the tug at the back of my brain that told me I was being selfish. The logical part of me was nagging, but I ignored her because he tasted too right to be responsible.

His droopy eyes opened, drunk on the feel of my fingers drawing circles in his hair. I pulled back, running my palms down the side of his face and over the glorious stubble that covered the bottom half of his face.

"I really like this," I found myself whispering aloud.

His eyes lit up, and he regarded me for a beat before wrapping his arms around the tops of my thighs and spinning me toward the ground. His hand caught the back of my head before I hit the floor and he lowered me beneath him.

"I was hoping you would," he said and my heart soared.

Riot's mouth hungrily covered mine again. One hand trailed down my stomach and began to unbutton my jeans.

"Tell me to stop, Nicolette," he whispered and I couldn't shake my head more furiously.

"I don't want you to stop, Riot," I replied breathlessly, lifting my hips in response, urging him closer. His palm absorbed the heat at the center of my body.

His finger separated me and my need for him overtook all my senses. Cautious desire surged through me. I pulled him tighter between my knees. He worked me from the inside out, his thumb drawing small circles around the little bundle of nerves. I felt my body stretch around his dexterous fingers. My limbs began to shake.

He reared back slightly to watch me, his eyes fixed to my face and I could tell he wanted to watch me fall apart. The look of pure adoration and appreciation tied our eyes together with intimacy so fierce it took my breath away. A reverent smile danced across Riot's lips as his eyes swept over my coiled body. His satisfaction plunged me over the edge. My body tightened and convulsed around his fingers, gratification still coursing through me when his head dipped down to inhale my moan of release.

It should have been enough to satiate me. But it only made me want more. It made me want to mount him and watch him come apart beneath me.

I hissed through my teeth, bringing my hands to the swollen erection that threatened to burst through the zipper of his jeans. I ran a firm hand down him. The arm that held his weight began to shake. I eagerly moved my fingers to the clasp on his jeans.

He pulled away and sat back on his heels. It was like he took my breath with him. I propped myself up on my elbows, gazing at him in protest.

"I'm not going to have sex with you, Nicolette."

My chest lurched and my face burned, my insecurities racing through my brain. He didn't want me. Not anymore.

Not after seeing that horrendous video.

He was just here to be nice. To make me feel better. I looked away, a pang of humiliation coursing through me. My hand searched for the shirt he'd given me. I blinked away the sting of rejection, but he put a rough hand on my stomach to still me.

"At least not *here.* Not right now."

My body inflated slightly. "Why not?" I asked, and I hated the pathetic, neediness in my voice.

A small smile touched his lips. "Because..." He hovered his body over me, his hands on either side of my head, caging me in. He leaned his face inches from mine, hesitating before brushing his lips down my chin, finding that spot on my neck that made me close my eyes again. "You've been through a lot today." My ears perked up, and I didn't understand what that had to do with it. But my thoughts shut the hell up again when his lips wrapped around a nipple, his tongue setting a punishing rhythm as it worked over the sensitive tip. I let out an audible sigh, enjoying the weight of him above me. He moved to my other side and my back arched of its own accord.

He pulled back and looked me in the eye, our noses barely an inch from each other. His hand roamed over the center of my stomach. "And it's all still on your mind."

I had to work to thread his words back together to follow his train of thought. *I'm not going to have sex with you. At least not here. Not now. You've been through a lot today. And it's all still on your mind.* I tried to concentrate on his words but I was numb to everything except where his skin pressed against mine.

Riot stilled his roaming hands and brought his attention back to my eyes. He whispered the rest of his thought, "And when I get to feel what it's like to be inside you... I want to be the only thing you're thinking about."

My stomach lurched with heat and I would do whatever he fucking wanted me to.

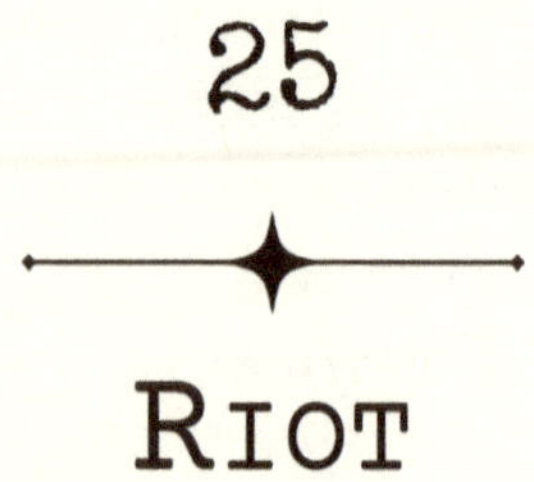

25

RIOT

It took everything in me to stop from diving inside of her. *Fuck,* I wanted her. But it didn't feel right after what had happened at the carnival. She was hurting and vulnerable and desperate for safety and comfort. And as much as I wanted to give her that, I couldn't stand the idea of having sex with her as a reaction to something someone *else* did to her. When I finally got to feel what the inside of her body was like, I wanted it to be about us and only us.

Still, it was a tough drive home. She kept casting side glances at me, a secret, knowing smile on her red, swollen lips. My fingers were raw from adjusting the zipper of my jeans all the way home. When I glanced over at her, she was squinting into her phone.

"Everything okay?" It was a stupid question. Nothing was okay but still, she looked perplexed.

"I finally got a note back from that doctor who consults for the DEA." She scratched her chin. "Kind of bizarre that something as deadly as a heroin-meth hybrid hasn't made the national news."

She shot me an inquisitive gaze and the look on her face was fierce. I found her even more amazing. After everything she'd been through today, she was still curious.

"He said they had a task force that was investigating it a few years ago but it was too difficult to track because it looks and is traded just like meth. Except whatever they do to it in the production process renders it almost invisible on the standard urine drug tests. It can only be detected through blood samples so it became too expensive and the DEA cut their funding so the investigation went cold."

I gave a humorless snort. "That's convenient." Nicolette regarded me, a question dancing on her eyebrows. "When I was getting released, there was talk about going to a halfway house but since my crime…" I cleared my throat. We had never addressed my conviction. Not directly and she'd never asked. "Since it wasn't drug related they determined probation was good enough. But I had heard what it's like at those halfway houses. Curfew is eight p.m. and they get drug tested every night with a urine sample. A drug that eludes urine tests would be pretty convenient."

Her eyes bore into me, unasked questions lingering on her puffy red lips. Something guarded flashed across her expression before softening again.

"I have to figure out how it all connects." She shook her head.

"You're still going to do a story?" I asked. "After what those people did to you?"

Disapproval flickered across her face. "It wasn't *those* people that did it, Riot." My eyes darted between her and the nighttime road ahead of us. "You know it was Katie, right? She must have loaded the file last minute."

That thought hadn't crossed my mind but the knot in my stomach was back. Did Katie have something like that in her? A sense of dread crept through me, knowing I'd have to confront her about it. I had several missed calls and messages from her but tonight was not the night to return them.

"Funny how it's always the *women…*" she muttered before finding my quizzical look. "The guy from the tape? I'm fairly certain it was his mother that released it. She and Katie should meet. Together they could slut-shame women back a couple of decades."

"I don't know if it was Katie," I said, and she bristled. "But whether it was or wasn't, I'm sorry it happened to you." I took a deep breath and kept my focus fixed on the road ahead. "And for whatever it's worth… I won't watch it. Not ever."

Her eyes glistened and the gratitude I saw in the smile on Nicolette's lips hit me in the heart. That primal territoriality made me want to wrap her in my arms and shield her from the world.

"That's worth a lot," she said.

How bizarre the world was. A few weeks ago I wanted her gone. I was desperate to ensure she didn't get too close. Didn't ask too many questions. The idea of her anywhere near my life terrified me. I was still terrified of her. But in such a heart-shaking different way. Now I didn't know what I'd do without her and that thought hit me like a wrecking ball. Godot was no longer her home. She had always, and still likely did, plan to leave.

The idea of her being gone was too painful to think about so I pushed it far away and let myself bask in the warmth of her presence for as long as I could.

When we got home, we did an awkward little shuffle in the kitchen where we'd normally split into our respective bedrooms. I didn't want to leave her alone but if we shared a bed tonight, I'd never be able to keep my hands off her and I needed to keep my word. She sucked in her bottom lip, peering up at me through her long, dark eyelashes and it went straight to my groin.

"What are your plans tomorrow?" I asked her, meandering to her sliding door.

She almost laughed. "Oh, you know, church in the morning, sex tapes in the afternoon." She cocked her head, and I chuckled. I saw her eyes dip to my lips. She lifted her hand and caressed my cheek. "I really do like this," she said, running a hand over my stubble.

"The scar doesn't make me look like a psychopath?" I asked.

Her smile turned my insides to mush when she shook her head. "No." She leaned in, running her nose along my jawline, planting a soft kiss on the scar. I held my breath. "It makes you look human," she whispered. My arms wrapped around her and I inhaled that scent I had come to memorize as so devastatingly *her*.

"Go to dinner with me tomorrow," I said after I'd loosened my grip, resting my palms on her waist.

She grinned and let her eyes roll. "You're asking me out on a date?" She raised an eyebrow and heat rose to my cheeks. I lolled my head back but met her eyes.

"Yes, Nicolette Parker. I want to take you out on a date. I want to pick you up and bring you flowers. I want to open your car door and pull out your chair at some fancy restaurant. I want to bring you home and I want to get nervous about kissing you goodnight."

She was trying to play it cool. Like she cared about none of those things, but her blush gave her away.

"Yes, Riot Asher, I'd love to go on a date with you." She bit the edge of her lip, wrapping her arms around my neck, kissing me on the cheek. She didn't pull away immediately. Instead, she pressed her body against mine and I could feel my clothes constricting. Her lips sent shivers down my spine, grazing my ear. "But if you *don't* kiss me tomorrow night, I'll be very disappointed. Because until then? You will be the *only* thing I'm thinking about."

Nicolette pulled away and smiled lasciviously before stepping into the screen room, sliding the door shut before pulling the curtain closed.

I almost doubled over with the ache between my hips. I crawled into bed and spent the next ten minutes picturing just how I wanted to finish tomorrow night with Nicolette Parker.

26

✦

NICOLETTE

Okay, so I wasn't leaving town *just* yet. I told myself it was because of the new information Dr. Moore's friend had given me but I knew that was a lie.

It was for *him.* Part of me was ashamed that I was deviating from my decision to leave Godot for a man. But the bigger part of me didn't care. Last night, Riot brought something to life inside me that I'd never felt before. The feelings I had for my producer back then were strong, but they felt dark. Dirty. Dangerous. The feelings Riot inspired felt like airy sunshine and safety. He made me feel desirable, cared for. Important. Plus, I couldn't remember the last time I'd been out on a date, and the teenager inside me was giddy.

That morning, I'd gotten the call that my car was finally ready to be picked up. Just as I pulled the front door open to head into town, I nearly jumped out of my skin when Chelsea appeared on the other side of it.

"Jesus, you scared the shit out of me." I pressed against my heart, slamming in my chest.

"Sorry," she said, eyeing me over curiously. "I would have texted, but I wanted to check on you and didn't want you to tell me not to come."

The sincerity in her eyes brought back yesterday's earlier events. I hadn't forgotten about what happened at the carnival. But what progressed with Riot made it feel a lot less important. Still, I was touched Chelsea was here, on my doorstep, making sure I was alright. She was such a good friend, I tried to not to let my mind wander to how much I *wasn't.*

I smiled at her and the "Thanks, I'm doing okay," was perched on my lips. But as I studied Chelsea's features, my words fell silent. There was something loaded behind her expression. A deeper sadness that went beyond sympathy for her friend.

"What happened yesterday at the carnival..." She took a shaky breath. "It was super shitty. Jeremy Blackwell said he's launching a full investigation." She rushed the words out. I really didn't relish the thought of Jeremy spending time investigating my sex tape.

"Chelsea, I appreciate that, but really, I'm surprisingly okay—"

"Nicolette." She said my name with such emotion I pulled up short. Her eyes were shrink-wrapped in unshed tears. She looked away and swallowed. When she turned back to look at me, the heartbreak I saw there made my throat tighten. "What happened to you yesterday... what someone *chose* to do to you... it wasn't right. And it isn't your fault."

Her words were sentiments I'd already accepted, but it was validating to hear it out loud. Still, the emotion came off her in disproportionate waves. My breath hitched, realizing it wasn't sympathy at all.

It was *empathy*.

I wrapped my arms around her shoulders. She sniffled once. We stood there for a silent minute. When I pulled back, a single tear streamed down her face. I pushed a lock of hair behind her ear.

"I have to grab my car at Riot's shop. Could you give me a ride? Then maybe we can grab coffee? If you have time?"

Chelsea gave me a watery smile. "I'd really like that."

Chelsea stayed close to me when I breezed into the auto shop. When the door chimed, Riot looked up from the desk. His eyes lit up briefly and my butterflies went wild.

"Hey." He stood, pushed his hands in his pockets and approached me with a knowing smirk. Maybe it was simply the lack of beard, but Riot looked lighter today. His blue eyes sparkled brighter and there was a levity to him I hadn't seen before.

"Hey," I repeated. We faced one another, a wave of comfort passing between us. Chelsea coughed and shuffled behind me. "Riot, do you remember my friend Chelsea?" I opened my body up to let her into the conversation. He gave a gentlemanly nod with a sheepish smile.

"Thanks for helping out yesterday, at the vendor booth," he said appreciatively.

"No problem," she said but her words were clipped, nervous.

She was afraid of him. He shrank away to grab my keys off the wall and my heart ached. He rifled through paperwork and I pulled my credit card out. Handing my keys over, he waved the card away dismissively.

"It's taken care of," he said with a confidence that made my neck flush with heat.

"You didn't have to do that," I said flatly but my appreciative smile gave away all the ways I planned to thank him later. He shrugged and winked and I had to take a deep breath to keep myself from throwing my body at him. "Well, thank you."

The shop was simmering with a quiet tension when a phony sex moan suddenly cut through our silence. Stifled boyish laughter followed and Riot's body went rigid. A small gasp escaped from Chelsea behind me.

"Tell me you want it..." someone mocked from yesterday's video.

My face burned but my attention was on Riot. The vein in his throat grew thick with fury as his fists clenched. He couldn't afford to get in trouble. Especially not over me.

He moved to whirl around, oozing danger but I grabbed his upper bicep to stop him. His lips parted to protest, but I slid my other hand slowly up his chest. I sliced my narrowed eyes to the work bays where the boys were standing, slightly slack-jawed. My wandering hand wrapped around the back of Riot's neck.

I glared daggers at each one of them before pulling Riot's face down to mine and kissing him so hard I think my bones turned to jelly. It was meant to show off. To show them I didn't give a fuck about whether they mocked me. To give them something better to blabber about. But as I melted into his body, I began to forget myself.

Riot was stiff at first, caught off guard by my public display of affection. But when his lips parted, and I swept my tongue lightly over his top lip, all the coiled tension in his body relaxed. His strong, calloused hand gripped my waist, almost for stability.

An impressed catcall pierced the air from somewhere behind us. When I felt his smile against my lips, I took a thick swallow and reluctantly pulled away. His sheepish eyes were hooded but shining with something I couldn't quite place.

"I'll see you at home?" I rasped. He bit the corner of a swollen lip and nodded once.

I threw one more deadly glare in the direction of the workers standing speechless, awkward in the work bays before turning toward the door. I didn't spare Chelsea a glance quite yet, a little nervous about how she'd respond to my affection toward Riot.

But she wholly surprised me when she turned to face the shop and yelled, "Hope you got a good look yesterday, boys. 'Cause those were the perkiest tits you'll ever see again for the rest of your life!" When I pushed the door open, I caught her throwing a middle finger at the men.

As I spilled into the daytime, my heart bloomed, realizing I had more people in my corner than I'd had in a long time.

The Coal Country Caffeine Stop was the best coffee shop in town. And not just because it was the *only* coffee shop in town. It was genuinely a great cup, which I was thankful for after spending a month drinking the *swill* Riot called coffee. Plus, they had makings for Irish coffee if you knew who to ask.

Chelsea twisted her fingers at our little table when I approached with two more steaming cups of Irish coffee.

"You gonna tell me what's on your mind? Or just sit there pulling your fingernails off?" I raised an eyebrow in her direction.

"That video. At the carnival…" she drifted off, darting her eyes all over my face like I was a puzzle she couldn't put together. "How are you okay?" Her question caught me off guard.

"What do you mean?"

She shook her head as if trying to rattle the sense loose. "I…" she cut herself off by taking a big swig of the hot liquid.

She gazed up at me, resolute.

"It was the night of senior prom. I was dating that guy from Charleston?" I didn't remember, but I nodded like I did. "We hadn't been dating long, but I really liked him and… well, he said he always wanted to remember our first time together." Her jaw worked up and down, afraid to continue and I felt my heart sinking. "I… I let him film us."

My mouth twisted into a frown. Chelsea's cheeks grew impossibly red. I reached over and put a palm over one of her hands.

"It was a great night. I mean senior prom, you know?" I didn't; I hadn't gone after all. I was already knee-deep in pencil skirts and blazers at that time. "Anyway… we broke up during the summer, after he slept with Lanie Mitchell. When I went to college, I forgot all about him." She took a breath. "Until someone sent me a link on skinflix.me." Her eyes flashed knowingly in my direction. "I don't know if he sold it to them or if he sent it to someone who put it up there…" Her curly brown hair shook across her face. "But I was devastated. It was awful; it was shared all around campus, and I had guys coming up to me asking when my next video would get released." She offered a humorless laugh.

"Jesus, Chels. I'm so sorry, I had no idea."

She shrugged. "My parents didn't have the money for a lawyer but this woman, Sadie, reached out to me and said she'd file a court order to get it removed, pro bono, if I wanted. It still took a while, but she got through to the hosting service and turns out they don't *like* when their content is revenge porn so they erased it pretty quickly." She chewed on her lip, eyes glistening as she stared into her coffee. "She offered to 'sue the shit-stained pants off the guy' but I told her I wanted to forget all about him."

I gave her hand a quick pulse. "I'm glad someone was there for you. And I'm really sorry I wasn't."

"You know, she reminded me a lot of you. So, in a way, you were." Chelsea offered a wry smile. "I ended up taking the rest of the semester off, which turned into the year. I opted for online classes after I met Bill." She lifted a shoulder before letting it slump down. "When I came over this morning, I guess I expected to find you as wrecked as I was back then. I should have remembered you were always so much tougher than me."

"Hey." I placed my other hand on top of hers and demanded her attention. "I was never tougher. I think I'm just more of an asshole." She laughed, and I was relieved to see her smile. "And for the record... I was wrecked. Wholly. You should have seen the fit I threw. I broke all of Riot's metalwork."

"I heard," she said through a watery smile. "I left to go check on the girls who were with Bill's parents while everyone was at the stage." Chelsea's eyes darted down and back up at me as if nervous to ask her next question. "So... you and Riot?"

The sound of his name brought a shy smile to my lips. "Yeah... I don't know. It's kind of fresh, I guess. He's taking me on a date tonight." Her eyes went a little wide before she recovered with an exaggerated nod. I wished I could help her see what I saw in him. "What are you and Bill doing tonight? Think his parents could take another shift and you two can double with us?"

For a moment her eyes were steeped in longing but her sad smile followed with a shake of her head. "That's okay. They're out of town. As much as I'd love to... Bill and I haven't been on a date in *years*. We've been saving up to fix our shower. The girls' bathroom is getting *real* crowded."

"The five of you are sharing a bathroom?" I immediately regretted the incredulity in my voice but Chelsea just laughed.

"We did always love 'The Simple Life', didn't we?" I thought back to the hours of the reality show we used to watch in my bedroom because Chelsea's parents never let her watch it.

The morning ebbed to the afternoon while Chelsea and I exchanged more stories from the past. Guilt crept up my throat for how I'd missed the worst period in my best friend's life. I pictured the excitement she must've had for prom night and even though her date had been a colossal asshole, a stab of ostracization pierced my insides.

Senior Prom. Homecoming. Winter Formal. It was a world I'd never been part of. Would that night have gone differently if I'd been there? I pictured myself in a sparkly pink dress. No, I wasn't made for something like prom.

After we parted ways, another pang of guilt lodged in my chest. I thought about the offers I'd been extended when my sex tape had been uncovered. Would it have made a difference? Would speaking out have done anything to prevent things like revenge porn and leaked sex tapes from happening to other men and women?

I sat on the edge of my bed, gazing out into the sunny afternoon, wondering how I could be so hypocritical. Here I was, priding myself on making a name uncovering injustices, holding people accountable, giving a voice to the unheard, and telling their stories. But I wasn't willing to give myself a voice about the things that happened to me.

A light knock on the sliding glass door pulled me from the vortex of my brain. Rising to my feet, I felt that vortex disappear like a dying windstorm because Riot stood on the other side of the door, a small bouquet of wildflowers in his hand. I'd return to the thought at some point. But for tonight, all I saw was Riot's boyish grin and endearingly outdated suit jacket.

Embers & Ivy was nestled in the recently developed downtown area of Lycon. It was a large standalone building that was a stone's throw from the lake and I had to admit that it was hard to believe we were only twenty-five minutes from Godot.

Inside, dim lighting illuminated the oak and cherry walls, casting an intimate ambiance throughout the space. The walls were decorated with fake gas lantern sconces. It smelled wonderful.

"Riot Asher, I should smack you for not coming in sooner. Come here, honey."

A woman in her late fifties came sweeping up to us, beaming from ear to ear. It startled me because, outside she-who-I-refused-to-think-about, not a single person ever greeted Riot with such warmth.

"Hi, Aunt Jen." He smiled and gave her a heartfelt hug. Her arms wrapped tighter around him, loaded with some ineffable grief.

Aunt? I wracked my brain to try to remember whether he'd ever mentioned her to me.

"This is Nicolette Parker." He gestured to me and she shook my hand zealously. "Nicolette, this is my dad's sister, Aunt Jen."

"Pleasure to meet you," I said.

Aunt Jen showed us to a table for two in the corner. "When Riot told me he was bringing a date, I had the best table in the house reserved." She smiled. The walls were deep mahogany and everything looked like it was made from solid oak. The chairs were thick and sturdy as Riot pulled mine out for me.

He was milking this whole "official date" thing. I promised to be a good sport when he insisted on opening my car door for me. I wasn't much for the overdone displays of chivalry, but it made him smile and I was a goddamn sucker for that smile.

Half an hour later we were almost through with the first bottle of wine and I had told him all about my crazy eco-parents and their hippie parents before them. Riot had never met his father's parents, which I found sad.

There was a special kind of love grandparents gave their grandchildren, an unadulterated, unburdened kind of love. His mother's father had been around when he was little but died in a mining accident. He said Grace used to go visit the mine every year on the anniversary of his death to lay flowers. A sadness washed over him, describing it.

"Tell me about Aunt Jen," I said. "You've never mentioned her before."

"She's my dad's younger sister. She used to live in Charleston but moved this way when my dad passed. She was planning to stay with us, help my mom with me and Brennan but..." he looked around. "They couldn't get along." Riot shrugged and spun the fork in front of him.

"I would think your mom would be glad for the help. Two boys couldn't have been easy."

He lifted his eyebrows. "We most certainly weren't. Especially Brennan. He and my dad were close. Dad was one of the few people who didn't treat him like something was wrong with him."

Realization passed over his face when he met my gaze.

"Kind of like you..." he said with a soft expression before shaking it off. "When he'd do things like repeat himself, my dad would just give him a pat on the shoulder and say 'I might be your old man, but I'm not so old you have to repeat yourself. I heard you the first time.'" Riot smiled, lost in the memory. "He was good with him. And when he was gone..."

I watched Riot's eyes search for some intangible reasoning somewhere on the ceiling. "Brennan was just more difficult. Aunt Jen tried to get him help. There was a therapist she wanted him to see. But my mom refused to let her take him to counseling. She said the church offered plenty for free and she couldn't afford to be driving him to and from Charleston twice a week."

Riot pressed his lips into an unfortunate line.

"That must have been hard to watch," I said.

His head bobbed a few times before meeting my eyes. "When I was younger, I didn't understand, so I just enjoyed being the *good child*, you know?" Remorse painted his features. "Then when football started to gain some momentum, I spent every waking minute I could on the field, in the gym. Anything to be out of the house." My heart ached for the little boy escaping his own family. "You know I was offered a football scholarship to Stanford too?"

My eyes widened in surprise. "I did not know that. Why on earth didn't you take it?" I tried to mask the disbelief but I still cringed when I heard it. If Riot was offended, he didn't show it because he just laughed.

"You know, I think I loved the idea of being the hometown hero." He shrugged and pushed a few pieces of lettuce around on his salad plate. "The idea of moving to a place where I'm just another face in the crowd scared me. I wanted to be the guy they all looked up to. I wanted to stand out." He offered a humorless laugh. My heart tightened, reading the thoughts all over his face.

He'd love to be just another face in the crowd now.

"I think about it often. If I'd taken it. Moved to California... How everything might have worked out differently."

A small shudder ran through him and I found myself holding my breath. He had opened the door to his mother's death, and I had so many burning questions for him. When he was just a name on a news article, I was cynical enough to believe anyone was capable of anything. I still believed that but now, after meeting him, after a tiny peek into his heart, I had so many doubts. I had studied his hands and fingers and I had tried to picture them wrapped around a bloody knife.

My mouth opened, the words perched on my lips.

"Riot, what happened with your m—"

"Dinner is served!" Our waitress appeared, balancing a large tray with our plates on it.

Our plates radiated the smell of warm food and my stomach rumbled. Besides the breakfasts at the diner, I couldn't remember the last real meal I sat down and ate that didn't come in a cardboard box.

I was about to dig in when I saw Riot dip his head and mutter something under his breath.

"Are you praying?" I asked, immediately regretting how critical I sounded. Riot looked up, surprised as if I'd caught him doing something wrong.

"Sorry. Just a habit, I guess." He took a sip of water and averted his eyes.

"No, I just mean, I'm surprised…" I backpedaled. "I guess after everything you've been through with the church, your mom… I'm just surprised, is all." I shrugged and offered an apologetic smile but was captured by the curious look he had on his face.

"I can't be mad at God for the things people voluntarily do in his name." He offered a distant smile.

"So, you're still into it? Like the whole white-bearded-man-in-the-sky thing?" I hated how dumb I sounded but he had piqued my curiosity.

Riot grinned, cutting a piece of steak. "I don't know about the man-in-the-sky thing but I believe there's a higher power or purpose for sure. There's too much evidence not to."

"Evidence?" Now my skeptical journalistic instincts were intrigued.

He tilted his head back and forth, considering before swallowing the bite of ribeye. "Think about it. We're careening around the sun at sixty-seven thousand miles per hour and still, we stay on this planet, planted firmly, and aren't launched into the depths of space. It's practically magic."

"I'm pretty sure that magic is called gravity," I teased.

He narrowed his eye victoriously through a bite of risotto. "Exactly!" He pointed his fork at me. "And gravity just… works. It *works*. Perfectly. Every day. Without fail. Because that's the way we have to have it to stay in orbit. It's just really wild how precise everything needs to be for the world to keep turning and *living* the way it does and yet," he gestured around us, "here we are. That, to me, is goddamn magic and I guess I'm hard-pressed to believe there isn't some kind of power that is responsible for creating all those perfect conditions." Riot lifted his shoulder one more time before returning to his plate.

I sat dumbfounded at the man in front of me.

"So, God is a master magician?"

He looked up, considering. "Yeah. At least that's how my dad used to describe it." Riot took a sip of water and a small humor returned to his eyes. "Or he could have just been trying to make light of my mom's obsession with us going to church on football Sundays." He gave me a wink and my heart did a little flutter.

As Riot returned to his dinner, I took a breath and opened my mouth. "Riot, about your mom—"

"How is everything?" Jen came ambling over, a fresh bottle of wine in her hands. "Wanted to treat my favorite nephew to a little Camus. On the house, dear." She plunked the fine wine on our table. Riot beamed.

"Why don't you join us for a glass?" I surprised myself by asking.

Jen looked between me and Riot who nodded before she pulled a chair up to our table.

Jen wheezed through her fits of laughter. "And then Brennan turns to the blonde and says, 'Even if I were interested, your peak child-bearing years have largely dwindled. If you had a younger sister perhaps...' And then that girl dumped an entire martini on his head!"

Riot pushed his fingers into his eyes, watery with laughter. "Man, am I sorry I missed that!"

"Oh, me too, honey. But that's what I get for being a Nosy Nelly and trying to hook him up with the staff." She patted his hand.

The restaurant had mostly emptied by the time we were finished with our dinners. But Aunt Jen had the wine flowing, and she was tapping into the high-end section of the cellar so I was here for it.

"That boy, I'll tell y'all... He'll either save this world or destroy it. But either way, he'll be single while he does it," she smiled, her laughter subsiding.

Her focus landed on me. "Have you met Brennan, dear?" Her southern accent got deeper with each glass of wine. Or my hearing got fuzzier, I wasn't sure. All I knew was that this calming sense of normalcy was foreign but welcomed.

"Oh, Nicolette and Brennan are quite fond of each other," Riot said with amusement in his eyes.

Jen made a high-pitched *mmm* noise.

"I have met Brennan. And I'm pretty sure he only tolerates me because I talk to him like a real human and not a slow adult."

Jen cackled. "Now that's a girl I can get on with. Riot, hang on to this one." She stood up and my gaze met his, our eyes tangling and my breath quickened. "Alright, I gotta close up. Don't be a stranger, boy. Nicolette, it was a pleasure to meet you. So long as I have a restaurant to run, I hope to see you around here again real soon." She gave Riot a wink before patting his head and disappearing into the kitchen.

"What'd she mean by that?" I asked.

Riot smiled distantly. "Some company has been trying to buy this place from her for years. With all the developments that have happened around Lycon, her taxes are doubling every year. She's trying to hold out until the real estate is worth what she needs to retire." He shrugged. I considered that. It *was* a large space and I could see it being valuable to the developers. It was a cozy restaurant but it didn't have the mark of newness the rest of the downtown area did.

My focus turned back to Riot and my chest hitched at the reverent expression on his face.

"What?" I touched my hair to see if it was out of place before running a hand over my mouth to make sure there was nothing on my face.

"You're incredible, you know that?"

A blush prickled up my neck and I rolled my eyes trying to dissuade the embarrassment from spreading.

"Of course, I know that," I said but softened further at his amusement. "But it's still nice to hear," I added. "So... Wanna come to my place for a nightcap?"

Riot grinned, and I became a puddle of mush.

27

RIOT

I jumped in my car with nervous, giddy energy and it was hard to mask my anxiety the closer to home we drove. I was nervous as all get out and I tried making small talk but it was hard to focus. It had been almost twelve years since I'd been with a woman and Nicolette wasn't just any woman.

She was beautiful. And talented. And sexy as hell and I was terrified I would disappoint her.

Naturally, I didn't want to make any assumptions but the way she threw scalding gazes down my body at dinner had me all but convinced I was the only thing on her mind. And now in the confines of my truck, I felt her eyes running up and down my thighs. As we pulled down the road that led to my property, we settled into a fiery silence, the air thick with tenuous anticipation.

When I finally threw the truck in park, she sat still, amused, while I jogged around to open her door. She slid down, and we were impossibly close. Her tongue darted between her lips, pulling her bottom lip in between her teeth.

"I have to send a quick video to my mom," she murmured. Her eyes lingered on my mouth. "Come by in ten?"

I swallowed and nodded but neither of us moved. I inched my face toward hers, holding my breath. If I inhaled her scent, it'd be all over and I'd never let her walk in that house. The image of us writhing naked in the backyard made my clothes feel tighter.

Her soft lips pressed against mine and every bit of tension, fear, or anxiety melted from my body.

I had always gotten nervous before football games too. The antic-ipation was the worst. Once the whistle blew, I was in it and I could rely on my practice and body to carry us to victory. It felt similar to Nicolette. Kissing her was like a magnetic pull. Like it was something I was supposed to be doing all my life.

Her lips parted, and I traced her mouth with my tongue. A soft ex-hale escaped her lips and if I didn't pull back, I never would.

Nicolette's eyes were heavy and those red lips remained parted.

"I'll be over in a few," I whispered, walking her to the outside door that led to her screen room.

I walked around the house and entered through the main door under the carport, smiling stupidly to myself the whole time.

"Hi Mom, I'm here, alive and in the flesh..." I heard her singsong voice muted through the closed door. The illumination from her com-puter cast a soft glow behind the curtains.

I walked to the bar and grabbed two wine glasses off the rack. They were old with weird etched designs on them and were way too dusty. I hurried to the sink to wash them before pulling out a bottle of champagne that I'd gotten earlier that day.

I ran into my bathroom to brush my teeth. I could still taste her on my lips and I began to harden.

"Fuck," I cursed down at my belt buckle. I remembered one of the guys in prison saying he jerked off before every date so he wouldn't finish too fast and I wondered if I had time to try to do the same.

I was just about to unbuckle my belt when sharp shouts cut through the night.

"No good, it's no good! I don't like it! Don't like it!"

My heart picked up an unnatural rhythm. I bolted from my room. It sounded like Brennan's angry growls were coming from the screen room. I didn't want to invade her privacy but when I heard Nico-lette shushing him, I let all reservations go and pulled the sliding door open.

They were facing each other just outside the entrance. He was tow-ering over her with a harsh scowl and her back was shrunken against the door. I made it across the lanai just as Brennan began to slap himself in the head.

Shoving myself between the two of them, I put my hands on Brennan's shoulders and eased him backward, further from her.

"Hey, it's okay, Brennan, just breathe and calm down." But he was fuming and what on earth had set him off? I eyed Nicolette to make sure she was okay. She had a curious look in her eyes, watching the two of us. "Hey, Brennan, remember that camping trip with Dad? We have to go fishing this year. It's almost season, right?"

Brennan started seething through his teeth but I could see that he was deescalating.

"I made a promise to you. That we'd go back? Just like you made a promise to walk away when you're upset, okay? Remember that? That was an important promise."

His eyes glared from me to Nicolette. What the hell had happened between them? He threw one last scathing look at her before stalking back to his house across the yard. I blew out a heavy breath of relief.

"You alright?" I asked, pulling my eyes over her body. Her face was etched with worry but beneath the surface, I could tell she was warring with something. She turned around and went inside without a word. The fear of loss gripped my heart.

She sat on the edge of the bed, appearing deep in thought and my heart picked up. *Had Brennan scared her away?*

"I'm sorry," I looked down at my hands. "He just has these episodes. Do you know what set him off?" I stole a glance over to her but she continued to stare aimlessly, her mouth twisted in regret.

I pushed a lock of hair behind her ear and her eyes floated down to her hands. She was wringing them so tightly. Trying to control my heart, I kept a hand on her cheek and her skin was so soft I wanted to sleep against it.

"Hey," I whispered, "what's going on in there?" I gazed at her forehead.

She turned her body to face me, pulling her face away and my stomach lurched but the look on her face wasn't one of withdrawal.

Nicolette Parker took my hands in hers and spoke the words that I'd always feared someone like her would speak.

The tightness in her voice didn't go unnoticed.

"You didn't kill your mother. Did you, Riot?"

Everything in my body went cold.

My heart stopped.

The cicadas froze.

The wind chimes moved in such slow motion I began to think I was dreaming.

The room felt far away.

My worst fear.

The only real fear I'd ever had.

Laid plain like it was being hung on a clothesline.

I was distantly aware that I'd pulled away and stood up, bringing my body closer to the open window so that my lungs might retrieve more air.

"It was Brennan, wasn't it?" Her voice was soft and tender and it cut through me like a finely sharpened filet knife. I wanted to lie. I'd done it so many times before. I had the whole spiel memorized by now and I should have gone into autopilot.

"I returned home after I'd received a phone call from my brother. He was upset. He and Mom had gotten into a particularly nasty fight so I drove home to try to diffuse the situation. But when I arrived my mother had gone crazy, she'd gone mad. I tried to get her to calm down, but she pulled a knife on me and my brother and I just snapped."

That was the story. For a dozen years now.

Until *she* came.

My voice was strangled in my throat. I closed my eyes, resting my head against one of the storm windows. The nighttime air was crisp and had a distinct chill.

The silence was teeming with energy, diluted by her words and my inexplicable incapacity to lie to her.

The worst person to give the truth to.

My body started to shake. I turned to face her. To face my truth. The truth only one other person on this planet knew.

Her chest looked concave and her eyes brimmed with tears. For me. For him. For Grace. My lips parted but my voice was caught.

Without hesitation she stood up and wrapped her arms around my neck, pulling my head down into the crevice of her neck and shoulder. When that lilac scent hit my nostrils, my chest hitched. All the anger and sadness I kept in came silently flowing out of me.

I'm not sure how long we stayed there. I'm not sure if my eyes shed actual tears or if I just imagined them but her raw femininity moved me and I could melt into her body.

She pulled back and ran a soft, tender hand under my eye and over my cheek before pulling my face to hers and claiming my lips like they'd been hers since the moment I saw her at that library.

A rush of need hit me like a tidal wave and my arms wrapped around her back. I pulled her tight against my chest.

Her lips and tongue tangled with mine and I was amazed at how her shape complimented me. She pushed her chest against me and I could feel the soft tips of her nipples. I needed more.

My hands began to roam, shakily, my fingertips grazing the skin of her belly, forming goosebumps in their wake. Our hips connected, eager to be closer, and it was all I could do to pull away so that she could pull my shirt over my head. She tugged hers off, and we paused, drinking the other in, our hair disheveled and eyes heavy with want.

She took a step closer and ran a hand over the zipper of my jeans and I couldn't help the groan of relief that escaped my lips. Her eyes lifted toward mine. She regarded me through her dark lashes and I swear I loved her.

Her hands moved me toward the bed. I fell to my back, holding my breath as she climbed on top of me. She found my lips once more before dragging her chin down my body. My breath grew shallower when I heard the clasp to my belt come loose. I was hardly aware of how exposed I was until I felt her lips close around me. My body went weak.

A deep sigh rolled through me, my body melting into the bed. I couldn't open my eyes; I knew if I looked down and saw that blonde head bobbing I would come that very second and her mouth was too good.

Better than good. Incredible. No. Mind-blowing. She took me in further and a deep shudder rolled through me.

My hand twisted itself in her hair. I leaned into her. She moved her tongue up and down my length a few more times before sliding her lips to the base and before I realized what I was doing, I squeezed the base of her neck. I knew I should let go. The closer I got, the tighter I squeezed but in that moment I couldn't physically let go if I tried. She had me completely incapacitated. My complete and utter surrender. And I would give it to her, unabashed and willing. She swirled her tongue around my tip before my breath started to come in short pants.

I finally chanced a glance down, not wanting to miss a moment of it. And as she looked up at me with sleepy eyes, it was my final undoing.

"I'm going to come," I warned but God bless her, she merely smiled with that full mouth and took me deeper. The pleasure surged through me like a wild animal, coursing through my veins. The world exploded around me. My body convulsed as she took every bit of me I had to offer.

Sounds faded and a deep peace washed over me. I wanted to close my eyes and die right then and there, wrapped in a warm blanket of bliss and calm.

I watched her, through heavy eyelids, rise to her knees. She moved toward the bathroom but my eyes landed on those swollen red lips. I needed them back on me.

I grabbed her wrist to stop her from getting off the bed and I pulled her on top of me. Her toned thighs straddled my hips and I could already feel the tension in my groin building again. I was worried it would take a while, but it was apparent I had underestimated my need for her.

Pulling her face to mine I slipped my tongue into her mouth and could taste the faint remnants on her lips. Me. I could taste *me* on her lips and that sent a fresh wave of heat through my body.

I didn't even bother to unhook her bra, pulling it over her head. Her hair fell in waves over her shoulders. I took a moment to take her in. All of her, laid bare above me. I pushed my hips up into her core and she let out a small moan.

Grabbing her hips with both my hands I lifted her off me to spin her down toward the bed. I ran my hands up her arms and laced my fingers with hers, pinning her to the sheets.

She opened her knees and I let one of my hands drift to the warm space between her thighs and the heat coming off her went straight to my core. I let a finger separate the soft skin there, and I almost came again, feeling how ready she was. I hardened almost instantly, pulling my hand away. Her hips bucked in protest.

I dipped my head down, running my tongue over her nipple and felt her sweet back arch into me. My cock throbbed, but I wanted to make this last. The way she moved beneath me was possibly the most beautiful thing I'd ever seen.

My lips trailed down her body, shuddering with soft gasps. Her head fell back as I kissed down the edge of her thigh, deliberately teasing her. Eager to hear that desperate moan one more time. I dragged my tongue lightly over to the center of her body.

"Please, Riot..." she panted, and hearing my name on her pleading lips sent my tongue deep into the soft folds of her skin. Her cry was music to my ears and her thighs fell further apart.

I pushed a finger inside of her. My tongue made soft circles around the swollen peak of her body. Her hands wove in my hair and I let her tell me where to go, where to touch her, where to slow down, where to speed up, where to apply more deep, unrelenting pressure. I listened to her hands like I was her puppet until her body began to shake. Nothing prepared me for the satisfaction I'd feel knowing I was the one capable of making her feel this way.

I slid a second finger inside of her, applying more pressure with my mouth, taking as much of her between my lips as possible.

The quaking of her body came to stillness. Her whole midsection rose off the bed, her scream of pleasure echoed off the ceiling and walls.

She tightened around my fingers and it was heart-stopping. I rode the rest of her orgasm but didn't wait a second longer before I climbed on top of her.

I hesitated for a moment, watching her. She picked her head up to look at me and although I could see a definite relief in her eyes, even more prevalent was the dark desire that called me closer. I moved to grab a condom out of the back of my discarded jeans but she stopped me.

"We don't need it, if you don't want. I'm on birth control and there hasn't been anybody..." Her eyes danced between mine, wondering the same from me. I nodded. *There hasn't been anyone else for me either*.

I wondered if there ever would be anyone else ever again. Not after this. Not after her.

I lined myself up at the center of her body and hesitated until I saw her nod her head, urging me forward. I took in every expression, every dip and curve of her open mouth, fixed in a silent *o* as I buried myself slowly. Pausing for a moment, I waited for that desperation in her eyes. She let out a breathy plea.

One last push and I was wholly consumed by her body. I wanted to live inside her. To grow and weaken and come and harden and give her everything within me until I had nothing left. I swallowed, needing to take a breath. Her eyes were softer now. Her legs wrapped around my waist, somehow plunging me deeper.

My head fell between my shoulders and her hands grazed either side of my neck, tender, bringing my lips to hers. I moved rhythmically inside her. Already, the heat and tension swirled in my lower abdomen. Our breaths came out in short, heavy pants.

God, she felt so good, like her body was made to receive mine and the thought only sent more blood rushing to my cock. She cried out like she felt it and I wouldn't be able to hold back much longer. But I needed her to come again. I wanted to feel what my fingers had when her body convulsed around them.

Her face contorted in a look of unbridled desire and pleasure and pain and wanting. Our eyes locked. Her lips parted in a silent cry. I picked up speed, close to losing control entirely. But I held back, waiting for her so that I would finish with her. Together.

Her body shook beneath mine. I pressed more firmly, burying every inch of me inside her with each stroke. Until her head fell back and her voice made the most wonderful sound as it garbled my name. Her body squeezed me tight, and I let myself go, spilling into her, warming the very little spaces left between us.

The pleasure shuddered through her body. I claimed her lips with mine, drinking in every last moan, praying for tomorrow to never come.

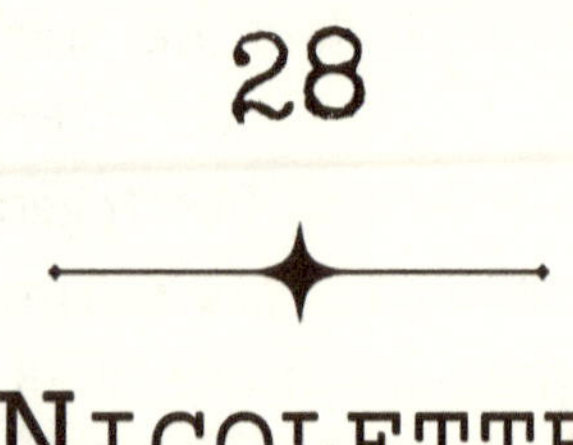

28

NICOLETTE

Apart of me had suspected Riot hadn't been the one to kill his mother after my first night here. I had looked into the eyes of evil men. I mean truly, evil, heartless, sell-your-own-daughter-into-slavery kind of men, and after I'd spent that day with Riot; the Center, our breakfast then him bringing me home like some kind of stray dog... something felt truly off about the story that he'd told and then retold so many times.

When he flew into Brennan's house after hearing us yelling while playing that robot game, I thought it was because he didn't want me too close to Brennan. He didn't trust me not to ask questions. But when he came outside once again with that wild look in his eyes, I realized he had never been afraid for Brennan. He'd been afraid for me.

I hadn't waited for an answer when I asked him. I didn't need one. The look of pure despondency in his eyes was all the truth I needed. But I still wanted to understand.

As we lay with our legs and bodies still tangled together in the top bed sheet, I wanted to understand. I needed to understand why he had given up everything; his scholarship, his education, his future, *his life* — for ten years. My fingers drew circles in the tiny curls of thin chest hair, my cheek pressed against the warmth of his shoulder.

His heartbeat was slow now, calm. I expected to see him asleep but when I gazed up, he was staring at the ceiling, a listless expression on his face.

I parted my lips to ask him a question, but he beat me to it.

"The summer after I graduated..." he began, and I stilled. "I went away to training camp in early August. I had been nervous about how they would do. She and Brennan never got along, especially after Dad died. It was like my mom's empathy and patience died alongside him. I had made a point to call home every couple of days. I called one Sunday and my mom picked up, we chatted, the usual. I asked to talk to Brennan, and she said he wasn't there. She had enrolled him in a program that would 'get him the help he needed'."

Riot's throat bobbed.

"She said it was some kind of therapeutic wilderness program. No phones allowed but I could write to him. I assumed he was getting evaluated by some social workers, behavior therapists, I don't know." He ran a hand over his chin. "He had always spent most of his time holed up in his room on the computer before that. I was glad he was getting out, maybe meeting friends in the *real* world." He laughed humorlessly, and I leaned in a little closer to him. "I wrote him a letter of *encouragement*." He shook his head, an expression full of shame. "I told him I was proud of him. That I hoped he could *embrace* the experience and that it was the right thing, the *good* thing for him.

"It wasn't until I came home Labor Day weekend that I saw what they did to him. Brennan was back but..." Riot shuddered. "His eyes. I knew something was wrong. He was a shell of himself."

Riot's chest hitched. He closed his eyes. "His skin was... translucent. He had these black circles under his eyes and would flinch at every sharp sound." Riot took one more deep breath. "As you may have deduced, Brennan has always been kind of *asexual*. Never showed any interest in girls growing up and I think he probably thought there was something wrong with him. So, Brennan being Brennan, needed empirical data. So, he looked up *gay* porn." Riot waved a hand. "I think to see if *that* did anything for him." He frowned sadly. "Mom went snooping on his computer. She found it and freaked." He turned his head, and we locked eyes for a fleeting moment and I thought I saw Riot's heart crumble to pieces all over again.

"You know, I don't think it was the possibility of him being gay that made her snap. I think it was some kind of loss of control. Her children were the only two things she recognized about her life and I guess she felt like she was losing him." His eyes narrowed in thought. "It's not an excuse, either way."

He looked down at our tangled bodies before meeting my eyes.

"It wasn't a wilderness camp, Nic." He blew out a breath. "It was a conversion therapy program." I furrowed my brow, resting my chin on his chest. "One of those camps that basically, if they can't pray the gay away, they'll beat it out of you."

My heart lurched and my mouth fell open.

"You're kidding."

"I wish I was."

"Those still exist?"

"Apparently."

"Jeez, poor Brennan."

Riot huffed out a chuckle devoid of humor. "I keep going back to that letter I sent him."

I wrote him a letter of encouragement... That I hoped he could embrace the experience and that it was the right thing, the good thing for him.

My heart broke open for Brennan who must have felt like he truly had lost everyone.

"He must have hated me because he didn't speak to me until... a few months later." Riot squeezed his eyes shut as if the words caused physical pain.

"It was a Friday night," he said to the ceiling. "Brennan had been chatting with some gamer online. It wasn't *romantic*." His chest rose and fell with his breath, exhaling a cathartic sigh as the story spilled. "But I guess they made plans to meet up in Charleston that weekend. There was some kind of Comic-Con convention." A laugh escaped his chest. "I mean, *real* nerd shit. When he told Mom his plans she forbade it, calling it some kind of *gay retreat*." Riot's head shook back and forth. "He was twenty-three years old, and she tried *grounding* him. When that didn't work, she decided that it was time to send him back to the camp."

I winced.

"When he heard her on the phone with the office, he took off in a panic. He said he'd rather die than go back there so he ran away and hid in the woods by the lake. That's when he called me. I could hear the devastation in his voice. *He* was different. He was terrified."

Riot was silent for a long moment. His breath caught in his throat, bobbing up and down.

"I told him I'd be there within a couple of hours and I'd pick him up. He could stay with me for as long as it took. I told him to go back home. To meet me there." A long exhale passed through Riot's lips and tears stung my eyes.

"So, that's what he did. He went home." Riot looked down and bit his lip. The guilt was all over his face and it made my chest hurt. "By the time I got there, he had already stabbed her three times. Brennan was practically comatose. Clutching the knife and rocking back and forth on the front steps. He just kept repeating 'I think she's dead. I think she's dead.' I went inside to check."

He took a shaky breath and his body trembled. "I'll never forget it for as long as I live. She was face down in the kitchen, a trail of blood leading from the living room like she'd..." his voice cracked almost imperceptibly, "like she'd tried crawling to get to her phone that was on the kitchen counter."

Something pulled distantly at my memory but I dismissed it. I let the silence hang heavy in the air, wrapping my arms tighter around him as if it would take some of his suffering away.

"I barely noticed the fire that had started toward the back of the house. I ran outside after that and told Brennan to run. He refused over and over but I told him that I was going to make everything right. And to do that... he needed to go." He shook his head in disbelief and that made me pause again.

"You didn't start the fire?" I asked, and he looked down at me as if just realizing I was there.

"No. The news reports made it sound like I did. Honestly, I kind of assumed Brennan had. My mom did love candles. She'd always have one or two burning so one probably got knocked over in their struggle." Riot's chest deflated. "Kind of ironic."

"What's that?"

"My whole life literally went up in flames." My throat tightened, and I found myself pressing my face harder into his chest. His right arm tightened around me in approval. "First Dad... Then Mom... Then my *whole* goddamn house." He breathed out a humorless chuckle.

"Why'd you do it?" I asked.

"What? Confess?" I gave a slight nod of my head. He exhaled a long sigh. "Brennan could handle the high school bullies... But you can't exactly talk your way out of getting assaulted in prison. Me on the other hand?" He tipped his head back and forth. "All-star college quarterbacks fair a little better than skinny white boys severely on the spectrum." His words punched me in the gut. "All I could think about was what would happen to him there. It would be fifty-fifty if he even made it out and I couldn't bear to think what would be left of him if he did make it." He shrugged helplessly. "My parents were gone. I couldn't lose my brother too."

Riot astounded me and I tried to consider how selfless a person had to be to accept responsibility for voluntary manslaughter because you wanted to protect your brother from what he *might* face in prison. I studied his face and my heart melted for the soul inside him.

"He didn't want me to. He begged me to let him confess, but I told him it was too late. I'd already done it and if he said anything it would get us both in trouble and it'd all be a waste. So I'd made him promise me that he would live his life and if he ever felt that kind of threat or fear or anger like he had that night, he would just run away. And until today, the secret was the two of ours and ours alone."

His eyes met mine and a fierce protectiveness struck me.

"I'll never say a word, Riot. I swear." His eyes sparkled against the nighttime darkness while he studied my face as if making sure there were no hints of deception. Satisfied with what he saw there, he pulled me closer. The night sky twinkled out the window while the reassuring rhythm of his heart sang me to sleep.

When the sun came streaming in the next morning, it took everything in me to get out of bed and shut the blinds. I yanked the old dusty curtains closed. When I turned around, Riot was watching me with a sleepy grin, a muscled arm resting behind his head. My eyes raked down his bare chest and I sucked in my bottom lip to keep from drooling. I blushed, realizing I was still completely naked.

Diving back under the covers a shiver crawled over my skin. Riot pulled me toward him and we lay there in quiet silence, feeling the sun warm the tiny screen room. Closing my eyes, I pressed my ear to his chest and found that strong, comforting rhythm.

Had I ever felt this at peace? Surely not with someone I was romantically interested in. The tryst with my boss was laced with danger and illicit, stolen moments. Complemented only by the defeating times I'd face him in public and he'd have to pretend I was nothing other than an employee. After that, I spent many years keeping everyone at arm's length, putting the entirety of my focus into my career, my stories, and the next big exposé.

Nestled against Riot's body, it was incredible to feel like I could rest. Like I could unload some of the weight I was carrying and feel as though another person might protect me as fiercely as I've had to protect myself.

The jaded cynic in me wanted to be critical. She wanted to chastise me for finding comfort in another person. She wanted to remind me that people were wired to let you down and to keep a guarded distance. But after everything my life had thrown at me, everything this town had thrown at me, that cynical voice got surprisingly quieter.

I'd spent so long playing offense, listening to that voice, being the strong one, having the upper hand, being one step ahead, that I'd forgotten what it felt like to be vulnerable with someone who wasn't there because they wanted something from you.

That voice was always going to have a place. A cautious dose of skepticism was healthy, it's what would keep me asking questions. But for now, breathing in the scent of Riot's skin, feeling his fingertips trace down my arm, listening to the unrelenting beating of his heart, an overwhelming sense of calm captured me and I was at peace.

I told him not to but Riot called in sick that morning and we spent the whole day in my bed, only getting up to make some quick snacks before getting back in bed. It was a strange experience. My few relationships had been mostly business-like. We went on dates. We met at functions. Sometimes we'd spend the night at each other's apartments. But I'd never shirked any responsibilities to stay home in a little love cocoon.

It felt nice. It felt normal and even though I was accustomed to looking down on the more *basic* human emotions, I think I understood what all the buzz was about. Sex with someone you cared about, *really* cared about was in a different category of its own. In the past, it had been almost transactional. With Riot, it was soul-shaking and I couldn't get enough of him. I was like a woman possessed.

"We can't stay here forever," I mumbled somewhere around dinner time.

"Shh..." I could hear the smile on Riot's lips. He wrapped a hand over my mouth. "You shush now."

We went on like that for several days, him only getting dressed to go to work and me to the grocery store. At night we'd tangle ourselves in a blanket, sometimes watching a movie. Sometimes just watching the stars.

We went for ice cream and I wish I could say I ignored the stares as we waited in line, hand-in-hand.

But where Riot would shrink away, I relished the critical scowls. Their disapproval only fanned my affection for him. It made me hold him tighter, laugh louder, and smile wider. Let the tongues wag. Riot brought me a sense of peace I'd never known and not even Katie Plainbottom's foul glare could poke a hole in my parachute.

There was a part of me that wished I could slap the truth in their face. After hearing the truth about Grace Asher's death, I was shook. It didn't feel fair that Riot sacrificed ten years of his life, but I had made a promise I would never say a word. I couldn't be the one to waste his sacrifice. This was one story that wasn't mine to tell.

Melody's assignment drifted in and out of my brain. The truth would absolutely wreck the entire plan for the episode. But a wrongful confession story? That could be developed into an entire series, if they wanted it to. Remorse twisted my insides just at the thought of it. Did I have it in me to betray Riot? A month ago, I would have said absolutely. Desperation made people do crazy things. But everything was different now. No, my heart couldn't handle the idea of breaking Riot's trust by using his selflessness against him.

Still, something irked me about the story he told me. Something that nagged at the back of my subconscious I couldn't quite put my finger on it.

My brain thought so too because this morning I had woken in a cool sweat from a bizarre dream. I was walking on top of a shallow lake, my surroundings black until I spotted a person standing in the distance. It was Grace Asher, standing still. Her face pale. Her eyes blank, drained of life. I asked what she was doing but there was no answer. Her appearance began to skip like I was watching a film before she started spinning in place. Slowly, at first, then quickened until she was spinning so rapidly she was a blur before the surrounding air sucked me in like a tornado. I never took too much stock in dreams but it left me with a feeling like I was forgetting something.

Before I left Easton for Godot, I poured over all the police records to familiarize myself with the facts. The crime scene, the court case, all of it. But the image of a twirling Grace Asher ate at me all day until I finally sat down at the little round table in my lanai. Maybe taking another look would jog something.

As I pulled my laptop open, I was ashamed to say I hadn't so much as turned it on since the night of our date. We'd been so wrapped up in each other that I had let my entire Chimera investigation fall to the wayside.

My computer was dead, so I plugged it in as my thoughts drifted back to the night of our date.

I had been in the middle of sending my mom a video message when the sensation of being watched hit me from behind. Brennan had been sitting in the corner of my room like a goddamn creep.

"Jesus, Brennan! You scared the shit out of me," I'd said but he just glared in response.

"Do you know how important cybersecurity is to me?" he asked, monotone.

"What?" I narrowed my eyes at him. Riot would be coming by any minute. I hadn't been entirely forthcoming about the little drone operation Brennan had helped me with. It had been a bust, so it didn't seem important.

"No devices connect to my network without going through a very thorough scan." His eyes narrowed at me accusingly and my neck prickled. "The media was pretty relentless when Riot first came home so you can understand why I take precautions."

It was incredible how even-keeled he was and I don't know why but it made me nervous. I searched my memory for anything incriminating that could've been on my computer and didn't think of anything until—

"You read the profile I wrote."

He didn't dignify it with a response.

"I don't like what you said about my brother."

"Brennan, I didn't mean it. I was angry. And hurt. I wasn't thinking straight. I'm sorry. I thought I deleted that document, I swear. No one will ever see it."

He eyed me with his dead stare and expressionless face and paused for a long beat.

"There were a few questionable emails I came across too. My brother's name appeared quite a few times. All were sent or received before you arrived in our lives. Why are you here, Nicolette?"

It was the most normal and coherent I'd ever heard Brennan. Like the social awkwardness went to sleep when he was feeling defensive of his brother. His voice was deeper, his accusatory tone cut through me like a looming guillotine.

I opened my mouth but hesitated when I saw Riot pass by inside.

"Can we go outside and talk about this?" I moved to the door, but he stood there, arms crossed, eyes narrowed. I stepped outside and held the door. Finally, he acquiesced. I glanced inside one more time before ensuring Riot wasn't nearby.

"Look, yes, I initially came here because I was assigned to get Riot's side of the story for this stupid documentary but I'm not writing it, Brennan. I swear to you, I'm not. That's why I'm looking into all this Chimera and coal mine stuff." I let the words rush out but Brennan started to shake his head. His eye twitched, and it was as if the past few minutes had exhausted his "normalness" and his madness started to take over. "I promise, Brennan. I care about Riot. A lot. Okay? Like, a *lot*." I looked at the ground before gazing back up at him. "Please don't say anything to him. I'll tell him, I promise. It'll be inconsequential soon enough, anyway." I waved my arms, accentuating the point. "Please? I just need it to come from me."

I waited for his response but he just kept shaking his head fervently, taking a few looming steps toward me. His breath came out in shallow, sharp exhales through gritted teeth.

"You're asking me to lie to my brother. I don't like it." His voice rose, and I prayed Riot couldn't hear us. "No good, it's no good! I don't like it!

Don't like it!" He had started hitting himself in the head and I backed up until my back found the side of the lanai.

I was thankful that Brennan had stalked away when Riot came out. I knew I had to tell Riot about the assignment before he found out from Brennan but I also knew it had to wait until I could make sure he believed that I wasn't doing it. And it'd be a hell of a lot more digestible if I had another story on deck.

Finally, my computer had enough juice to come to life. Determined, I opened up the court case notes and began re-reading but nothing stuck out. I moved to open the crime scene report and began reading from the top. There had been signs of a struggle. End tables were knocked over. Shattered glasses on the kitchen floor. I scanned down to the description of the body.

Victim was found lying on her back between the dining area and kitchen—

"Hey!" My attention snapped to the sliding door where Riot stood in all his masculine glory. His biceps, round and pronounced, gripped the door frame above him.

I clapped my laptop shut and bounded to my feet, throwing my arms around his neck. His smell was intoxicating and the bubbly levity of youthful infatuation turned my limbs to jelly.

His lips pressed against my ear, sending a shiver down my skin. "There's a drive-in movie at the ball field tonight," he murmured. "Wanna be my date?"

I grimaced through my school-girl grin. "Do they do those as, like, a nod to nostalgia or something?"

He pulled back and raised an eyebrow at me. "No?" He seemed genuinely confused by my question and my heart melted.

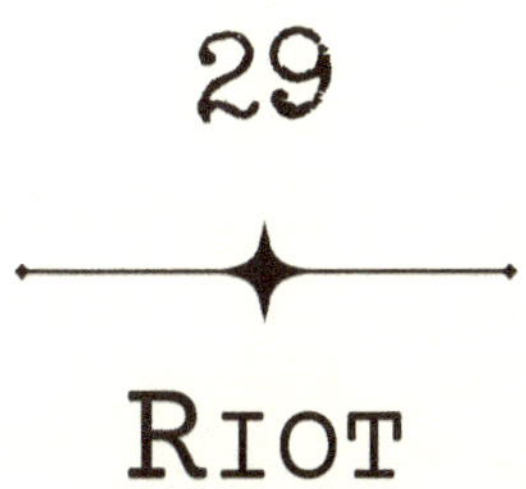

29

RIOT

I'd be lying if I said it didn't make me nervous. Nicolette knowing the truth. For over ten years my greatest fear had been a reporter or someone with her *credentials* finding out what happened that night.

And even though an innate sliver of doubt still clung to my subconscious, a sense of comfort settled over me, knowing *she* knew the truth. For the longest time, the only person I had no secrets from was my brother. It was like a ten-ton weight had been lifted off my chest when Nicolette whispered those words to me.

We shared a secret from the whole world and although it was a secret that could destroy what little was left of my family, a part of me was exhilarated to know that *she* was the other half of my secret now.

"What do you think?"

I turned to see Nicolette emerge from the lanai, her perfect body draped in a small sundress, red with small white flowers. She didn't wear a lot of color often, I'd noticed, so it was almost like seeing her for the first time. She did a little spin, and it fanned around the tops of her thighs and I could feel the heat shoot right to my groin. Her long legs had a crisp tan now and the way the white flowers complemented her skin was captivating. Her hair, normally pulled up high, now fell in waves around her shoulders. It, too, fanned around her while she spun in seemingly slow motion.

"I take it from the extended silence and ogling that you're a fan. Good." She smirked, and I cleared my throat.

"Yeah, wow. Um, you look really nice," I stammered. Glancing at my watch, I snagged my keys off the hook.

When we'd parked in the back of the ball field, I fiddled with the ra-dio, tuning it to the station that broadcasted the sound of the movie, something about a dog, I wasn't sure.

"Did you go to prom?" she asked abruptly. I looked over, and she was squinting like she'd never heard of the term.

"I did." I nodded, cautiously curious. She nodded, a vacant expression on her face. "I was Prom King," I muttered.

She raised her chin like a memory was flooding back to her. "Yeah, I think I remember hearing that. I didn't pay much attention but I remem-ber Jeremy being butthurt about it." Nicolette looked over at me and the subtle sadness in her smile pulled at me.

"You went with Jeremy," I stated almost like a ques-tion. Had I known that? The sound of his name burned a little hole in my confidence.

"For about an hour." She rolled her eyes. "I never went to mine." A contorted smile twisted her lips and I couldn't tell if I saw sad-ness or regret there. A few ideas danced in my mind as she fiddled with her jewelry.

"Could you help me with this? It keeps getting tangled." She mo-tioned to the thin gold necklace that was unclasped around her neck. I swallowed hard. She inched over, flipping up the armrest so there was no barrier between us. My heartbeat caught in my throat as she swept the wavy mass of hair over one shoulder, handing me the clasp of the delicate chain. We'd spent all week exploring each other's bodies but every moment I spent with her was like the first time and I was a jumbled mess of nerves.

My fingers fumbled. Small goosebumps spread over her skin where my fingertips touched her. The overwhelming urge to press my lips to the back of her neck was interrupted by a motion out the front window.

We turned our gaze to see two women, one holding the hand of a toddler staring at us through the windshield. One muttered something to the other, and she shook her head, distastefully.

Before I could process the judgment, Nicolette whipped her head around and grabbed my face in her hands, pulling her lips to mine with eager desire.

Out of the corner of my eye, I saw one of the women bring a shocked hand to her mouth before ushering her child away. I drank in the light grin on Nicolette's lips. Something bloomed in my chest at how fearless she was, how possessive of me she'd become. I wanted to consume all of her.

My hands moved to the back of her neck, that soft, tender skin I knew lit a fire in her. I parted my lips, letting my tongue explore her mouth. She met me, motion for motion, just as she always had, not backing down, not shying away, but greeting everything I offered with passion and fire of her own.

"They're gone," I murmured against her teeth, her lips spreading into a mischievous grin.

"I know," she whispered low and lascivious, moving closer. She pressed her chest into me and I was undone.

My arms wrapped around her backside. I pulled her closer to me. She slid her right leg over my lap and I could feel my strained erection pushing into the warm center of her body. A low curse hissed through my teeth. Her thighs fell to either side of my hips.

I wove my fingers through her wild, blonde locks and let her golden hair fall over me. She was a tidal wave of lilac and beauty and fierce femininity.

Her hands moved to the top of my jeans. I sucked in a breath. "Someone might see," I said, pulling back to gaze into her eyes.

"Let 'em watch," she replied huskily. We had parked in the back but, still, I scanned the crowd. Everyone appeared to be nestled into their seats, their attention on the screen ahead.

My heart ticked up another beat in anticipation when she unzipped my jeans, letting me spring free before running her hand along my length. My head rolled back, eyes squeezed shut, reveling in the feel of her lips on my neck, her body pressed against my chest. She seemed eternal, perched there on top of me and I'd never get enough.

I opened my eyes and studied her face. She positioned herself right above me. I slipped a finger beneath the lacy cotton under her dress and sensed the wet heat there. Pulling it to the side, I let my tip slide easily across the slick opening to her body and I memorized the perfect arch of her parted lips. Her eyes flashed open and met mine.

Something tight passed between us. Tender, but heavy. Her expression was serious and sincere when she lowered herself on top of me, stretching her body to envelop me entirely. I clutched her to my chest, wishing her heartbeat could touch my own as she moved rhythmically above me.

"Riot…" she exasperated and her words tightened my lower abdomen. Our collective breath fogged the windows with the warm exhalations of our shared air.

As her head tilted back I brought my lips to her breasts, pulling down the neckline of her sundress to expose her beaded pink nipples. I let my tongue lave over her and the small noises I heard in her chest were everything.

Her forehead crushed itself against mine as she tightened around me. A high-pitched squeak escaped her throat. Her fingernails raked through my scalp and it was all I could do to stay in one piece while I shattered underneath her, endlessly inside her.

We remained entwined there for several minutes, our breath catching up to us. I inhaled everything about her. She lifted herself off my lap.

We were jolted out of our little reverie by the loud sound of a horn honking. My eyes bolted wide, and a humored chuckle exhaled from her lips. Her ass had hit the horn on the steering wheel.

Her cheeks reddened. She clamped a hand over her mouth and I tried to muffle a snort but couldn't help myself. I let my head roll back, a deep laugh rumbled through my chest.

"So much for not bringing attention to ourselves," I muttered and she snickered harder.

As she collapsed against my chest, I brushed my fingers through her hair. After a minute I grabbed a small towel from the backseat to clean ourselves. She shifted next to me but settled into my arms, her warm cheek pressed against my chest. I loved it there. I loved *her* there.

30

NICOLETTE

I had almost dozed off in Riot's arms when his stomach growled. He clutched it and groaned.

"Sorry, I guess you make me ravenous." He smirked down at me. I grabbed my wallet out of my bag.

"I'll get us some snacks."

I hopped down from his truck in time to catch his eyes wandering over my ass as my dress fell around me.

At the concession stand, I ordered a large popcorn and a pack of Twizzlers and was pleasantly surprised to see they had beer in the cooler so I snagged two of those.

When I spun around, I smacked directly into Geoffrey Brown. I recoiled at his proximity.

"Miss Parker, how are we doing this fine night?" His greasy little sneer was all-knowing and my stomach turned at the smell of him. His crooked teeth were yellow, and he reeked of stale nicotine.

"Hi Geoff, lock anybody up against their will lately?"

"I don't know, Miss Parker. Stick your nose somewhere it doesn't belong lately?" He took a step closer to me and I wanted to back up but wouldn't give him the satisfaction. I stuck my chin in the air.

He regarded me with a suspicious glance. "You know, you Godot women have a really bad habit of poking around the wrong rattlesnake bed." My face flushed, and I opened my mouth. *I'd show him who the rattlesnake was.*

"Geoff!" Pastor Blackwell appeared, clapping him on the shoulder. "Not making any more trouble with the locals, I hope?" Blackwell let out a hearty laugh, shaking his friend deliberately.

"Course not, Elias. Just having a friendly chat with Nancy Drew, here." He shot me a look, and I caught a quick, silent glare of warning from Pastor Blackwell. *Weird.*

"Well, you know what they say about talking during the movies... why don't we all head back to our respective cars, hm?"

Why was Pastor Blackwell so eager to get me away from Geoff? He was a dick, sure, but he had that same nervous glint Riot had had when he first introduced me to Brennan, like he was afraid I was going to get the wrong information out of him.

As I walked back to Riot's truck, I stole a glance over my shoulder but the men were no longer at the concession stand. I spotted them at the edge of the ball field in a heated conversation. Blackwell looked angry and Geoff was gesturing wildly and shaking his head.

"Did you have to go out and pick the corn?" Riot grinned but hesitated when he saw my perplexed expression. "What's up?"

"Nothing," I shook my head, dismissing the brief exchange. "Just ran into that dick Geoffrey Brown who locked me in the basement of the records room."

Riot's eyes darkened and his body tensed. "What happened?"

I waved it off. Riot sat straighter, craning his neck around. "It was nothing. Pastor Blackwell pulled him away before he said anything."

Mundane interest passed over Riot's features.

"Good to know those two are talking again," he muttered.

"What do you mean? Isn't Geoff Jeremy's godfather or something?" Riot scowled briefly at Jeremy's name.

"They *were* best friends for a long time, yeah. Geoff moved here from Baltimore shortly after the Blackwells did. He followed them here on purpose for a job at the church. To be honest, I think he had a thing for my mom."

"Geoff?" I looked surprised at him. "But he's so... gross."

Riot chuckled. "Yeah, but he could be a charmer when he wanted to be. The last ten years weren't kind to his face." Riot looked up, considering. "Or waistline. I'd come home from school some days and he'd be sitting in our dining room, drinking *tea*. I pretended I didn't see him sneak whiskey in it. He'd try to ask me about football and school. Girls. He'd call me 'son' and I wanted to hit him but my mom seemed to be happy around him so I let it go."

"What happened?"

"I'm not sure really, I was pretty wrapped up in football my senior year and then when I took off for summer training, I guess he and Blackwell had some kind of falling out. Brennan mentioned overhearing an argument. Something about stealing from the church? I don't know, I wouldn't put it past Geoffrey Brown to get sticky fingers around the collection plate, though."

"So, your mom found out he was stealing? Did she ever tell anyone?"

Riot shrugged. "I don't know, I wasn't around. But I'm assuming Elias found out because Geoff was pushed out of the church and got a job with the water authority, which made him move out of Godot proper. He wasn't seen around town for years." Both our gazes fell to Geoffrey in the distance, stalking away from the ball field.

We tried to settle in to watch the rest of the movie but every time Riot's body moved, mine came to life. He stroked the back of my hair. I ran my palm down his thigh. He kissed my ear. I ran my tongue along his scar. How was it possible I still hadn't had enough of him. Heat pooled between my thighs.

"Should I climb on your lap again?" I whispered, tracing his ear with my tongue. His chest rattled with a groan.

"You deserve better than a truck twice in one day. I want you in a bed. I want to lay you out and take my time with you." His voice was all gravel and thank god the movie was over.

When we finally heard engines revving, I looked up to see most of the cars in line to leave.

Riot's lips trailed my neck and a delicious chill ran down my arms. I whined when he pulled away, a satisfied smile outlining his perfectly white teeth.

"I'm going to hit the head quick then we'll head home?" His eyebrows jumped up and down and I wrapped a sweater he'd given me tighter around my shoulders, inhaling his residual musk on the cotton. *Home.*

"Yes, please."

He hopped down and I watched him walk away. His tight little ass wore those jeans so perfectly it should be illegal.

Collecting our garbage from the truck, I pushed the door open and jumped down, spotting the nearest garbage can a few yards away. After tossing it all in, I let my mind wonder if I could unbutton his jeans with my teeth.

"You're going to ruin him, you know." Katie Plainbottom's voice cut my daydream short. My smile dropped like an anvil.

I spun around and narrowed my eyes at her, letting my distaste seethe from the sneer on my lips.

"What's your obsession with him?" I asked. "Please don't tell me you're one of those prison groupies who gets off writing to inmates because they're trapped and vulnerable."

For a moment she looked mildly surprised, and I wondered if I'd gone too far but then I remembered this was the woman who most likely put a graphic video of me on a large screen projector in front of the whole goddamn town and maybe I didn't go far enough.

I took a few strides closer to her, squaring my shoulders and standing taller. "He's a human being, Katie, not a dress-up doll for your hero complex," I bit off.

She took a deep breath, getting ready to respond, and some territorial part of me stirred to life. She tried to match my stature and it appeared she might bite back with some retort but after a moment she deflated, breaking eye contact with me.

She blew out a breath, appearing almost defeated.

"I care about him, Nicolette. And if you did too, you'd leave town and let him be. He is working for my family and maybe one day could own the shop. He could have a *real* place in this town again and I know that doesn't mean much to *you* but it does to him. More than you know."

All I wanted was to buy a massive piece of land for my sweet, homemaker wife and our basic, predictably beautiful litter of children. I wanted that life, okay?

I shifted my weight, remembering his confession.

"Riot was almost there before you blew into town and ruined everything for him. He was earning respect back and people were starting to see him like the hometown hero they remembered instead of the man that brutally murdered his mother." She stared daggers into my eyes and paused to let me absorb that. *Except he didn't kill her,* I wanted to scream. "And now he's put himself back *years* just for associating with you. Let him go, Nicolette. Leave town. I'll take him back. If you leave right now, I'll forgive him for choosing you but that window is closing. If you two stay together much longer, there will be no going back for him and you know he's mandated here for five years."

My chest hitched. *What the fuck?*

Katie sneered at the opportunity to catch me off guard. "He didn't mention that to you, did he?"

My brain flipped through all our conversations and I scanned my memory... had he told me that? I knew he was on probation but I didn't know for how long.

"Yeah, the condition of his release. Probation for five years and let's be honest... palling around with you is *definitely* going to end with him violating it and then it'll be even longer." She paused and tilted her head. "If you care about him, you'll break it off and leave town. Somewhere deep down even *you* know I'm right."

She started to back up but my pride wouldn't let her get the last word.

"He doesn't love you," I called after her.

Katie looked back at me and frowned, a deep sadness mapped on her face.

"I know that." She looked at her feet before meeting my eyes again. "But he could learn to. And we could be happy enough. But you? You destroy people, Nicolette." She threw her arms up and her words hit my chest like bullets. "It's just what you do. You ruin people and companies and towns and you leave a trail of bodies when you leave. Don't make Riot just another casualty of your ambition."

With that, she turned around and disappeared into the night. I covered my eyes with my palms with the sinking realization that Katie was right. She didn't *feel* right. But her words hit a truth inside me that split my heart open.

I did ruin people. Mostly they were people who deserved to be ruined and had earned every bit of the criminal charges or public scrutiny they faced when I was done with them. But it was also true that there were always casualties, unwilling accomplices also prosecuted, jobs lost, and relationships ruined.

Riot didn't deserve any of that. He deserved better than that. He deserved better than me.

31

RIOT

I emerged from the bathroom and blinked when I saw Katie walking away from Nicolette who stood a few feet outside my truck. I frowned at the look Katie threw me in the brief passing. Her face was flushed, and she nodded at me before disappearing in a sea of cars.

My eyes shot over to Nicolette who stood frozen in the same spot. Her gaze was unfocused, and I was brought back to the expression on her face when she'd stood on stage and withstood public humiliation at the carnival.

"What the fuck did you say, Katie..." I muttered to myself, hustling to the truck. I scrambled to her side but Nicolette waved me off, pulling the passenger door open herself and climbed in. I walked to my side and did the same.

She made slow, small, deliberate moves to buckle her seat belt. I turned myself in my seat to face her, my heart picking up a beat at the look of desolation on her face. She kept her eyes fixed out the windshield but I didn't start the car. Finally, she sighed and looked over at me half-heartedly.

"What happened, Nic?"

"What do you mean? Nothing. Ready to go home?"

"No." I wasn't moving until I could help wipe the despondent expression off her face. "What did she say to you?"

Nicolette looked down, and I hated the way she looked so... *dethroned.* "Nothing, just small-town, jealous girl stuff." She wiped her hands on the skirt of her dress and took a breath before meeting my gaze. "Really, Riot. It was nothing." She smiled, but it didn't touch her eyes.

I shook my head. "Nope, sorry, but I'm not going to let you do that thing where you pretend like everything is okay so you can stew on whatever is bothering you alone in silence. Not now. Not after everything."

Nicolette scowled at my stubbornness and I was glad to have a little piece of her back. She picked at a cuticle.

"Why didn't you mention that you have to stay here five years for probation?"

My heart clenched. It wasn't like I had been trying to keep it from her. Part of me assumed she knew, everyone knew everything about me in this town. But the other part of me was too afraid to bring it up. Things had been so good the last few days and I wasn't ready to pop the bubble by having the What Are We Doing talk yet.

I shrugged. "I guess I wasn't sure where your head was at. For the last few weeks, all I've known is that you're here temporarily and you're planning to leave soon." I saw her nod as if she understood. "And these past few days have been the best days of my entire life and if I brought up my probation, that would bring up your plans to leave. Just the *thought* of that conversation happening was enough to delude myself into pretending it wasn't inevitable."

I took her hand and squeezed it, trying to bring her back to life. "I'm sorry, Nicolette, I wasn't trying to hide it from you—"

But she waved dismissively. "No, no it's okay. I get it, Riot. You didn't owe me that information. I guess it just sucked hearing it from Katie." She leaned back and let her full head of blonde hair bounce against the headrest. Her head lolled to the side. She gave me a soft look. It stirred something in my chest but I was bothered by a piece of what she said.

"Nicolette, it may not have come up or been the right time to talk about *future* plans. But you need to know..." I made sure she was listening carefully, "that I do owe you. I owe you *everything*." My throat tightened, and I mentally kicked myself in the nuts to keep it together. But, goddamn, if this woman didn't bring me to my fucking knees.

My heart split open and the rushing urge to give her everything overwhelmed me like a massive dam that was finally breaking. "I was in prison for ten years and for ten years I thought that the day I got out, I would feel like a new man.

"I made all kinds of plans and I pictured how my life would be different. And then I came home to a place that no longer felt like home. I've spent eight months here feeling like I was just in a bigger prison cell." I found her eyes again and I steeled my voice. "And then you came back and suddenly this place felt like home again."

Nicolette bit her bottom lip and tilted her head. "Is that what you want?" she asked, her voice low. "To make Godot your home? If there was a choice, I mean. Probation aside."

I paused to think about it. I had never pictured a life anywhere else, probably because I'd never been anywhere else except for a few weekend trips here and there. I took a breath. My head began to spin. I shrugged helplessly.

"I don't know, Nicolette. I've been trapped inside my circumstances since I was eighteen. I've never considered a life outside the present tense."

She looked out the front window and nodded.

"What do you want?" I asked her, holding my breath for the answer. None of this mattered if she didn't want *me*. My chest ached at the thought. She was quiet for a long moment.

"I don't know either, Riot." The words stung, but I understood. "I know that it would be next to impossible for me to have a career here. And I'm not sure I *want* to make a home somewhere so many people *vehemently* dislike me." She looked defeated, and I desperately wanted to hold on to her. "I guess, I just had this *plan*... I was going to come back here and bust open some huge scandal about the church owning the town or some drug conspiracy cover-up—"

She got quiet and then lurched forward. She spun her large eyes to face me and her entire expression lit up. She pulled out her phone and started tapping.

"What's going on?" I tried to keep the alarm out of my voice. I wanted her to finish her thought. I wanted to know what she had been thinking. Was I enough? Could she wait until my probation was up to start a life elsewhere? That was selfish of me to think but I'd follow her anywhere.

"I'm not   sure…" She continued swiping on her phone until she pulled up a dark photo I couldn't make out. She zoomed in and turned the overhead light on.

She pushed the photo in front of my face and I jerked back. I could make out some kind of commercial truck parked next to the water tower. My eyes darted between her and the photo. I tried to see what she saw, but I had no clue what I was looking at. But the energy radiating from Nicolette was positively *brimming*.

"What am I looking at?" I asked.

"That is a truck from Echo Chemicals pouring fluoride into the town's water supply," she said excitedly. Despite the fact that I still had no idea what she was talking about, I did love the look of pure glee on her face. She looked like a little girl going to a birthday party.

I shook my head, still confused. "They put fluoride in the water supply?"

"The fact that Blackwell is doing it under the cover of night so the town doesn't know is kind of ridiculous, I mean who doesn't want healthy teeth?" She rolled her eyes.

"Pastor Blackwell admitted to dumping chemicals into the town water?" My eyes went wide.

"Yes, I mean, no, that's not the point. It's fluoride, most of the country does it by default." She waved dismissively.

"Then what does it mean?"

"Nothing on its own but when I found out that the church was essentially the sole source of funds for the Center, I confronted Blackwell about where all this money is coming from. It has to cost thousands of dollars for this much fluoride and upward of *hundreds* of thousands to keep the Center up and running. They're a church. Not even a mega church."

"What's a mega church?"

"So, I asked where all the money was coming from?" She ignored my question. "He said almost thirty years ago he started investing all the money that people donated into hedge funds." My eyes went wider and I opened my mouth but she held her hand up to shush me. "He said the money has been paying out hundreds of thousands of dollars in dividends every month so on top of all the money people donate, the *real money* is coming from the success of the investments."

She paused and slumped in her seat, frowning. I nodded, still unsure where she was going. "Okay... that sounds like a pretty smart move. What's wrong with it?"

"He mentioned the money was invested into real estate and medical. But he pulled out of real estate before the market collapse *and* before the news of the class action against the builder who put up the valley homes."

Her eyes darted around like she was reading some invisible text in front of her, working out her thoughts in real-time. "Therefore *all* the church's money is wrapped up into investments in the medical field. I thought maybe Echo Chemicals could be one of the investments, which I guess isn't a conflict of interest. Besides... a tiny little fluoride order for a town the size of Godot would never be enough inflate Echo Chemicals' stock price. And I guess a chemical company doesn't exactly fall under medical." She rolled her neck around. *Fuck,* she was sexy when she was thinking.

"Yeah, well that's an old truck," I told her. She whipped her head in my direction. "Brennan worked for them for about a year before they had a massive merger about ten years ago and laid off half the staff. That must be an old truck, 'cause they're no longer Echo Chemicals."

"What are they now, Riot?"

"Echidna Pharmaceuticals."

32

NICOLETTE

"I need to speak with Dr. Moore right away," I barked into the phone as Riot pulled up to the house. I was out the door before he even put it in park.

"I'm sorry he's not here tonight. I can take a message?"

"I need to know how far along one of the Echidna Pharmaceuticals drug trials is."

Irritatingly enough, the woman laughed. "Oh, honey, I'm just the night nurse, I don't know that information. I can leave a message with the doc—"

"Yes, please, tell him to call Nicolette Parker back. It's urgent."

"Is that Nicolette with one L or two—" I hung up. He'd never get the message, anyway.

I flipped my laptop open, my knee bouncing in anticipation. Riot entered the house behind me.

Remorse pricked at me for derailing our date but let's face it, Katie had already done that and our conversation was headed nowhere positive. Glass clinked around in the other room before Riot appeared in my doorway, two glasses of red wine in his hands. My computer stirred to life.

I smiled and pulled out the chair next to me. I opened a browser and searched for companies running drug trials for cancer treatments. It took a few clicks to find a list, but I clapped my hands together, spotting Echidna Pharmaceuticals on the list. But so were about sixty other companies. I knew better than to jump to conclusions but holy shit, I might be on to something here.

My fingers tapped furiously, searching for Echidna Pharmaceuticals' latest SEC filing. I put a request in for the full report. Within twenty-four hours I should have the basic details of their top shareholders in my email. I shut my laptop and sat back in my chair, satisfied, taking the glass of wine from Riot.

I looked over to find him watching me with a strange gleam in his eyes.

"Sorry, I disrupted our date." I grimaced, hoping he wasn't disappointed.

He smiled at me and wrapped a warm hand around the back of my neck. He leaned in close.

"Do you know how fucking sexy you are when you're excited?" He pulled his bottom lip in between his teeth and my face flushed with a crazy mix of embarrassment and desire.

I leaned in to meet his lips, the warm, dark taste of red wine still fresh. His tongue bathed my mouth in ownership. I pressed closer to him, setting my glass on the table before climbing into his lap, my knees on either side of his hips.

A long sigh escaped his throat, and I drank it in. His strong hands wrapped around my back and he pressed my body tighter against his. All the heat in my blood rushed to my center. I couldn't help but clench my thighs together to relieve the pressure but his body was between them and a soft, needy whimper slipped through my lips. He pushed his hips up into mine and I let my head fall backward.

Riot moved his mouth expertly down my neck and I shivered at the scratchy way his close-cut shave scraped against the most sensitive parts of my skin. I pushed my chest up closer to his chin and drank up the breathy exhale he let out when I ran my fingers through his hair.

I was about to start moving my hands down his chest when he pulled back. I groaned, giving him my best pout. He smiled, and it was a grin that touched his eyes.

"Stay with me tonight. In my room," he whispered. I bit my lip to keep from grinning like a fool, realizing I had never been in Riot's room. We'd been holing up in mine all week. I had often wondered what it looked like, what his bed felt like, but something told me his space was private to him.

Still, it was hard to ignore the echoes of our conversation from earlier. He saw the hesitation on my face, and he jumped into it before I could.

"Look, I know we don't have any resolution about what tomorrow looks like. I'm here for another four years and change and believe me, the thought of being stuck here without you is practically crippling because the truth is, these last few weeks have been the best of my goddamn life. I don't know what the tomorrows after you will look like but believe me when I tell you I'd follow you anywhere, Nicolette. And I know I can't. But I want you anyway. And if that's going to make all the tomorrows after you hurt even more when you leave then so be it. Because I can't live another second without your hands on me so, please, at least for tonight, right now is all that matters. Please, stay with me. Tonight."

My chest warmed. I knew that he wasn't just asking me for tonight. I didn't know how to answer about tomorrow or the endless tomorrows after that one but I also knew I couldn't live another minute without *his* hands on *me*.

I drank in his scent and his masculine shape and relished the hot heat that rose between us. I pressed my lips, thick and wanting, against his to give him my answer.

I expected to find Riot's bedroom messy, like a typical boy's room. But I was saddened to walk in and find it almost bare. It had light-gray walls with almost no personal effects. The only thing I spotted was a series of photos wedged all around the border of the mirror that sat on top of his dresser.

They were all of his parents. Family photos, couple photos, individual photos. It was the first time I realized there had been none around the house.

"I didn't know how Brennan would react if I hung her photos up around the house. So, I kept them to myself in here," Riot said, reading my mind. My heart ached for him. His fingers ran over the pho-tographs.

"She's beautiful," I said.

It was wild how different she looked in the younger photos with her husband and the boys. Beyond looking young, she looked *happy*. Care-free. Her brown hair was loose, blowing in the wind. She smiled care-lessly, holding Riot's hands.

There was a noticeable shift in her appearance when the boys were older. There was little color to her cheeks. Her hair was flat and her clothes were buttoned tightly to her neck. Her smile nev-er touched her eyes.

"She wasn't a bad person. She wasn't a bad mother. Not to me at least." Riot's chest heaved slowly. "From the beginning, she just didn't know how to be a parent to someone like Brennan. When Dad died, it was like all of a sudden she woke up in someone else's life."

I thought about what it must have been like, to kiss your husband goodbye for work in the morning and never see him again. To come home to two young boys and have to manage the entire family by your-self. My heart ached for the young couple in a Polaroid, taken on their wedding day.

When I looked over at him, Riot's eyes were filled with sadness.

"It's okay to miss her, you know." I took a step closer. He exhaled a breath through a doubtful smile.

"I know. It just feels like I'm betraying my brother somehow by wish-ing she were still here." My hand roamed the massive expanse of his back. "I've been angry for so long and have had nowhere to put it. Angry at him for taking her away. Angry at her for sending him to that camp. Angry at myself for not being around to take better care of them." He put down the photo and turned to face me. "When you're around, I forget about that anger. You make it feel like it's not such a hurdle after all. Like I can finally put down the anger and move on."

His words fell over me, making the bridge of my nose sting.

"Whatever happens, Nicolette. Thank you for giving me that."

It was the middle of the night when I woke up. My body was still thoroughly spent and my limbs were limp from the peaceful blanket of bliss Riot and I had created. But I'd had another dream about Grace. She was in the backyard this time, standing still, unmoving until I approached closer. Once again she started spinning as if she were a ballerina standing on one of those music box platforms. She sped up until the surrounding air created a vortex and I was sucked in.

My eyes popped open, and I needed water. I gazed over to ensure Riot was still asleep. I padded out of his room into the kitchen where I downed two glasses, trying to wash away the minor wine headache.

On my way back, I slipped into my room and opened my computer, pulling the crime scene report back up that I had been looking at before Riot invited me to the drive-in movie.

Victim was found lying on her back between the dining area and kitchen. Victim's body was face up with three distinct puncture wounds in the abdomen.

There was an outline of a body with three Xs, which indicated where the stab wounds were found.

Mobile device was found shattered in the corner of the dining room.

I paused, recalling Riot's words.

She was face down in the kitchen...

Her phone...was on the kitchen counter.

Could it be possible that Riot misremembered? It didn't seem right. I'd interviewed enough trauma victims to know that they often recalled the tiniest details correctly.

The police report was short, written by Godot's best and brightest, which wasn't saying much. But it contradicted what Riot said. Even for a cut-rate, backwoods West Virginia police force, it was unlikely that anyone with two eyes and a semi-functional brain could get simple details like that wrong.

I found the name of the reporting officer.

Officer Emery Plainbottom.

Plainbottom.

Fuck, this town was small.

I did a quick White Pages search and found he was Arthur's brother, which made him Katie's uncle. I also uncovered his last known address, which, of course, was still in Godot. He was in the Valley, though, which I found interesting. I had assumed that the Plainbottoms were a well-off family given how involved with the church they were. I needed to talk to Emery, and I needed to get my hands on the crime scene photos.

I snuck back into Riot's room where he slept, shirtless, draped in the soft white sheet. He looked young. Innocent. Vulnerable. A wave of guilt ran through me.

If I'm going to be asking questions, I should tell him why I came back to Godot.

I should tell him that I had been assigned to root out the very story he trusted with me earlier that week. And that I had also killed it (in my head, at least) weeks ago.

As I climbed into bed, I scanned his face, the moon casting a soft glow on his features, a peaceful warmth relaxing his brow. I hated the idea of him distrusting me, but the longer this went on the worse it would be if I didn't explain myself.

"One more day, Riot," I whispered inaudibly, snuggling next to him. "Just give me one more day."

33

NICOLETTE

The Farmer's Market was already packed with vendors by the time Riot and I arrived. He stood in the bed of his truck, pushing the artwork to the tailgate. I unloaded his new pieces onto a push cart, noticing how different they had been lately. More colorful, more hopeful.

When I arrived in Godot, his pieces were dark with sharp edges and almost all rusty, black steel. Now the animals had colored eyes, and he used mirrors and glass to cast sparkling rainbows against the walls.

Some of the vendors were already coming over to eye the work. These were going to go fast and I couldn't help but beam with pride watching him carry the last one in through the bay door. His black t-shirt clung to his chest and arms in all the right areas and I tried not to blush, remembering the devastatingly wonderful way he woke me up this morning. His fingers tracing my nipples and his lips trailing lower.

"Excuse me, are all of these from the same artist?" a woman interrupted my thoughts.

"They are," I nodded. Riot bent down to place the heaviest piece on the floor.

"Are you Riot Asher?" she asked with wide eyes.

I groaned. *Here we go.* I understood why Riot didn't want to man his own booth. To be subject to open scrutiny. I steeled myself for the tongue-lashing I was prepared to give this woman if she brought up his criminal record. But I was stunned when she stepped right up to him, extending her hand.

"I saw your piece at the Godot Field Days a few weeks back. Oh, my God, I'm so glad I got to meet you in person. My name is Avery Adams;

I own an art gallery in Charleston and I simply *must* talk to you about a showing."

Riot stood there, looking like an invalid who didn't speak English. Part of me realized he probably never had this reception before. His eyes flitted to me and I nodded encouragingly. He shook the woman's hand.

"Thank you, yes that was a good piece. I was... proud of it." His cheeks pinked and his eyes flitted to me quickly. It was adorable how he stumbled over his words.

Avery linked her elbow through his and began walking. "I'm thinking we could do a limited-time showcase later this summer..." As she passed by she gave me a not-so-subtle wink. "Well, he's sure marketable, isn't he?"

A splash of anxious possession hit me and my eyes narrowed at the old bat. But I stood down because this was the first time Riot got to interact with anyone but me about his artwork. I couldn't keep his talent to myself forever.

Look at me and my personal growth.

We were once again almost sold out before the market was over. Riot had just returned from his walk with Avery the Art Collector and he was teeming with nervous energy but trying to be cool about it.

"She said if it took off in Charleston, it could maybe be a traveling showcase. There's a tour going to Charlotte and Asheville later this fall."

I smiled and stood on my tiptoes to kiss his cheek and brush a loose lock of hair off his face. "That's awesome, Riot. You should be proud. I know I am." He smiled at the repeated words he'd written on my article weeks ago.

"I couldn't have done this without you, Nic. Seriously, thank you." He wrapped his arms around me and I wondered why I wasn't feeling more joy. Something in my heart tightened at the idea of Riot going on an art tour.

If it was how he made his living, he could get a limited exception to his probation. He'd done it before for a show on Hanniqua Island. So, why wasn't I more thrilled? Deep down I knew it was because if Riot's art career took off, I wasn't sure where that left me.

Where did I *want* to be? What was next? I shook the thought away. He pulled back and smiled down at me.

"What do you think about going to the diner and getting a giant stack of sticky French toast?" he asked. My heart floated at the hopeful expression on his face.

"I would love to but I have to make a quick visit to the Valley to follow up on that clinical trial study." It was only a partial lie but it sat in my gut like rotting fruit.

Riot pouted briefly before kissing me on the forehead. "Okay, see you at home?"

Home. There it was again. Said plainly like second nature.

I pressed my lips into a thin smile and nodded. He hesitated a moment, seeing the tightness in my face. I didn't want him to worry.

"Hey, what do you think about going back to the lake tonight? Maybe pack a tent and do a little mini-camp trip? See if Brennan wants to go?" I offered and Riot perked up, happily preoccupied with my distraction.

"That sounds like a great idea, I'll throw some stuff in the truck."

Before he turned to go, he pressed his lips wholeheartedly against mine one more time, inhaling softly, his dark lashes closed so I followed suit. I felt drunk, frozen in place when Riot pulled away, flashing me another grin before walking to his truck. I studied his firm figure, the way his hips and backside flexed as he walked. I stood there and the only way I could admittedly describe it was *swoon-worthy*.

I had to come clean with him. I just needed today.

Chelsea hadn't been kidding about the Valley going downhill. It was startling. I drove into the small community. Front lawns were so overgrown that you could hardly see the dorm-like townhouses that were built there. It was hard to believe that only a mile or two down the road sat beautiful, sprawling farmhouses and suburban colonials.

People sat on the front steps of their homes, gathered in groups of four or five every few houses. I saw a few kids running through a sprinkler that sat nestled in a foot of tall grass.

The homes were basic and kind of cute but even the ones that were well taken care of were overshadowed by their deteriorating neighbors.

Eventually, even the most beautiful flowers will get choked out by the thickness of overgrown weeds.

My knuckles rapped on Emery Plainbottom's door. Brief rustling subsided to silence.

A man who should be my father's age stood in front of me. Only he didn't look my father's age. He looked at least twenty years older. His speckled skin was thin and sagging as if melting off him. An oxygen tube ran under his nose and hooked behind his ears. He was hunched over at barely five foot five. Despite his decrepit appearance, he had bright brown eyes that were inquisitive despite the redness around his retinas.

"Hi, Emery Plainbottom? I'm Nicolette—"

"Parker, yes, I know. You went to school with Katie, right? Come on in."

He waved me in and retreated inside without even knowing why I was there. Sometimes southern hospitality had its perks. He gestured for me to sit on an old floral-print couch. A coffee table sat in the middle of the room scattered with prescription bottles and a tea kettle.

"What brings you to the Valley, my dear?" His wrists shook violently while he tried to pour hot water from the kettle. I reached out to grab it but he waved me off. "I gotta do it on my own. Keeps me sharp." He gave me a toothy grin, sitting in the oversized electric lounge chair.

"Well, it might be a sensitive topic and I want you to know that everything is off the record. This is purely human curiosity."

He nodded, rolling his eyes. "Dear, I'm too old for niceties. What can I do for you?"

Straight to the point then.

"Grace Asher," I said her name clearly and studied his reaction. A sincere sadness washed over him, his head bobbing up and down. "I'm hoping you could tell me about the crime scene. As much as you can remember at least."

He was surprised. "I'll never forget *that* day." He blew out a long breath before taking a sip of tea and leaning back into his chair. "I'm curious why you ask about her, though. That case has been closed for some years now. Time served and everything."

I chose my words carefully. "I've been renting out a room on the Asher property for the past few weeks. I guess I'm trying to better understand what happened that night. I'm having a hard time connecting such a brutal death with the two men I share a space with. They just don't seem the type."

Emery looked at me pointedly. "The first thing you should know is that *everyone* is capable of *anything* given the right circumstances."

I nodded like it was a profound thought but the truth was, I had learned that a long time ago.

"Of course. I read the police report and there were just a few things that seemed inconsistent with how R—" I paused, "um, how the *boys* remember it. Do you remember where you found Grace?"

"Oh yes, I might be full of cancer and drugs but the image of that poor woman will be burned in my brain until the good Lord calls me home." His grim expression held a hint of humor. "Which should be any day now."

I offered him a sympathetic smile.

"The way their house was laid out — the kitchen opened up into the family room. The dining room was off to the side here." He gestured with his hands, resting his head as if looking off into some distant memory. "She was lyin' on her back, halfway between the kitchen and dining room. Eyes still wide with fear." He shook his head despondently. "Couldn't imagine the terror, your own boy..." His tongue made a clicking noise, and I masked my indignant bristle.

"You're sure she was face up toward the dining room? The boys seem to remember everything happening in the living room and... *ending* in the kitchen."

"Oh, I'm sure. I'm not going to call myself a forensic specialist or nothin' but I'll never forget that look of terror on her face."

"I thought the house burned down. Her body was still... identifiable?"

"Oh, yes." Emery nodded assuredly. "The fire department arrived pretty quickly to extinguish it. Only the outside was burned beyond repair. Most of the inside was almost untouched."

My insides buzzed.

"The fire started from the outside?" I tried to mask the rising flurry inside.

He nodded with a sad frown. "That's how I know Riot didn't have a devil in him."

I quirked an eyebrow. "How do you mean?"

"Picture it... you've just stabbed your mother. If a person's soul is truly evil, you burn the body first, give it one last indignity. If you have remorse in you — you burn the house from the outside, because you can't stand to see what you did."

Only Riot didn't do anything. That fierce defensiveness gripped me. Over both of them. I'll never say what Brennan did was right, but he was out of his mind with fear and I found it understandable for a mind that brilliant to do what it thought it had to for self-preservation. I took a breath to dispel my thoughts.

"Do they know where the fire started?"

"I can't recall, but I think I've got a copy of the case records in the basement. I'm not supposed to share them but I don't reckon it'll do any harm now. You're welcome to take a peek." I nodded fervently. He clicked some buttons to move the chair to help him stand.

I followed him down the narrow stairs. A tick of anxious energy picked my heart up a beat, remembering how I was locked in the records room the last time I followed a man down into the basement. That reminded me.

"Did you know Grace before that?"

"Of course. Sweetheart, she was. Helped shape that church right up."

"Was she in a relationship with Geoffrey Brown?"

He paused on the bottom step and attempted to turn to me over his shoulder. "Hm, I don't see that being likely. I always thought Geoff was kind of a doofus." I hid my smirk.

"Riot said he was hanging around a lot that summer before she died. Said they got into an argument. Something about stealing money?"

Now Emery turned to give me his full attention. He studied my features almost as if he were looking at the ghost of Grace Asher herself. The little color that was left in his face drained and he gazed down, to the side, remembering something.

"You know, she called me a few days before she died. Said she wanted to talk to me about something she thought she uncovered. I never got the chance to call her back." His eyes turned down. "Poor woman. Your own boy..." He shook his head and continued deeper into the basement.

Emery fumbled with a string that made a free-swinging lightbulb come to life. There were dozens of boxes all labeled with different years and names.

"Not exactly the most secure filing system, is it?" I muttered.

"There was a big movement a few years back to digitize most of it. They planned to shred and destroy the original copies. I snagged a few of the cases. Felt like an insult to the dead to just burn all their stories, even if they were backed up in some kinda rain cloud or harsh drive."

He raised his arms to a box labeled "Asher, Grace" but bent over in a coughing fit. It sounded like chunks of his lungs were dislodging in his throat.

"'Scuse me," he said with a hand to his mouth. "The drugs help with the inflammation, but the dust still kills me."

I hurried to grab the box down before he attempted it again. An eager excitement sent a tingle over my skin. Inside were dozens of file folders. I flipped through until I found the fire marshal's report. I scanned the paper.

Origins of the fire began in the back of the house.

Signs of accelerant detected.

Extreme damage to the back porch's outer walls.

Riot thought one of his mother's candles had been knocked over. My heart began to pick up, realizing just how many inconsistencies there were.

The next file that caught my eye was the official autopsy report.

I pulled out the Xeroxed copy of the handwritten notes that were scribbled all over the official report page.

Reading the official cause of death, a cold chill crept up my body.

Asphyxiation

I spun to Emery and held up the paper. "This says Grace Asher died from asphyxiation." My tone was more accusing than I meant for it to be.

He nodded grimly. "Why do you think that boy only got voluntary manslaughter instead of murder one?"

"It was a crime of passion, murder requires premeditated intent."

"Sweetheart, he drove three hours home in the middle of the night. The prosecutors would have *painted* him with intent." I frowned, knowing he was right. "If the smoke inhalation hadn't killed her, the stab wounds probably would have."

"Probably?"

He shrugged. "Hard to tell with belly wounds. With immediate medical attention, it's not a death sentence but she was already gone before the responders got there and Riot was already claiming responsibility."

I frowned deeper. Did Riot know the official cause of death? A fresh wave of dread washed over me. I had to tell him about the assignment and I had to do it soon. The truth would be the only explanation for why I had spent so much time looking at the police reports. It was the right thing to do. And now I had information that might help put his mind at ease.

I dug through the box a little longer. A chill ran down my back when I spotted the knife, still wrapped in an evidence bag. Deep rust-colored splotches still speckled the instrument.

Something about it pulled at my heart. The last person to touch this was Riot, a terrified eighteen-year-old boy who just lost his mother and was facing the likelihood of losing his brother too.

Underneath it, I spotted another evidence bag containing an older model cell phone, cracked on all sides.

"Did they find anything on her phone?"

"It was busted, we couldn't even power it on and didn't have the resources or even see the need to send it to the state's tech department."

"You didn't see a need?" I asked, incredulous.

"Sweetheart, the case was open and shut." He watched me with a flat, albeit sad, frown. "Believe me, I was heartbroken like the rest of them. I watched Riot Asher grow up. Coached him *myself* in football during elementary school." Emery smiled fondly like he'd been some kind of mentor. "He was going to put this town on the map with those athletic talents of his. I didn't want it to be true. That he had it in him to kill his own mama. But he had the weapon. He admitted to it freely on every occasion. The boy was given the opportunity to plead not guilty. Heck, part of me was hoping he would so that he could stand trial. I don't think you'd find twelve people in this whole state who would have sent the pride of West Virginia football to prison. But he refused. Said he did it and that the remorse was crippling. He wanted to start paying for his crime. He didn't want to drag his family through any more of a media circus with some big investigation and court trial."

'Cause he didn't want to risk them finding out it was Brennan. Then Brennan would have stood trial, which most certainly would not go the same way Emery predicted Riot's would.

"Can I borrow this?" I held up the bagged cell phone.

"Oh, no, I'm not even supposed to be letting you go through this stuff."

"Please? I just want to find some old pictures of the family, share them with the boys, you know."

He shook his head. "Sorry, Miss Parker, I may be retired but chain of custody is still important."

I smiled and nodded. "Which of these other cases were memorable to you?" I asked, batting my eyes, feigning curiosity.

"Oh, let's see. There was one back in ninety-five, missing twin…"

When he spun around, I snapped a few pictures of the autopsy report, the fire report. I paused at the crime scene photos. I didn't get a good look at them but I could tell it was gruesome. I snapped pictures of them plus the autopsy photos while Emery dug through a box.

"Poor thing was lost in the woods for three days…" he went on.

"Wow," I said admirably, keeping my eyes on the back of his head. "The family must have been so relieved."

As Emery went on about how he brought the little girl home, I started to pack all the files back in the Grace Asher box, picking up the top and blocking any possible view of my hand swiping the bagged cell phone. I pulled the phone out of the bag and secured it in the back of my waistband. Closing the box, I stepped beside Emery and pushed the evidence box back into place.

"Well thank you, Mr. Plainbottom. This was a big help." I smiled sincerely.

34

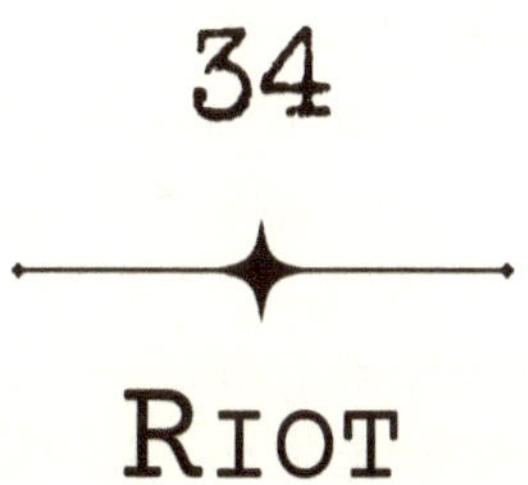

RIOT

I was brimming with excitement at the prospect of making some real money with the wind chimes and whirligigs. Reassurance and inspiration wove in my gut when Avery approached me, recognizing me not for the violent crime I'd been convicted of, but for the artwork I'd spent so many hours on.

I was eager to get home and start working on some new pieces but first I needed more materials. I had scavenged the dump and Benny's scrap yard pretty thoroughly. There was only one other spot in town I thought I might be able to scrounge up some new materials.

Hank Taylor was one tough son of a bitch as the Fire Commissioner when my dad worked for the department. At least that's how ten-year-old me remembered him, seeing him around town. He owned an antique junkyard now not too far from my house. I prepared to knock on his door when a voice from the corner of the porch startled me.

"What can I do for you, Riot?" Hank sat in the corner, a glass in his hand resting on the arm. His gray hair was still thick and cut tight.

"Sir," I nodded, regarding him, pushing my hands in my pockets. "I was hoping I might buy some of the antiques you got here. For a… project I'm working on."

Hank's face remained impassive. His narrow eyes held me for a long beat, the only sound the slight creaking of his chair against the wood porch.

"Don't see why not. Come see me after you pull what you need."

I didn't wait for him to change his mind.

It didn't take me long to pick some pieces I thought I could use. I was idly aware of Hank's eyes on me from the porch. I wondered what he was thinking but to be honest, I'd always been a little afraid of him.

When I re-approached Hank, I pulled cash out of my wallet from the market sales earlier that morning.

He held his hand up, dismissing me.

"No point in paying for garbage, son. Sit a spell. Let's catch up."

My stomach dropped and I could feel the anxious restlessness start to hit me. But you did what Hank Taylor told you to do.

He picked an empty glass off the end table next to him and pulled a bottle of light pink wine from underneath it where it had been sitting in a bucket of ice. He extended me the glass.

"Rosé?" he offered.

It might've came off as rude, but I paused for a long moment, staring at the glass. Out of all the alcohol Hank Taylor could have been drinking, rosé was not on the shortlist I would have predicted.

"Rosé," I stated. I tried to mask the surprise, but he caught it.

"I'm too old to pretend to like the brown stuff." He waved dismissively and lifted his glass. "It's delicious and I enjoy it." He punctuated the end of his sentence and it was the end of the discussion.

I brought the sweating glass to my lips and let it slide down my throat. *Touché, Hank.* It was delicious.

"You know it was your mother who first brought me a bottle of this." His words drained the color from my face and I swallowed hard, waiting for his follow-up. But it didn't come.

I nodded. "She wasn't much of a drinker," I said with a nervous laugh. "Probably didn't even know what she was buying."

Hank smirked, and it put me at ease a little.

"You know, she'd spend hours at that church, praying for that brother of yours." His head shook slightly and my breath grew shallow. My heart picked up. But if he was looking for answers from me, he didn't give it away because he just kept going. "I used to tell her, 'You wanna point that boy in the right direction, you go be a good mama *and* daddy. Teach him to cook a meal, make him set the table, teach him how to wash the dishes properly. Hold eye contact while talking to adults. Keep him close but not too close, otherwise, he'll just get bent.' But who am I to give a widow that kind of advice? Our kids were grown when Sally passed." He continued to rock back and forth, watching the grasses blow in the light breeze. "But she always said God would answer her prayers one way or the other."

"She *was* a God-fearing woman," I sighed.

"Not always," Hank droned. My surprised eyebrow lifted in his direction. "She was always devout in her faith, no doubt. She loved that church. But before your father passed, she was just like anyone else. Church on Sunday and the holidays, volunteer here and there but after he died? That was when she dove head first."

Hank rocked back in the creaky wooden chair, a familiar expression on his face that I couldn't quite place.

"That kinda grief has a way of... gripping people. Makes 'em lose themselves in an endless pit of sadness. By the time they claw their way out, the world looks different. Something they can't recognize. Something they can't understand. So, they turn to the things they *do* understand. For some that's the bottle, for others the needle. For your mother it was God. At least the church's version of him, anyway."

I smiled, remembering the brief conversations my dad and I used to have about my mom's faith.

"You know my dad used to say that the church is some kind of social construct. People created it to apply tangible theory to something inexplicable. It's a physical place you can go. The Bible is something you can physically hold in your hands. Take all that away and all you have are a bunch of people blindly talking about magic."

Hank raised an amused eyebrow. "They burned women at the stake for less." He coughed out a surprising cackle and took a sip of his glass. "That daddy of yours was her balance. Without him..." His words drifted off and his eyes gleamed with a distant memory.

That was when I understood that familiar expression on his face. Guilt. Technically, my dad had died under his leadership.

"Dad respected the hell outta you." I rested my elbows on my knees, peering over to him. His eyes flashed to mine, albeit briefly. A moment passed between us and I saw his nearly imperceptible nod.

We sat there for another ten minutes, drinking our pink wine in silence, a distant air of understanding and forgiveness settling between us.

When I got home, I unloaded all the pieces Hank had let me take for free. I was covered in rust and grease and I wanted to be clean when Nicolette came home.

There was a strange sense of closure after I'd left Hank's property. I couldn't put my finger on it but this day felt like it almost belonged to someone else, in another life. A life I was leaving behind.

I stepped into the shower, contemplating the foreign feeling. Between waking up next to Nicolette in my bed (a complete first for me), to the art collector offering me a spot in her gallery, and then the bizarre exchange with Hank, something felt different.

It was as if life was starting and I wasn't scared. Quite the opposite. I was beginning to feel like my life was happening and a warmth bloomed in my chest when I thought about that life with Nicolette. She didn't want to stay here, and I still had a little over four more years to serve probation in Spokane County. There was a chance I could get permission to join the art tour but the exception to my probation for Hanniqua Island had been grueling and they warned me it wasn't likely to happen again. I had told Avery I probably couldn't be there in person but she waved me off, telling me agents represented artists on tour all the time.

I blew out a breath.

If I had to let Nicolette go, I would let her go. I wouldn't be the one to hold her back. And in four years, three months, and eighteen days I'd go search for her, if that's what it took.

Because I loved her.

A soft tingle started across my back and wrapped around my chest. I whispered the words, "I love her," to myself.

My lips curled into a smile. Even if she didn't feel the same, it was a wonderful feeling, to love someone. It was glorious and terrifying and uncertain but hopeful and inspiring.

As I let the water cascade down my face, the feeling grew in my chest until I thought I might burst if I didn't tell her. I imagined a number of ways I could do it. A date. Flowers. In bed. *In the shower*. My cock jumped at the thought, and I was once again reminded of how fiercely my body loved her too. It didn't matter how I told her. I just needed it to happen soon.

The scratchy sound of tires against gravel sent my heart bouncing into my throat. I grabbed a towel, hearing a car door slam shut. Jumping into gym shorts, I ran toward her room but was derailed by a knock at the front door.

A deep growl buried itself in my throat when I saw her Uncle Jacob standing on the other side. Draining the oil from his car wasn't enough. After the carnival, I made the mental connection of why Nicolette had jumped from the second story window to get away from her uncle. She'd found her video all over his computer. Disgust and vengeance swirled inside me. Nicolette and I would never have a future if I went back to prison, so that had been the only thing holding me back from beating the living day lights out of him over the last few weeks.

I paused at the door. He had a stupid, wide grin on his face. When I didn't return it, his smile faltered and became defensive before it landed on pompous.

"What can I help you with, Jacob?" I kept my voice neutral.

"Is my niece here?"

I pressed my lips into a thin line, unwilling to give him any information about Nicolette. He narrowed his eyes at me before taking a long look around me and then down the driveway. Her car wasn't here, so I wasn't giving much away.

"She's not here. Not sure what time she'll be back. Can I give her a message?"

Jacob sighed before handing me a small binder.

"This came in the mail for her. I wasn't expecting anything for her so I opened it. Please give her my apologies." There was that shit-eating grin again.

I took the binder from him without looking at it. I lifted my eyebrows, asking if there was anything else.

"Well, I'd better be going then," he said.

I nodded a strong confirmation.

He took a backward step down. Before I could close the door, he turned back and added, "You know, I think it's great you're finally telling your side of the story. I look forward to catching it on the television." He smiled patronizingly before disappearing to his car.

A chill went down my arms and I couldn't help but look down at the binder in my hands.

Reading the cover page, my blood went cold.

Athena Studios

Feature Episode Treatment

Beyond Bizarre: Season 3 Episode 2

The Riot Asher Story

A Golden Boy's Fall from Grace

Black spots appeared at the side of my vision and began to close in. I screamed at myself to move. To do something. I shook my head. It couldn't be what I thought it was. Nicolette swore she would never tell anyone.

When had this binder come for her?

I studied the torn envelope he'd handed to me underneath it. The post date was over three weeks ago. Before she'd even uncovered the truth about my mother's death.

I made every excuse for her in my head. I convinced myself, my breath growing shallow, that there had to be some kind of explanation.

She was under duress. The studio kidnapped her parents and threatened to kill them unless she came here to finish the story. Or maybe she'd been injected with a lethal poison. The only way they'd give her the antidote was to get me to talk.

But I knew that was ridiculous. And when I read the handwritten sticky note on the inside cover, my heart crumbled to a thousand pieces.

Nicolette - Here is the official treatment for the featured episode.

There are three possible narratives we can end with. You let me know what you think will make the most sense with Riot's version of events.

If anyone can crack him, it's you, Bloodhound!

Go get him! -Melody

I began to flip through the binder, the unfiltered truth slapping me in the face with each page turn.

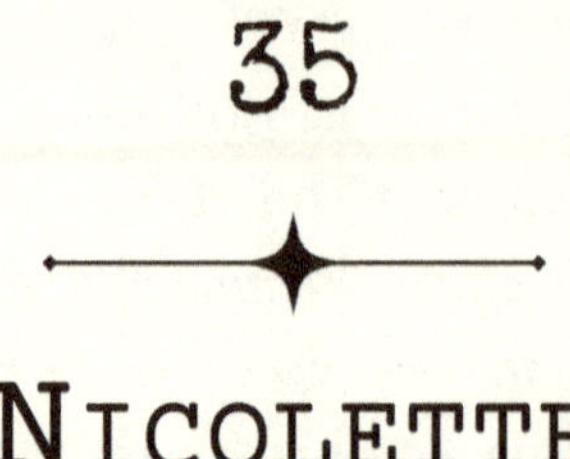

35

NICOLETTE

Back in my car, I drove a few streets up before pulling over to re-trieve the phone from my back. For grins, I hit the power button but the cracked screen remained black. I searched for the power port and another wave of excitement lit me up inside. It was a standard USB Micro-B port. I needed to get this phone plugged into my laptop. I already had recovery software, and I was hoping the memory on the phone wasn't destroyed.

I sped to the library, knowing I couldn't go through this stuff at Riot's house yet. I sent all the photos I'd taken to my email so I could go through them on a larger screen.

When I entered the library, my phone rang. I answered after see-ing that it was Dr. Moore.

"Dr. Moore, thank you for calling me back."

"What can I do for you, kiddo?" He sounded like he was in the car.

"The cancer drug trial that they're running at the hospital. It's with Echidna Pharmaceuticals, right?"

"Yes, I believe that's the one."

"How far along is it?"

"It's already in the FDA's hands for approval. I'm heading to a con-ference now where they're going to go over the results. I hear the latest trials were quite a success."

"And what happens if the drug gets passed?"

"Then it goes into mass production."

"And Echidna Pharmaceuticals' stock?"

He paused, taken back by my change in direction.

"Well, I would imagine that stock would become extremely valuable."

"And its shareholders?"

"Would stand to make a heck of a lot of money."

I gleamed with validation. "Dr. Moore, I think the success of the drug is a little premature."

"Oh?"

"The trial volunteers. The ones from Godot. There is a good possibility that they're still addicted to that Chimera drug I've been looking into."

"Well, everyone's drug tested at the beginning to make sure they're eligible for the study."

"With a urine sample?"

"I would assume so..." Doubt crept into his voice.

I shook my head as if he could see me. "The results are no good then, Dr. Moore. Your DEA consultant? He sent me a note saying that their investigation into Chimera was dropped because it was too hard to trace and track since it *doesn't show up* on standard urinalysis."

Dr. Moore was quiet. "Nicolette, if that's true, there are going to be a heck of a lot of angry people and very disappointed investors."

"Do me a favor. Keep this discreet. If you have to, only bring it up to someone you know you can trust."

He sighed. "Be careful, Nicolette. There are a lot of things that go into these trials. A lot of money and that means powerful people. Just be careful, okay?"

In the library, I opened my laptop and fished out the charger to my Kindle. I plugged it into my computer and opened the recovery program.

I was no Brennan, but I had picked up some basics. It was standard recovery software available to the everyday Joe Schmoe. Of course, most of it went to use by people who dropped their phones in the toilet or suspicious spouses checking into their partner's whereabouts. It wasn't so-phisticated by any means but anything could help.

While it ran in the background, I opened up my email to scan the photos I'd sent. First, I caught the shareholder report for Echidna Pharmaceuticals. I eagerly opened it up and started scanning the names. I knew that it wouldn't say *Redeemer's Church* but I was hoping I could recognize something.

Vanguard

Dodge & Cox

Fidelity International

Typhon Industries

I paused, a memory pulled at me. Jeremy's face popped into my head, shaking hot sauce onto his breakfast plate.

Something Industries? Titan? Triton, maybe?

I searched Typhon Industries and found very little information. There was only an old, outdated website that read *Typhon Industries - Property & Wealth Management.* It listed a PO Box in Charleston and a phone number. I copied and pasted the phone number into another tab and searched. A few mismatches came up before I scrolled down to discover it was a Baltimore area code.

The hair on my neck bristled.

"Gotchya," I whispered to myself.

I moved back to the recovery software. There wasn't much, but it was able to recover a few photos and voicemails.

A tender smile hit my lips when I heard Riot's younger voice, full of bright enthusiasm. The voicemail was choppy but still audible.

"Hi Mom, we've got our home opener this Friday if you and Bren want to come. I can reserve tickets for you in the friends and family suite. Just let me know by Thursday, okay? Love you!"

I pressed play on the second one which was from a day before she died.

"Grace, I need to talk to you," the familiar voice said in a rush. "I know you think you know what you're doing but please, we need to talk. Before you do *anything*. Please, just don't do anything *stupid*, Grace." The threat echoed underneath the tone so violently that I could hear it even through cutting in and out.

I saved the file in my email drafts.

I clicked through a few photos. Most were of the church services or events, and most were heavily pixelated. I scanned the dates and pulled up the ones from the week she died.

"Shit..." The photos were dark, almost black. There were splotches of light here and there. It wasn't the software. Wherever the photo was taken was just dark.

I frowned and ran the program again before pulling up my email to go through the photos of the documents.

The crime scene was grizzly but Emery Plainbottom had been right. Grace's body was lying on her back in the doorway between the kitchen and the dining room. There were blood smears on the door jamb and more photos of the trails like Riot had described from the family room to the kitchen. He'd been right about those. If she was still alive after Riot left the house, it was possible she dragged herself into that final position.

But something bothered me about all the blood spatter around her. I could see a chair knocked over in the dining room and her phone in the corner, already smashed.

I clicked on the next file. It was a close-up of Grace Asher's head and shoulders on the medical examiner's table. She looked cold and my heart ached for Riot and Brennan. She might have gone a little crazy, but she was still their mother. A sense of intrusion plagued me to be examining her like this but my journalistic instincts wouldn't let me stop now.

I almost clicked off when something else in the photo caught my eye. I zoomed in and my blood ran cold.

"Holy, shit..." I hit the print button.

Slamming my laptop shut, I scooped everything in my arms up and ran to my car.

I had to get home to Riot.

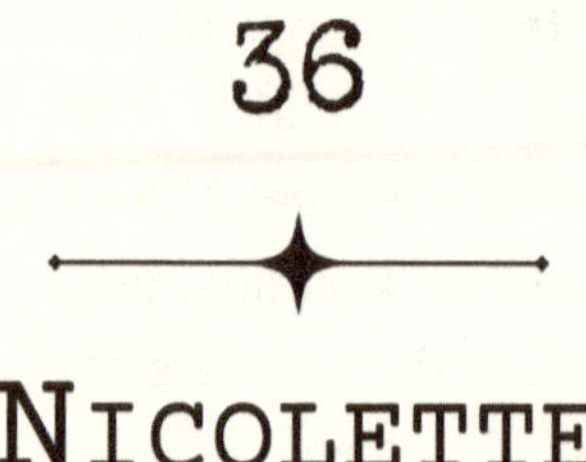

36

NICOLETTE

"Riot?" I called. Sweeping the double-wide, I scanned the kitchen and living room but they were empty. "Riot!" I peered into his bedroom but it, too, was empty.

A light ruffle caught my attention, and I spun to cross the length of the house to the sitting room at the opposite end.

Riot's head was bowed, flipping through pages of a small binder.

"Riot?" My voice was weaker and something hit my stomach hard when he didn't look up at me but I ignored it, too eager to care what he was looking at. "Riot, I have to tell you something I found today—"

"You know, I found something interesting too." Cold eyes gazed up at me. "Your uncle dropped this off earlier today. He opened a package he didn't realize was addressed to you."

"That can wait." I tried to reign in my impatience but I was about to burst. "There's something I should tell you f—" I froze in place. My uncle dropped off a package addressed to me? My throat tightened, remembering the only thing that I had anticipated getting in the mail at his house.

No, no, no...

Riot closed the binder and threw it on the table in front of me.

My heart stopped when I saw the cover page.

"Riot, no, this isn't what you think..."

"No? Because what I think is that this is some kind of outline for an episode of that garbage documentary series. But it isn't finished. It's missing an ending. And what I think—" he rose to his feet and crossed the space between us, "is that *you* are here to try to help them finish it."

When I didn't acknowledge the binder, he picked it up and shoved it to my chest. I stumbled backward. The adrenaline of what I'd found about Grace was still coursing through me. But a whole new rush of adrenaline was fighting for my attention.

His distrusting eyes were cold, assessing me and it broke my heart.

"Riot, I never wrote the story."

Riot's angry expression faded to sadness and disappointment and my insides continued to unravel.

"So, it's true. This is why you came back." There was so much despair in his voice. He'd been hoping he was wrong. He had been hoping there was some kind of explanation.

"Yes, initially," the words rushed from my lips, "but I never wrote the story, I decided very early on that I wasn't going to. That's why I've been poking around all this Chimera stuff with the church. I was looking for a bigger story and, Riot, I think I have it. Your mother. I went back over her autopsy report."

"You *what*?" His words were laced with such heat it sent shivers down my spine.

"Riot, it's good. It could exonerate you."

His mouth dropped open, and he stumbled backward, sitting back down on the couch and raking his fingers through his hair.

"You're unbelievable," he whispered to himself. "I can't believe I trusted you." He kept shaking his head. I went to sit down next to him but he shot to his feet and backed away.

The hurt on his face cut through me. I just had to make him understand. I began to explain, but he cut me off.

"Ten years, Nicolette... Ten fucking years!" I jumped. His voice seemed to rattle the whole house. "I gave up ten goddamn years of my life to protect the only family I had left. And you're willing to throw that all aside for a fucking story!" He began to stalk close to me and I instinctively backed up.

"Riot, it's not like that. Calm down and let me explain."

"So you can spin me more lies about why you're here, pretending to care about me?" his voice choked, and I moved toward him but he put a hand up.

"I'm not pretending, Riot! None of that has been a lie." Panicked tears stung my eyes. Everything in my head was swirling, whooshing, making it hard to think straight. I tried taking a breath but my throat was too tight to swallow air.

Riot kept shaking his head, repeating how dumb he was to trust me, how he knew he would regret helping me and my heart splintered with the fear of loss. The idea of Riot walking away struck a panic in my soul and a hollowness was carving itself out of my heart. I had to stop him. I had to make him understand. He had to know the truth.

"Riot, please, I love you!"

We both froze. My heart inflated at the surprise passing over Riot's features. But it fell back into betrayal just as quickly.

He took a calculated step toward me. "No, you don't." His words dripped venom. "You've never loved anything besides yourself and your career. Well congratulations, Nicolette, you have the ending of a lifetime. Don't mind us while my brother goes to prison, effectively causing me to waste an entire third of my life! What difference is a third from a half because they're definitely throwing me back in for goddamn perjury!" His voice roared at me and I flinched.

His face was impossibly close and I could see the vein in his neck and temple throbbing. I tried blinking away hot tears.

"That's not going to happen, Riot, you need to see what I found. There were inconsistencies with the police report and what you told me—"

But loud, heavy knocks landed on the front door, interrupting me and calling our attention away.

Riot exhaled through his nostrils and stalked toward the front door. I tried to take a breath, recalling the breathing exercises I had been taught in case I found myself in compromising positions. But this was different from being held at gunpoint by some Middle Eastern militia. Somehow, this was worse. Because I knew in my heart, it was all my fault.

Riot pulled open the door. Hearing voices, I padded over to find two sharply dressed adults, a man and a woman, standing shoulder to shoulder in Riot's doorway. They were tucking away what I assumed to be badges and anxiety spurned inside my stomach.

"We need to speak with Brennan Asher," the man stated.

"What's this regarding?" Riot was struggling to keep his voice even.

"We need to speak with him directly," the woman affirmed.

"I don't know if he's in. If you leave a card, I can have him call you," Riot nodded like it was the end of a discussion when choppy static mumbled from a distant radio.

The woman smiled, pleased. "Sounds like he's in and already on his way to my colleague's car."

On cue, additional footsteps pulled Riot's attention to the right and his face paled.

"Don't say a word, Brennan! I'll call a lawyer. Don't say anything!" Riot shouted.

With my heart in my throat, I ran to the window just in time to get a glimpse of Brennan ducking into the backseat of a black sedan. *No, no no...* None of this made sense.

I burst through the entryway to where they were all standing.

"Stop, you have the wrong guy!"

"Who's this?" The woman flinched, and I saw her hand move to her belt. They were too well-dressed to be regular police officers but seemed too young to be detectives.

"Nicolette Parker and I have evidence you need—"

"Stop it!" Riot pleaded. His voice split me open.

"Riot, it's going to be okay. You have to trust me."

He laughed and turned his gaze to the ceiling. "You've got to be kidding me."

"Why don't we take the conversation back to our satellite office where there won't be as many distractions?" The man smirked humorlessly.

"Are we under arrest?" I asked indignantly.

The woman's smile faltered, almost irritated. "No, but we have questions. For the both of you actually, thank you for making this a one-stop pick up."

I'd dealt with law enforcement in my career plenty. I had to be careful not to underestimate these two. Usually, the rule was the greener the cop, the dumber they were. But the older ones never listened to any theories other than what proved to be the easiest close. The young ones still fancied pretending they were in a cop show and would be the next one to "blow the case open". If I went with them, maybe I could convince them to look into what I'd discovered.

"I'll go," I said, grabbing my bag off the counter. Riot's incredulous eyes followed me.

"Then I'm going too. You should know *this* one is a chronic, pathological liar."

37

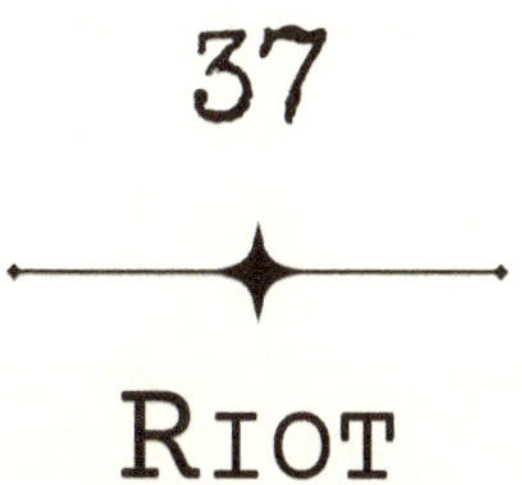

RIOT

Hurt, pain, disappointment, devastation, anger, heartbreak. I couldn't think of a single word that encompassed the utter hollowness I was feeling. I liked the anger. It felt good. It felt hot. I knew when I stopped being angry I would start to break so I held on to it for dear life. Betrayal wracked my body, leaving me hollow and shaking.

As we got into the backseat, the questions flooded my brain. *How could she?* Had it all been a game? Had it all been for the story? Was I just another plot angle? I knew her professional career was in the toilet but did she have it in her to use me like that for a *job?*

I stared out the backseat window, the distant but distinct memory of the last time I'd been in the back seat of a law enforcement vehicle flashed into my brain.

The lights, the sirens. The smoke coming from the house they extinguished. And then there was the panic. Not knowing what was going to happen to me. Or to my brother.

It felt different this time. These weren't Godot officers, and I wasn't in handcuffs. There wasn't even a partition between the back seat and the front.

When we parked outside the town courthouse, I searched for the other car that had taken my brother away but I didn't see it. Dread crept through me with its skeletal hand.

I could feel Nicolette's eyes on me, begging me to look at her but I couldn't. I knew I would see pleading mixed with wide-eyed fear and despite how viciously I told myself I hated her, her tear-stained face would melt me and I wanted to hold on to my anger.

I never wrote the story, I decided very early on that I wasn't going to.

Could that be true? I hated myself for the hope that bloomed in my chest.

I avoided her gaze as the two officers led us into a small study room in the courthouse.

"We'll be right back, make yourselves at home." I wanted to punch the condescending tone right out of his voice box.

When the door shut behind them we were alone and I braced myself for Nicolette to launch into more defense, but when I stole a glance over she was quiet, gazing around the room before her eyes landed on the door.

"Who did you tell?" I seethed through gritted teeth.

She spoke without looking at me. "I didn't tell anyone, Riot." The solemnness on her face almost made me believe her. "When you opened the door, and they showed you their badges, what did it say?"

I didn't like the tightness in her voice. "They said they were federal agents."

Her eyes whipped to me. I saw her chest rise and fall and despite myself I let my focus fall to her mouth before meeting her gaze, our eyes tangled with unspoken questions. She turned back around in her chair and scrunched up her eyebrows.

"What would federal agents want with us?" she whispered to herself.

"Sorry to keep you." The female agent re-entered the room with a folder, and two cell phones in her hand.

"What are we doing here?" I demanded.

The woman paused. She looked mid-forties, had a slight frame, and piercing green eyes that were innately trustworthy.

"I'm Agent Billings. But you can call me Sam." She sat down and clasped her hands together across the table like we were ordering lunch.

"Where is my brother?" I demanded. Nicolette softened next to me like she was telling me to tread carefully.

"Brennan is being questioned by a colleague of mine," she stated. "At our office in Charleston."

Fear gripped my chest. Would he know to call a lawyer? My phone hadn't rung, so he hadn't called me yet, which meant maybe he wasn't under arrest. What the fuck was going on? I opened my mouth, but Sam placed one of the phones in the middle of the table and pressed play on an audio file.

She sat back and studied us.

I think I stopped breathing when my own voice cut through the speaker.

"'So, that's what he did. He went home… By the time I got there, he had already stabbed her three times. Brennan was practically co-matose. Clutching the knife and rocking back and forth on the front steps. He just kept repeating 'I think she's dead. I think she's dead.'"

I didn't move. I didn't speak. I didn't breathe.

She'd recorded us.

Any trace of hope that Nicolette wasn't a conniving liar evaporated into the stale air in the room. I didn't look at her. I wouldn't. But I could tell she was frozen solid in the chair next to me.

"Where did you get that?" she seethed. The anger in her voice surprised me. "I didn't record that. West Virginia is a one-party consent state and neither of us consented to being rec—"

Agent Billings held up her hand and frowned dismissively.

"We intercepted this audio file as it was being sent to local law enforcement." She studied us, her face impassive. "I need to know which of you sent it."

We both stared at her. I was speechless. Neither of us spoke.

Sam took a deep breath. "Okay… how about you tell me where you both were around twelve-thirty this afternoon?"

It took me a moment to search my memory earlier today. That binder. Nicolette's betrayal. It had cut my life in half and everything that came before seemed like it was wrapped in a dream.

"Uhm… I was picking up some scrap metal at Hank Taylor's junkyard."

The female agent studied me, scribbling the name down. Seemingly satisfied, her eyes moved to Nicolette, who sat quietly.

I stole a glance over and through the curtain of blonde hair, I could see the guilt mapped all over her face and the knot in my gut grew tighter.

"I was visiting Emery Plainbottom."

Her words punched me in the chest. Agent Billings didn't even blink. It appeared the name meant nothing to her.

It meant something to me, though. Emery Plainbottom had been my arresting officer.

Fucking hell, Nicolette, what did you do?

The agent studied us for another long minute before standing up. "Okay!" she exclaimed. "You are free to go. My partner will drive you back home."

"That's it?" Nicolette's voice registered surprise and relief. I don't know why that gave me a modicum of comfort.

"That's it. We'll be in touch if we have any more questions."

She disappeared.

We both let out a long breath simultaneously.

"Riot, I don't think—"

"Stop," I commanded. "I don't want to hear anything more you have to say."

The car ride back was silent. The wheels turning in Nicolette's mind were almost audible but I was glad she wasn't trying to speak anymore. If I heard one more lie fall from her lips, I would snap.

The rage that bubbled within me was boiling. The depth of her betrayal, staggering.

God, I hated her. I hated her for lying to me. I hated her for recording that whole goddamn conversation. I hated her for throwing away ten years of my life. And as my thoughts drifted to my brother, I hated her for taking away the last member of my family. But mostly, I hated her for making me fall in love with her while she did it. I hated her because throughout everything, she was still the one person I wanted to lean on right now.

When we got back to the house, my resolve began to crumble, my rage reaching a violent pressure point. As I darted for my room, she called out.

"Riot, I didn't send that audio. I never recorded that conversation! I have no idea how they have it!"

And the rage bubble burst.

"Why should I believe *anything* you say?" Her face was inches from me and I towered over her cowering frame. "You've been lying to me since the day you got here! And now my brother is facing criminal charges in Charleston because of *you!*"

"Those are federal agents, Riot. They can't possibly be interested in a small-town murder investigation. I understand how upset you must be—"

"Clearly, you don't because if you *did* understand how up-set I am, you'd be packing your bags before I cut the goddamn screen room off the goddamn house!" My voice echoed and the whole room might have been shaking.

"There is no reason for the FBI to look into a closed murder case."

"Then what could they possibly want with my brother, Nicolette?" I fumed. Her expression registered a thought.

"He helped me with the drone... maybe it has something—"

"Then it's *still* your fault! Somehow *you* are at the center of all of this either way! And now, thanks to you, they have audio evidence my brother *killed* someone!"

"Riot, I had no idea that existed."

"Why *does* it exist, Nicolette? How the fuck could you let that happen? I would have thought of all people, *you* would be more cautious about fucking recording devices!"

The wounded hurt on her face stoked my anger. Her eyes narrowed.

"What's that supposed to mean?"

"It means disaster follows you, Nicolette. It follows you everywhere! At some point, you're going to have to take a hard look and recognize that *you* seem to be the source of it."

I was wrongfully blaming *her* for that sex tape and even though I didn't believe that, I wanted to hurt her. I wanted to wound her beyond repair so that she would walk out of my life and leave me to try to put the pieces back together, yet again.

Nicolette looked as if she had been punched in the chest and I couldn't stand to see the despair on her face anymore.

"Get out. Now. Out of my house. Out of my town. Out of my life."

Without another word, I spun around and slammed my bedroom door shut so hard something clattered to the floor.

It tugged at the memory of our first kiss when I'd pushed her against the wall and a frame fell over. The memory added a whole new level of pain to my soul. I leaned against my closed door and let the events of the day flood back to me. They were so overwhelming I started to feel dizzy.

Collapsing on the bed, I raked my hands over my face. A sob choked in my throat. Angry, devastated tears rolled from my cheeks onto the pillow, where they mixed with the haunting scent of lilacs.

38

NICOLETTE

My body shook violently, making it remarkably more difficult to pack my things. The nausea overwhelmed me and I had to stop a few times because I was sure I'd get sick.

Just get out. Get out and get some air and try to straighten it all out.

As I threw the bag in my car, I took one last look at Riot's house and my heart split open, driving away.

I blew out a long exhale, catching my breath before turning off the engine and letting my eyes land on the library.

The world had no sounds. The tears dried on my face, creating a mask, fixing my features in despondency, holding the pain there permanently.

I couldn't bring myself to think about Riot. About how much I already missed him. How I wish I could explain. So, I thought about anything and everything besides him. I banged my head on the headrest, screaming in frustration.

Here I was again. Sitting in my car in the library parking lot, the powerful sun sinking to the valley. Nowhere to go. No story to be told.

What had been the point of these past few weeks? I was back where I started and the humiliating realization that I didn't care about any of it hit me like a bus. I didn't care about the story, the research, the drugs, the trial, the investments. I didn't care that I had nothing to give Melody. That it likely meant the end of my whirlwind career. I didn't care about any of it.

None of it.

All of it came back to Riot.

I didn't understand how they could have that recording. As I flipped through the possibilities, my phone rang. My mother's face flashed across the screen. She'd be alarmed if I told her what was going on but I couldn't think of anything that would give me a shred of solace, if not my mother.

"Hi, Mom."

"What's wrong?" I had tried to make my voice sound even, but she knew me too well, and that somehow made me feel worse. A cracked sob escaped my throat. I rested my head on the steering wheel, too exhausted to hold it up anymore.

When I managed to get a hold of myself, I swallowed. "I hurt someone I really care about, Mom. And I don't think I'll ever be able to make it right. I just got so wrapped up in this case with the church and the drugs and the mines... I never stopped to be honest and now it's too late to make it right with him."

"Honey, I'm sorry. I *knew* something was wrong when I never got that video you promised."

Waves of realization hit me like a rainstorm. I had been taking a video to send to my mom the night Riot told me the truth. But I'd been interrupted when Brennan came in. Had I not paused the recording? I remember folding my laptop down but maybe I never closed it. *Fuck, it had recorded the whole goddamn night.*

I cringed, realizing that it *was* my fault that the recording existed. Everything in me deflated. The profound sea of sadness pulled me under, its weight pushing the air from my lungs.

"It's all my fault, Mom. And now the people I care about could be in a lot of trouble. And I'm not sure I have enough to stop it."

"Nicolette, is what you're doing dangerous?"

"I don't think so," I lied.

"Okay, you said you don't *think* you have enough. That means you have something?"

"I do," I offered weakly, pointing my gaze to the seat next to me where the printed photos and files sat.

"Well, honey. When it's too late to make it right *with* someone, the only thing you can do to bring closure to a broken heart is to do right *by* that someone."

I was quiet for a long moment.

"I loved him, Mom." The past tense forced a hot tear to roll down my cheek, falling into the corner of my lips where I could taste Riot's salty heartbreak.

"Then do right by him, Nicolette." My mom listened to me breathe for a minute before she perked up. "What on earth were you checking out with the mines?"

I shook my head like she could see it. "It was more about the company that manages them now. They're an investor in this drug trial."

"Bizarre that anyone still manages those mines."

My heart skipped a little. "Why is that?"

"Those mines were going dark twenty years ago when we first moved to Godot. There's definitely no coal left in them by now."

It was dark by the time I reached the other side of town where the Godot Valley Coal Mine was located. Whatever I was missing had to be in those mines.

The dark pictures on Grace's phone flashed before my eyes. I never thought in a million years that her death could somehow be connected to all this but after the autopsy photos and the voicemail, the pieces began to become clearer, like a magic eye image coming into focus.

The entrance to the Valley came into view. A thought pressed on my brain and I scanned the decrepit houses until I spotted a rusting bicycle on someone's front lawn.

I snatched it up, promising to buy the kid a new one once this was all over. It stuck out of my trunk but I wasn't far from the mine, now. I parked my car almost a mile away so that if anyone did pass by, it would look like I was visiting the Valley houses. I rode the bike the rest of the way there.

I passed by the locked-down airfield on the other side and a pang of guilt hit me.

It's still your fault, Nicolette! Somehow you are at the center of all of this either way!

Riot's voice, angry and hurt echoed in my brain, bouncing off the walls of my skull, making me dizzy.

Then do right by him, Nicolette.

The mines were gated, a chain-link fence with barbed wire issuing a fierce warning to intruders like me. I discarded the bike at the entrance.

I scoured the perimeter until I spotted a loose section where the fence separated from one of the poles. Holding my breath, I was able to shimmy through.

I crept across the field toward the towering, black entrance. Of course, it was chained off with a heavy lock.

Thank God I was a good listener, though. Back at the prom, I remembered Jeremy boasting about how he and a few buddies had snuck into the mine to smoke weed. They went through a small service entrance that was used for maintenance on the elevator. I scoured the opening until I spotted it. Prying it open with my desperate fingers, I took a breath. Stale air and peculiar smells wafted from below. The cage was at the bottom but there was a narrow ladder that I could reach on the inner wall.

I took a deep breath and stepped inside, feeling my pulse in my throat. I grabbed the rungs of the ladder and began to descend several stories into God knows what.

Prying open the elevator doors, it was almost pitch black. I could see equipment, coats, hazmat gear, and hard hats hanging to my right. I pulled out my phone to look for the light switch, praying beyond hope the electricity was on.

The light was low and red, almost like backup generator lights, but it was enough.

I turned to face the cavern in front of me. My eyes went wide.

"Holy shit..." I breathed out. I started to record a video. moving through the massive operation. I had no service, of course, but I attached the video file and more photos and documents to an email to Dr. Moore anyway, hoping it would send if I walked into a bar of service.

The vindication flooded through me and I struggled to keep a level head.

I could do right by Riot. And Brennan. And Grace. And this whole town. A tinge of disappointment clouded my victory. Part of me had hoped I was off track. But not now. Not after this.

My mind started to reel, spinning in so many directions that I didn't hear the chain on the main doors unlock until they swung open. I held my breath, pushing myself against the wall, my eyes darting around for escape routes.

Inching my way back to the elevator entrance, I warily peered up the shaft.

"Just couldn't leave well enough alone," the familiar face peered down, and rage boiled inside me.

"You..." I growled.

39

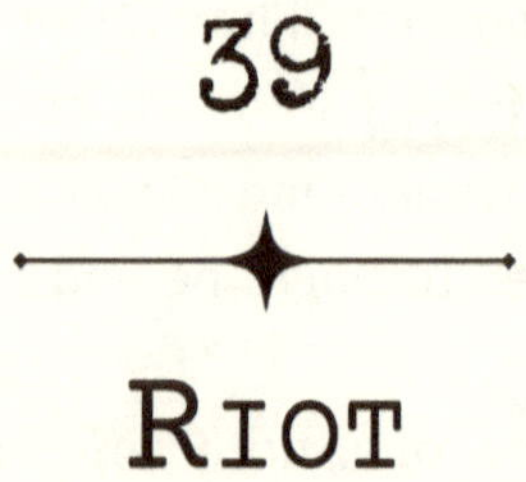

RIOT

I didn't sleep a wink that night. I tried to distract myself by searching all kinds of federal laws about false confessions but the more I searched, the deeper into a vortex I went. None of it was good. But Nicolette had made a valid point — why would a simple domestic manslaughter case interest the feds?

The thought of her name gripped my heart in a bitter ache. I would never understand how someone could hurt another person like this, let alone a person they claimed to *love*.

The despair clung to my hollow chest. I replayed her words, her expression, her body, all of it.

Riot, I love you!

The words had sent me flying. It was exactly what I had been hoping to hear less than an hour before. And now they were the worst words in the entire world.

Because they were either a lie or worse. They were the truth, and she was a person willing to betray someone she loved.

The next day was a frantic scramble of phone calls. I called my attorney, who was out of the office because it was Sunday. I couldn't find an FBI office in Charleston so I called the police department.

"We've got nobody named Brennan Asher anywhere in our custody."

"No, I know that. He was taken by two federal agents. They said they took him to an office in Charleston. Sam Billings and someone named Gibbons."

"We don't have any officers by those names, sir."

I wanted to scream. Break something. I hung up and found the generic number to the FBI but that was a black hole of pointlessness. When I *did* get through to a human being, it was a lot of "we can't give out that information" or "we're uncertain at this time".

No one I spoke to had any idea what I was talking about and I began to doubt that I was even awake.

Had I dreamed all of it? A wisp of hope drifted past my chest at the thought. This was all a bad dream. Brennan was home, holed up in his little adult tree house like usual. Nicolette was never assigned to do a story on me and she was here because she loved me and I loved her. My probation would get cut short, and we'd travel together. Her finding stories. Me selling art. Together forever.

But the chilling silence of the entire property snapped me back to life. And the overwhelming vacancy in my lanai bore a hole in me so big I thought I might fall into it forever.

That was the only *forever* allowed to me now.

It had been a full twenty-four hours since the agent took my brother away and I was starting to panic. Spinning like a top, I'd never felt so helpless.

As the day waned into night, I almost pulled a bottle of bourbon out so that I might get some sleep. But I needed to be sharp. In case they came back. In case he came home. The agonizing hope remained wrapped around my brain until sleep finally claimed me.

When Monday morning rolled around, I couldn't go to work. I called in sick and even though Rodger gave me attitude and said he'd have to report it to my parole officer, I didn't care. I was most likely going back to prison for perjury according to the internet.

My lawyer was still out of town and I begged the receptionist for anyone to talk to.

"Please. My brother... he's not well. He's not good... at talking to people. I told him I'd send a lawyer."

"Where is he being held?"

I closed my eyes. "I don't know. I need help to figure that out."

The line was quiet. "I'm really not sure what to tell you, Riot. Unless we get more information regarding his whereabouts, there's nothing we can do."

I slammed the receiver down and ripped the phone off the wall.

I woke up with the sun the next day. Called in sick again. Nothing seemed to matter. Not without my brother. Not without *her*. I laid in bed all day and waited for the sheets to swallow me whole. Her scent was beginning to fade along with the fire and the hope that had kept me going the last few days.

So, I gave in and laid down on the bed that was once hers, her scent stronger than ever. Where it once filled my heart, it now stung my eyes. I could lay here forever, wrapped in the only piece of Nicolette I'd ever have.

I couldn't let myself think about her anymore. I got out of her bed and stalked into the living room where I slammed the sliding door shut, locking it behind me and vowing not to go back in there until the captivating smell of her skin and hair had faded.

When night began to fall, I had promised myself that I would get some sleep tonight. I was losing my mind with exhaustion and I was starting to see dinosaur shadows everywhere I went.

I had just pulled a reserved bottle of bourbon from underneath the bar when my cell phone rang. Sluggishly I pulled it out of my pocket and my eyes opened a bit more when I saw it was the lawyer's office.

"Riot," Allan Catalano barked into the phone.

"Allan, thank you so much for calling back. Did anyone find Brennan or at least find out why he's being held?" I stopped breathing, holding my breath.

"Not sure about that, but I ran that name Agent Sam Billings by a couple of my contacts. I can't reckon what they want with your brother but that agent is assigned to a very specific division of cyber intelligence. Now, as far his release goes..."

But his words were lost when I saw headlights turn down my road. My heart lifted when the black sedan pulled into my driveway. Suddenly alert, I darted to the front door, slamming it open with a bang, idly aware I had dropped my cellphone.

Brennan emerged from the backseat, looking stricken but not terribly much more than usual. I moved faster than I thought my feet could go and my body slammed into his chest, wrapping my arms around his shoulders.

He didn't hug me back, just stiffened in the normal way Brennan did when people touched him. My heart flooded with relief.

I stepped back but kept my hands on his shoulders, afraid he might disappear if I broke contact with him.

"Are you alright? What happened?" I looked him over. "What did they do, Brennan? What did they say? Where have you been?"

Brennan leaned in. "Which question would you like me to answer first?"

A long sigh escaped my lips and at that moment his answers didn't matter. I pulled him into the house.

"Can I make you anything? Are you hungry? Did they feed you?"

Brennan blinked at me and repeated, "Which question would you like me to answer first?" It was one of those times his quirky mannerisms were frustrating. I took a deep breath, trying to remain patient.

"How about I heat some SpaghettiOs and you can start from the beginning?"

They kept Brennan in the dark, as they did to me and Nicolette when we were brought in. They kept him waiting even longer though, only questioning him once that Saturday evening and it was the same question they had asked us.

"They played the recording of you confessing the truth to Nicolette." Brennan blinked at me and my face flushed.

"Brennan, I'm so sorry about that. She was halfway there on her own and I thought I could trust her. I promised it was yours and mine only and I broke that promise and you have no idea how sorry—"

"They said they had traced its origins back to this property." I didn't think my heart could break into more pieces but now that I knew Nicolette had lied about that too, I was hollow all over again. "Then they asked if I was aware of who sent it."

"Yeah, they asked us the same thing." My eyes grew dark, the anger beginning to replace the sadness. "Of course, Nicolette lied and pretended to know nothing about it. I swear if I ever see her again—"

"It's unlikely she knew about the audio's existence."

My hand stopped stirring the pot in front of me. I turned to face him.

"How would you know that?"

"Because when I first accessed the file, it showed no signs of modification since its origin. I suppose she *could* have known about it but she'd have to have pretty extensive knowledge of metadata erasure and while I would not underestimate her—"

"What do you mean when *you first* accessed the file?" My voice climbed higher.

Brennan clasped his hands, and he looked down.

"What do you mean, Brennan!" The volume of my voice startled him and he stood up, taking a step back, his eyes darting all over the room, landing everywhere but on me.

"I overheard you two talking." His words were aimed at the ground. I turned the stove off and threw the spoon in the kitchen sink, a fresh wave of dread creeping up my throat. The sensation of falling made me grip the counter. "On Friday night. You said the last few weeks with her were the happiest you'd ever been." The feeling of falling came to a sudden halt and it was as if I had smashed through the plate glass door of the screen room. "You said having to be stuck here without her would be crippling." The shards of his words pierced my soul.

"Brennan, I didn't mean it like that. I wasn't referring to you—"

"You've done everything for me, Riot." His eyes still shifted around awkwardly but they hovered closer to my head. "I was supposed to be the big brother."

His lower lip quivered, and I was stunned. The last time I saw Brennan emotional, it was at our dad's burial. I was incarcerated for our mother's but I somehow doubted he managed to shed a tear.

"I thought if I sent that recording anonymously and they heard the truth, it might shed just enough doubt that you could at least be released from parole sooner." He twisted his gaze around, sheepish, before meeting my eyes with so much sentiment I think my heart might burst.

"*I* was supposed to be the one to take care of *you*. And I never did. I never could." He shook his head apologetically. "I never could handle being in the world where you lived. I wanted to. I should have tried harder. But those things don't come to me like they come to other people. You were always the strong one. The one people understood. The one who could make sense of the unkindness of the people around us. You knew what to say, always knew what to do.

"When I heard you talking to Nicolette on Friday about not being able to be with her because of the probation... because of *me*. Well, it was the first time I ever knew what to do. I just knew, Riot. I had to take care of you. For once, I had to be the big brother."

I tried to be angry. But as tears glistened in his eyes, I watched one spill down his cheek, and the only thing I felt in that moment was love.

It took us some time to let our moment pass. I was okay with the silence that ensued. We both slurped SpaghettiOs on the couch. When we were just about done, I regarded him, red sauce smeared on the corners of his lips.

"Alright, what happened the rest of the time you were there? Saturday you told them you were the one to send the file. What about the other three days?"

"Well, they were closed on Sunday, so I wandered around Charleston."

I frowned. "And you didn't think to call me? Brennan, I was losing my mind!"

He paused and blinked at me. "I tried calling the house. But it said it was disconnected." We both turned to where I'd ripped the landline off the wall.

Well, shit.

"I stayed in a motel next to the office building. On Monday, they were very interested in watching me demonstrate how I sent the audio file, which is peculiar because it wasn't all that sophisticated of encryption. I was sending it to the Godot Police Department, so I didn't bother masking my IP address. I erased the metadata from the audio so that—"

"Brennan." He paused mid-narrative. "This is all very interesting, but what did the FBI want?"

He frowned. "I cannot know for certain."

Ignoring the tick of irritation, I reminded myself how relieved I was to have him home. "What questions did they ask?"

"They asked about my work. They asked about you. About Nicolette. About Mom and Dad. About our childhood. My hobbies. Countries I've visited. My religious affiliation."

"And what did you say about Mom and Dad?"

"They asked if what you said on the tape was true. I told them it was. But the recording was taken illegally so it was inadmissible in court. I offered to give them the true recounting if they met my list of requirements."

A heavy weight settled in my chest.

Ten years.

I spent ten years. I hung my head between my shoulders and covered my eyes with my palms.

"I insisted that you not face any repercussions. That your probation be cut immediately and your record be entirely wiped clean." He grinned proudly.

"What did they say?"

He frowned, curiously. "They didn't seem too interested. I noted Agent Gibbons didn't even write any of it down." Brennan scrunched his face up but then shrugged like it was a joke he didn't get.

"Ughh!" I growled and leaped to my feet. I wanted to strangle him. "These are our lives here, Brennan! What happens next?"

His lips turned downward. "Sorry, brother. I don't know. They said they would be in touch with any more questions."

Solemn quiet settled over us. When I looked up, Brennan was shifting uncomfortably.

"Ahem, you can rest assured, though..." His eyes darted around the room like someone might be listening. "There is no record of the events that... *preceded* your confession." His face went red. I furrowed my brow. What—?

Oh shit.

"Right, yeah..." I dragged the word out.

"I didn't listen to it." Brennan's face twisted like hearing two people have sex was the most repulsive idea, ever. "And there are no copies. In theory, I may be able to scale the same protocol to erase the adult video of Nicolette from the web..."

He scooped the last bits of SpaghettiOs into his mouth before perking up, his eyes landing on the locked sliding door to the screen room.

"Where is Nicolette, anyway?" he asked, looking around and my stomach clenched at his hopeful tone.

A heaviness weighed my head down. "I kicked her out. She's probably halfway to L.A. or New York by now."

"Why would you kick her out? I was the one who sent the audio file."

"Yeah, I'm aware of that *now*, Brennan!" A heavy sigh inflated my chest. "It's more than that. She was only here to try to get me to participate in this stupid TV documentary. She was lying to us the whole time."

Brennan was quiet, and I saw something flicker behind his eyes.

"Did you know about it?" I asked suspiciously.

"I did see a few e-mail exchanges referencing the assignment."

In-fucking-credible. "So, I've been the only schmuck in the dark this whole time?" I let my head roll back to stare at the ceiling. "The two people I..." Brennan stood to regard me apologetically. I waved him off. "I need to lie down." I stalked to my bedroom door. But I paused before disappearing inside.

I said quietly to the floor, "I'm glad you're home."

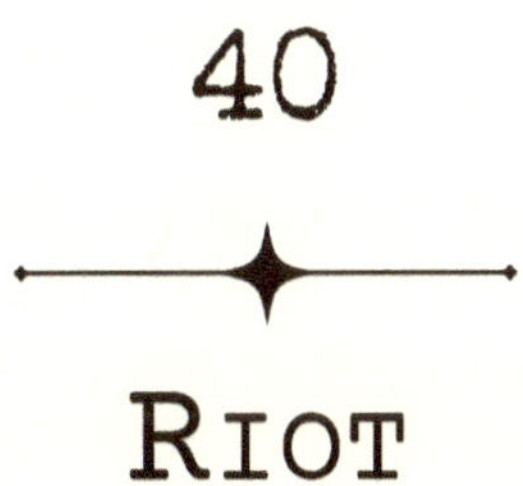

40

RIOT

When the next morning rolled around and I remembered that my brother was asleep, just a few yards away, like he was supposed to be, the feeling of hopelessness left my body.

With that gone, I was left with nothing but raw hurt. I was loath to think that I was settling into my new reality without her. But here I was, pulling on my stupid mechanic uniform to go to work like it was just another day. It was normal and so incredibly abnormal at the same time.

I was still pissed at Brennan for not telling me he knew Nicolette had ulterior motives. But the one thing he actually *could* confirm was that she really didn't know about the recording. She hadn't known it existed, and she hadn't been the one to release it. A wave of guilt crashed over me. All those terrible things I said to her.

Unable to stand it any longer, I sent her a text message.

I waited for the confirmation that it was delivered but it didn't come. *Not Delivered* under the message mocked me like a dancing monkey. What did that mean?

I could ignore it. Let Nicolette Parker slip into my past where so many other people remained. I should put it to rest. Delete her number and let her do whatever it was she wanted with her life. I should be the mature one and stand by my decision to ask her to leave...

Yeah, fuckin' right.

I pressed the call button immediately.

"Hello, you've reached Nicolette..." My heart pounded with fear and hope at the same time. Did that mean she blocked my number? Or was her phone off?

Damn, I was clueless with this shit. I needed to ask someone who understood what any of this meant and I didn't want to involve Brennan, even though he could probably pinpoint her location.

"You look like shit, bro," Evan greeted me warily when I walked into the auto shop. I nodded in his direction, taking my position in the bay beside him. The morning was uneventful until an old Cadillac was called in. My heart sparked with hope but it wasn't hers.

She's gone. You told her to leave town.

I remembered the way her beautiful skin was marred with a red flush and the way her eyes were swollen and how she cowered into her shoulders as if she was trying to disappear inside herself while I screamed at her.

I pulled my phone out.

"Hey, uh... Evan?" He looked up from underneath the Chevy he was working on. "If a message says 'Not Delivered' does that mean I'm blocked?"

An amused, mischievous grin curled around Evan's face. He stood up, wiping his hands on a rag.

"You're busted up about a girl."

I scowled. "I'm not. I'm just... Wondering— I've never used... I don't know what I am," I stammered.

His eyebrows rose in amusement and I scowled deeper. "Oh yeah, you're definitely busted up. Let me see." I handed him the torturous piece of technology.

He ran a hand over his chin. "Could mean you're blocked, could mean her phone is off."

I sighed in frustration, snatching the phone from him, I hit the call button.

"Whoa, dude, what are you doing?" Startled by his reaction, I hit the end button before it connected. "You can't just *call* her!"

"Why not?" I asked.

Evan stared at me blankly as if he didn't know the answer. "I dunno... you just can't. You gotta find a mutual friend, and have them ask her if she's mad at you or if she blocked you. Then wait for that person to get back to you and tell you whether you're blocked or not."

I stared at him, trying to make sense of his foreign social language. Is this what Brennan felt like all the time?

Without breaking eye contact with him, I hit the call button again and brought it to my ear. He shook his head like I were a lost cause.

"Hello, you've reached Nicolette..."

My heart deflated. "It goes right to voicemail," I whined.

Evan closed one eye, thinking. "Yeah, that means her phone is off."

"You're sure?"

He hesitated. "Pretty sure."

Frustrated, I went around the service area to the front desk where I picked up the regular goddamn telephone.

"Don't do it, man. Two calls from two numbers borders on stalker status!"

That didn't sound right. One of the guys in my cell block had been there for stalking and this didn't feel anything like the stories *he* told.

I carefully punched in her number, copying it from my phone.

"Hello, this is Nicolette Parker, I'm sorry I missed you..."

I hung up. "Right to voicemail," I shouted over to him.

"Phone is definitely off. That's good. If you didn't leave a voicemail, she won't know you called when she turns it back on. You won't look desperate."

"Evan!" Rodger called, throwing a set of keys to him. "PD got a report of an abandoned vehicle in the Valley. Need it towed to the impound out back."

"Righty-O, boss!" Evan jogged away, and I was left with the aching, unsettled feeling of unease. Did I *want* her to know I called? Why was her phone off? It was almost one o'clock in the afternoon.

The men's room stunk, but I needed to get a hold myself. I threw water on my face and hunched over the sink. I really did look like shit. The scar on my chin stared me in the face. It had made Nicolette smile. It had made Katie cringe.

Katie. I hadn't thought about her in weeks.

As if my mind conjured her, the front door chimed and her singsong voice trilled through the shop. I cursed under my breath, walking back out.

She regarded me with a smug, disapproving grin. After a moment, the pretense appeared to fall from her face and she looked genuinely sad.

"I'm sorry, Riot. But it's for the best. Nicolette was never going to stay here."

I narrowed my eyes. "What are you talking about?"

"Well, she left town, right? I mean that's the only reason she could have missed the Field Days recap meeting, right?"

"Sure... It couldn't have possibly been that you publicly humiliated her on stage."

I rolled my eyes at Katie's shock.

"I don't know how that clip got in there. Maybe when we assembled it was just part of the download, I don't know. But it doesn't matter. She's gone and we can get back to life as usual." But her voice was too high.

She sat down on the edge of my desk and smiled warmly at me. I blinked and averted my gaze.

"I forgive you, you know." Her words were patronizing and the urge to flip the desk was overwhelming. She put a hand on my cheek to make me look at her. "Everything is going to be okay, Riot." Her words and touch were so tender they almost made me soften. "I feel like

I haven't seen you in weeks! The Fourth of July Celebration is going to be incredible this year! Oh my gosh, and did you see that the elevator to the old mines collapsed this weekend? And did you hear we're finalists for the tourism grant? I think we can win it..."

But I tuned her out, her hand reminding me of the way Nicolette used to run a fingernail over the scar on my chin and then through my hair, down my back when I hovered above her.

Fuck.

Maybe Katie was right. Maybe getting back to normal, at least the normal before *her* would help me come to terms with the normal *after* her.

"Hey! How about I bring dinner over for you and Brennan tonight?"

I held her gaze for a beat too long, considering what it would be like to try and go back to that. No, the idea of trying to pretend like I could go back to before was ridiculous.

"Katie..." I started.

She looked at me with such wide, expecting eyes, it crushed the last bits of my shattered heart. "We can't go back to the way it was before. I'll never be able to thank you for how you helped me when I first got back." I saw the light in her eyes start to dim. "I mean it. I'm grateful for you now and always... But I feel like you might have some expectations that I'll never be able to meet." She deflated, and I'd never felt like more of a piece of shit. I could tell she was biting back tears.

"But... But Nicolette is gone, Riot. She left. She's not coming back and you're never going to see her again." Her words struck me in the chest. The assurance in her voice gave me pause.

"I know, Katie. And I'm sorry if I gave you the wrong impression here. I appreciate you more than you know but I'll never be able to pursue a romantic relationship with you. And I've gotten the impression that's what you might be looking for. You're an amazing woman and you deserve to be with someone who can love you as fiercely as you love them."

A red flush colored her cheeks as she looked around. Her jaw worked up and down like she was trying to figure out something to say and this whole exchange was painful.

"Riot..." she started. She looked around again as if the answers were somewhere hidden in the old auto garage. Finally, something resolute passed over her face. Her shoulders rolled back, and she plastered her best Katie Plainbottom Smile on her face. "I appreciate you being honest with me." For a second I thought she was going to stick out her hand for a handshake. But instead, she nodded once before turning on a heel and leaving the shop.

I expected tears, if not perhaps a little more pleading. But Katie swallowed my dismissal like it was a college rejection letter.

I blew out a breath once she was gone. I shook my head, thankful that was over.

Half an hour later, the nose of Evan's tow truck pulled in. I rose to help him when the front door swung open, almost shattering when it bounced off the backstop.

"The fuck did you do to her, Asher!" Jeremy Blackwell stormed through the entrance and raged toward me, the vein in his forehead popping. He didn't slow down, storming my desk. I stood, towering over him. A rush of blood and ten years in prison instantly put me on the defense.

"What are you talking about, Jeremy?" I sighed, narrowing my eyes.

"Don't play dumb with me, you piece of shit!" My blood rose. "What did you do to Nicolette?"

The sound of her name made me pause.

"What are you talking about?" I repeated with more intention this time. "She left town Jeremy. Three days ago," I added sullenly.

"On what, a bicycle? You know, if you're going to make a habit of murdering women in this town, you really should learn to do a better job of covering it up. Dumping her car in the Valley? Not exactly pro status."

What?

The window to the back impound lot snatched my attention. It parked and lowered the golden midsize sedan. I would recognize that old relic anywhere. An anxious alarm sent the hairs on my neck to atten-tion.

I pushed past Jeremy, ignoring his warnings for me to stay put and sprinted around back. I was idly aware of his presence be-hind me but nothing could stop me. My chest slammed into the driver's side door and I yanked it open.

My nostrils filled with her scent and it clouded my focus.

"Where did you find this?" I demanded, whipping around to face Evan.

He appeared unperturbed. "A few hundred feet down the road from the Valley entrance. The guy called it in after it had been sitting there since Sunday morning.

My blood went cold. "Sunday?" I tried to mask the rising panic in my voice but the fallout of last weekend suddenly didn't seem important.

"They never saw the driver?"

Evan shrugged helplessly. "I just picked it up, man."

I spun around and found myself face-to-face with Jeremy.

"You're going to pretend like you know nothing about this?" he seethed, almost appearing to care.

"I swear, Jeremy. We fought. Saturday night. I kicked her out, and that was the last time I saw her." I moved around to the passenger side and pulled the door open, sifting through papers on the seat there.

"You fought," he repeated matter-of-factly. "Saturday night. Which means you were probably the last person to see her."

I ignored him, my world coming to a shattering halt. I held up a pic-ture of my dead mother on an exam table. What the fuck had she been looking into? Her frantic words from Saturday came rushing back to me.

Your mother. I went back over her autopsy report.

She had been overwhelmed with the urge to tell me something but the blind rage of that binder made her words fall on deaf ears.

"Alright, Riot. I'm going to need you to come down to the station with me."

Irritation bubbled within me. "If she's been missing since Saturday night we don't have time for this, Jeremy." My words rushed out, scooping up the papers on her seat and running to my truck out front.

"Brennan," I barked into my phone. "I need you to find Nicolette. Track her phone. Anything you have to do."

"Okay," was all my brother replied before he hung up.

At least some people didn't waste time.

I pulled my car door open but Jeremy's tone halted me in my tracks.

"Don't move another inch, Asher." He had his gun drawn, and I reluctantly put my arms up. More irritated than afraid.

"Jeremy, there's no time for this."

"*I* tell *you* what we have time for. I'm taking you in for an official statement. This is a missing persons case now. You can either come willingly or I can put you under arrest for violating parole by refusing to cooperate."

Rage boiled through me but I lowered my arms and acquiesced.

As Jeremy slammed the rear door to his cop car, I couldn't help but dwell on the rapidly growing dread in my heart.

Jeremy radioed his colleagues that we were coming in and he was filing an official missing person report on Nicolette Parker. The words gripped my chest and disbelief marred my thoughts. Everything tangled in my brain at once.

I shot Brennan a message that I was being taken to the police station. I didn't ask him to call my lawyer. My message ended with three pleading words.

Please find her.

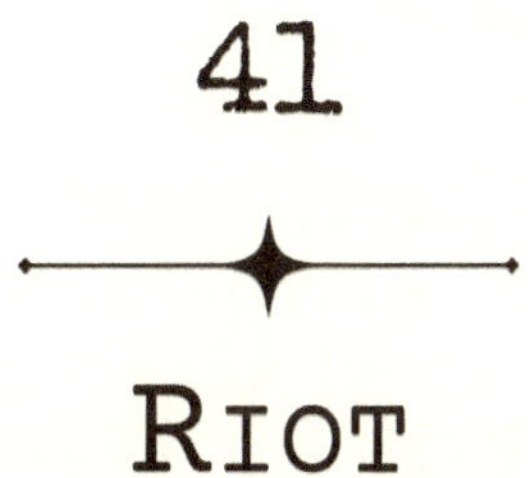

41

RIOT

There was no actual interrogation room in the Godot Police Department so I sat on a wooden chair across a desk from dipshit Blackwell in an empty office. While Jeremy kept me waiting for over an hour, my mind descended into madness with every second that ticked by.

"I don't know what else to tell you, Jeremy—"

"It's Deputy Blackwell, now, Riot." I refrained from rolling my eyes. "You look awful nervous." He leaned back in his chair accusingly. My legs bounced up and down wildly. I was running out of patience.

"We're wasting time, Jeremy. Nicolette was looking into some things, and I think she's in danger."

He smirked. "I have a whole crew sweeping the Valley houses right now."

I shook my head. "She's not in the Valley."

His eyes widened suspiciously. "And you know that how?"

"Because her car was parked *outside* the development. Nic isn't afraid of anything. Or anyone. If she was going to the Valley to talk to someone she would have parked right outside their goddamn house."

"You seem to think you know *Nic* really well."

I glowered deeper, letting his mocking tone linger in the air between us. Was he really going to let his jealousy get in the way of finding a missing person?

Not just any person.

My person.

A knock landed on the door and another officer poked his head in, gesturing for Jeremy to come out.

"Don't go anywhere," he smirked at me and I wanted to hit him. But then I'd be cuffed in a cell for sure.

I put my head down on the table, staring at my shoes, and pulled my phone out, desperate for a message from my brother but there was nothing. I hit my head against the desk twice.

"Psst."

Spinning around, a new wave of relief hit me. Brennan was at a window behind me.

I unlocked the window and slid it open, my heart eager for some kind of news.

"Let's go," Brennan tilted his head in the opposite direction.

"What? I can't leave now. They'll think I'm running because I'm guilty."

Brennan blinked at me. "I can't operate the tablet and drive at the same time. Now, if they had taken my recommendation under advisement to install a full operating system in the dashboard—"

"Brennan! What about a tablet?"

He grinned that spooky, vintage-dummy, grin. "I found her last location."

I heard the sirens before we were even out of the town center. *Fuck,* I was definitely going back to prison now. But I didn't care. Gunning the gas, Brennan tossed me a tablet that had some kind of map on it that I didn't recognize.

"What is this?"

"It's ground-penetrating radar that tracks the changes in thermal dynamics." I shook my head, not understanding. "It's a heat map, Riot."

The car swerved, and I clutched the door. "Say, Brennan, did you ever get your license?"

"Nope. But I've watched you." At that moment he jerked the steering wheel, and I almost went flying into the back of the cab.

"Why am I not driving?" I asked, trying to keep the panic out of my voice. We would never find Nicolette if we were dead in a car wreck.

"Because you need to jump out of the car when I tell you to and go find our friend."

I tilted my head back and forth, considering. "Okay, what am I looking at?" I asked, turning my attention to the tablet.

"It's the coal mine. Her last location was marked off a cell tower between the airfield and the Valley. She had asked me to help her look at the mines a few weeks ago. I figured she went to investigate it herself but I can't find any trace of an active mobile ID."

"What is this picture from?" I studied it. It had topography outlines, but it was mostly black with splotches of yellow and one circle of burnt orange. "A satellite?"

"It's a drone."

I paused and caught his gaze. He looked guilty. "I hacked into the airfield next door and launched one of the drones that identify thermal disparities." I frowned at him disapprovingly. "If I couldn't find her location with the mobile ID, then the only way to find out if she was in the mines was thermal detection, okay? So, don't yell at me."

I stared incredulously at him but I didn't have time to scold him. At that moment, I wanted to kiss him.

"And?" I prodded.

He tapped a finger on the burnt orange blob in the center of the screen.

"That's her? Does that mean she's in there? And alive?" The hope I heard in my voice was heartbreaking.

"It's *somebody*..." Brennan hesitated, slamming on the brakes and taking a left turn down the road that went to the Valley. He looked shifty, and I stared at him hard. "It registers a thermal signature, but... Riot, it's weak. Okay? We don't have a lot of time. Whoever it is... their body temperature? It's getting colder."

Utter panic gripped my heart.

"Shit... Katie." My eyes darted around, searching my memory. "She said the elevator entrance to the mine collapsed this weekend." My heart shattered into a million pieces. "Brennan, she's been down there for almost four days."

The sudden jolt of the car pulled me out of my brooding. A police car appeared in front of us and we careened down an embankment.

"Shit!" The sirens were blaring, the lights lit up against the fiery sunset behind them.

"Almost ready to jump?" Brennan shouted, nearly hysterical, a twisted smile on his face. "I'm going to get close to the woods. Roll out, and hopefully they'll just keep chasing me."

"Brennan—" I opened my mouth to protest.

"No time, Riot, we're close!"

"Brennan!" I shouted to make him look at me, my palm on the door handle.

For a moment, the sounds faded. Brennan offered me a weak smile.

"It's okay, Riot." He nodded in quiet understanding. "Time for me to be the big brother."

He smiled again, letting the silent moment breathe all on its own.

He unlocked the doors. "Now!"

The passenger side door scraped against the bushes. I cracked it open just enough to slide out.

My vision was a whirlwind of sticks and rocks and bushes and weeds. Sharp branches stuck into my ribs as I rolled to the ground. I lay there, holding my breath, watching the taillights grow more distant. Two police cruisers sped past me, gaining on my truck where I swore I heard a harrowed voice shout, "I'm a leaf on the wind!"

When I was sure they hadn't spotted me, I rolled out of the bushes and began to sprint in the direction of the mine entrance. I pictured that orange dot getting smaller and my legs pumped harder. The front gate was unlocked but covered in caution tape. No one was dumb enough to wander into an actively unstable mine that had collapsed.

No one except me.

That was when I spotted it. It looked like a miniature airplane. Sleek black. And it hovered several hundred feet above the minefield. It looked dangerous. Like it would drop bombs any second.

"What did you get into, Brennan?"

"Nicolette!" I screamed into the void that once was the elevator entrance. Now it was just a hole in the ground. The hoist house had fallen in on itself, but still, I searched for any equipment I could use to see in the utter, complete dark.

She was down there, getting colder, possibly buried by blown rock bed.

I grabbed the longest rope I could find and found the largest entrance down into the elevator shaft that remained.

My heart hammered in my chest.

"Nicolette!" I shouted repeatedly. But no voice returned my call, and I tried to ignore the tightening in my throat.

The entire elevator shaft was one giant hole plunging to what seemed like the center of the earth. The service ladder hung on the opposite wall, dangling by one rung. I prayed it held long enough to at least get me down there.

The metal whined to give way. I took hurried, tentative steps down. I cringed and looked around. Maybe I could fashion a harness out of the rope.

"Stop!" A distant voice shouted. More muted lights approached. No time.

I held my breath and tried to alleviate my weight when I could, but I could feel the ladder losing its hold. A dark shadow loomed above me. The drone moved, eerily to hover right above the entrance. Suddenly a spotlight shone down from it so bright I had to close my eyes.

Panic raced through me before I realized that it was helping me see down the blown elevator shaft. *Thank you, Brennan.*

The first level was only a few yards farther down. I hurried to descend the last few rungs, and I reached out to grab the elevator door frame but at that moment the ladder finally gave way. I leaped, slamming my gut hard into the floor of the first level. A burning sensation speared my abdomen, feeling a rib crack.

"*Ughfph!*" The air blew out of my lungs. More commotion stirred above me. I scrambled to my feet. The spotlight did nothing to illuminate the first level. I reached for where the light switch used to be but it was shot. She could be anywhere.

"Nicolette?" I yelled into the black void. Fuck, I couldn't see anything. "Nic!"

Just then a clang cut through the dark. It was soft, something like metal on metal but it definitely came from deeper inside the cavern.

"Nic!"

I listened, and it clanged again. I moved toward it but slammed my head into a fallen beam. I groaned but pressed forward, keeping my arms in front of me, shuffling my feet.

I called her name, again and again. The soft clang echoed a few more times before something clattered to the floor and it stopped.

"Nicolette, please. Please. Stay with me. Listen to my voice!" But the cavern grew smaller and smaller, the ceilings groaned and I was aware it could collapse further at any time. My feet shuffled faster until my toe tipped something soft.

In the darkness of the cavern, I knelt down to feel the soft skin, cool and damp. My heart flooded with so much relief I easily dropped to my knees. Her hands were outstretched, a small pipe in front of them. There was a beam tipped over her.

"Just hang on, Nic. Please, just hang on," I begged, running my hands along the wall, looking for anything to illuminate the impossible darkness. My hands met all kinds of equipment and I was distantly reminded of an old science lab. *What the hell was down here?*

My fingers found what felt like a grill lighter. That would do.

In the dim light of the flame, I could tell there were all kinds of industrial equipment.

I hurried back to Nicolette and a fresh wave of relief and worry hit me like a truck when I saw her blonde hair fanned out on the ground, her face covered in dirt. The beam that was over her wasn't pinning her down. I ran the tiny flame down the length of her body to make sure nothing was punctured before grabbing her hands and dragging her limp body from underneath the beams.

I was acutely aware of the searing pain in my ribs but nothing compared to the gaping wound in my chest knowing I'd cast her out and this is where she'd wound up.

More commotion had grown at the top of the mine entrance and it was the first time I was thankful that I was being hunted like a nine-point buck. I got as close to the edge of the mine shaft as I dared.

"Help!" I screamed. More shadows and lights beamed down. I sat down against the metal elevator door and pulled Nicolette into my arms, cradling her. My tears fell onto her face, leaving streaks of dirt and rusty blood on her skin.

I pressed two fingers to her neck for a pulse and screamed for help again when I couldn't find it. My hands were shaking so hard I cried out in frustration. I leaned my ear to her lips. Was that a breath I felt? Or was it the hope in my heart playing a cruel joke on me?

"Don't move!" A gruff voice from above. I shielded my eyes from what I now saw was a helicopter hovering overhead, beaming that glorious light onto us, illuminating Nicolette's beautifully damaged face.

I pulled her tighter to my chest, trying to warm the translucent skin that covered her lifeless form.

42

NICOLETTE

I was floating. No flying. In circles. Up and up. Higher and higher, the glaring white light stinging my eyes.

Fuck, I'm dead.

My throat tightened.

I was dead.

I died.

How the fuck had I let *that* happen?

My mind reeled back to my last moments...

I had hit send on all the various emails I had drafted initially just to hold them. But I had learned I always needed a failsafe, so I sent them all to Dr. Moore. I wanted to send them to Riot. But it felt weird, to send pictures of his dead mother to my ex-lover. The thought made my chest hitch.

He wasn't even an ex because we were never together, not really. We were cut short before we could begin.

"Just couldn't leave well enough alone," the familiar face peered down at me, and rage boiled inside me.

"You..." I growled. "Really!" My voice echoed up the elevator shaft. "The water guy?!" I shrieked. Geoffrey Brown's ugly, fat face stared down at me.

"Sorry, sweetheart, but nothing happens in my lab without me knowing about it. I have cameras on cameras filming other cameras. They come

in real handy. Especially when nosy little Nancy Drews trespass in the middle of the night."

I mustered all the confidence I could.

"Oh, you have no idea what kind of shit you're in. All of this is on its way to the press right now," I lied. He squinted at me but I could tell he was calling my bluff.

I had to double down, but I also had to keep him talking while I figured a way out of here. Because as confident as I was pretending to be, I was terrified. He had the upper hand. I discreetly pulled my phone out and tried calling 911 but it was too dark and I couldn't see if it was connecting.

"It was only a matter of time before someone at the pharmaceutical company figured out the study was pumped with ineligible candidates. The results are no good because they were all hooked on your little Chimera drug." I waved to the industrial meth/heroin lab behind me.

He nodded, smugly. "Yeah, I suppose it would have been. I'll have to call up my broker and tell him I have a... bad feeling about Echidna Pharmaceuticals. Seems like a good time to short the stock."

From behind my back, a faint "whoosh" confirmed the sent email. I had to work to conceal my smile. Whatever happened from here? At least someone else had what I had now. Someone else could do right by Riot if I never made it out of here.

The thought of that lit something primal in me and I wanted to get back to him. I had to get back to him.

"And what about Grace, huh? She went to lay flowers on her daddy's death site and saw this whole operation getting set up, didn't she? So, what — Elias Blackwell sent you as his dumb muscle to shut her up?"

The echo of Geoff's guffaw bounced down the shaft, slapping me in the face. "Yeah, right. That dumb hick couldn't add four quarters to make a dollar. I made him every dime he has and we're about to come into a whole lot more. FDA approval or not."

He disappeared and started rustling for something and I gauged how long it would take me to climb the ladder. Just as I was about to jump for it, he reappeared.

"I was sorry about Grace, I really was. I liked the woman. In another life..." He drifted off and the surprising thing was that I believed him. "But she threatened to blow the whole operation before it ever got started." Geoff tsked sadly.

He pulled something out from the box he brought into view.

"I gave her a chance. I tried to reason with her. Told her my vision. Tried to get her to see how much good she could do with the church when our investments came through but she had a hard head. A lot like you, I reckon. I had a soft spot for my Gracie." He looked up to the black night sky. "It blinded me. And I swore I wouldn't make the same mistake twice." I saw him fumble with something in his pocket. "Almost lucked out when that wacko boy of hers nearly took care of it for me. But naturally, that queer wasn't man enough to finish the job."

I growled, blood boiling at his vicious summary of my friend. He had seen Brennan's fight with his mother. And he let Riot go to jail for it. If I had air in my lungs I would have growled, I would have given him a tongue-lashing so fierce he wouldn't be able to sit down for months.

But I couldn't breathe because as he spoke I realized what he was fumbling around with.

"You see, I let my Grace go, hoping I could change her mind. But then she had to go and call up that Plainbottom cop..." He gazed down at me. His lighter flicked to life. "That's why I can't let you go, sweetheart. I'm sorry. I really am. But I'm too close to let some Nancy Drew call anything into question."

I watched, almost in slow motion. The fuse to the stick of dynamite sprung to life like a tiny, deadly little firework.

There wasn't time to think about anything. About my regrets, what I would miss. The things I wish I had done. The people I wish I never involved myself with. The places I had always wanted to go.

I let a certain peace wash over me. The lit stick floated down past my face and all I could feel was the warm palm of Riot's outstretched hand, as he offered it to me so many times. I pictured his handsome face, smiling in the driver's seat of his truck as we took turns turning up the music.

I closed my eyes and felt his lips on me, his scent overwhelming me. Eclipsing me. I heard his voice, whispering my name.

Riot Asher was the last thing I saw before the dynamite fell to the bottom of the elevator shaft and the world around me exploded, pitching me into an endless abyss of nothingness.

And now, fucking hell, I was dead.

The bright white lights of Heaven descended on me, piercing my eyeballs, goading me to open them to see the pearly white gates that would be my eternity.

Wait, did Heaven really smell like bleach?

And did I *honestly* think there was a Heaven? Especially one that would let *me* in?

The smell of bleach pricked the back of my sinuses and it woke up something in the back of my head, a throbbing ache that paralyzed me.

Being dead shouldn't hurt this much, should it?

One eye blinked open. The overwhelming ache of my body finally hit me.

As the bright room around me came into focus, Riot was the first thing I saw. He was pacing around at the foot of my bed, horrible concern fixed on his face.

Holy shit, I was alive. Not only was I alive but Riot was here. In the same room with me. Everything came rushing back to me. The treatment, our fight, the recording, him kicking me out. Was he still angry with me?

I tried parting my lips to speak, but I began to choke violently. Oh, God, I couldn't breathe.

I felt Riot's hands press against me but I was too focused on ripping out whatever was in my mouth.

"Hey, easy, Nic, easy." His words were comforting, but I still coughed and hacked until I saw the end of the tube that was down my throat come out of me. He shouted something to someone but the echo of the mine explosion still ricocheted off my brain.

I tried sitting up to catch my breath but the pain in my neck and spine was excruciating, so I attempted to roll to my side. Riot's warm hand ran across my back, drawing heartfelt circles. I grappled for his other hand. He gave it over willingly and I put it to my cheek, inhaling the smell of his skin. Silent tears rolled down my cheek into his palm. He rubbed my back and I clutched onto his hand for dear life.

When the doctors told me they had put me in a medically induced coma for the past few days, I freaked out.

Ignoring the searing pain, I sat up and started screaming something about Geoffrey Brown and the Chimera lab. It took two orderlies to restrain me while another doctor administered a sedative. I thought they were going to stick a needle in Riot's neck too, the way he tried to fight them off me.

Once that sedative wore off I was remarkably clearer.

When I peeled my eyes open, Riot was dutifully posted in the chair next to my bed. He perked up when our eyes connected.

"He blinked, Riot." My voice was dry and hoarse. I tried to swallow.

"Who did?" Riot's voice was strained, his gaze fixed fiercely on me.

"Pastor Blackwell. When I told him I knew he shorted the stock for the builders. He just... blinked. I thought he had a really good poker face." I blew a breath out. "He had no fuckin' idea what I was talking about." I scoffed and attempted to shake my head but a jolt of fire shot down my neck and I grimaced.

Riot leaped to his feet, concern mapped all over his face. He knelt at my bedside and slipped a hand over mine, weaving our fingers together.

I tried not to let hope bloom in my heart.

He didn't want me dead. But that didn't mean he forgave me for lying to him.

"The Center was kept funded so it could be a constant source of Chimera addicts for the drug trial to yield false-positive results. When it got passed, Typhon Industries stood to make millions. I don't think Elias knew anything about it. It was all Geoffrey Brown." The thoughts flooded back to me. "Riot… Brennan didn't kill your mom. At least, she didn't die from the wounds he inflicted on her. Geoff Brown was there that night."

Riot didn't look surprised.

"Your doctor friend there?"

"Dr. Moore?"

Riot nodded. "He stopped by the house yesterday looking for you. He told Brennan that he got all these weird emails from you. When you weren't answering your phone, the house was the only other place he could think to find you. I've been going through everything here the last few days but was only able to make sense of a few things." He gestured to a stack of papers and a laptop sitting on a chair across the room. "I also found the picture from her autopsy in your car. I saw the circle you drew over the ligature marks on her neck." He looked up and laughed humorlessly. "You know, I don't even think that I knew her official cause of death was asphyxiation? How good of a son am I?"

"You couldn't have known. Even the police assumed asphyxiation meant from smoke inhalation at a quick glance. They had a body, a confession, and the alleged murder weapon. No one bothered to dig deeper.

"Until you," he whispered. His blue eyes glistened with intensity, studying my face. He leaned toward me an inch. "Are my pupils dilating?"

The affection punched through my attempt to hold back hope. I crumbled, choking back a laugh-sob while his hand caressed my forehead.

"Riot, I'm so sorry I didn't tell you about the assignment…"

"Shh," he interrupted me, leaning over and placing a warm kiss on my temple. "It's okay, Nicolette. I'm sorry too. I should have listened to you.

I should have trusted you. I'm ashamed of the way I spoke to you. Can you ever forgive me?"

My chest hitched, my heart swelled, and I was so tired of crying but the happy tears were cathartic and I laughed and nodded. I held my arms out and Riot sank into them. God, he smelled better than I remembered. The muscles in his back were tense.

"Riot, where's Brennan?" I asked quietly.

Riot pulled back and shifted uncomfortably. "He was taken into custody by Godot PD," Riot nodded and my jaw dropped.

"Oh, no, Riot, I'm so sorry... Was it the audio file? Because we can prove he didn't do it now."

Riot smiled sadly. "First, we can't prove anything, Nic. Nothing nails Geoffrey Brown to my mother's death. Besides, it's a closed case. Either way, it won't help Brennan."

"What was he taken in for?"

"He went on a little joy ride, running from the cops." Riot's eyes went wide. "He was held for a day or two," Riot's head bobbed. "Until those federal agents swept in and took custody of him, cleaning out every record of his presence in Godot."

The air I sucked in burned my sore throat.

"What? No..."

He shook his head helplessly. "They've told me nothing. I have no idea where he is or when he might be back. *If* he'll be back." Riot plopped down on the chair, defeated. "But he told me he'd be okay. And that I should trust him. It was the last thing he said to me when I went to see him at the police department." Riot shrugged, and it sent my mind spinning.

"Well, I have to get out of here. We have to turn all this over before Geoffrey Brown gets wind of it..." He held a hand up to stop me.

"*We* aren't going anywhere. Jeremy Blackwell already has everything that was in your car. Plus, you need to rest. They said if your scans are clearer tomorrow, I can bring you home Monday." He gazed down and shuffled his feet shyly. "That is... if you *want* to come home... with me?"

My chest blossomed with the flush on his cheeks. I grabbed his hand and his eyes met mine.

"Riot, I can't think of anything that I would like to do more than come home with you."

43

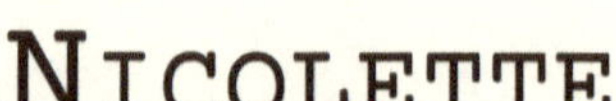

NICOLETTE

My body still ached something fierce when Riot pulled up his rental car to the house. His truck was going to be in the shop for quite some time, thanks to Brennan's last joyride.

As I limped into the house, I instinctively moved toward the sliding glass door.

"Nuh, uh. Where do you think you're going?" Riot wrapped a hand around my elbow, pulling me against his chest. I looked questioningly between him and the lanai. He leaned in and I was dizzy, maybe it was the painkillers or maybe it was the intoxicating scent of *him*. "I'm not letting you out of my sight for at least a year." He pushed a lock of hair behind my ear. "You're staying in my room," he whispered and a peaceful swoon took me willingly. My lips curled in a shy smile. "If that's okay with you, of course."

I bit my bottom lip to try to mute my stupid grin. I nodded. "Yeah, that's okay with me."

With the brightest smile I'd seen yet, Riot dropped my bag and scooped me into his arms. I was aware of the dull ache in my spine but somehow his arms supported me in all the right places.

My face flushed with desire. He laid me down on his bed. He moved to leave, but I grabbed his hand, pulling him back down to me.

"Where do you think *you're* going?" I gave him a suggestive smile and frowned playfully, turning his own words on him.

"Nic, you almost died. Less than a week ago. You're not even approved to drive a car right now, let alone—"

"Riot, I was down there for what felt like weeks. The thought of seeing you, touching you, being near you — it was all I held on to. I swore if I ever saw you again I wouldn't waste a minute being afraid or cautious. Please. I need you."

A few weeks ago I would have been mortified, ashamed, even, to have behaved this desperate toward a man. But the unending waves of relief and warmth to be back in his bed were so overpowering I couldn't think of anything other than the weight of him on top of me.

He wavered and groaned. I saw his eyes drag down my body. He crawled into bed next to me, laying on his side, propping his head on his hand.

"You know even with hospital head, you're still the most beautiful creature I've ever seen." He grinned, and I blushed. A wave of sincerity darkened his eyes. "I love you." The words made him smile and all the blood rushed to the center of my body.

I grazed my palm across his cheek, running my thumb over the scar on his chin before weaving my fingers through his hair. "I love you, too, Riot Asher."

Riot kissed me through his smile, running his fingers gently over my body. His tongue explored my mouth, and I relaxed into his bed, feeling as though maybe I really had died and this really was Heaven. I pouted when he pulled away.

"I love you," he repeated. "I love you so goddamn much and that's not going to change. So, we can afford to wait a few days until you're stronger." My bottom lip stuck out childishly. He bit it playfully before wrapping my wrecked body in his arms. It felt intimate. Real. Honest. It felt *final.* I didn't know what that meant for us tomorrow or any of the tomorrows after, but I was content to let this be for today.

The days that ensued were a whirlwind of statements and conversations, unanswered questions and frustrations.

Geoffrey Brown was in the wind. The night I was found alive he emailed in his resignation to the water authority and took off. After the allegations of tampering with the clinical drug trial, the SEC came calling for him with charges of insider trading.

With the power of the SEC behind it, I had no doubt the search for Geoff Brown would turn him up soon. Of course, it would be a long trial and he might only get slapped with fines. There was no way to prove he knew that the Chimera addicts would skew the clinical trial. It burned me that he still wouldn't face charges for what he did to Grace Asher. Or to me for that matter. But the rumors were already flying and in the court of public opinion, Riot's guilt was called into question.

Still, he wouldn't be exonerated from his mother's death. There simply wasn't enough evidence to overturn the conviction. But he did receive a new parole hearing.

The day he was scheduled to be in court, we were almost late. That morning, after spending an hour pinning him to the bed and touching every *inch* of his skin, we heard a car door slam.

"Hello?" Brennan's voice ripped us both out of our sweaty afterglow.

Riot jumped into sweatpants faster than I'd ever seen him move. I was still moving slowly but managed to pull on an oversized shirt of Riot's.

When I emerged from Riot's bedroom in nothing but his t-shirt, Riot was still embracing his older brother. Brennan's eyes popped before his face morphed into a sneaky grin like he caught his brother stealing extra cookies. His eyes darted between the two of us. Giggles erupted from his throat.

I had been right about the federal agents. They didn't have any interest in a small-town manslaughter charge.

But they *did* have interest in the person whose IP address had been identified as a national security threat after it hacked into a federal UAS airfield and hijacked a drone. They took him in after that same IP address popped on their radar when he emailed the audio file to the police. They knew the IP address was linked to

Riot's property but they weren't sure which of its three residents it belonged to.

After they took us all in for questioning, it was abundantly clear it was Brennan. They spent the next few weeks vetting him to make sure he wasn't already part of some terrorist organization. When they were satisfied that he was just a brilliant nerd with no social skills from podunk West Virginia, they offered him a job.

"It's incredible!" I'd never seen Brennan so animated and I had to work to hide my amusement. "It's a new program with twelve people in my class and they're all *just* like me! Can you imagine it? A room with twelve of *me*?" He grinned expectantly but I just pressed my lips together with a smile.

I looked at my watch. "I'm sorry to break up the reunion but, Riot, we really need to get to the hearing on time."

Brennan didn't come with us. We thought one Asher brother would be enough for the town to handle.

As I sat in the room while Riot made his case, I studied the parole board. They didn't seem convinced one way or the other and in reality, they appeared bored. That irritated me. When he was done, the head of the committee turned her focus toward the back of the room.

"Does local law enforcement have anything they'd like to add?"

I spun around to find Jeremy glowering in the back and I saw Riot's chest deflate. I grabbed his hand encouragingly and squeezed it twice.

Jeremy took a few steps forward, narrowing his eyes, drinking in the attention. My stomach turned. How was Riot ever expected to have a life when his future was in the hands of the guy I had rejected for him?

Jeremy's gaze fell to me and I withheld my instincts to scowl at him. Instead, I looked at him with hopeful, pleading eyes.

"Riot Asher has had some pretty serious run-ins with the law." The balloon in my chest popped. "But his intentions have always been good. There are people in this very room, *important* people, who wouldn't be here today if Riot Asher hadn't gone to heroic attempts to save their lives."

The air left Riot's body, absorbing the shock of Jeremy's endorsement. Once again the sting of joy warmed my eyes.

"Furthermore, more evidence has come to the department's attention that suggests Riot never received a fair investigation. And while there is nothing we can do in retrospect to rectify that, I think it's only fair to advocate for his complete and total clearance of all future parole and probation sentences."

My jaw dropped. I eagerly watched the woman who held Riot's life in her hands listen to Jeremy intently. When he was done talking, I held my breath.

"While I don't particularly like the suggestion that a closed case's sentence could have been mishandled," she shot a disapproving glare at Jeremy, "we are relatively blind in these areas and rely on the recommendation of the community and its law enforcement to advise what's best for its future."

She scanned the room before looking Riot in the eye.

"Congratulations, Mr. Asher. Granted you stay out of trouble, you face no more parole restrictions. Next case, please."

Riot stood there, stunned. I grabbed his arm, but he was frozen solid, his eyes fixed on some distant thought.

He whispered to no one in particular, "Jeremy *fucking* Blackwell."

I wrapped my arms around him and heard the smile crack his lips. He embraced me, lifting me off my feet and spinning me around. I winced in pain but didn't care because now our future was infinite.

44

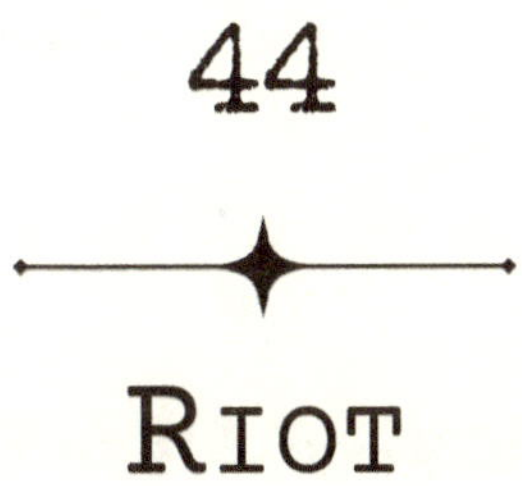

RIOT

When Brennan went back to the Cyber Intelligence program, he couldn't tell us where it was. But the smile on his face was all I needed for reassurance. Before he left, he winked at Nicolette and told her not to worry, he'd be back in no time so she could kick his ass again in Rock 'Em Sock 'Em Robots.

I had laughed but Nicolette looked perplexed. Later that night, my beautiful little bloodhound sat straight up, scaring the bejesus out of me. She didn't even put her shoes on before running to Brennan's house and slamming open the door.

I followed her groggily and found her tearing apart his house, room by room. She overturned pillows and shelves until she found the robot game stashed under his bed with all the other action figures he'd saved.

"Aha!" she exclaimed, flipping over the game to reveal a USB drive taped to the bottom.

"What is it?" I cleared my throat. She ignored me and started running back toward the house.

I made it back in time to find her parked at the breakfast bar, opening her laptop.

"Brennan kicked *my* ass in Rock 'Em Sock 'Em Robots last time."

"Maybe he got it wrong." She shot me a flat look. *Has Brennan ever been wrong?* "Yeah, okay, fair enough."

"I knew he was trying to tell me something."

It was almost three in the morning. She plugged the USB drive in.

Immediately a text box popped up. The letters appeared as if someone was typing in real-time.

Greetings Earthlings,   I have come with an important message…
Kidding.
It's me.
Brennan.
This was the last thing I was able to recover before I broke Riot out of Godot jail.
He tried to wipe the server.
But you can't wipe Brennan!

The text box disappeared and a normal file folder appeared with one file in it.

"Maybe you shouldn't—" But as I said the words, Nicolette was already double-clicking.

A black and white video popped up from a security camera. I recognized the entrance to the mine immediately. At least what it used to look like before it was blown up by the stick of dynamite that Geoffrey Brown was lighting.

Nicolette laughed. "He got the security footage from that night."

It was a clear shot of Geoffrey Brown dropping a lit stick of dynamite into the mine shaft where a blonde girl peeked out from the first level.

My heart ached at the image. At the resigned expression on her face. I never wanted her to feel that way ever again. In that moment I knew I'd do anything to keep her safe. From now until as long as she'd have me.

I held her tighter that night. We talked endlessly about what we should do with the footage. There was no audio to the video, so his confession about my mother wasn't tangible. Believe me, that irony was not lost on us.

The federal marshals had caught Geoffrey Brown trying to get on a boat to the Caymans. He was currently locked up as the SEC's investigation swirled around him. Nicolette brought up the valid point that if we turned the video over, then he would be facing attempted murder charges and there could be a turf war. The attempted murder investigation could get in the way of the SEC investigation, and it could jeopardize both.

I wanted to nail his ass. Make him pay. But ultimately, my brilliant girlfriend won the argument (boy, did I love using that word). She said we should hold on to it. There was no statute of limitations on attempted murder in West Virginia. So, we would wait to see how he fared during the SEC trial.

When the SEC got to town, people were wary of them. They didn't understand what the SEC was, let alone what they were looking for. Nicolette was quite helpful, however, with their investigation. They put us under a gag order from going to the press with any of it. Making it public before the investigation was over could jeopardize Brown's indictment.

The lead SEC investigator, Lucas Wilder, was friendly, but in a deadly kind of way. His smile was genuine but I could tell he had something ferocious inside of him and he reminded me of Nicolette. He had dirty blonde hair and fierce blue eyes and I had to admit even *I* was jealous of his jawline. I caught him checking her out at one point and if he wasn't a federal agent, I might have said something.

When she turned everything she'd found over to him, he kept her aside for at least twenty minutes after the meeting was over. I started to get antsy. I peered through the small square window in the door. As he spoke, I could tell Nicolette was considering something.

They shook hands before exiting.

"What was that about?" I asked, trying to make my voice sound casual. It didn't work. Nicolette smirked at me.

"I think he might have offered me a job…" She sounded cautiously intrigued. "Not officially or anything but he said they often take on 'consultant contractors' to help out with investigations. I guess he was impressed by my *investigative acumen.*"

"What did you say?" I looped my arms around her waist and pulled her tighter to me.

"I said I'd consider it. I told him a lot is happening in my life right now. Not sure where my next stop is."

Her words hit me somewhere in the chest. The last few weeks had been such a whirlwind that we hadn't talked about how my parole release could impact our future. There was a lot to consider but as long as she wanted to do it with me at her side, I would be there.

45

NICOLETTE

With his permission, I told Melody the truth about Riot Asher. That not only had it not been Riot, it wasn't even one of her sons. It had been one of Grace Asher's colleagues from the church who strangled her so she wouldn't uncover the major drug operation he had been building in the old coal mine.

It was a better story. Wrongful conviction. Brother sacrifices himself for brother. A villainous church treasurer deceives everyone for years. Drug distribution. Stock manipulation. Insider trading. All wrapped up in a love story.

It was a *way* better story. But it no longer belonged in *Beyond Bizarre* so the episode was squashed.

Melody would come calling if the producers were interested in what happened in Godot, West Virginia. I told her I couldn't guarantee Riot would talk and I wouldn't ask him to. If he wanted to tell his story, it was going to be his choice.

That could mean burning one of my last bridges with Melody. But journalistic integrity and my career standing didn't seem nearly as important as they used to.

It was scary. Having no direction. No purpose. No *objective*. But it was the first time in all my years that aimlessness didn't worry me. A part of me was exhilarated at the endless possibilities.

The following Sunday, I didn't want to go to church with Riot. But we had gotten wind that it was Pastor Blackwell's last service, so I felt obligated to go since I was the one who almost got him arrested.

He was questioned at length about the investments, the clinical trial, the building contractor that later got sued, and the stock shortage. They found it hard to believe that he had no knowledge of it. After all, anywhere that Geoffrey Brown's name appeared, Elias Blackwell was right there next to it. *I* found it hard to believe that he was completely guilt-free, even if his crime was looking the other way.

What's crazy is that, in the end, it wasn't the claims of insider trading that forced him to step down. It wasn't his connection to the coal mine that ended up being the very place that caused half of his parish to fall victim to addiction. It wasn't even the fact that he commissioned a community to be built on land that was so high in radon that it gave one out of every six people some form of lung disease.

Nope. It was the goddamn fluoride.

The good folks of Godot were most upset that he asked for fluoride to be added to the water without their knowledge. The absence of a *choice* for healthy teeth and gums was what didn't sit well with the community. They demanded his removal.

Fucking wild, I know.

I rapped twice on Elias' office door.

"Pastor Blackwell?" I peered in to find him packing up his personal effects and I couldn't help the stab of guilt that struck me.

"Nicolette, please, call me Elias. No longer a pastor, and all."

I entered the office but remained a good distance away. "I'm sorry about all this." My eyes roamed over the packed boxes.

He waved a hand dismissively. "Don't be. You were following your instincts. And you have good instincts. Geoff was my best friend for a very long time. He was always the smart one. I used to think he had good instincts too. Turns out those instincts were quite... *manufactured*." Elias twisted his mouth in contemplation. "Given all the facts, I would have assumed the same thing about me."

"You really didn't know? Anything he was up to?" He shot me a flat look. "Off the record, I swear." I held my hands up. "Purely human curiosity."

He sighed and sat down, steepling his fingers. "I like to think I didn't but if I'm being incredibly honest with myself... Some part of me had to have an inkling. When the dividends started coming in after the lawsuit..." His tongue clicked. "Well, it was just a lot of money. And I guess I didn't want to ask where it came from. I was eager to believe the lie that it was from a legitimate investment." He shrugged. "It was almost time to pass the torch anyhow."

"Yeah, who's planning to take over?"

"Excuse me!" I cringed at Katie Plainbottom's singsong voice, brushing past me.

I smiled ironically at her. "You know, *you* should have been my first guess."

She ignored me, busying herself with unpacking a box.

Elias Blackwell took his opportunity to excuse himself. "Be well, Nicolette. Whatever you do. Go with your heart." He hugged me before disappearing down the hall.

Katie and I were alone. I took a step toward her and she eyed me warily. She peered around the large office as if trying to distract herself.

"Not sure I really need all this space. More for the optics, I guess..." Her shoulder shrugged with a nervous giggle.

"To be the senior pastor, don't you have to be, like, I don't know, a good person? You know someone who would never *intentionally* humiliate someone in public?" My heart thrummed with adrenaline.

She appeared defensive at first and then sighed, shrinking away like a dog that had been caught chewing the new couch.

"That's what I thought." As I turned to go her voice followed me.

"It was an accident!" she finally choked out.

Spinning around, I stalked toward her. "Pardon?" I cupped an ear in her direction. Her pink cheeks reddened.

"It was an accident, I swear. I've taken on way too much with the church this year, so when Jeremy asked me to put together a highlight reel for you... I cut some corners. I heard about this AI tool that was supposed to make my workload easier. I asked it to give me the most popular clips of Nicolette Parker and..." She looked positively miserable. "I never double checked what those clips were."

My eyes narrowed in her direction. "I'm supposed to believe that?"

The guilt on her face was only eclipsed by the shame. "I swear I didn't know. I would have *never* put something like that in front of the Field Days." She swallowed. "But it *was* my responsibility. And..." She sighed with closed eyes. "And I definitely took advantage of it."

She looked genuinely disappointed in herself.

"I should have taken accountability and apologized immediately. But I didn't." Her breath sped up and it was as if I was watching something burst inside her. "It was just so hard to watch Riot fall away from me the *moment* you waltzed into town. He was..." She looked me square in the eyes. "He was everything. And he was supposed to be *it* for me. He was my happy ever after, you know?" She shrugged, a tear rolling down her cheek. "I've never been like you, Nicolette. You shine. Brighter than all of us. And it was like he saw you coming from miles away. With everything I'm part of, everything I do for this town... I can't even remember the last time someone asked me how *my* day was. Or how *I'm* doing. I don't shine for anybody."

I wanted to scoff at her crocodile tears but her final words hit me like a gut punch. The words carried an undertone of relief and I wondered if she'd ever admitted this to anyone. The grief that flashed across her brow almost made me feel guilty.

The woman had literally quit seminary school to help Riot, harboring the dream of being his wife one day. It was batshit crazy but there was something respectable about that level of self-sacrifice.

"None of this would have anything to do with Jeremy's sudden one-eighty for Riot's endorsement, would it?"

Katie's eyes went a little wide.

"That was mostly Jeremy. He knows his department screwed up all those year's ago. But I may have nudged him in the direction of how to start fixing it. Anyway," she continued. "I really am sorry. I don't deserve your forgiveness but I'll spend the rest of my life praying for it."

I choked back a laugh, picturing Katie kneeling at her bedside, asking God for my forgiveness at night. I didn't want to forgive her. But did I really want to be a prayer on this woman's lips for the rest of my life? I crossed my arms and leaned against the door jamb, chewing on the inside of my mouth while I assessed her. Her tiny frame dwarfed by the massive office. An idea snaked through my brain as I regarded her.

"You want to make it up to me?"

Her eyes lit up. "I'll do anything I can."

Emboldened by the two women flanking my sides, I strode right up to Jacob's massive porch and landed three hard knocks.

When the front door opened, his eyes registered surprise. I took up as much space in the doorway as possible.

"Hi *Uncle Jake,*" I said, pushing past him, without an invitation.

"Nicolette," he feigned happily. "What... are you   doing here?" he asked with a phony smile.

"What, I can't drop by my uncle's house for a visit with some friends?" I bat my eyelashes.

He chuckled nervously. "Well,   of   course   you   can! If I'd known you were bringing company,   I   would have tidied up a bit." He clasped his hands, looking around.

I stepped toward him. "No need actually, Jake. This is your official eviction notice." The smile dropped from my face like a rock plunking into water. His phony grin faltered. He blinked away the confusion.

"I'm s-sorry, wh-what?" he stammered.

I pushed an open palm in Katie's direction, never letting my eyes divert from his uncomfortable, confused twitches. Katie placed a short stack of papers in my hand. I pushed them into Jacob's chest. He fumbled with the packet.

"Transfer of ownership? Nicolette, what is this?"

I walked deeper into the farmhouse so that the three of us encircled him.

"You see, my best friend Chelsea here has been holed up in a tiny little two-bedroom ranch with three little girls and one bathroom for several years now. She needs more room. And you need to leave Godot. So, I thought, what a perfect opportunity for you to pay your *good fortune* forward. You're going to sign this over to her and then you have twenty-four hours to vacate the premises."

A practiced smile stretched across my face. I clasped my hands, mimicking his position. I waited and watched a rainbow of emotions flash across his face, soaking up every bit of his discomfort.

"And why would I do that?" His voice dropped an octave. *There's the conniving little opportunist I knew was lurking there.*

"Because I'm asking nicely. And I'm only going to ask nicely *once*." I took two strides toward him, pulling a pen out of my back pocket. "But you should know, I'm prepared to get mean. So, *please, test me.*" He swayed, ready to call my bluff. "Because the next question I ask will be in a lawyer's office, reexamining my Aunt Shirley's will that we *graciously* did not contest."

His features darkened, and he finally dropped the façade of innocence.

"The will was clean. You'll waste thousands in legal fees."

I pushed my lips together in a smile. "Thousands my parents and I will *happily* spend after I tell them just how many times my dear old uncle went searching for my illegal sex tape."

His face paled.

"Eww…" I heard Chelsea mutter. Katie let out a little gasp. I hadn't told her why I needed to use her paralegal skills, nor did I tell her why I asked her to draft up the proper real estate paperwork to give Chelsea complete ownership of Jacob's farmhouse and all the land he owned around it.

Jacob studied me for a moment, eyes swirling between Katie and Chelsea. Air flew in and out of his flared nostrils.

I held up the pen, quirking an eyebrow. "You have ninety seconds before I get mean."

The color of fury returned to his cheeks, but I let the glory of victory bloom in my chest as he snatched the pen from my hand. The girls twittered with triumph.

Katie joined him at the table to point to where he needed to sign.

"You didn't have to do this," Chelsea said, facing me. "This was your aunt's money, you should do something with it."

I brushed her upper arm. "I'm doing exactly what I want with it." She offered me a watery smile. "Sell that little ranch, invest the money for the girls. I hear housing and healthcare are killing it." I gave her a wink.

Katie returned with the paperwork.

It felt like solid gold retribution in my hands. I started toward the door.

"*Pleasure* visiting with you, Uncle Jake!" I tossed over my shoulder.

When I crossed the threshold into the outdoors, I was pleasantly surprised to find Riot leaning against the porch beam, arms crossed over his chest like an angry security guard. The black t-shirt he was wearing hugged his muscled chest, and he looked like the perfect victory snack. I stopped in front of him, raising my eyebrows. He leaned in and I got drunk at his mere proximity.

"Nicolette! This isn't over—" Jacob's voice approached from inside.

Riot's body moved with precision and speed. He arched over Jacob before I even saw him move, a firm hand on Jacob's bony chest, stopping him in his tracks.

"Nope," he growled, and it was so fierce it sent shivers down my back. The danger in his voice was chilling. And incredibly sexy. "You don't talk to her. Ever again. If I get wind that you *thought* about her? What I do to you will give them a *real* reason to put me in prison." Riot gave Jacob's chest two firm pats, sending him stumbling backward.

As the front door slammed, I turned back to Riot, unable to mask my graciously defended honor. His eyes grasped mine and although there was fire there, his lips tipped up.

"You *honestly* think I'd let you come back to this house without me?" he said, flashing me a wry, knowing grin. My mouth twisted and the butterflies turned to jellyfish under his appreciative stare.

Riot made his way back to his truck. I regarded the two women who'd helped me today. Chelsea was close to tears as she filled Bill in on what was happening over the phone. But Katie still cowered between her narrow shoulders, afraid to meet my gaze. I pushed her gently.

"Hey. How's your day going?" She peered up at me, blinking almost in confusion. "You doing okay?" Her chest exhaled a relieved laugh. She nodded with a watery smile. "Look," I continued, "you're still obnoxious but..." I gave her an appreciative nod. "We're good." The air whooshed from her tiny body. She shuffled again and shifted like she was about to hug me.

"Should we—?"

"Nope!" I held up a palm to stop her from getting closer. "Not necessary."

Katie nodded. Her eyes darted quickly to Riot whose arm was hanging out of the truck window, the other arm pressing his cell phone to his ear.

"Treat him well, okay?" I almost threw her a sarcastic smile but the raw, authentic crack in her voice hit me in the chest. "He deserves to be loved. So... love him honestly." I dipped my head, both dismissing and forgiving her all at once.

Chelsea spun to me. "I seriously don't know how to thank you. You have no idea what this is going to do for our family."

My breath hitched. "You remember our deal? The terms?" I gave her a serious look.

She smiled and nodded. "I will be sure to have the girls plant a lilac patch named after Auntie Nicolette."

I promised to keep in touch with Chelsea wherever I ended up. And unlike the last time I left, I knew I meant it this time.

The passenger door to Riot's truck squealed when I pulled it shut.

"Okay, thank you. Yes, I'll let you know as soon as I can." His eyes connected with me fiercely. I quirked my eyebrows up at him. He peered down at his phone, appearing confused. "That was Avery - that art dealer. She offered me an official spot in the showcase. It opens in Asheville for three weeks in September and then moves to Charlotte for a month and a half. She said we'd see how those two shows went and then we'd go from there."

My cheeks ached from the smile that the news put on my face.

"Riot, that's amazing," I said sincerely, twisting my fingers.

"Come with me, Nicolette." Riot's intense gaze bore into me with a questioning plea.

"What?"

"Come with me," he repeated. "To Charlotte, to Asheville. Everywhere. Anywhere. Come with me. Please. I'm not asking you to give up what you want to do," he added hurriedly. "I would never ask you to change that. I never want you to compromise your passions for mine." He ran a hand through his hair. "I don't know what your tomorrow looks like, but no matter what you do or where you go... you're always going to need a home base." His eyes found mine and my breath hitched with the intensity. "Let *me* be your home base."

Rising to my knees, I grabbed his face between my palms. I gazed into the eyes I would get lost in forever before kissing him more honestly than I ever had. And when I pulled back, I told him the most honest thing I'd ever said.

"My tomorrows? Look a lot like you."

EPILOGUE

Riot

"Do you know how much sugar is in that punch? Or any idea how that sugar is processed? How it continues to eat away at your body even after—"

"Wash, dear? Can we put the healthy pomp and circumstance away for one night, please?" Nicolette's dad, Graham said to Brennan's new best friend.

Wash was a non-binary physics genius that Brennan met in his program. When he told us he was bringing someone on the camping trip to Alum Creek Park that we'd finally been able to plan, we were excited. Naturally, we were curious if it might be a love interest, but it had been nearly a week since the camping trip started and I hadn't seen any signs of romantic interest whatsoever. They laughed. They argued. They fought. But still, they slept in separate tents and I never saw them embrace or show any physical affection toward the other.

Wash made Brennan happy and if company was all a person really needed, then I'd be happy to have Wash as part of the family.

"T-minus two minutes, people. Riot, you ready?" Graham gazed over at me anxiously.

I finished hanging the lights and plugged in the extension cord. A small chorus of *ooo*s erupted from behind me.

"She's gonna hate it," Brennan stated matter-of-factly.

"Hey, now. I'm her dad and I get to say what she will and won't like." He admired the decorations we'd spent the past half hour hanging, tilting his head back and forth. "She... might whack you for being corny," he admitted through a grimace.

But I just grinned, resting my hands on my hips, appraising the handiwork.

"Corny's perfect," I whispered to myself. I stood back to admire the campsite.

The sound of a car pulling up sent anxious jolts through me. I fixed the collar on the dress shirt that I had on underneath my suit jacket. We had instructed Nicolette's mother, Darlene, to park beside my truck, which blocked the view of the campsite.

They had gone for a mother-daughter hike that afternoon and I could see the small glean of sweat that shimmered off her neck when she stepped out. She spun to find me standing on the other side of the car, dressed in a suit, my hands clasped behind my back.

I tried to look handsome with some kind of sexy scowl or pout but it was too hard to keep the shit-eating grin off my face.

"Riot, why are you dressed like that? It's August and getting hotter by the minute."

"I'll leave you two alone." Darlene's eyebrows danced.

Nicolette's suspicious eyes turned to me. "What... is going on?"

I approached her, taking her hands in mine.

"I wish I could remember the moment I first laid eyes on you. But let's face it. We both were pretty wrapped up in our own ambitions in high school to see the person we were meant to be with was right there all along." I could feel her hands getting a little clammy. Or maybe it was mine, either way, I kept going. "But looking back on it all, I think I loved you from the moment I first stumbled upon you sleeping in your car."

"What?" Her mother faintly admonished. "She was sleeping in her car? Why—"

"Shhh!" Graham hushed.

"Your fire." I brushed a hand over her face, pushing her hair back. "Your beauty. Your intelligence." I leaned in and lowered my voice so no one else could hear. "Your incredibly hot body." She snorted, and it broke the tension, albeit slightly, that had crept across her brow. "I knew at that moment I wanted to give you everything you deserved. All the things you never experienced. I admire you, Nicolette. You're my goddamn hero and I want you to know that today, tomorrow, and all the tomorrows after that. Your dreams made you grow up fast. I want to spend each day giving you back a piece of that carefree adolescence you don't even know you missed."

I took a deep breath, sinking to one knee. I watched her eyes go wide in terror, shifting from me to all the members of our family staring at us. "Nicolette Parker..." I reached into my coat pocket. "Will you do me the great honor..." I pulled out the floral corsage, "of being my date to the prom?"

She blinked. Her face fell into confusion. For a moment I thought she was angry, and that I had read her all wrong, until she snorted and rolled her eyes, pulling me to my feet.

"You're a dork. Don't scare me like that."

"I'm serious," I said through the sheepish grin I couldn't wipe. She stilled and stared dubiously at me. "You left before your senior year, which means you never went to your senior prom."

She nodded in understanding. "Riot, you know that kind of thing didn't hold a whole lot of value to me then." She arched an eyebrow, and I nodded in agreement.

"No, I know. But a woman as beautiful as you should get to dance at the prom." I held open the elastic on the corsage. Her smirk subsided to something resembling gratitude as she slipped her wrist through it.

I led her around the cab of my truck where the illuminated campsite came into view. We had hung Edison bulbs from the trees, strategically weaving them around an open space to create a dance floor.

Her expression transformed back to that seventeen-year-old girl I used to pass in the hallways. The lights twinkled off her eyes, making them shimmer more than they already did.

She ran her finger over the picnic table, which we had covered in a bright plastic tablecloth. An obnoxiously large punch bowl (filled with rum and Coke) sat at the forefront with another equally large bowl of cheese balls.

And of course, a canister of Twizzlers sat on the end.

"This is ridiculous, Riot." But not even the Bloodhound of New England could keep the amused smile from her face.

I gazed down at her. Brennan pressed play on the speakers we had stashed in a low tree branch. The opening drums to "One Headlight" rolled through the late summer air.

"May I have this dance?" I bowed, offering her my hand. She stared at my outstretched palm with a funny face before taking it.

We danced all night, only pausing to take a dinner break. Brennan, with the strategic help of Wash, had caught a few massive bass and Graham knew just how to dress and season the fish over a fire. I smiled sadly, wishing our dad could see us now. I took comfort in upholding his promise to take Brennan fishing. I found myself wishing our mom could see us too. Because even though things wound up tragically in the end, they hadn't always been that way.

There was a time when we had been a family. A happy one, or so I liked to think. Imperfect in our choices but devout in our love for each other. I gazed over at Nicolette who was catching cheese balls in her mouth that Brennan tossed at her face. Her dad kept score while her mom shook her head. My heart expanded with the distinct hope we'd be a real family again soon.

"Thank you for a wonderful prom, Riot Asher."

Later that night, we stretched our bodies over the sleeping bag in our tent. Nicolette rested her chin on my chest, gazing up at me with those eyes I would never get enough of.

"You should have seen your face," I smirked. "You know, the sheer panic in your eyes was almost a little disparaging?"

She slapped me playfully. "You know what's disparaging? Fake proposing to a woman. Besides, you caught me off guard. Everyone was just standing there. Listening and... gawking. It was all so... not intimate."

I brushed my lips to her forehead before nestling into her ear.

"Don't you worry, Nicolette Parker. When I propose to you? It'll be just you and me." Her blush goaded me on but the curl in her lips told me everything I needed to know. "And there will definitely be fireworks," I whispered.

I sensed the smile on her lips, which proceeded to drag down my chest.

When our naked bodies found each other moments later, I knew it was going to be the last time I made love to her as my girlfriend.

After all, the fireworks were already loaded in the back of my truck.

Like what you read?
Leave a review!
Reviews are the lifeblood of an author's success. Especially one just tryin' to cut her teeth in the industry. So, if you liked what you read and want more even faster, review and share!

Want more Nicolette and Riot? Sign up for my newsletter to unlock an exclusive, steamy bonus scene!

Want to know what happens to Katie and Jeremy after Nicolette and Riot ride off into the sunset? Keep reading for a sneak peek at *Circle Circle, Dot Dot*; a small town friends to lovers romance.

Acknowledgements

Thank you to everyone who helped make *The Tomorrows After You* come to life!

Writing a story is easy. Making it readable is hard. From my endless posts seeking feedback and advice in Facebook groups to all the beta readers that gave me such valuable feedback- everyone had a hand in making this come to life. Without you, Nicolette and Riot would be sitting in a Google Doc, taking up data space.

When you're just starting out, the most valuable asset you have is your network and I'm reminded on a daily basis what a fantastic bunch of people romance readers and authors are. I'm floored at how much time and intelligence you all are willing to lend to someone who you've never met and owe nothing to. It is my hope, one day, to be able to give back to all of you!

A big thank you to my parents who have supported and believed in me all my life. I wouldn't be who I am today without you and I'll never be able to express just how lucky and grateful I am that you are such a big part of my life.

To the incredible women in my life who read and shared and never stopped encouraging me. My Wolf Pack is amazing and you are the driving force behind the courage I have to give this whole thing a shot.

To my husband, who has been patient through all the midnight writing with the emanating glow and tap, tap, tap of my laptop or phone. Here's to making it all worth it, love.

And, of course, to my son. Who is notably less patient. But you're three. So that's okay. Because I wouldn't give up a single second of the time I get with you. I hope I make you proud one day.

Circle Circle, Dot Dot

Annie Ritter

1

Katie

I lay out my makeup brushes like a surgeon about to operate. Despite the record-high temperatures expected for the Fourth of July Celebrations, I can't wait for it to get underway. I examine my hair to ensure I haven't missed any locks before unplugging my straightener.

"This is it," I mutter to myself. "You have it handled. You have it all under control."

My painted reflection stares back at me. The tube of red lipstick feels dangerous in my hands. It's probably too much. But this is my chance. My day to show all the people of Godot that I can handle being president of the board for Redeemer's Church. My acting presidency will be voted on to become permanent in two months. So, today? The audition begins.

That means I can't be Regular Katie. I can't be the same, dull little girl who runs around collecting bakery donations and reminding parishioners of the potluck dinners Sunday night. I have to be Grown Up Katie. I have to be a woman. A strong, sure-headed, shiny woman.

And I'm pretty sure those women wear lipstick.

The dull patter of footsteps pulls me out of my morning affirmations, and an anxious tick spurs me forward. I put the finishing touches on my eyebrows, ensuring they're perfectly arched. I give myself one last appraisal in the mirror.

The lipstick is bold. But I need to be bold. At least I need people to see me as bold, even if my insides are on the verge of panic.

I have it handled. I have everything under control.

As I flick the lights off, my cell phone buzzes. I pull it out and blink twice at the familiar, unsaved number. I hit the silence bar and drop it back into my pocket.

∞

"Ohh, don't we look sassy?" Miriam winks at me as I gather the volunteers in a group at the front of the church foyer.

"Out looking for a husband today, are we?" says one of the other women, puckering her lips.

I clap twice, blinking away the side commentary.

"Alright, everyone! Thank you for your help today. If we can get through the Family Field Days, then tonight will be a breeze!" I smile at the group of about a dozen volunteers.

"Hopefully *this* event won't have any smut videos worked in," I hear someone murmur.

My smile doesn't falter. "Excuse me?" I ask sweetly. "Was there a question?"

Cherry Mitchell lifts her head. "I was just thinking maybe it's best if one or two of us go through the slide show?" she offers with phony concern. "You know, make sure nothing untoward got slid in at the last minute." Her knowing sneer threatens my façade as a few murmurs roll through the group.

"Thank you, Cherry, but that won't be necessary." I smile as kindly as I can. "I spent all night going through every detail of today's celebration. There should be *no* surprises. Now, if everyone who is working the food stands could move over—"

"I'm sorry, Katie. But weren't you in charge of it the last time, too? And look how that turned out." I blink twice at Cherry, drawing in a calming breath.

"I have it handled. I have it all under control," I speak the words through gritted teeth. "Now, *as* I was saying…"

I give everyone their respective stations as we make our way out to the fairgrounds.

But not before running to the bathroom to wash the lipstick off.

It's humid and I should be sweating, but I'm fine. Because I'm always cold these days. Regardless, I pull my compact mirror out of my back pocket to make sure my makeup isn't melting down my face.

"Hope the heat doesn't scare people away," the male voice comes from behind me. I quickly snap my compact shut, concerned that whoever it is would deem me shallow and vain for staring at myself in the mirror.

But it's just Jeremy.

"Oh, it's you," I say, shifting to face him. "Thanks again for what you did for Riot at the parole hearing." I fidget with my fingers. "He probably wouldn't have gotten released otherwise."

Jeremy shrugs. "It was the right thing to do. I still think he's just another over-hyped ex-jock..." Jeremy rolls his eyes. "But after everything Nicolette uncovered, it was clear he never got a fair investigation. And turns out I'm not one to stand in the way of *true love*," he adds grimly.

I can't help but wince at the image of Riot riding off into the sunset. Without me. My chest aches, but I don't have time for hurt. I keep my eyes focused, blowing out a breath.

Jeremy scans the sprawling park that serves as our fairgrounds and gazes at the people bustling around. "I'm sure there will be a whole new scandal by this time tomorrow," he says.

"There better not be! This is my first major event as Redeemer's acting president, and it needs to go *perfectly*." I shoot him a warning.

"Hey." He holds his hands up and gestures to his sheriff's uniform. "My guys and I are here to keep the peace. That reminds me. The fire marshal asked me where you plan to set up the fireworks."

I frown. "I'm not sure. It's the same company we used last year, so I'm sure they know where to set up."

Jeremy's head twirls. "Shouldn't they be here by now, staking off the area?"

∞

"What do you mean you never received the payment? I mailed the check a month ago!" I try to control my voice, but I'm panicking.

It is July-gosh-darn-Fourth and there are no freaking fireworks!

Jeremy leans against a tent pole, examining his fingernails as I pace back and forth, trying to keep myself from hyperventilating.

"I'm sorry, ma'am, but if we don't receive payment and the signed waiver at least two weeks out, we cancel the order."

"Well, it would have been extremely helpful to call me and let me know that! I have over a thousand people coming to this event tonight. What do I have to do to get someone out here?"

"Sorry, ma'am. We're booked up. July fourth and all."

I pull the phone away from my ear and let a frustrated noise escape my throat. I take a deep breath and close my eyes, letting the air exhale slowly as I try to calm myself down. The heat rises to my face, and I know I need to keep my composure. Jeremy's eyes register amusement and I want to kick him.

"Okay, thank you for your informative help."

I don't wait for him to respond to end the call. I rack my brain, trying to recall when I had mailed the waiver and the check. The stamp had gone on the envelope a little crooked, so I know I mailed it. Not a single box in my event planner was left unchecked. What did it matter...

I sit down on a thin rental chair and put my head in my hands.

"What am I gonna do?" I groan. "Cherry Mitchell is going to destroy me." My empty stomach feels sick and spoiled.

"Let me make a few calls," Jeremy sighs.

Gazing up at him, he looks bored and apathetic. It aggravates me. This is his town, too. I feel my breathing accelerate. Sweat beads down the center of my back, and it feels like hot insects crawling over my skin, leaving trails of insect tears.

Why isn't he more upset? I grit my teeth and close my eyes to try to fill my lungs with air, breathing slowly in through my nose and blowing the air out cleanly through my lips.

"I have it handled. I have it under control," I whisper to myself. When I open my eyes, Jeremy is looking at me like I sprouted a second head.

"Want me to get you a drink or something?" he asks warily.

"No," I bite off. I square my shoulders and toss my hair over my shoulder. "I need to stay sharp."

Jeremy raises his eyebrows and forms a little 'o' with his lips. "Oookay, I'll let you know what shakes out." He turns and walks away as he throws over his shoulder. "Don't worry, doll. It all comes together!"

He intends to reassure me but his words only aggravate me more. I silently utter a desperate prayer to help me rectify this.

I have it handled. I have it all under control.

I call nothing short of twenty fireworks shops. The majority are closed for the holiday, and the others laugh me off the phone if they don't hang up first.

It's less than half an hour from dusk, and I'm fighting a full-on panic attack.

On the inside, of course.

On the outside, I smile widely. I walk with my shoulders back, and I shake hands with every gosh darn vendor and sponsor we have, thanking them profusely.

People are settling into their places on the large hill that spills into a flat field on the edge of the fairgrounds, staking out their spots with blankets and throwing popcorn at each other.

My heart beats in an unusual rhythm.

"Katie..." Cherry Mitchell's awful singsong voice blisters my eardrums from behind me. "Doug, you know my husband, Doug? He works for the Town of Lycon Fire Department. He told me the strangest thing." I spin around slowly. "He said *Lycon* was using Premier Fireworks this year. You know Premier Fireworks? The company that has always done our show for the past five years?" Her red lips mock me as they curl into a smug smile.

Why hadn't anyone called her *sassy?*

I freeze as my entire world feels like it's being catapulted into space. I try sucking in more oxygen between my lips but the air just feels hot on the back of my throat. I can feel the sweat beading from my scalp, and I know any minute now my meticulously straightened hair will turn into the unruly mane I've kept secret for nearly thirty years now.

I need to pull it back. I need to get inside before anyone sees it. I need to keep it under control.

But here's Cherry Mitchell, standing in my way like a finely-taloned raptor, ready to pick me apart with her manicured claws.

I feel weak. Physically. Mentally. Like I can hardly stand up. My eyes steal a glance at my watch. It's already half past 8 pm, and the show was supposed to start ten minutes ago.

I scan the families huddled on their blankets, the kids plunked in their parents' laps in collapsible lawn chairs. I can feel their impending disappointment wash over me, tightening my throat and stinging the back of my eyes.

It's time to call it. Even the best generals know when to surrender.

"Cherry, I have to tell you something... I don't know how it happened but—"

And just as the words leave my lips, I hear a soft but distinctive explosive *POP!* followed by a sparkling sizzle. I spin around to see what can only be described as stardust from the freaking heavens falling from the sky, rescuing me from what would have surely been permanent social ridicule.

"Sorry, we're a little late!" Jeremy yelps as he trots up next to me. "Apparently there was a... *misunderstanding* with Premier Fireworks' schedule." He eyes Cherry in a speculative way I don't quite understand before he claps and turns his attention to me. "But never fear! Good thing the Blackwell influence still reaches far and strong." He curls an arm up and flexes, showing off biceps I don't remember being so defined...

"Hm." Cherry smiles and puts a hand on his muscled upper arm. Some tiny voice growls at her affection toward him. "Always rely on a Blackwell," she chimes before taking her time dragging her raptor fingers over his skin and walking away.

Another beautiful, wonderful, gracious firework launches into the sky and explodes with multiple colors over our heads, and it feels as if every explosion is breathing fresh, cool air into my lungs.

I observe Jeremy who just smiles at the sky before fixing his gaze on me.

"I don't know how you did it, but I could kiss you right now," I let out a long exhale and watch as his eyes dart to my mouth so quickly I might have imagined it. He scrunches his nose up.

"I don't want your cooties," he says through a smirk.

"Circle, circle, dot, dot," I mutter, sticking out my tongue. He rolls his eyes and pushes me gently on the shoulder. I nearly stumble over before he catches my elbow.

Something passes over his features before he asks, "How about that drink now?"

I pause, considering it. "Okay, you get the beer, I'll get the ice cream."

His eyes blink slowly, and he nods before jogging away.

"Wow," Jeremy exclaims slowly. "You haven't changed your ice cream order in over twenty years?"

I sit down next to him, handing him a cup of strawberry ice cream with chocolate sprinkles and a waffle cone upside down on top.

"It felt appropriate." I shrug, but I hope he doesn't see me blushing. My insides are warm because a part of me can't believe he remembers.

We couldn't have been older than six when Jeremy and I first became friends at the day camp the summer he moved to Godot.

Jeremy had been teased relentlessly at first. His ears were too big for his head and stuck out like a caricature. He mostly got rude, unoriginal nicknames like Dumbo or Bugs Bunny.

One particularly humid day, the camp had brought in an ice cream truck. Filled with sugar and malicious youth, two older boys started throwing M&Ms at him, trying to hit his ears. He had ducked but lost his balance and all of the chocolate and vanilla swirl had fallen off his ice cream cone.

I immediately ran up to the truck to get him another one but they were already closed.

"Hi, I'm Katie. Do you want some of my ice cream? Mama made sausage and grits this morning so I had a big breakfast, and I won't eat all of this. I'd hate for it to go to waste."

It was a lie. I hadn't eaten anything that day. It had been one of Mama's *bad* days. She hadn't even gotten out of bed before I left for camp.

Jeremy looked at me warily as if I were trying to trick him as he sat down on the bench next to me.

"Why do you get it in a cup? It's more fun in a cone." He twisted his face but pushed his nose closer to my cup.

I scooped a small spoonful of strawberry and held it up. "No way. Look. No drips. No sticky fingers. You get more ice cream with it. And..." I pointed my eyebrows together in the direction of the blob that was already being mauled by ants. "You don't have to worry about it falling off." I shoved the spoon in my mouth and admired how clean it came out.

I offered him the spoon, but he twisted his face again in a grimace. "I... I don't want your cooties."

I frowned at him, pausing a moment before taking the now-empty cone from his hand and plopping it on top of the ice cream. I looked at it momentarily before using the cone as a scoop to collect some ice cream. I passed it to him.

He nodded in approval, and I remember the incredible feeling of doing something right.

"You know how to protect yourself from cooties, right?" I asked, enjoying the feeling of imparting knowledge. He raised an eyebrow.

I grabbed his wrist and drew two circles then poked twice inside each one. "Circle, circle, dot, dot. Now you have a cootie shot."

He looked at me like I was crazy but shook his head as he scooped up strawberry ice cream in silence.

We were best friends after that, inseparable for years. Jeremy was the first person to bring me to Redeemer's Church where I promptly got involved in every activity I could. I started going to his house for dinner several nights a week. We'd have sleepovers on the weekends. Ate strawberry ice cream with chocolate sprinkles at the drive-in movies. We did everything together.

For a few years anyway. Then puberty happened and suddenly it wasn't cool to hang out with girls you weren't dating. And we *definitely* weren't dating. I tried to pretend it didn't hurt when he barely nodded to me in the hallways when he was with his friends. Or when I was no longer the first person he called to complain about how Mr. Meaney would pick on him in wood shop. And I made excuses for why he no longer sat with me in the cafeteria, even though we had the same lunch period.

I had exclusive eyes for Riot Asher throughout most of high school, so it wasn't like I was yearning for Jeremy to ask me to prom. But I missed my best friend.

Maybe that's why I never really replaced him with anyone except more clubs and youth groups. Maybe I thought I would find a new best friend that way. But it never happened.

I liked to think I was friends with everybody, given how involved I was. But I still found myself going to movies by myself or celebrating my birthday alone.

I didn't spend any time being bitter at Jeremy. There was no point in that.

We'd drifted apart. That was all.

When Riot was released from prison, I envisioned how I'd sweep him back into the fold of the community. How he'd take me on dates to the movies and bring me a cake on my birthday. But that didn't happen either.

Just thinking his name still makes my chest hurt. There is a very empty, very obvious Riot-shaped hole where he'd once taken up so much of my heart and soul, and now he's just... gone.

Stop, I reprimand myself. Riot's happy. Isn't that what I had wanted for him?

Jeremy hands me a beer as I cross my legs beneath me on the blanket. Happy faces radiate from the field below us, illuminated by the fireworks.

"Thank you for this." I bump his shoulder with mine. He waves me off. "Seriously, how did you do it?"

He smiles impishly, and for a moment, I think he isn't going to tell me. "We've only used Premier Fireworks for the last handful of years." He glances over at me knowingly. "Who do you think put on the show before that?" He raises his eyebrows.

His grin is contagious, and I feel my face stretch into the first unforced smile of the day. I take a small sip of the beer, and the bubbles catch in my throat.

"I guess I never put that part together," I admit.

"Yeah…" He studies the grass between his feet. "It was our summer tradition. We'd spend a day hitting all the good spots." Jeremy leans in, and I catch a quick whiff of his clean scent. "Dad was a bit of a fireworks connoisseur. Didn't talk about *that* much in his Sunday sermons, but it was *ours*. Then every year we'd set up right over there." He points to another peak of the hill a few hundred feet away. "There was a regular crew of us. So I made a couple of calls."

"And you just so happened to have a few thousand dollars' worth of fireworks on hand?"

Jeremy shrugs before returning that impish smile to me. "We pooled resources."

I let my face go serious. "Thank you, Jeremy, really. If you hadn't gotten this together today, Cherry would have *absolutely* called a board vote to try to oust me. I'm barely holding it together as it is." I shake my head and lick the strawberry ice cream off the eco-friendly wooden spoons I'd insisted on. "For a moment today…" I blow out a breath. "I don't know. I started to think I'm not cut out for this."

Jeremy leans away as if he'd heard me wrong. "Are you kidding? You're Katie goddamn Plainbottom."

I drop my jaw, feigning shock. "Your dad has been gone a few weeks, and you're already taking the Lord's name in vain." I tsk and shake my head. "What would the good pastor think?"

"He would think 'nobody's perfect'. Not even the Pastor's son. Although *you* give perfect a run for its money." He rolls his eyes.

"I like things in order. Under control. It's cleaner that way. It allows the plan to roll out without a hiccup."

He raises an eyebrow at me. "Oh yeah? How well did that work out with Bonnie and Clyde?" He snorts.

"*They* weren't Bonnie and Clyde." I shake my head with a flat expression at his dubious smirk. "Come on, Jeremy. Bonnie and Clyde were the bad guys, and that would make me the good guy. I can cut it anyway I want to... I wasn't the good guy with what happened with Nicolette and Riot." I gaze down, picking at a blade of grass. The sound of Riot's name on my lips makes my ribs ache, and I want to stop thinking about him.

Jeremy opens his mouth to protest, but he struggles to find the words. "It was an accident. You didn't know her sex tape was one of her 'top viewed' videos. If anything, it's a cautionary tale against asking A.I. for help," he offers, but not even he's convinced. I smile at the effort to make me feel better, though.

We settle into a comfortable silence as the miraculous colors pop, fizzle, and sputter across the clear night sky.

I close my eyes and uttered a silent thank you to the Lord above for the miracle I'd hoped for. As I open my eyes, the sound of my mother's voice floods back with some of the last words she'd ever spoken to me.

"You can pray all you like for a miracle. But God doesn't give you miracles, Kitty Kat. That would be too easy. No, instead, he hides them. In places that you'll only ever look when you really, I mean, truly need one."

And as I glance over at the profile of the boy I'd known all my life, outlined by the illuminations lighting up the sky, I can't believe I'd found a miracle hidden in Jeremy Blackwell.

<h1 style="text-align:center">2</h1>

• ❤ • ❤ • ❤ • ❤ • ❤ •

<h1 style="text-align:center">Jeremy</h1>

Boredom buzzes in my chest as I wait for the board meeting after the Fourth of July to start.

I hadn't wanted to take an active role in the board of Redeemer's Church but the weight of expectation on the Blackwell name was my sole responsibility now. As my dad packed up, he made me promise to do right by the town. I thought dedicating all my time to becoming police chief would be enough. But the church was the most influential entity in the entire city. With as much land as Redeemer's owned, their issues were the town's issues. Which meant they were my issues. It could be a lot, but this town afforded me a lot of opportunity, ensuring it was taken care of was a responsibility I took seriously.

That sense of duty didn't make the board meetings any less mind-numbing, though. They had hardly been necessary while my dad was President. He and Katie had this place flourishing like blueberry bushes in springtime. But without the charm, candor, and authority of Elias Blackwell, suddenly half the board was ready to descend on the open leadership position and Katie was the gazelle up for the chase.

The thing is, most of these people are more vultures than lions. They prefer an easy meal versus a deadly chase. Opting to pick over carrion, delighting in the spoils of others' work. They want to complain, but they don't want to write the necessary letters to petition the bylaws. They want someone else to do it. Someone who knows the ins and outs of this place like their own complexion. Someone like Katie

The board meeting that follows the July Fourth celebration is no exception. It begins by high-fiving everyone involved. Katie sits perfectly straight at the center of the head table as acting President. My dad had delegated the role to her when he stepped away. Since the fiscal year ends at the end of August, the board accepted his decision instead of going through the rigmarole of calling an emergency vote.

Which, honestly, wouldn't have been difficult, but once again; no one actually reads any of the bylaws, so they don't know that.

I'm happy Katie's in the position. If anyone's earned it, it's her. She looks six inches taller as she sits in that chair, and some strange part of me beams with pride that I haven't earned.

I scan the agenda, and my stomach rolls when I see *Leadership Concerns* at the bottom.

It doesn't take long to get there. Cherry Mitchell, board secretary, is practically frothing at the mouth to speak. I cringe when she stands up.

"We all know what an *unfortunate* loss it was to have Elias step away for the rest of the summer."

I withhold my snort. *Please*. They shamed him into walking away under the threat of unseating him, which wouldn't look good to *any* future place he tried to go. All because he asked a private company to put fluoride in the town's water supply without official approval.

"And while our *acting* President has *clearly* worked *tirelessly*—" I watch Katie wince before blinking the hurt away and opening her eyes brighter, as if that would eliminate the small dark circles under her eyes that had appeared the last few weeks. "I wonder if it would be best suited to name an *interim* President who can also double as our senior clergyman for Sunday services. While the seminary students are... gaining wonderful experience with their Sunday sermons... attendance has dropped off significantly."

Everyone's eyes swivel to Katie. Her cheeks are flushed as her jaw works up and down to defend herself. But before she can speak up, someone lobs another accusation.

"Is it true that you're playing *cartoons* in Sunday School?" asks a board member. "My daughter came home and said it was the second week in a row they watched cartoons all morning. Cartoons!" She throws her hands up like animated television is drawn by the devil himself.

Katie is shaken. Her expression reminds me of a deer cornered by a pack of wolves.

It rattles me more than I expect it to. We'd been close as kids, but we grew apart the way teenagers do, and I haven't given much thought to her outside everything she did with my dad when he was the head of the church. Until my high school crush, Nicolette, came back to town earlier this spring. Of course, she shacked up and eventually took off with the man Katie had planned to marry. Needless to say, we'd spent some time commiserating over the last few weeks.

"I didn't have time to build the curriculum the past two weeks with the summer events," Katie says defensively. Their doubt burns into her. Her tiny mouth drops open and shut defensively before she throws up her hands. "It was Veggie Tales!"

A few snickers roll throughout the room. My rising hackles surprise me.

"Look, I'll find a temporary pastor." Katie rights herself. "I have only a few more credits before I, too, receive my ordination. I'm returning to seminary school for the fall semester." She smiles and scans the group, searching for supportive glances. I try to give her a quick nod.

Cherry laughs out loud before putting her fingers to her lips. "I'm sorry. That's *wonderful,* dear. I just think it's going to be *awfully* difficult to live up to the standard Elias has set. The congregation expects a certain degree of...*maturation* in its senior clergy." She cocks her head disparagingly at Katie and I want to tell her to sit the fuck down. "I think we should have a board vote to nominate an interim President for the remainder of the term."

I stick two fingers in the air. "Sorry to interrupt." All eyes swivel in my direction. "But choosing an interim President is not up to the board.

That's something the entire congregation has to vote on." The room is quiet.

We had just gone through this with my dad. It was the reason they accepted Katie as acting President in the first place. When you left a decision up to the congregation, which essentially was the *entire* population of Godot... *anything* could happen.

"I'll find a pastor," Katie says forcefully with more conviction.

"By when?" Cherry's voice falls flat, undercurrents of doubt dripping from her injected lips.

Katie's mouth pressed into a thin line, a phony smile, as she blinks twice.

"By this Sunday, of course."

I drop my head into my hands.

She gave herself two days. I want to smack her upside the head.

A small ripple goes through the dozen or so people in the boardroom. And Katie, ever the optimist, takes it as encouragement.

"Yes," she exclaims as she rotates to acknowledge everyone around the table. "This Sunday, we shall have a new guest pastor. Let everyone know that it certainly won't be one to miss! Now, if there aren't any more agenda items, I'll motion to end the meeting."

"Seconded!" I shoot my hand up. Katie's eyes soften in appreciation.

Cherry scowls, but the majority of people are already out of their chairs and dispersing.

I stand up, stretching my legs. I find myself hanging back, waiting for Katie to be done with her handshakes and polite nods.

When we're finally the last people in the room, she rushes over to me with wide, desperate eyes that somehow manage to punch me in the gut. She grips right above my elbows with firm, tiny hands.

She leans in fiercely, and I'm surprised by the delightful scent of vanilla I find near her. Her panicked expression locks on me.

"Jeremy, *please* tell me you have another miracle in you."

3

❤ • ❤ • ❤ • ❤ • ❤

Katie

"This is a little out of my realm, Katie." Jeremy sighs.

I part my lips to speak, but feel my cell phone ring. I pull it out, and the same number from two days ago flashes hauntingly across the screen. The blood pounds in my ears, and I need to focus on one disaster at a time. Shoving it back in my pocket, I turn my eyes to Jeremy, who's frowning curiously at my hands.

"You don't have any ideas? I mean, can I hire someone on the Internet?" Hope pours through me, but he just laughs at me, incensing my mood more. "This isn't funny, Jeremy!" I feel the hot prickle around my neck again as my breath speeds up. "This is serious!" His skeptical, nonchalance fuels my outrage. I surprise myself, and him, by giving him a forceful shove on his chest, amazed again by how smooth and firm that chest feels under my palms. I shrug the thought away. "It's serious," I repeat, softer. "This is all I have left, Jeremy. This job. This role. This church. It's all I have left, and I can't lose it."

Sympathy softens his gaze. Or is it pity? I don't care. He looks around as if the answers are somewhere on the walls.

"Maybe try the church in Lycon? It's not nearly as popular as ours but they have a full staff. One of the guys at the station said they have, like, four senior clergymen." Jeremy shrugs. "Just bat those little doe eyes at them and ask for a favor to step in this week. It's barely half an hour away." He touches my chin with his fingers and narrows his eyes playfully. I feel my breath catch in my throat, caught off guard by the familiarity of his touch. "They won't be able to resist you."

He smirks and walks away, and Jeremy Blackwell once again gives me the clue I need to find my next miracle.

∞

Lycon is different from Godot. Where Godot has roots in the early English settlers (or at least claims to, verification has proven difficult, but I'm still trying), Lycon is brand spanking new.

Despite being only a thirty-minute drive, it might as well be a universe apart. It sits on the other side of the lake, and once they realized they could lean into the nautical theme, the developers came. Shortly after came the large, seasonal tourist population. Some might call it "upscale". It has things like condos and chain restaurants, and shops that exclusively sell novelty clothing with the town's name on it.

Lycon seems to expand further out every year. Sometimes I wonder how it's taken so long for anyone to notice how beautiful the landscape is with the lake not far from the rising mountains.

I check my reflection in the mirror one more time before heading in.

"Hi, I'm Katherine Plainbottom from Redeemer's Church in Godot. I spoke with Pastor Simmons on the phone this morning." I flash my brightest, most confident, I'm-not-desperate smile at the woman who sits in the front office. I opt for my full name, believing it sounds less like a teenager and more like a mature, soon-to-be clergywoman.

She peers up at me through half-lenses and purses her lips.

"Oh, right. Yes," she nods. "He's not here today..." I deflate. "But he said our Associate Pastor is available to speak with you." Her eyes linger on me for a moment. "I'm sure he'll grant you some time."

I almost catch an eye roll that I don't understand, but nod profusely. "That would be wonderful, thank you!"

She lifts the phone from its cradle and punches a few numbers. "Atherton. I have a Katherine Plainbottom from Redeemer's Church here to see you."

She pauses a moment, her eyes flitting over me again. When she speaks, her voice is lower this time. "I don't know, a young woman from Godot." Another irritated pause. "The town across the lake! I'm sending her in." She hangs up the phone without another pause. She blinks her eyes rapidly. "He's down the hall, sweetheart. Atherton Ames. Last door on the left."

I nod in appreciation and make a mental note of the small flower arrangement on her desk. Lilies. I'll have to send her some lilies.

I don't know who I expect to find when I walk into the last door on the left, but the man in front of me is not it.

The associate pastor is usually the second most senior member of the clergy, so I guess I expected gray hair, a hunched posture, weighed down with age and experience. Maybe some robes. Someone more resembling The Sandman. But Atherton Ames is a far cry from The Sandman.

His wavy dark hair frames his face in thick locks and contrasts perfectly with a light tan that spreads over his skin and under the light stubble that adorns his square jawline.

And, God Bless his blue eyes.

Darker than Riot's. But just as intense.

He blinks expectantly, almost impatient as I try to regain my focus. The man can't be more than ten or fifteen years older than me, and I'm ashamed to admit the disappointment I feel when I spot the glint of gold on his left hand.

Get it together, I scold myself. I blink several times, but Atherton's face is barely amused, accustomed to rendering women speechless.

"Hi, I'm Katie- um, I mean- I'm Katherine, acting President of the board at Redeemers Church." I stick my hand out, feigning confidence.

But he doesn't take it. Instead, he tucks one arm under the other and brings a finger to the side of his lips. He takes a few steps towards me, frowning. He advances until we're nearly toe-to-toe. I hold my breath.

"Are titles supposed to impress me, Ms...?"

"Kather- I mean. Plainbottom. Miss Plainbottom." Cringing at the sound of my voice after accentuating the Miss part, Atherton finally softens a bit. His eyes take their time assessing me, and I feel like a cattle up for auction.

Finally, he takes a step back, and I blow out the air I'd been holding. He moves around to the opposite side of a large, ornate desk and gestures for me to sit.

I acquiesce without thinking about it.

"What can I do for you, Miss Plainbottom?" He leans back in his chair, stretching the dress shirt over a defined chest, and I catch myself before it's too obvious I'm staring.

"Please, call me Katie. Or Kate, I mean Katherine." I suck in a deep inhale before smiling apologetically. I shake my head in disbelief at how rattled I am. This isn't me. I'm put together. Calculated. No one uncans me. I offer a coquettish smile. "You know, you can call me whatever you like."

He finally smiles, and holy mackerel, is it suddenly warm in this office...

"Mm..." He narrows his eyes as if considering. "I like Katherine. Tell me, how may I be of service, Katherine?"

I almost wince. The only thing I hate more than being called Kat was Katherine, but Atherton could call me whatever he darn well pleased if it meant he'd perform Sunday services.

I launch into the pickle I'm in, giving him the cliff notes, probably focusing too much on the boring details of the board, but unable to stop the words from spilling from my mouth.

"So, while you'd be doing *me* a huge favor, it's really about the people of Godot." I hear the earnestness in my voice, and I hope he does too. "Sunday services used to bring us all together. Pastor Blackwell somehow knew how to reach into everyone's soul at the same time and make us all feel like we were powerful. Loved."

Using the past tense in talking about Pastor Blackwell makes my heart hurt, and suddenly my aching heart combined with the Riot-shaped hole next to it feels as though it might consume me. The bridge of my nose stings, and I detest the loss of control.

He looks skeptical. And worst of all, unconvinced.

"I'm not asking for forever," I implore him, leaning across his desk. "I just need this Sunday. That will give me a stay of execution with fourteen unruly board members. I won't bother you again. Unless, of course, you wanted to join us." I try batting my eyes like Jeremy said, but I feel ridiculous.

"Katherine…" he sighs my name, and it does funny things to my insides. He shakes his head, the refusal already perched on his lips. A momentary pause ends with a curious glance at me. "You have fourteen board members?"

"Fifteen, including me. Two seats are empty, but they'll be filled by the end of the summer."

His bottom lip protrudes, and I can't help but wonder if it's as soft as it looks.

"We've got a full-time staff of over forty people between clergy, admins, teachers, maintenance…. Our board is only eight."

I feel like I'm on fire under his gaze. He hasn't asked a question, but that doesn't stop me from blathering on.

"Oh yes. The President and Vice President are traditionally our only paid full-time employees. Everyone else is a volunteer, or we sometimes offer trade in kind with our tenants."

"Tenants? People live in your church?"

I shake my head. "No, sorry. The church owns a majority of the real estate in Godot. Mostly, people manage the properties themselves. We don't have to be landlords or anything." Why do I feel like I have to sell him so hard? I just need one Sunday service!

Atherton studies me for a moment longer before sitting up abruptly.

"I'm hungry," he says with a smile. "How about you? Why don't we finish this conversation over lunch? There is a wonderful little Mexican-Italian fusion bistro near my apartment right in town. You can tell me more about what kind of sermon strikes the best chord in your congregation."

My heart picks up speed. This has to be a good sign. I breathe a giant sigh of relief and briefly close my eyes. Once again, thanking God for burying another little miracle that Jeremy helped me uncover.

4

·❤·❤·❤·❤·❤·

Jeremy

I check my phone for the three hundredth time Saturday as I brush my teeth to see if Katie got back to me about how it went in Lycon. I don't know why I'm so curious. It doesn't affect me. It isn't even nine o'clock, but I'm beat. I worked overtime through the holiday and am looking forward to nearly a whole week off.

I should go out. Maybe get a few buddies to take a rowdy trip into Charleston for the night. Find a woman to drown my sorrows in.

The image of Nicolette wrapped in Riot's arms still burns hot in my brain. She had never been mine. Not even close. But it burns nonetheless. Poking little cinders into wounds I swore I closed a long time ago.

I knew a woman like Nicolette would never call Godot home. Hadn't I known there was never a future there? Maybe that's why I pursued her so intently. Because I'm a glutton for punishment. Relishing the little burn I get when I once again prove to myself that I'm not enough to stick around for.

Moving on from *that*...

Maybe a reckless night of casual sex is what I need. It isn't something I do often. The infamous Godot rumor mill taught me long ago not to sleep with local women unless I'm in a serious relationship.

And I haven't had one of *those* since my last one tore my heart out seven years ago.

So my romantic life was reserved for nights out in Charleston. But the thought of putting on a dress shirt and meeting strangers at a bar makes me tired.

I contemplate what's happening to me that I would really rather sit here alone and wait to find out whether Katie filled the pastor role?

Maybe I should have gone with her.

It dawns on me why I care so much about Katie keeping her position with the church.

I feel guilty.

We'd been friends once. Best friends. And when high school hit, I had distanced myself from her.

It's hard to remember why exactly, but I recall getting teased about how obsessed she was with me. Instead of telling people we were close friends, like I probably should have, I stopped hanging out with her in school. I cringe at the shameful memory.

I was thirteen, maturity hadn't exactly been priority one.

We interacted plenty as adults but never got back to the friendship we once had. And she never really found her *people,* so to speak. She was one of those girls that was involved in everything but never had a core group of friends. She seemed to belong to everyone.

But between everything that happened with my dad and our former high school crushes, the more time I've spent with her, the more I was reminded of how easy and natural our friendship came to us.

I was a dick for pushing her away all those years ago.

I owe her. So, I resolve to stay home Saturday night and crawl into bed by nine o'clock. Just in case she needs any more help.

I hardly doze off when I hear my phone ring. I leap to answer it, expecting to hear Katie's voice, either ecstatic or dejected.

But to my surprise, the number comes up as the Lycon Police Department. I groan. I'm supposed to be on vacation.

To my chagrin, I answer.

"Blackwell here."

"Jeremy. It's Griffin."

I almost smile at the sound of my training partner's voice. We were in the academy together and started at Godot PD until he moved to Lycon a year later.

"Griff! Hey, man, what's going on? Keeping all the socialites outta trouble?"

He chuckles. "You know I'm tryin'... Wish it was a social call," he says. I feel my vacation slipping through my fingers. "But it's more of a... courtesy call I suppose. Off the record." I grimace.

"You're calling me from a landline, bro, y'all don't record your calls?"

He pauses for a long moment, and I shake my head. Griffin was a workhorse, but he wasn't the brightest in our class.

"Yeah... anyway, I've got a chick here in holding that claims to be your sister?"

For a moment, all my muscles tense.

"Now I told her I don't recall you having a sister but she seemed to know an awful lot about you." He pauses. "Sisterly things and the like."

There are only two people left in the state of West Virginia who know about my half-sister, and I'm one of them. The other is most definitely *not* my half-sister, who I'm pretty sure hasn't left California in years.

I rub my eyes.

"Thanks, Griff, I'll be right there."

The Lycon Police Department instills all kinds of envy in me. Everything is state of the art. The best, most expensive technology and equipment money could buy. I pass through their kitchen, which is stocked with food and drinks, and opens up to a patio outside that features a grill and a commercial-sized Blackstone.

I whistle.

"Don't I know it?" Griffin grins at me. "Could always use a man like you on the force here, brother. After that big drug bust, there can hardly be any crime left in Godot."

I nod dismissively, but the truth is, he was right. Most of my time and my team's hours have been spent flagging traffic and being security at all the town's events.

"Where is she?"

He nods towards a set of doors as he places his palm on a scanner, making the doors slide open. Really? A bioscanner? What was wrong with a keycard?

When he opens the door to the holding cell, I do a double-take.

Katie's the only other person who knows about my half-sister. It's not like she's a secret, but she and my mom left Godot behind twenty-five years ago. It would be silly to still be sore about the way my mother took her and left us, so I'm totally over it.

But it's still not something I discuss a lot.

So, I knew Griffin had been talking about Katie when he called. But I assumed there had to be some mistake. Katie doesn't have so much as a parking ticket on her record.

But as I stare at the woman draped over the bench in the holding cell, I'm thoroughly confused.

"Katie?"

The young woman snaps her head up, and I watch those familiar lips break into an unfamiliar grin.

"Jer! My white knight!" She lazily puts her feet on the ground and drifts towards me. "You're here to rescue me, hm? You always were my hero."

It's her. But it isn't.

The woman before me has thick, wild, unruly brown hair. Is it wet? Either way, it's a far cry from the pin-straight, silky brown hair I see nearly every day.

She has on chunky black sunglasses and a set of Lycon PD sweats that are so big for her that she looks dwarfed, even thinner than usual.

Dropping my eyes to her mouth, I see a hint of smeared lipstick.

"Well? Can we go?"

And her breath. It smells like a frat house floor on Sunday afternoon.

"You... are drunk."

She giggles with her lips closed and sways back and forth.

"Did you figure that out with your detective skills?" She smiles in a way that's supposed to be seductive but only reveals a smudge of red lipstick on her teeth.

I take a deep breath to soothe my nerves. I roll my eyes and turn to Griffin.

"What'd you pick her up for?"

Griffin tries to mask a chuckle. "She went swimming in the public fountain in the town center. Was about to go skinny dipping with some bachelor party until it was called in. The guys scattered, but she..." he shakes his head in disbelief. "She just sat there. Because someone told her she couldn't leave."

I hate everything about what he just said. The only thing I'm thankful for is that Katie hadn't scattered *with* the bachelor party to pick up their activities somewhere else.

I rub my palms over my face. "What do you need me to do, Griff?"

"Griff!" Katie exclaims. "That's a great name, Griff. I was calling him Hot Cop."

A flicker of irritation blooms in my chest when she pulls her bottom lip in, chewing on it in Griffin's direction.

I see him blush and put myself between them. "Paperwork?" He nods, and we move toward his desk.

"Careful bringing her home," Griffin mutters. "She's been on the verge of bootin' face for an hour."

I cringe. "Ugh."

"Oh, fuck you, Jeremy. I wiped your ass after you shit yourself sophomore year at Lanie Mitchell's field party," I hear Katie jab from the holding cell.

I whip my head in her direction. It's the first curse word I think I've ever heard come out of her mouth. I can't see her eyes through those irritating sunglasses, but I can *feel* the smug grin on her face. I stalk toward her.

"Do you think this is a joke?" I seethe. "You do realize I'm doing you a favor here? I could very well leave you in here."

Her jaw moves up and down as if she's working on something to say. Finally, she scoffs, twirling around and slumping back down on the bench on the opposite end of the cell. I nod, satisfied, and turn back to Griffin.

"Thanks, man. I appreciate it. I'll rein her in. She's just going through it." Going through what, I have no idea.

"Look, I'm happy to help where I can, but between us? We gotta keep our houses in check." He lowers his voice while raising his eyebrows. "There's rumblings again about consolidation."

Wispy fingers of dread weave around my ribcage.

"Damn." I run a hand through my hair. "I thought that was squashed four years ago."

Last election season, one of the county executive candidates had run on the platform to use tax money more efficiently, he would look at inter-municipal consolidation, rendering Godot a mere subdivision within the Town of Lycon. It would mean sharing most public resources, and that meant emergency services. Me. The man didn't win, but the mere discussion about its benefits had done what he intended... make people think about it. It had been a few years since anyone brought it up, but election year was coming, after all.

Griffin shrugs. "Got a few people lobbying for it. So, just keep your head down and don't put resources into anything you don't have to."

I grumble. "We're operating on a skeleton crew as it is...." I frown. "Thanks for the heads up, man. I appreciate it."

As he unlocks the holding cell door a few minutes later, Katie grabs the bars and swings herself outside.

"Thanks, Hot Cop! You're a doll. Let me know if you want to... detain me again sometime."

She pushes herself against Griffin and presses her pointer finger to the base of his throat, and begins to drag it down his chest. Christ, she's making a fool of herself. Even though Griffin isn't pulling away.

I snatch her pointer finger and grab her hand, dragging her away from him as I shoot Griffin a disapproving scowl. He shrugs and smiles impishly.

∞

The night had cooled down. It's still humid, but at least it's breathable. I was hoping the fresh air would help sober Katie up, but she doesn't appear to be fazed by anything at the moment.

"Slow down, will ya? Let's do something!"

I spin around angrily. "No, you hurry up. And, no, you've done enough tonight. We are getting in my truck, and I am bringing you home."

She giggles again, and my agitation is about to bubble over. I could just go home. She must have a car here somewhere. She could find a place to sleep it off and return to Godot in the morning. But as I picture leaving her by herself somewhere, something feels off about it. It feels like how I imagine it would feel to bring a dog to the forest and walk away.

"I'm not going home. I'm not ready." She plants her feet and crosses her arms. The ridiculously large sweatshirt twists, almost looking like a straitjacket, and right now I'd kill for one of those.

"Welp!" I shout, turning away from her. "Train's leaving. You're either on it or off it."

She makes an audible harumph and says indignantly, "Then I'm off it. But I appreciate you stopping by."

That's it. I whirl around and push my finger in her face. "Stop being a brat! I don't know what happened to you today or what's gotten into you, but it's not cute! None of this is cute. So, get in the goddamn car and let's go, I'm serious!" I don't mean to sound so harsh, but I'm done babysitting. I spin around but immediately feel something solid hit my shoulder. I turn back to glare at her.

"Did you just throw a shoe at me?"

"No, Jeremy! I'm serious!" She whips those stupid sunglasses off to glare at me dead in the eye for effect. I stall. Realizing what she'd done, she hurriedly puts them back on. But I already saw her face.

I take two long strides until she's only inches away. Snatching the glasses off her face with one hand, I tilt her chin toward the street lamp with the other. I can see underneath her puffy, bloodshot eyes, one side of her cheekbones is already starting to register a bruise.

"What happened?" My tone is more aggressive than I intend, but some carnal protectiveness squelches my irritation, spurring it into agitated concern.

"Hot Cop told you. I went swimming." She enunciates her words carefully. "In a fountain. It was wet. And slippery. It was made of stone. Or granite." She giggles and takes a step back. "Or probably diamonds. I mean, can you believe this place?"

It's the first time all night her voice almost sounds like her. For the time being, I choose to believe her. She isn't a drinker. Not at all. It's entirely plausible she's a klutzy drunk. No one would ever know.

She twirls in circles, taking in the immaculately coiffed town square.

"There are more flowers in this square than in the entire town of Godot!" She huffs and then sags a bit. "What the actual fuck are we doing wrong, Jeremy?"

I almost choke on my tongue again hearing her swear. She used to have a swear jar at town halls. For adults.

I examine her with more discerning consideration and feel my chest constrict.

She's spinning out. Something happened that catapulted the typically perfectly perfect Katie Plainbottom into this deep vortex of reckless abandon. I soften, reminding myself that the only responsibilities I have for the next week are Sunday services tomorrow. My heart clenches.

"You didn't get anyone to fill in tomorrow, did you?" I ask quietly.

She tilts her head and smiles at me. "Oh, I sure did! And wait until you meet him. He... is a doozy! Atherton Ames. Sounds like something out of a Jane Austen novel, huh? We had a lovely lunch." I can't read the tone of her voice, but something about it makes me nervous for her.

My brows knit together. "So, this Atherton took you to lunch and got you drunk?"

"Nope!" she says with a pop of her lips. "Atherton took me to lunch and got me tipsy." She smiles distantly before it transforms back into goofy. "The bachelor party got me drunk." She giggles and snorts, and my irritation threatens to return.

I feel unseated. I knew Katie better than I thought I wanted to, and seeing her completely unwound is like waking up to a green sky.

She bounds in my direction, putting both hands on my shoulders.

"Oh, my God. Jeremy! Have you ever heard of a Kastapology shot?"

I squint. "A what?"

She frowns and tries again. "A cosmokazee shot." She tightens her pressure on my shoulders, sliding her hands slightly over my collarbone as if my body held the answers, and the idea of that sits strangely in my gut.

"A kamikaze shot?" I offer, and her eyes light up.

She touches the tip of her finger to my nose and smiles, nearly collapsing into my chest. "That's the one. They. Are. Awesome. Come on, let's go find some!" She pushes off me, but I grab her hand, swinging her back towards me.

"Hell naw," I drawl. "You're going home."

She snorts and covers her mouth, and her reaction confuses me. "What home?" But before I can ask a follow-up up she rights herself and puts her hands on her hips, pouting her bottom lip. Have her lips always been so pink and full?

"Come on, Jeremy. You're off the clock. Let's go out. Have one drink with me. For old time's sake." She arches an eyebrow and pouts her bottom lip. I'm suddenly brought back to high school, watching her eat alone at the lunch table with the cafeteria monitors while I was surrounded by dozens of people.

"Fine!" I throw my hands up. She bounces up and down joyfully, and I try to keep my eyes on her face. "But only one, and we're going back to Godot for it. The last thing I need is to get pulled over by another Lycon hot cop for drinking and driving." I roll my eyes and start toward my car.

She yanks open the passenger side door and scampers up like a puppy finally being adopted.

I toss her the bag Griffin gave me, containing her wet clothes and belongings. Her phone slips out from under my feet, and I pick it up to hand it to her. The home screen lights up, and I see she has four missed calls and two voicemails from the same unsaved number. It's a Spokane County area code, but she snatches it from me before I can study it too closely.

Dumping the contents of the bag in her lap, she frowns down at herself as if just realizing what she has on. I pull onto the main road that leads back home just as Katie yanks her sweatpants down around her hips.

"Jesus, what are you doing? Are you even wearing underwear?" But she doesn't answer, and the thought makes my abdomen tighten, which feels like a betrayal. This is Katie. Goody-two-shoes. Class one clinger, undateable, perfectionist Katie. Still, I shuffle in my seat, trying my damnedest to keep my eyes on the road. After pulling on torn denim shorts, I see her grimace at a tiny tank top she pinches between her fingers.

"Are those even your clothes?" They're entirely too skimpy for Katie, who probably adds more top buttons to her blouses.

"Nope. There was another girl with the bachelor party." She grins over at me. "We switched clothes." Her head swivels around to my back seat.

Before I can protest, she snatches a light button down that I stashed back there. She pulls the oversized Lycon PD sweatshirt over her head. I hear my breath hitch as her wild curls come unfurling down her bare shoulders. I try to avert my gaze, but she's at least wearing a bra. It's thin and white, and I almost audibly groan when I see her nipples pucker under the damp, thin fabric. I shift in my seat as subtly as I can.

She tries to suppress a sly smile, and I'm loath to know she catches how her nakedness affects me. I'm loath to know it affects me at all.

Purely biological, I tell myself.

I watch her thin, delicate arms slide through the sleeves of my shirt, and I exhale once she's finally dressed.

∞

It isn't even midnight by the time we saddle up to Benny's. I order two light beers, and for nearly half an hour we drink in silence. I'm beginning to feel a little lighter, and suddenly the gravity of the evening doesn't feel so crushing.

"What was so special about Riot Asher anyway?" I croon. "I mean, before all this nonsense, back in school he was just some dude who could throw a football. What's so special about that?"

A wistful smile passes over Katie's lips, and her eyes become a bit dreamy. A scoff catches in my throat.

"Well, for me, it began in seventh grade. We had just entered the high school. I had stayed up all night trying on clothes and jewelry to find the perfect outfit for the first day." Her focus drifts off into the memory. "Riot was one of the first boys I saw. His locker was right across the hall, and he had those eyes." Katie closes her eyes and sways on the barstool as if listening to her own Riot-themed song. "Well, I went right up to him and introduced myself. And you know what he said?" She quirks an eyebrow in my direction.

I narrow one eye at her and humor her with a shake of my head.

"He was with all of his friends, and he could have ignored me, but he didn't. He said, 'Hi, Katie. I like your headband. It's the same color as your dress'. And I was a goner!" She puts her hands on the bar as I notice her little southern drawl coming out stronger with each drink.

I don't have the heart to tell her Riot was probably mocking her back then. And I won't tell her now.

"Of course, he paid me no mind then." She rolls her eyes as if it were a silly mistake. "He was into sports and all, and I... wasn't. But when he was released, I knew it was fate telling me we finally had a second chance." The smile on her face slowly fades as her eyes lose focus. "You know what adds more insult to injury?" she drawls, propping her right arm on the bar and holding her head in her hand. "It's bad enough Riot rejected me after everything I did for him, but I put seminary school on pause the day Riot came back to town. And now that he's gone, I can go back. But it's just a *little* too late, after all, I can't complete it by *tomorrow*." She pinches her eyes shut.

I roll my eyes. "Please. You weren't doing all that stuff for Riot." She squints at me. "You were doing it for you. You were roping him into owing you so that when you deemed it was time, he could repay you by proposing. It's fuckin' twisted, Katie. Especially for you." She drops her jaw.

"What about you? All dopey-eyed for Nicolette, trying to relive what-ever Prom Night Special you're still clinging to."

An insecure growl nestles in my chest.

"At least I went to prom," I tease.

"Hey, I went to prom."

"Yeah, as a chaperone."

"I was on the planning committee! So, you're welcome for having every teenager's dream prom night."

"You didn't have a date, did you?"

She rolls her eyes, and I soften my banter. Maybe she just needed some direction. Some insight from an *impartial* male.

"You're a cute girl, Katie. If you had just chilled out a little bit, you could've had more boyfriends. But you were always so... obsessive, and guys don't like clingy."

Her head whips towards me, eyes narrow as she sits straighter. "I. Am not. Clingy," she says through gritted teeth. I hit a nerve. Good. She's been fucking with my nerves all night.

I raise my hands. "Just what I heard."

She lets out a sharp laugh. "Ha! Katie the Clinger. Yeah, I remember that one.... Bartender!" She holds a hand up in the air even though he's only four feet away. "One cazapolee shot, please!"

He frowns. "She means kamikaze," I mutter to him, holding up two fingers.

"Yeah, Katie the Clinger. That was a real original one by *Steve*." She sneers, saying his name.

It was the one boyfriend I'd ever known her to have in high school. They went out a handful of times, but he'd told everyone that she was already making plans for kids after they graduated. Hence the nickname Katie the Clinger. I had to admit it had slapped her with a fairly vicious 'updateable' label for the next few years and the indeterminable future.

The bartender sets the shots down, and she swiftly takes hers back. Slamming it down on the bar as she continues.

"You wanna know why he started that rumor?" She blinks at me, expectantly.

"Because when you were sixteen years old, you were already planning your engagement party on the third date?"

She laughs down to the floor before looking up, humorlessly. She leans in and whispers, and I can't help but catch that faint scent of vanilla and cinnamon as her curls fall towards me. It mixes with a trace of another man's cologne, and I don't like it. "It's 'cause I wouldn't fuck him." I pull back at the blunt words and shoot her a skeptical frown. "Mhmm. One more kazakazee, bartender!" Her intentional stare finds me, filled with haunted emptiness.

"I told him I wanted to wait. At least until I was eighteen." Her voice is even. Sad, almost. "Or married. Whichever came first!" Her lips press together. "That last part had been tongue-in-cheek. But he *sure* didn't retell it that way."

I watch her throw her head of wavy hair back as she downs another small glass of the green numbing agent.

"Nope. I wouldn't give it up at fifteen, so *Steve* told everyone that after a mere month of dating, I was planning to marry him and have his babies as soon as we graduated. After that, Katie the Clinger just... stuck." She snorts and takes a long swig of beer before waggling it towards the bartender, signaling another. "Alliteration is a bitch."

I suddenly feel incredibly sober.

My chest thuds like I've been hit with something, and I have the most random urge to wrap my arms around her. To tell her Steve was a dick and I was sorry that I'd ever listened to him and God, forbid, repeated anything he'd said.

"Katie..." I begin softly.

"Nope!" She puts a hand up dismissively. "No apologies necessary! We all do things we're not proud of. Hell, I accidentally released a revenge porn sex tape! We've all got to be the villain sometime."

My heart feels like it's cracking, and I try to make sense of what I'm feeling but I'm so far outside the bubble Katie and I usually live in that I can barely see her as the same person. I study her as she avoids my gaze, fixing her eyes on the army of liquor bottles behind the bar. I want her to look at me. See the apology in my face. But she doesn't.

"I sometimes wonder what would be different if I had done it," she says to the wall.

"He probably would have just told everyone how easy it was, and you would have walked through school with a different but equally awful nickname." Her mouth twists into a sad, agreeable smile. "Sometimes there's just no winning with high school boys."

Her face falls slowly. "Doesn't stop at high school," she mutters into her beer bottle, and I don't like the tone of her voice, but before I can ask her a follow-up, the bartender interrupts.

"Closing time, folks."

I gaze down at my keys. I'm in no shape to drive her home.

"Look, my house is walkable." I try to sound apathetic. "I've got a spare room if you want to sleep it off."

She studies me warily, and it hurts more than I anticipate to think she might be sizing up how much of a threat I pose. I almost rescind the offer, but I breathe a sigh of relief as she nods and hops off the barstool.

∞

The walk home is quiet. The nighttime air and physical movement have a surprisingly sobering effect. Back at my house, which is a short walk from the town center, I throw her remaining wet clothes in the dryer and lay out the smallest sweats I can find.

When she emerges from the bathroom in my old sweats, she looks ten years older. Her face pale. Eyes red.

"Thanks," she clips nervously. "For this." She gestures to the clothes, but her eyes say more.

I nod, remaining seated at my kitchen counter. "Of course. The spare room is upstairs to the right." She shifts her weight like she feels like she needs to say more. "I'll be up in a bit. Just gonna wait for your laundry."

Her pink lips press together in a thin, appreciative smile, and she says nothing more before she disappears up the stairs.

I don't mean to fall asleep on the couch. I plan to rest my eyes while waiting for the dryer but the beer and shots had done more of a number on me than I thought. I pull her clothes out and neatly fold them on the kitchen counter. I quickly check the fridge to see what I have for breakfast food. She's going to need something greasy and digestible.

Traipsing up the stairs, I mentally plan out when I need to start cracking eggs so she'll get to church on time. I turn left to my room, but stop when I hear soft noises coming from the spare room. I take a few slow steps toward her room and realize the door is slightly ajar.

Peering in, Katie is curled up, under the covers, and I watch her body shake gently, sobs escaping her throat. They aren't "I drank too much and feel like a fool" sobs. They are "something viscerally hurt me and I can't catch my breath" sobs, and I hate how helpless I feel. I've never seen someone more in need of a friend in my life.

Pushing into her room feels like a violation, but as I move to walk away, that feeling of abandoning a dog in the forest hits me like a truck, so I knock softly and step in.

Her sobs pause, but she doesn't look up. I stand there like an idiot.

Purpose. I need a purpose.

I grab the box of tissues off the dresser and pad over to the side of the bed she's facing away from. I reach over and deposit the box next to her shoulder. She chokes out a tearful sound of appreciation, but still doesn't speak.

My hands shake, and I feel more awake than ever despite it being three in the morning. I can feel my heart pounding as I gently reach over and rest my hand on her shoulder. She feels colder than a person should, and I'm suddenly unsure if she's shaking from the cold or tears. I press my palm into her soft skin as if that could warm the parts of her that need it.

I sit there for what feels like hours, but has only been a few minutes. Eventually, her sobs fade. I take a breath.

"Do you... want me to go?" I ask softly. She's still, and for a moment I think she's fallen asleep, but as my weight shifts off the bed, I see her head shake quickly back and forth. Anxious yet inflated, I peel back the covers and lie down next to her. My movements feel mechanical and wooden, moving deeper into this unfamiliar territory.

I lay on my side facing her back, leaving a few inches between us. I gently return my hand to her shoulder, and her body curls towards me until her backside is flush against my chest. I curse my body, sure she can feel how aggressively my heart is hammering. Taking a shaky breath, I extend my left arm around her until my hand comes to rest on her forearm. She seems to calm under the weight of my arm.

At first, we're both stiff, and I know she must feel as displaced as I do. I relax as I feel the tension slowly ebb, in time, from both our bodies as if we'd absorbed each other's unease.

I don't know what went on before I picked her up at the jail. I might never know. But something feels right about being here now. And when

I feel her breathing come to a slow, rhythmic pace, I finally let my eyes close.

When I wake up the next morning, Katie is missing from my arms. All that remains is a small indentation of where her body had been and the faint smell of vanilla on the pillow next to me.

Pre-order *Circle Circle, Dot Dot*
Available in ebook, paperback and free with Kindle Unlimited
on November 1!